In the peaceful land of [...], the death of a young child stirs the simple countryfolk to vengeance against their ancient enemy. Across the Strait of Balomar, in the sylvan kingdom of Simbala, another mysterious death breeds suspicion and fear, and a newly crowned monarch struggles against treachery to avert a war. And in the unexplored Northlands, a timid inventor seeks an answer in a terrifying twilight land of winged legends.

"Visiting this land of Dragonworld—where windships and dragons, secret missions and hidden passageways, love ... pageantry and simple living are everyday matters—is an exquisite experience. The beautiful line drawings by Joseph Zucker add much to the story, giving life to the characters."

—*Indianapolis Star*

"The text of *Dragonworld* is as charming and faerylike as the illustrations ... The book is indeed a magic casement."

—Philip José Farmer

"*Dragonworld* goes far beyond the flashy pyrotechnics of contemporary fantasy and fantasy illustration. Joe Zucker is a superlative and original illustrator, and he reveals a rare and astonishing gift for infusing a richness of character into his pictures, which do justice to Byron Preiss's and J. Michael Reaves's compelling story."

—Maurice Sendak

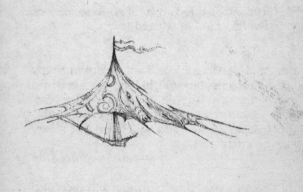

Dragonworld

Byron Preiss and Michael Reaves

Illustrated by Joseph Zucker

BANTAM BOOKS
TORONTO · NEW YORK · LONDON · SYDNEY · AUCKLAND

DRAGONWORLD

A Bantam Spectra Book

Bantam Trade Edition / September 1979
2nd printing ... November 1979
Bantam rack-size edition / August 1983
4 printings through December 1985

Book design by Alex Jay
Cover painting by Joseph Zucker
Produced by Byron Preiss Visual Publications, Inc.,
128 East 56 Street, New York, N.Y. 10022.
All rights reserved.
Copyright © 1979 by Byron Preiss Visual Publications, Inc.
Illustrations Copyright © 1979 by Byron Preiss Visual Publications, Inc.
Dragonworld is a trademark of Byron Preiss Visual Publications, Inc.

ISBN 0-553-25857-5

Published simultaneously in the United States and Canada

PRINTED IN THE UNITED STATES OF AMERICA

O   13   12   11   10   9   8   7   6   5

Acknowledgments

This book is a major effort for the three of us. I hope you will find some of the love and excitement involved in producing it reflected in the story.

Many people helped us with their friendship and support, but there are two who played very special parts in *Dragonworld*'s publication. The first, our editor, Roger Cooper, not only supported *Dragonworld* from the first day he saw it, but stayed with us through all the changes and developments that ensued. His enthusiasm, commitment, understanding, courtesy, and personal friendship are so special and so important that they deserve to be viewed as a beautiful gift.

Our manuscript editor, Betty Ballantine, is not only a warm and wonderful person, but the first lady of the American paperback business. To have the benefit of her experience in the editing of this book was a rare pleasure, and she has our respect and affection.

We also wish to express our thanks to Kenneth Leish, manager of Bantam trade paperbacks, and Beverly Susswein, administrative editor, for their extraordinary understanding.

Michaelyn Bush, an assistant editor at Bantam Books, has been a good friend and compassionate liason to the network of administrative offices of our publisher. Shirley Feldman, our fabulous typist, persevered through many tight deadlines and revisions. Both have shown rare patience.

These people have also given support during the production of *Dragonworld*—Edmund Preiss, Pearl Preiss, Ian Ballantine, Joan Brandt, Sydny Weinberg, Alex Jay, Len Leone, Lurelle Cheverie, Michael Deas, a talented and considerate artist, Mary Inouye, Neal Adams, Ralph Reese, Joe D'Esposito, Maurice Sendak, Bunny Kerth, David M. Dismore, Dena Ramras, Bea Decker, Robert W. Shea, Lisa Goldstein, Chris Lane, Theodore Sturgeon, Norman Goldfind, Richard Lebenson, Seth McEvoy, Tappan King, Mark Passy, Sheryl Sager and Phyliss Asman, Gary Reinhardt, Ira Turek, Buni Stensing, Richard Egielski, Don Goodman and Katherine Rice. To these people, and to others accidently omitted here, thanks.

I would like to thank G–d for giving us the ability to do this book.

Byron Preiss

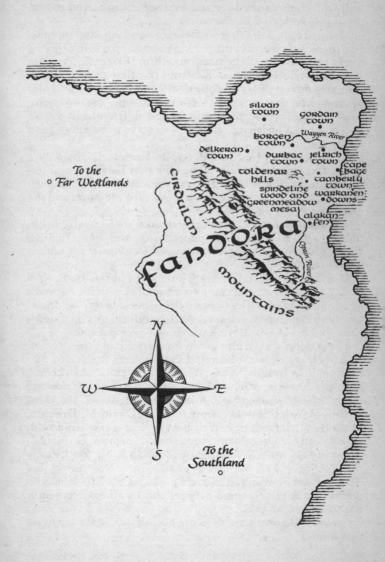

Dragonworld

I

It was well after midmorning when Johan, son of Jondalrun, stood on the edge of the cliffs and looked out over the Strait of Balomar. He wiped damp blond curls from his forehead and shaded his eyes against the sunlight. Johan was tired; he had begun the climb in predawn darkness, carrying the Wing tenderly as he made his way across the bushy hills to the northern escarpment. Even with his care, the stretched leather surface and wooden frame of the Wing had been scratched by hookberry vines and sharp rocks. The last part of the climb had been the steepest, and the sea winds there had made the Wing jump and buck like a stallion. Yet Johan had persevered. He intended to fly this day, and he would settle for nothing less.

The boy now sat upon a huge rock, having carefully anchored the Wing behind it. He ate a nectarine from his father's garden, and gazed up at the foamy clouds as the breeze dried the juice on his cheeks.

He was a farmer's son, young but strong and limber. The friendly wind played with his hair, tickling strands against his face. Johan hugged himself, as much in delight at his daring as against the slight chill of the Fandoran spring. His father, Jondalrun, would be angry. Risking safety for pleasure was a silly, Simbalese thing to do, but Johan had seen Amsel one beautiful morning, drifting above these very clouds, soaring as free as a fabled dragon, and he knew that to fly was far more than pleasure and truly worth the risk.

1

Taking the Wing had been easy. The giant tree that formed part of Amsel's house rose up next to Greenmeadow Mesa, and its massive upper branches grew flush with the cliff's edge. Johan had simply walked onto the tree, descended to the limb where the Wing was kept, and left with it by the same route. He cautioned himself against falling into the easy habit of thievery. Just this once, and never again. He would apologize to Amsel when he returned it later.

He was rested now, and the nectarines were all eaten, and there would be no better time for flying. He carried the Wing with him to the cliff's edge. A hawk sailed by far below him, close to the cliff's face, wings motionless. Wait for me, Johan thought. Hawk, I'll show you flying.

Standing at the edge, he carefully aimed the Wing into the wind. As the leather flapped and boomed in the updraft, he gripped the steering bar beneath the frame and slipped his feet into the thong loops, as Amsel had once shown him. That done, he stood facing the ocean, far below. For the first time he felt cold fear spreading under his heart. What if flying were not as easy as it looked? But it was too late now. The weight of the frame pulled him forward, and he could only push with his feet and turn a sudden descent into an awkward leap. Sea air slapped his cheeks, and he cried out in terror. He was falling! Amsel's invention had failed, and Johan prayed that he would not die. Eyes squeezed shut, he twisted his body desperately, this way and that, and after an eternity felt air catch beneath the leather sail. Suddenly he was not falling, but rising. He opened his eyes: a cloud of indignant gulls exploded about him, protesting his invasion. He was flying!

Held aloft by the laughing wind, Johan experimented with his body weight, learning the rules of flight. Mastery came swiftly as he flew over the water. The sheer beauty of it! Johan had known little more in his eight years of life than plowing and sowing, harrow and harvest. This was totally new, this was wonderful! Air burned sweetly in his lungs, then exploded from his lips in a shout of delight as he swooped and circled.

As the first euphoria faded, Johan began to study the scenery below. He was hovering in a steady updraft just over the vertical cliffs. The Strait of Balomar separated his

land, Fandora, from the dim purple shoreline to the east. Through the mists above this shore was Simbala, home of the mysterious and distrusted Riders of the Wind.

On his rare days of play, Johan would often come to the cliffs with his friends Doley and Marl, and they would sit for hours, staring eastward, hoping to see the magnificent slow-moving windships of Simbala. It was well known that the Sim were magicians and sorcerers, and that even the smallest of them could shrivel cornstalks with a glance. Though Johan and his friends knew they should not be fascinated by the crafts of the sorcerers, still they came, hoping to glimpse the sails of the distant windships in the clouds.

No Fandoran had ever seen a windship at close range.

Until last week, none had ever crossed the Strait of Balomar. Johan remembered the wide-eyed accounts of the couriers who had brought news of a ship that had swooped out of the sky without warning, its sails flapping like Old Witch Winter's cloak as it crashed into a high town-house garret in Gordain. A shower of embers had been cast from the small boat beneath the sail, and the resulting fire had caused damage to a half-dozen homes. No rider was found in the ship, and its descent had been blamed on the sorcery of Simbala.

Johan sailed dizzyingly in a wide arc over the water. The Sim, the couriers had said, must be magicians. How else could they make boats fly? Yet, Johan thought, here I am, flying as swiftly as any Sim, and I am not a magician. He had seen Amsel build the Wing himself, without sorcery. What if the Sim had built their windships just as Amsel had built his Wing?

Many folk, his father included, were worried about the possibility of another attack by the magicians of Simbala. What if they were not magicians, but humans like Amsel and Johan himself? Perhaps the Sim were not people to be feared, after all. Perhaps Amsel was right when he said that the unknown should not be feared just because it was unknown.

Filled with the joy of flight, Johan was sure that he could convince his father, and everyone else, that Amsel was a man

of vision. Johan's dreams soared higher than the Wing he rode, and in them his friend Amsel, that shy and strange man, would teach the Fandorans marvelous things. And he, Johan, would become his apprentice, and be privy to all the wonderful secrets and inventions that filled Amsel's forest home. . . .

Johan flew through the bright day, happier than he had ever been. He flew, and dreamed, and, occupied by his dreams, was blind to the nightmare coming until far too late.

The sight and sound of terror came simultaneously: as Johan swooped over a white sickle of beach two hundred feet below, heading inland, he saw his small shadow over-

taken by a vast bat-winged blackness. There was a deafening screech, and then a hurricane hit him, born of giant wings. Then swiftly the dreams fell to darkness, and the dreamer to death. Johan had hardly time to comprehend the casual shattering of his life; the torn leather and broken frame fell and he fell with it, screaming and grasping at the mocking wind. As he fell, he caught a single glimpse of the dragon, its mouth open, blotting out the world. The pain was mercifully brief.

•

The lad was late. The day was falling toward evening, and Johan had not returned to lead the plowhorse through the north field, or to wring the yithe fiber dry. His dinner of bannock leaves and fish had grown cold on the table. He was late, as he had been late before, and Jondalrun, his father, was angry.

Jondalrun was a gray and dusty man, a farmer of Fandora. He owned two small fields, a cottage and a barn, and he worked from dawn to darkness tilling soil and tending livestock. In summer he carted his produce daily to market in Tamberly Town, a mile from his farm. He was an Elder of the village, one of the three who sat in occasional council on the problems and grievances that are a part of any small community.

Jondalrun seldom smiled; he seldom had cause. The skin about his eyes was as furrowed and brown as the fields about his house, and his hair and beard flowed almost to his waist. He carried a sturdy oaken staff, and so gnarled were his hands that it was hard to tell where human limb ended and tree limb began. He was a man who felt that he had no quarrel with his lot in life. Yet there were times when he would ram his plow through the rocky soil, wielding it like a sword in battle, or thresh the harvested grain as though he were using a whip. He had been a farmer for thirty years and a father for twenty. He thought of his first son, Dayon, who had left home four years ago, and scowled, shaking his head. Was Johan turning out to be a vagabond, as his brother had become? Why didn't the boy understand that there was always work to be completed? Life was hard, as it should be. People were not meant to live like the Simbalese—the wealthy, decadent, perfumed Simbalese.

Jondalrun climbed slowly up the winding trail toward

the cliffs. He had raised Johan as best he knew how, as he would have raised a crop of millet or barley, with methodical care and devotion. The devotion was seldom shown, though always there. It had been enough for him as a child—it should be enough for any child. Evidently it had not been enough for Dayon, and did not seem to be enough for Johan. . . .

Worried, he shook his head. The fault did not lie with him. Johan had no business playing when there was work to be done. Jondalrun tapped his staff grimly against his hand. He did not carry it solely to aid his trek to the seaside cliffs, for though he was old, the decades of farming under the hot sun had baked him brown and hard. He carried it also because Johan had a lesson to learn. Like his brother before him, he was too play-minded. It was time he grew up.

Jondalrun knew that his son's mischief had to be connected with that madman Amsel, the wrong-thinker, the fool who constantly filled his son's head with dangerous notions. He recalled Johan once saying that, according to Amsel, everything was alive—the rocks, the air, the wattle and mud-daub of Jondalrun's barn—everything. The only difference was the amount of life in something— "consciousness," Amsel had called it. Johan had balked at breaking up dirt clods in the furrows after that, for fear of killing them. Jondalrun shook his head grimly. Amsel was dangerous, no question about that. The hermit had to be Simbalese. Jondalrun was sure that Amsel had something to do with the Sim attack on Gordain Town.

He topped the final rise in the trail and stood on a precipice overlooking the sea. He blinked at the sheer blueness of the ocean and the grandeur of the spires and natural towers of the cliffs. The iron-rich earth was banded in shades of brown and red, which merged with the white sand far below. Jondalrun watched the waves comb themselves free of seaweed on the rocks, and listened to the gulls' sharp cries. He took a deep breath, and reluctantly let himself savor the salty air. When he had been a lad, many a happy time had he spent exploring the caves and crannies of these cliffs. It gave him an odd feeling of comfort to know that they were still here, unchanged from his youth. He stood for a long, quiet moment, contemplating the beauty of it, feeling guilty for letting himself enjoy it. Then he suddenly

remembered something his wife had told him years ago about Dayon. "A pair of young legs cannot constantly tread the same beaten path from barn to cottage," she had said. "They must be able to climb hills and run through the surf as well." Jondalrun stared at the sea. His wife was dead now,

and Dayon was long gone. Johan did do his chores, albeit late at times. Jondalrun remembered evenings of his own youth spent watching the cliff fishermen cranking laden nets up the sheer rock walls, listening agape to their legends of giant seaworms and dragons. Jondalrun stood there, quietly musing, lost in the memories of his childhood. Then he remembered the reason for his trip. He frowned again, seeking to recapture the anger he had somehow lost. He tried to rekindle it by thinking of Amsel, but even that did not make him feel sternly toward Johan. His son was a good boy. Well, Jondalrun thought, perhaps the lad's shoulders would not sting quite so hard this time. Perhaps they would not sting at all. He did not want to lose another son. . . .

It was then that the old man saw the twisted wreckage on the beach below him, pushed gently by the waves, and the silent body whose clothes he knew.

There followed a gray time of rocks and pain. Jondalrun hung from crumbling ledges, slid down steep slopes of talus, and twice he fell, jarring the breath from him for some time. Afterward, as he crouched moaning, holding Johan's broken form in his arms, he looked up once at the cliff and wondered fleetingly how he had managed the impossible descent. But there was no room for thought of that, no room for anything but the grim, wordless sorrow. He remained on the beach for a long, unnoticed time, until the moon had risen and the advancing tide soaked his legs. Then he pulled Johan gently up the beach. The boy's broken legs were tangled in rawhide ropes, and for the first time Jondalrun examined the wreckage.

It belonged to Amsel, the hermit—he would have known that even if he had not seen the distinctive rune branded into the leather sail. Jondalrun had heard tales of the hermit's flying Wing. So Johan had flown, like some young, untried bird, seduced by Amsel's mad stories. Jondalrun looked about. The wreckage was scattered over a wide area, as though something had caused the Wing to come apart in midair. Also, the heavy leather sail was ripped, as were Johan's clothes—ripped and slashed. Jondalrun looked up, seeking a reason. He stared across the water at the distant moonlit shores of Simbala, and, against the gibbous moon, saw the silhouette of a windship moving slowly toward the east.

Jondalrun stared at it, trembling. Slowly he raised his staff; it gleamed, struck by moonlight, a cold fire of rage. "My son is dead," he said. "My son is dead!" he shouted. "For that I'll see your trees burn! I'll see blood run your rivers and stain the sea! Warlocks or no, you'll fear my coming! My son is dead, and he will be avenged!"

II

It was nearly suppertime in Tamberly
Town, and the evening air was made
pleasant by stews simmering and bread
baking. Dogs sat beneath unshuttered
windows, licking their jowls and whining
for scraps. The white-limed walls of the
houses were crowded together along the
narrow streets, along which a few peddlers and knife sharp-
eners still walked, calling their wares. From the Graywood
Tavern came the sounds of ale mugs clinking as Waymen
boasted of various bounties collected.

In the small town square, a Courier had just left his thirsty
horse at the watering trough and was posting on the town-
house wall a notice of a grain and livestock sale in Cape
Bage. Tired women in long, kitchen-stained skirts chased
laughing children into the houses for supper. Lanterns
hanging from rusty sluiceways or rafter ends were lit,
throwing light onto the streets. It was a happy, relaxed time
of day, and yet, in the midst of it, there came a gradual
lessening of the street sounds. The wheels of a peddler's cart
ceased to squeak and trundle on the cobblestones; street
musicians stopped playing in mid-note; the happy cries of
the children faltered into silence. Walking slowly, painfully, into the main square of Tamberly Town was the Elder
Jondalrun, his stare fixed and stony, tears glistening in the
wrinkles of his cheeks, and in his arms the broken body of
his son Johan.

The people on the street watched in silent horror. Jondal-

17

run entered a pool of yellow light from a lantern, stopped, and cried, "Justice for my loss! My son has been murdered!"

The cry carried throughout the town, filling it with painful echoes. Sashes were raised and shutters opened, as the inhabitants peered out. Jondalrun continued down the street, repeating the cry every few steps. Behind him, ahead of him, along the length of the street, murmurs began to grow, at first questioning, then sympathetic. A young man, fired by the scene, leaped from window to steep roof to street and marched alongside the old farmer, shouting, "Aye, justice!" He was quickly joined by several others, and what was one man's cry had become a procession's chant by the time they reached the Chief Elder's house.

Jondalrun paid no heed to any of them. He continued on his way, his pace stiff and somnambulatory, stopping only to voice his lament. The townsfolk stepped aside, clearing a path for him and his followers. Jondalrun stopped before the house of Pennel, the Chief Elder. The crowd that had followed him stood watching and waiting. If ever a town held its collective breath, Tamberly Town did so then.

"Pennel!" Jondalrun shouted. "Justice for my loss! My son has been murdered!"

There was no response for a moment. Then a kitchen shutter opened a crack, and a woman with a bun of gray hair peered out. Her eyes grew wide, and she withdrew, closing the shutter quietly. Again, silence; then, the sound of footsteps within. The iron-hinged door swung open, and Pennel came out onto the step.

The Chief Elder was a thin, small man with large eyes that peered nearsightedly. He had been napping before dinner, and so his clothing and hair were rumpled. He stepped, yawning, from his door, tugging hair away from his eyes, and was confronted by the father and the dead son, both of whom he had known for years.

The crowd waited.

Jondalrun said simply, "Bring Agron. We will talk." Then Jondalrun turned to a horse and cart that stood nearby. Tenderly he laid Johan's body on the straw, climbed onto the bench, and picked up the reins. The man who owned the cart, standing in the crowd, made as if to protest, but Pennel gestured him to silence. Jondalrun snapped the reins, and the horse began to trot, its hooves loud against the stones.

No one moved until he had turned a corner of the winding street and the echoes of his passage faded. Then, as though released from a spell, the townsfolk broke into small groups of excited conversation. Pennel put his hands on the wooden railing before him and squeezed hard. He let his breath escape in a great sigh, blinked, and looked down at the man whose cart had been taken. "Find Agron," he said. "Tell him to meet me at Jondalrun's farm."

He watched the man run down the street, filled with importance at carrying the Chief Elder's order. He looked at his hands again. They were trembling.

He did not know what had brought murder to Tamberly Town, and he was very afraid to find out.

●

Agron was also a thin and small man; in fact, he was close enough in appearance to Pennel to be his brother. Their temperaments were similar as well; both were taciturn, spoke softly and to the point, and were conservative in outlook. Each thought the other overly curt and reserved. They agreed on one thing, however—their affection for the cantankerous old man who completed the trio of town Elders. When Agron learned of Jondalrun's loss, he hurriedly saddled his horse and rode out of town along the dusty road that skirted the Toldenar Hills to the south, to Jondalrun's farm.

In the barn, several unmilked cows lowed plaintively. Pennel and Agron hurried up the stone steps and into the house, where they found Jondalrun collapsed on the fleece rug next to his favorite chair. In the bedroom, Johan's body lay on the bed, the quilt now stained with dark blood.

Pennel looked at Agron. "We must do it right for him," he said. Agron nodded, and together they brought the hide cot down from Johan's loft room. Agron stoked a fire in the fireplace, for the chill evening was drawing on, and put the bed-warming pan next to the flames for Jondalrun. While the house filled with warmth, they carried Johan to the cot, set well away from the fire, and arranged him as best they could in a position of rest. This took courage and strong stomachs, for the lad's death had left him broken almost beyond recognition.

In the bedroom they changed the quilt and managed to get Jondalrun's massive form onto the bed. Fatigued, they quickly completed the necessary chores outside, then retired to the fire, where they sat, side by side, watching the logs burn down to rosy embers. They spoke seldom through that night, and when they did, it was only to comment on the night's chill, or similar things. They said nothing at all about Jondalrun or about Johan. Or about the future.

•

Southwest of Tamberly Town were the Warkanen Downs, a desolate reach of dark sand, scraggly grass, and thistle patches. Here and there lay rounded hillocks, just high enough to hide various monsters of the imagination. Wind-twisted trees were thinly scattered, accentuating the barrenness. In them larks and lapwings would sometimes perch, and sing with the wind about loneliness.

No birds perched and sang now, however, for it was night. The moon, nearly full, was touching the western horizon, and the wind blew in chill gusts that stirred sand and leaves. A pair of wagon ruts called Warkanen Road ran across the downs, curving about the low hills and copses. Along this road came a single traveler—a young girl, wrapped in a dark green cloak. She walked hurriedly, casting anxious glances over her shoulder at the setting moon.

Far overhead, a silent shape moved against the stars.

The girl was young, in her early teens. Her name was Analinna. She was a shepherdess on her way to a tryst with a boy from Cape Bage, a smith's apprentice named Toben, whom she had met while bringing her father's wool to town. His brown eyes and charming speech had captivated her, and they were to meet at the crossroads and go from there to a nearby abandoned drover's hut. She looked anxiously behind her again; the moon was almost down, and she was late.

Above her the unseen shape grew larger, a black cloud that moved with terrifying purpose.

The road wound past a final hillock, and Analinna saw the crossroads before her. There was no sign of Toben. She paused, confused, then moved slowly toward the signpost. It was tilted at an angle, its base secured by rocks; the two cracked gray boards pointing directions were like skeletal fingers. The left indicated the way to Cape Bage, where, unknown to Analinna, Toben slept soundly in his room behind the smithy's shop, exhausted after a hard day's work. The other sign pointed toward the Stairs of Summer, the place of High Council for all the towns' Elders. But she could not see which direction was which, for it was too dark now to read the signs.

As she stood uncertainly, a sudden gust of wind seemed to come from directly above her. Puffs of dust rose. Analinna stifled a sneeze and looked up. She saw nothing, but faintly heard something, a sound like the bellows Toben had used to fan the furnace in the smithy shop, only much deeper and slower.

She turned about once, twice, looking at sky and land. The moon was gone now, and high clouds were blotting out the stars. It was growing very dark, too dark even to see the road. A sudden fear, so great that she was unable to run, overcame Analinna. She stood in the middle of the crossroads, breath held, listening, waiting.

The bellows sound came again, much louder this time. An instant later, a wind like a blow from Old Man Autumn himself sent her sprawling on the ground. The crossroads sign swayed. Dust and sand filled Analinna's eyes. She staggered to her feet and began to run.

She ran without direction, in blind terror. *Something* had passed over her in the darkness, something unseen and gigantic. Its presence filled the downs with a breathing horror. She ran, hopelessly, too frightened to scream, until she tripped over a rotting log and fell.

She heard the sound again, approaching. It sounded to her now like the flapping of mighty wings. Analinna knew of no creature so huge that could fly. She tried to scream, to scream for her father, in the unreasoning hope that he could somehow come and save her. But before his name was half-formed, it was cut off by an explosion of wind, and she was lifted from the ground.

The sound of wings faded slowly, until the downs were still again. Like a dying bird, a scrap of green cloak floated to the ground, landing in the middle of the crossroads.

III

Morning came fresh and clear over the Spindeline Wood, to the west of Tamberly Town. Songbirds greeted the sun's first rays. Within the wood, where the trees grew close against Greenmeadow Mesa, stood a large old house. Its walls were stone and wood, and its thatched roof was in disrepair. The rear end of the house was built right into the hollow trunk of one of the wood's largest trees. A rivulet flowed alongside the house, turning a waterwheel with a comforting, regular sound.

Amsel came out of the house, carrying a barrelful of scraps to be buried in his garden patch for mulch. He sat down on a weathered wooden bench and took a deep breath, watching it frost in the early-spring air. It was his habit to listen to the flowing water and the singing birds for a short time in the morning. Amsel was a small man, small and wiry, with a great explosion of white hair under a floppy hat, and a face that could claim any age from thirty to fifty. He was dressed in loose-fitting green and brown clothes, covered with pockets. In the pockets were all manner of things: a thong-bound parchment notebook, a quill pen which carried its own ink supply (Amsel's own invention), a lodestone, a small hammer (for chipping off interesting rock specimens), a small net of tanselweb (for capturing interesting insect specimens), and a pair of spectacles (also Amsel's invention). He believed in preparing for any eventuality.

He lived alone in this old house, away from town and

23

neighbor, and was aware of no lack in his life because of it. It seemed the best kind of life for a person with his insatiable curiosity about nature, and his many researches. He was well-adapted to it, although some of his habits were eccentric; he tied his clothes to the waterwheel to wash them, and he often talked to himself. This he did now. He rubbed one temple with a knuckle and mused, "Now, what was on the schedule for today?" He closed his eyes in concentration, then sighed and gave up by pulling his notebook from one of his pockets. With a nod and an "Ah-ha!" at one of his closely scribbled pages, he turned and walked around the outside of the house and down a path toward a clearing, where his experimental garden waited. There were rows of rare and unusual plants here; Amsel stopped at one and contemplated it. It was a bush covered with small knobby-skinned black pods. Amsel thoughtfully pulled one free of its stem, whereupon the pod burst, giving forth a strong, yet pleasant odor. It was almost citric, reminding him of nectarine blossoms. Amsel sniffed it in surprised pleasure, then carefully collected several pods and went back into his house.

In his workroom he examined a pod closely, then pulled his notebook from his pocket and made an entry with his pen. His workroom was spacious and well-lit, with a low beamed ceiling. Several shelves held a variety of things: almanacs, scrolls, parchment and vellum for writing and drawing, a huge collection of fossilized bones, and earthenware containers filled with herbs and liquids. There was a huge workbench with a great variety of tools on it. Other instruments, from garden equipment to an astrolabe, stood in corners or were suspended from the beams. Scrolls and experiments in progress were scattered about the room—Amsel was not the best housekeeper. He deposited the pods in his pocket for later examination, then busied himself by checking bubbling alembics and weighing proportions of various elements.

Ordinarily he was perfectly content to spend most of the day thus occupied, but today he found his interest in laboratory work gradually waning. He felt restless; his home, usually so secure and comforting to him, seemed confining. He looked out his window at the upper branches, swaying in a slight breeze, and abruptly made up his mind. Today was a day for outside. He would indulge himself in play and call it work—he would take his latest invention, his gliding Wing, out to Hightop Pass and spend the day probing the mysteries of flight.

Thus decided, Amsel went outside and around to the huge bole of the tree, where a series of steps led up into the leafy heights. He climbed quickly up to a large broad limb that lifted itself out of the foliage and into the clear sky.

This was where he kept his larger inventions. The limb extended itself out over the flat top of the mesa, and so he could step from wood to grass and use his lens tube to count the craters on the moon, or ride his pedalwheel cycle on some of the flat barren rocks that covered the center of the mesa. Amsel looked over these and several other contraptions proudly, then blinked in concern. Something was missing. He took careful mental stock and realized that his Wing glider was nowhere in sight. He looked at his notebook, to make sure that he had not put it somewhere else and forgotten about it. There was no note to indicate a change. Amsel raised bushy eyebrows.

"It appears that I've been robbed," he said.

●

"Where is my son?"

The voice awoke Agron and Pennel, dozing in front of the cold ashes. For a moment they were both confused and disoriented, and the slam of the bedchamber door did not help them regain their composure. Before they could gain their feet, Jondalrun had crossed to the cot, where he stood staring down at Johan's body.

Then he spun about, swiftly for all his bulk, and glared at his fellow Elders, standing by the hearth. "What happened?" he said, his voice half a growl. "I wanted to talk to you . . . tell you."

"You collapsed, Jondalrun," Agron said gently. "It is no reason to be ashamed."

Jondalrun looked about as though searching for something to vent his rage upon. Pennel said, "Why don't you tell us now—"

"By the seasons, I will!" Jondalrun shouted. "I'll tell the town . . . the country! The Simbalese have killed my son!"

"What?" Pennel and Agron spoke in unison.

Jondalrun spoke with such passion that at times they were forced to restrain him from breaking the furniture. The treacherous warlock Amsel, whom he had long suspected to be in league with the Sim, had tempted his son Johan with sorcerous powers, and by them entranced the child so that he could fly. He had done so knowing that the boy would be easy prey for a Sim windship. Whether they had meant to capture his son or kill him, Jondalrun did not know, but the plot had resulted in Johan's death. "It is an act of war!" Jondalrun, his face brick-red, hammered his fist on the table. "The Simbalese are toying with us," he shouted, "and I say to you that we must show them they cannot murder our children! We must attack!"

The intensity of his words shocked Pennel and Agron—they had known Jondalrun to be belligerent and excitable, but never to such a degree. The sorrow he had felt at his son's death had been transmuted into rage, a rage that would sustain him, that was an anchor for a life cast into turmoil.

"We must call a High Council!" Jondalrun concluded. "The Sim and that murderer Amsel must be punished!"

They tried to calm him, but he would not be calmed. "You do not believe me! What about last week's attack on Gordain Town—"

"What you say is not impossible, Jondalrun," Pennel said. "But we have no real proof that the Sim wish us ill. We must investigate these—"

"Proof, you say? Here is proof!" Jondalrun interrupted, pointing to his son's body. "There will be more proof, and soon—you can be sure of that." He turned toward the door. "Let's return to town. I must post notice of my son's funeral."

In silence the three of them rode back to Tamberly Town, the two horses trudging behind the cart. The morning was bright and cheerful, as though Spring had no inkling of the cruel disaster. Jondalrun stared at the road ahead, brooding. He had never, for all his bluster, been a particularly vengeful man. But he carried his resentments within him, festering. Chief among these were the Simbalese. Like most Fandorans, Jondalrun had little real knowledge of Simbalese life-styles and customs. In common with most of his people, he believed the Simbalese to be witches and warlocks. He resented the tales he had heard of their luxurious lives, but he had always grudgingly admitted that Simbala had never harmed Fandora. What meager trade the Fandorans had with the nations to the south was mostly in grain and woven products—it did not conflict with the Simbalese, who traded the jewels from their mines, their crafts and rare herbs. Simbala had never taken any hostile action against Fandora—until a fortnight before, when a windship had crossed the Strait of Balomar and attacked Gordain Town. The resultant fires had destroyed part of the town, including a warehouse filled with grain. That had been disaster for many people, but to Jondalrun it was less than nothing compared with the loss of his son.

Jondalrun was convinced that the Simbalese were indulging their fancied superiority—wantonly flaunting it. Their windships and their magic made them feel invulnerable, immune to reprisal. Well, he told himself grimly, they would soon learn how vulnerable they were.

In Tamberly Town, the mood of the folk was subdued and pensive, as though they awaited a verdict that would affect them all. This tension, the Elders learned, was not due solely to last night's sorrow. Where Jondalrun had stood before Pennel's house the night before, there now stood a shepherd, old and grizzled, his face set in grim lines of sorrow. Clenched in one hand was a scrap of green cloth.

He did not move, but began speaking in a slow monotone as the cart stopped before him. He did not look at the Elders, but spoke as though to himself.

"She went walking last night, went walking, after I was asleep, and she didn't come back, didn't come back. Soon as it was light, I began to search. I didn't search far. This"—he looked at the scrap of cloth, clenched tightly in his fist— "this I found at the crossroads on the downs. Not far from there I found her, I found her. She . . ." He stopped, his face twisted with grief. "She'd fallen . . . a long ways. . . ." He closed his eyes. His shoulders shook.

Pennel swung himself down from the cart and led the weeping man into his house. Jondalrun looked at Agron. Agron took a deep breath and let it out slowly. "You said there would be more proof," he said. "You were right, apparently."

Jondalrun nodded. "I will post the notice of my son's death," he said. Then, he added silently, I am going to see Amsel.

•

On all worlds, in all times, there are always those who are the curious ones. Amsel was such a person. He asked questions about everything, pried into secrets where others saw no secrets, and, like most with a mind given to wonder, did not fit well with his contemporaries. He was mistrusted and ostracized by the dour majority of Fandora, those for whom life was what they could wrest from the ground and sea.

Amsel was quite aware that he was not well-loved by his countrymen, and he considered himself indifferent to the fact. Despite their distrust of him, they had never offered him harm. He had occasionally prescribed healing poultices and remedies for minor ailments to some of the farmfolk, and so won tolerance by them. At times illness or misfortune had been attributed to his "magical" abilities, but the Chief Elder of Tamberly Town was a just and sensible man who refused to take action without evidence.

Now, it seemed, a person had dared to beard the "sorcerer" in his den. Amsel was both sad and angry. He had put a great deal of design and work into the building of his Wing, and now it had been stolen, and he had no idea where to begin looking for it.

He had been sitting there pondering the problem for some time; now he stood and slowly began his descent. But before he had gone far, he heard a rustling in the underbrush below, a pounding as if someone were knocking heavily on his door, and a voice crying out his name.

"Up here!" Amsel shouted.

He stood and waited. Very rarely did he have visitors; he could not imagine who it could be. The leaves rustled, and then the farmer Jondalrun, one of the Elders of Tamberly Town, stepped from the trunk stairs onto the limb. Amsel gazed at him in astonishment. The old man's face was haggard, his eyes wild, even slightly feverish. Without a word he lurched toward Amsel, both hands grasping for the hermit's throat. Amsel glanced over his shoulder quickly, then stepped off the branch into empty air, fell twelve feet, and landed with practiced ease on another wide limb. Jondalrun glared down at him in baffled rage. "Traitor!" he shouted. "Filthy Sim!"

"What do you mean?" Amsel said, bewildered.

Jondalrun did not answer. He climbed clumsily down to Amsel's new perch and lunged at him again. Amsel leaped out of the way, landing feetfirst on a thin springy branch that hurled him upward. He rose past the disconcerted Jondalrun, seized and sat himself upon a bough over the farmer's head, looking down at him.

"Jondalrun, what has happened?"

"You know what has happened!" cried Jondalrun. "And you shall pay for your part in it!" Panting, he lifted his staff to throw at Amsel.

There was no reasoning with the Elder, so Amsel leaped down in front of him. Before the staff could be used, Amsel pulled it from Jondalrun's grasp. Pushing the Elder back quickly into the fork of two limbs, Amsel wedged the staff between Jondalrun and a tangle of smaller branches. The Elder was trapped.

"Now," Amsel said, "tell me what has happened."

Jondalrun struggled, but to no avail—the staff held him firmly. He kicked at Amsel, who nimbly dodged the boot. Finally he spoke.

"You know . . . what you have done." The old man's voice came in bitter, broken gasps. "You tricked Johan . . . into following your evil ways. Now he has paid for it . . . with his life!"

Amsel grew very pale. "Johan," he said softly. "Johan took the Wing." It made terrible sense—fool that he was not to have seen it earlier. The boy had always been particularly fascinated by the Wing, and had begged Amsel often to be allowed to fly it.

"You Sim are murderers of our young. You are afraid to attack openly!"

"Jondalrun, what are you—"

"Don't try to deny that you are a Simbalese, Amsel! You've been sent here to undermine us with sorcerous terrorism!" Jondalrun spat at him; Amsel jerked his head out of the way. "A Simbalese windship attacked Gordain Town, burned half of it to the ground! Another has killed young

Analinna! And still another has torn my son from the sky, where *you* sent him!"

Amsel shook his head in confusion. It was obviously impossible to talk sanely with Jondalrun—he was raving. Amsel watched the old man warily, his memory filled with young Johan, one of the few friends the hermit had ever had. "Jondalrun," he began, "I had no idea Johan was—"

"You knew! You gave him wrong thoughts to think! You encouraged him to break the laws of nature, and he has died because of it! I swear, hermit, that I will have revenge on you and all of Simbala for this!"

With a massive effort that left his face purple, Jondalrun broke the staff that imprisoned him. Amsel leaped back quickly. They faced each other.

"I cannot win against you here," Jondalrun said at last. "You know these treeways too well. But there will be a reckoning, Amsel, and not all your magic will save you from it!"

He turned and descended the wooden steps. Amsel watched him go.

The sound of Jondalrun's passage through the forest faded to silence. Amsel still stood, unmoving. The old man was not insane. Johan was dead. Johan, for whom he had come to feel parental affection, was gone from the world— and he alone was to blame.

Amsel sat down slowly on the branch, put his face in his hands, and began to cry.

IV

ondalrun returned to Tamberly Town. He rode his horse down the winding streets, looking neither left nor right, paying no attention to the whispers and stares of the townsfolk. Tension filled the air, taut as a bowstring. A newly posted notice told of an impending High Council of Elders, the first in years, to be held at the Stairs of Summer. Couriers had already been sent to all the towns and hamlets of Fandora, even as far away as Delkeran on the western border. Jondalrun paused for a moment before the town-house wall and looked silently at the crisp, unweathered paper that fluttered in the breeze next to his announcement of Johan's funeral. Then he rode slowly to the house of the town stonecutter to order a headstone carved.

That afternoon, he buried Johan. The sun, heedless of his sorrow, shone in a cloudless sky. The day was bright and cool—the kind of day, Jondalrun thought bitterly, that Johan had always loved, with crisp, clear air that brought a snap of red to the cheeks. On such days Johan would hurry to finish his chores, that he might run and play touchstone with his friends in the Toldenar Hills near the farm. Jondalrun decided to bury him on the highest hillcrest there.

It was the Fandoran custom to bury the dead quickly and privately, and afterward to receive condolences from mourners. With his mattock and shovel Jondalrun loosened the ground and cleared a deep grave, then tenderly lowered the small enshrouded form into it. He stood looking down at it, still in the grip of a grief that would not let him fill in the grave and hide the sky and sun forever from his child. Like most Fandorans, he was a religious man, and now he prayed that his son might enjoy an eternal spring. After the prayer was done, he stood looking down, motionless. It was hard, very hard, to throw that first shovelful of dirt.

"M-mesire Jondalrun . . ."

Jondalrun turned and saw two small boys standing on the nearby ridge of rocks that ran like a spine along the first hill. He recognized them—two of Johan's friends, Marl and Doley. They stood forlornly in the bright sunshine, their jerkins and breeches dirty and tears streaking their faces. Jondalrun stared at them, not sure what to say. It was improper to interrupt the private burial. Yet, stickler though he was for tradition, he could not find it within him to send them away. He merely stood and looked at them, not knowing what to say.

The shorter boy—he could not remember which name belonged to whom—held a small toy in his hands. He held it out to Jondalrun.

"Johan l-lent it to me," the child said. "It was his favorite, but he lent it to me. I thought he might want to keep it now."

Jondalrun slowly opened his weathered hand, and the boy placed the toy in it. Then, as though released from an obligation and grateful to be off, they both turned and walked quickly, not quite running, down the hill toward town.

Jondalrun looked at the toy. It was a small wooden horse and cart, whittled from interconnecting pieces, so that the cartwheels turned and the horse could be unyoked. Jondalrun's hand tightened then in a sudden spasm that almost crushed the fragile thing, for he had suddenly recognized its construction. It had been given to Johan by Amsel. Jondalrun stared at it, trembling slightly. He loathed the very touch of the thing upon his palm—it was unclean, a Simbalese creation, a product of the same hands that had sent Johan to his death. Twice he raised it over his head to cast it down and crush it underfoot, and twice he stopped, remembering that it had been Johan's favorite toy.

At last he turned, his movements stiff, and, bending down, laid the toy upon the still form. His eyes averted, he began to shovel. He tossed the loamy soil into the grave quickly, his breathing ragged, until the body was covered. He worked more slowly then. When the grave was filled, he affixed a makeshift marker that would serve until the headstone was finished. Without gazing at the mound of earth, he collected his tools and walked heavily down the hill.

●

Word spread slowly across the steppes and hills of Fandora. A merchant, his cart filled with dried fruits, mentioned the tragedy to the inhabitants of several tiny hamlets. A Courier came to Silvan Town, feverish from an infection contracted by stepping on a spikebush during his run and not taking time to treat the wound. The word went out: for the first time in a decade, a High Council of Elders had been called.

Words from drovers and Waymen had already instigated rumors that were bandied about in marketplaces and taverns. There had been an invasion of Simbalese windships in the north of Fandora that was even now moving southward and westward. Sorcerers from Simbala in the guise of wolves and bears were stalking the countryside. Elders were hard put at times to keep panic from overflowing as the stories chased each other to the south and west.

In Borgen Town the speculation had reached a feverish height. Old women and gossips leaned daily from windows beneath peaked roofs and regaled each other with figures of imaginary casualties. Some even took to laying up corned and salted meats, bread and cheeses in their stillrooms and larders.

Tenniel, the sandalmaker, had just finished replacing the leather wrappings on the head of Old Ma'am Mehow's cane when a young boy came to the door of his shop and told him a meeting of the Elders had been called. Tenniel had been listening politely to Old Ma'am Mehow's theory that all this excitement was only a plot by those venal cliff fishers to increase the price of puney fish. He nodded polite agreement and ushered her out of the shop, then closed up and hurried down the street, rubbing his hands together to rid them of the softening oils he had been using on the leather. He was one of the youngest Elders in any town in Fandora—only twenty-eight—and his appointment to the post had not been without controversy. Tenniel had been keenly aware of this the times he had attended a meeting of the Elders. The responsibility of the post frightened him, but he had managed to keep his fear in check by his determination to do his best for the town in which he had been born. He loved Borgen Town devotedly; he would, when work permitted, spend hours simply wandering about the village, gazing fondly at its cottages and houses, at the noisy open bins of the marketplace, the fruit groves outside of town, the various heralds and coats of arms over doorways.

It was because of his passionate love for his town that he had been chosen an Elder at his young age. Few people had a deeper understanding of the town and its ways, and few were more anxious to serve.

Rushing through a lane behind the Court of Wells, he speculated on the sort of problem that had arisen to require a special council. It was not hard to guess that it must be concerned with the rumors of war with Simbala. As he turned the corner and came into view of the Chief Elder's house, he saw Axel, the third Elder, just entering, and ran the rest of the way so as not to be too far behind him.

Talend, the Chief Elder, was an ancient man of seventy or more, with one foot twisted and useless from a hunting accident that had happened long before Tenniel was born. Axel frowned as the young man sat down, puffing slightly. Axel was also much older than Tenniel. He was a sour-looking Elder who owned several of the shops in the town, and he wanted to own Tenniel's as well. The younger man steadfastly refused to sell his shop—it had been his father's, and he made a good living from it. As a result, their encounters were often tense.

Talend affected not to notice this conflict. As Chief Elder he had selected both of them, subject to approval by the townsfolk, and he felt that he had made a good decision. He thought that Tenniel's youthful views on things balanced his own nicely.

In a voice that Tenniel always found surprisingly strong for its age, Talend began to read the proclamation that had been brought to him by courier. The Elders of Tamberly Town had requested a High Council of all the townships of Fandora, to discuss and decide what action to take concerning the recent attacks by Simbalese windships.

Tenniel sat rigid with excitement. A High Council! The last such one had been held when he was seventeen, and had been called to decide how best to aid the flood victims of three towns when the Wayyen River had overflowed. If a meeting was deemed necessary now, then the possibility of war must be very serious indeed.

Talend squinted at him and Axel and said, "One of us must attend."

"Do you think it is possible that there will be war?" Tenniel asked, and was relieved that his voice was steady. There had been no war in Fandora, civil or otherwise, since it had been settled over two hundred years ago. There had been no desire by any other country to annex this land of high and barren steppes, rocky hills, and low marshes. There had been no desire by the Fandorans to war upon themselves or others—the business of making a living was hard enough. The concept of war was unbelievable to Tenniel at first. In fact, it was hard for him to conceive of Fandora as a country united enough to wage war.

"This is not to be decided by the three of us," Talend said in answer to his question. "Our task is to decide which of us will represent Borgen Town in the High Council. I am old and lame—I could not make the journey and be at my best. Therefore, it is between you two."

Tenniel said immediately, "Axel must go." It was so obvious that it hardly needed stating. He was older, and therefore wiser and more qualified to go. It was in the best interests of Borgen Town—therefore, Axel would go. Tenniel told himself that he was quite content to stay in this town that he loved, even though he knew that was not true. He did want to be part of this meeting, to aid in this decision that might well be one of the most important ever made in Fandora. Yet he also wanted what was best for his town, and so he voted for Axel.

He fully expected Axel to vote for himself, and for Talend to approve. Axel was not given to false modesty. Therefore, Tenniel was astonished beyond words of protest when Axel said briefly, as was his way, "Tenniel goes."

Tenniel was sure he had not heard aright. He could only stare at Axel in amazement. But his amazement had yet further to go, for Talend nodded and said, "I agree. Tenniel, you are to represent Borgen Town at the High Council."

"I? But . . ." Tenniel was literally beyond words; his jaw moved up and down and from side to side, like a marionette with loose strings. Talend chuckled, and even sour old Axel was moved to twist one side of his mouth in a smile.

"Yes, you, sandalmaker," Talend said. "We all know it can be no other. You have the energy, and the devotion which the High Council requires. It is a long trip and a difficult mission." His voice grew serious. "There will be enough there to represent the sage and hoary point of view. Let youth also be there, since youth is always the cutting edge in war."

"Aye," Axel said. "Your devotion to Borgen Town is known to all, and second to none. You will not use us ill, I think."

Tenniel looked at Axel with surprised gratitude. Axel snorted gruffly, as though to take some of the compliment back from his words.

Later that day, Tenniel packed a small satchel in his room behind his shop and left Borgen Town. Nedden, his horse, wore the finest saddle Tenniel had made. The sandalmaker was proud. He was having to readjust the scope of his loyalty—to widen it from the small town in which he lived to include the entire country of Fandora. It was an exciting concept. He knew next to nothing about the Simbalese, but how could their loyalty and devotion to their townships possibly match that of the Fandorans? However, he thought, war was more than just a matter of loyalty and enthusiasm. He knew that the concept of war was a simple one to most Fandorans: great bunches of men ran at each other from opposite directions, brandishing swords and firing arrows, and in a few minutes a victory was won, and the losers stood sullenly by while the winners had their pick of the spoils, which were usually fine silks, jewels, and sometimes princesses.

There was certainly nothing wrong with that, but he wondered if it would really be that simple. For one thing, the Sim were well-known to be versed in all forms of magic, which could be a formidable weapon. Something would have to be done to negate that. Tenniel felt that if it came down to a vote for or against war, he would not vote for it unless he knew the Sim magic could be challenged. He felt sure that he and his fellow countrymen could triumph over any normal army that came against them. It would certainly be a great adventure. As he rode toward the east, he recalled a bit of an old war song he had once heard sung by a traveler from the southern nations, and he sang what he recalled of it as he rode, substituting his name for that of the hero. It sounded very good.

•

Lagow of Jelrich Town was both woodwright and wheelwright to the town, and as such he made quite a decent living. Many of the houses and shops in the town were built by him, including his own—a fine two-story affair, with garrets and pantries and a wine buttery that was the envy of many. His wife of twenty-seven years was named Deena, and he still complimented himself occasionally for choosing her; she matched him length and breadth, he thought, in common sense. She had borne him two sons and a daughter. He had lost one of the sons to the raving fever, years ago, but that sadness had passed, and now his other son was learning to take over the business. His daughter was being sought by several very promising young men. It was a good life for Lagow of Jelrich Town, a life ordered and comfortable. He was proud of himself and his family, and proud of the fifteen years he had served as an Elder to the village. He felt he had earned the right to a peaceful old age, and so he was not at all pleased at being selected for the High Council.

"An absurd business," he grumbled, watching Deena pack his bags. "Disrupting an old man's life for such nonsense. I'll tell them so. See if I don't."

"You do that," Deena said crisply. "You're not that old, Lagow. Forty-eight isn't old."

"It isn't young, by far."

"Look upon it as a compliment. They value your opinion."

"If they value it that much, let them come here for it. Why must I haul my poor old body all the way to the Summer Stairs just to tell that excitable fool Jondalrun to come to his senses?"

"Listen to you! As if the man were a dotard in your charge!"

Lagow snorted. "I met him at the High Council when we

discussed the floods. He was high-tempered back then, and it doesn't sound like he's changed. Grown old and set in his ways, I'm sure."

"You haven't?" she asked, handing him his bags and pulling a cap down over his ears. She changed her tone slightly as she said, "Be kind with him and watch your tongue, husband. I heard in the market last week of his loss."

Lagow sighed. "I hear you, Deena. I know the man's hurt deep. But he's stirring up more hurt with his grief, and only ill will be left of it. I think it's my duty to tell him that."

She sighed. "Then be prepared to buy some beefsteak for your bruises, if what I've heard of Jondalrun is true."

He went down the stairs and out the door, where his son stood holding the horses yoked to his best shay. Lagow tossed his bags in the back, gripped his son's hand firmly, then turned and kissed Deena, a kiss which lasted long enough to surprise both of them. He saw his son grinning broadly. "What're you laughing at?" he roared in mock anger. "Hear me well, now—I want that spinning wheel for the widow Annese finished and polished by the time I'm back. And don't go sitting on your hocks when that's done—hustle up more work, if you want a wall between you and the witch next winter!"

They laughed and waved, and he smiled and waved back as he chucked the reins and started down the road. The smile did not sit right on his face, however. This talk of war—this was a serious thing, a very serious thing. He was worried about it. Not only for himself—though it would be a bitter thing to be denied a comfortable old age after he had worked so hard for it—but also for his son. War was so much worse on youth. He had never been in one, but his grandfather had told him of the Southern Battles, after which the founders of Fandora had come over the mountains to settle the steppes. Lagow was glad to have missed that war. He wanted his son to miss this one. He hoped that would be the case.

•

The sheer cliffs of Fandora rose sixty to ninety feet out of the sea, and their depth below the waves had never been measured. That part of the ocean was treacherous; undersea caves and grottoes produced sudden currents and whirlpools that could drive fishing craft against the cliffs.

Yet fishing was done here regularly; in fact, the community of Cape Bage made its livelihood by it. For only here, in these deep waters, could they find the large telharna fish, whose skin dried into a tough yet supple leather, and whose oil lit many houses during long winter nights. Also here were the schools of puney, the small, bland-tasting fish that, when seasoned with temwood spice, was one of Fandora's dietary staples.

The fishing was done by great winches and poles which lowered nets into the water from the top of the cliffs. The arrangement of the ropes and nets was complicated, and the end result was a sieve made of yithe fiber stiff enough to resist the currents, yet flexible enough to trap fish.

Tamark had been a cliff fisherman of Cape Bage since the age of twenty-two. His father had been a fisherman, and it was his grandfather who had invented the fishing nets. Tamark was a huge man, with a bald head that gleamed as though anointed with telharna oil, and an aggressive tuft of beard. His nose had been broken years before, when a winding lever had slipped from his hands while the nets were on the way up. His large hands were scarred with rope burns and callused to shining smoothness from winding the winches. He was a strong man, too, for it took a giant's strength to haul the nets full of gleaming, struggling fish up the cliff as often as forty times a day.

He stood now in one of the Baskets—the railed wicker platforms that overhung the cliffs—and looked down at the lines that fell away into the fog-hidden sea. It was a gray and gloomy day at the coast. Behind him there came a strange hollow sound, like the wailing of a wolf in the hills. Tamark did not look around. A moment later a fine mist moistened the fish-hide jerkin he wore, as a pounding wave far below was pushed up through the network of tubes and passageways in the cliff, to vent at last through some hole in the ground as water vapor and a moaning wail. Tamark hardly heard or felt it—it was as much a part of his life as the smell of fish.

It had been a bad day for catch—the mist and fog seemed to depress the fish as much as they depressed the fishermen. The nets had been let down twenty times, and they had filled barely three carts with fish. Tamark stared moodily down into the mist, the clammy billows that seemed like the edge of the world. Three carts of fish would bring barely enough waxings in his share to buy a decent meal. The life of a fisherman was hard at times. On days of poor luck like these, Tamark sometimes wished that he had not returned to Fandora, to his father's trade—that he had instead stayed a traveler. He had thought to see the world when he had been a young man, and so he had signed up as a merchant's apprentice. The caravan (such as it was: four horses and a few carts loaded with cloth goods, but to him it had been a caravan, and an impressive one, too) had traveled to Bundura, one of the Far Westlands. For several weeks they had stayed there, and Tamark had been dazzled by the comparative wonders of Dagemon-Ken, the capital. It had stone pipes in the city square from which water spurted in fountains. The streets were paved with jointed flagstones, not rough cobbles, and some of the buildings were huge, as much as three stories high and containing ten rooms or more. There were colonnades filled with taverns and shops, and peacocks wandered the streets. An impressive wall surrounded the city, and soldiers with cuirasses of beaten brass and bearing spears stood guard at the gates—and the women there! He had fallen madly in love with the doe-eyed daughter of a livestock baron. But he soon learned that his love was not reciprocated—she had tolerated him merely as a curiosity, someone whose bumpkin manners and mistakes could be counted on to amuse her and her friends. Tamark had returned home when he discovered this, and swore that he would never again leave the town of his birth.

He sighed. That was many years ago, and though he was still asked on occasion to tell of the marvels he had seen in his travels, he seldom felt the same surge of excitement and adventure at the memories that he once did. He was now a fisherman of Fandora—nothing more than that—and that was what he would be until he died. True, he was also an Elder of Cape Bage, but these duties, though he discharged them conscientiously, he found difficult to take seriously at times. Settling disputes such as which chicken belonged in whose pen, or deciding who owned the apples that fell on the other side of the fence, were scarcely problems requiring knowledge of far-off climes and cities. Tamark sighed again. He wished he had the opportunity to do something of value, for himself as well as his city, as his grandfather had done by inventing the nets.

It had come time to haul up the catch, and so he stepped out of the Basket and took his place at one of the winches. Twenty or so other fishermen were doing the same; Tamark watched them, waiting until they were all at their posts, hands firmly gripping the worn wooden handles. "Pray for a good catch this time!" he shouted, and was rewarded by a few despondent looks. At least he was not the only Fandoran dissatisfied. "Crank, then!" he cried, and they tugged the cranks toward them in unison.

The effort should have been rewarded by a fairly heavy resistance, a weight that they would overcome slowly but surely. Even a full catch did not pose a back-breaking strain for twenty fishermen. So Tamark was surprised when the crank turned perhaps half a revolution and then stopped, as if he had run his knuckles against an invisible, unyielding wall. He looked at his fellows—they looked as puzzled as he did. It had to be a catch heavy beyond precedent.

"Again . . . crank!" Tamark shouted, and they pulled once more. The lines came in half a yard, and then the heavy poles of wood, grooved to allow the passage of the lines, creaked alarmingly. Whatever they had caught weighed enough to threaten the winch; if not handled properly, it could pull the entire rigging into the sea.

Tamark looked at the ropes. They showed none of the familiar thrashing that accompanied an unusually large haul of fish. But they fairly hummed with tension. He had never seen them under such a weight; even the occasional wrecks dredged up in the nets had not caused such tension. He hoped the ropes would withstand the weight. No diver could be sent into the currents below to untangle them, and to cut loose the precious weavings of yithe fiber that formed the nets was unthinkable. It would take months to replace them.

"Pull!" Tamark shouted again. "Pull hard! Turn those cranks and lift!"

They put their backs into it, their muscles bunching along their shoulders and sides. Tamark felt himself sweating, the foggy air cold against his skin. The gray sky seemed to press down from above, and the fog was rising; trails of mist crept over the cliffs. Tamark listened to the subdued roar of the breakers far below, as if it might hold a clue to their unknown cargo. The creaking of the winches filled the air, punctuated by the gasps of his men.

The fog was a gray ghost all about them now. Tamark was suddenly seized with the strong feeling that whatever was in the net was not something that should be seen by man. This leaden weight was ominous in its resistance, its reluctance to leave those lightless depths from which it was being dredged. He had to breathe hard to keep from letting his sudden fear overcome him. But he did not order the ropes to be cut, for the nets were not something to be lost to childish fears. He set his teeth, shook his head, and kept turning.

They could tell when the nets broke the surface—the cranking became slightly easier. None of them could step to the edge and see what was in them, however—it took every man to turn the wheels. Slowly the ropes creaked through the grooves, layering about the huge drums with dreamlike slowness.

"Almost!" Tamark suddenly gasped. His single word of encouragement was taken up by the others: "Almost! Almost!" By the length of rope coiled about the drums, he could tell that the nets were about to swing into view. He longed to have it over with, to let the muscles rest. Yet, deeper down, he dreaded it.

The nets cleared the cliff.

For a moment, the fog hid them. Then a vagrant sea breeze dispersed the mist. The fishermen stopped cranking. They stared at what hung there entangled in the nets, shrouded by the fog.

It was the white, clean-picked skeleton of a sea creature, the like of which Tamark had never seen. It was gigantic, well over fifty feet long, its head larger than a horse. Long, serpentine vertebrae told of a sinuous neck, mounted on a body which, judging from the length of the ribs, must have been ten feet thick. Not a scrap of flesh still clung to the bones—the sea scavengers had seen to that. Yet the skeleton still held together, for the most part, by ligaments and tendons that had hardened like cables. The skull was missing the lower jaw, but the huge curving teeth of the upper showed without doubt that it had been a hunter. Two of the teeth were longer and thicker than Tamark's arm. Water dripped from the black eye sockets—a disturbing suggestion of weeping.

No one moved. No one spoke. There was not a sound, save for the creaking of the ropes. Then, from behind, came the rising eerie moan of air forced through the fissures of the cliff. At the other end of the line, one of the men let a cry escape from his throat.

As though severed by the sound, one of the ropes holding the massive tail snapped with the strain. The sudden shifting of weight was all that was needed; one after another, the ropes parted with sounds like breaking bones. The men barely had time to brace themselves against the sudden release of the weight. The thick poles whipped up and down like riding crops, and as the last rope snapped, the gleaming skull seemed to nod at Tamark with a strange, dreadful intelligence. Then the skeleton, together with the tattered nets, plunged downward. Several fishermen ran to the cliff's edge to watch it vanish into the cottony mist, and to hear the splash, dim and filtered. Tamark did not move. He stood still and staring, his mind filled with the eyeless gaze of the monster that had seemed to single him out.

The men stood stunned, both at their loss and at the creature that had caused it. Gradually, isolated voices penetrated Tamark's shock.

"What was it, then?"

"Never seen a sight to match it."

The high wavering voice of old Kenan, the netmender, cut through the speculation. "I'll tell ye what ye caught," he said. "That were the remains of a seaworm, a serpent of the ocean—Old Shipcrusher, we called them. They could wrap about a fishing boat and snap it to kindling. I only saw one once, from a distance, looping in and out of the water like a darning thread through a jerkin. It were forty years ago, but I never forgot it."

The discussion swelled again, the story already growing in the telling. Tamark turned and lumbered away from them. There would be no more fishing today, nor for many a day in the future, until nets and ropes could be fixed. The men started back to their small quarters or to the taverns of Cape Bage.

The Elder breathed heavily, as if to banish the dark air he felt around him. He had been dissatisfied with his lot in life, though it was better than most in Fandora. Very well, he thought ruefully, perhaps it would be taken from him. Something was looming in his future, of that he was sure. He was not eager to learn what it would be.

When he entered his rooms behind the village bakery, he found a brief message summoning him to a meeting of Elders in Tamberly Town. Tamark read it quietly. He had been wanting a chance to do something momentous for his village, to make a contribution equal to that made by his grandfather, years ago. Perhaps the chance had now come, he thought. He was a man with a sense of the dramatic, and the arrival of the letter and the terrible experience at the cliffs on the same day was a coincidence he could not ignore.

He sat down on his cot and put parchment on the stool in front of him. With the treasured writing skills he had learned in his travels years ago, Tamark laboriously drew instructions for the men to follow in his absence.

Then he rose, taking two or three small waxings of local currency from his taboret, and rang a small window bell which would summon a messenger to his door.

After the young boy had left with the message, however, Tamark still found it difficult to banish the feeling of unease within him. Despite his dreams, he was not looking forward to the council.

V

Tamberly Town was alive with the sounds of children, of angry parents and disgruntled Waymen, of anxious bartermen and gossiping farmers. There was an excitement in the town square unlike any the Fandorans had experienced in years. There was also tension; townspeople walking the street in the day or at night were apt to suddenly crane their heads skyward, as though they expected to see a Simbalese windship swoop low over the village.

The talk was of the Simbalese and the threat of war. The possibility frightened them.

"I hear they're devils, you know," Dame Sarness said to her sister. "I hear tell they can change themselves into any shape or form in an eye-wink; they could turn into bees and spiders and creep into your house, and then throttle you in your bed!" and she gave such a graphic pantomine of it that her sister bleated in fear and ran home, where she spent a vigorous afternoon cleaning her house of pests.

"Oh, yes, magic," the barber said to the butcher knowingly. "Why, all they needs is a lock of your hair, or a cuticle from your finger, and they can make you do things you wouldn't do in your worst dreams!"

"If they come near me, I'll cut off more than a lock of their hair," the butcher promised, testing his cleaver with a callused thumb.

"Don't believe the tales you hear," Agron reassured his

wife. "The Simbalese are as human as we are, and they're no doubt just as scared of the idea of war."

"It's not the ones who are scared of it that worry me," his wife said. "They're the sensible ones. But the ones that want war—they frighten me."

Little children played war in the streets and alleys, fighting with swords made of thistlesticks, turning carts and baskets into windships by children's magic. Many a mock battle was fought and won behind steps and in corners, and many imaginary Simbalese sorcerers died there.

"Would you really go to war?" a young lass asked her beau as the two of them sat on a hill overlooking the town. "Would you wear a uniform and carry a sword and all, just like in the Dancers' story tales?"

"Sure would," her beau said. "Would you wait for me to come home, all covered with medals?"

She looked coy. "How long would you be gone? Years and years?"

"Not near! We'll whip those Sim and be back before the week's up, with more treasure and jewels than you can imagine!"

It had been a week since Jondalrun had summoned the Elders of the neighboring towns. As was the custom, the village whose Elders had sent out the call for the council would play host to those who had responded, and so, on an exceptionally crisp and clear spring evening, Tamberly Town turned out to greet twenty Elders of Fandora.

The tension of the past week seemed diminished by the festivity of the occasion. A banquet fit for royalty had been arranged in the town square, and the entire village had taken part in the preparations for the event. Banners hung from the windows of the higher buildings. Children watched excitedly as Couriers strung lanterns across the streets. Sandalmakers found themselves with twice the usual waxings, as townspeople paid handsomely to have their shoes repaired for the reception. Dancers—young men and women in costume and makeup—entertained the visitors with pantomimes of legends and dances.

The visiting Elders were impressed with the results. Lagow of Jelrich Town dined happily on the first piece of striped sole he had eaten in years. As he picked through the tender white bones, he learned from another Elder that the fish had been a gift from Cape Bage to Tamberly Town. Lagow was pleased. Tamark of Cape Bage was a generous and experienced Elder, and the gesture was befitting his status. When Lagow spied the fisherman sitting under a bright red banner, he hurried over to thank Tamark for sending the dish.

Minutes later, he was surprised at the change that had come over Tamark since their last meeting. The fisherman's words were short and moody, filled with cynical observations on the gaiety of the event. At first, Lagow thought it might be the effects of the wine, but then, at the mention of Jondalrun's name, Tamark's wit resurfaced.

"It seems to me that death should not be synonymous with justice. Is there any reason, Lagow, for us to throw our young men into battle with sorcerers? If Jondalrun feels the Sim are to blame for our tragedies, why does he not send a messenger to Simbala, as is our custom with the Southland?"

Lagow nodded. "I sympathize with you, Tamark, but Simbala is not the Southland. No Fandoran has ever set foot in Simbala, and it would take a mission of justice to force any to their shores. It is obvious to many the Sim are to blame. Jondalrun feels that a messenger will lose for us the element of surprise."

"Surprise? When we do not even know the truth about them?" Tamark raised his cup of ale and traced the foam on its brim with his finger. "Surprise itelf is valueless. A tiny skyfish can surprise a telharna, but the telharna will eat him just the same. Surprise without knowledge is like this"—the fisherman lifted a cloud of foam on his fingertip and blew it at Lagow—"wet air."

The youngest Elder, Tenniel of Borgen Town, was negotiating his second turkey leg when he felt a heavy hand clap down on his left shoulder. He looked up and saw with surprise the face of Jondalrun. He quickly wiped his greasy hand and extended it to the Elder. "A pleasure to meet you, sir!" he said. "Are you not the very man who fought off a Simbalese windship in an attempt to save your son?"

Jondalrun stared at him, then snorted. "So," he said gruffly, "that is how legends are born." He appraised the confused Tenniel. "You are very young to be wearing the sash of an Elder."

"I'm twenty-eight," Tenniel said, a little defensively.

Jondalrun shook his massive gray head. "Amazing. I should like to visit your village sometime. No doubt the smithies are manned by babes, and farmers plow in swaddling clothes." Before Tenniel could protest, he continued, "As to your question, let me tell you the story as it really was." He then explained briefly what had happened, his voice trembling with emotion toward the end.

Tenniel felt sorry for him. He was also astounded by the fact that the black-hearted Amsel still lived in his tree house. "Why have the villagers not gone out with torches and staves and brought him to justice?" he asked. "I think we should go right now and—"

"These things will be done by the laws of Fandora!" Jondalrun said sharply. Then, feeling a pang of dishonesty, he added, "I attempted to do that very thing earlier, but I was maddened with grief at the time. We are not conscienceless lawbreakers, as are the Sim. We will do things properly!"

"As you say," Tenniel acquiesced, but privately he wished that he could come face to face with this Amsel.

●

Amsel decided to leave the Spindeline Wood that evening. He would spend some time at a large dry cave which he had furnished as a way station for long field trips. It had occurred to him that the story of Johan's death would grow in the telling, and that eventually there might be action taken against him. He had much to think about now, and he preferred a quiet, austere place in which to do it.

It was still almost impossible for him to believe that Johan was dead. He remembered the first time that he had met the lad—near the edge of the wood, on the banks of the small stream which ran by his house. Johan had been playing with a turtle, spinning it about on its back.

"Do you intend to eat that old snap-jaw?" Amsel had asked Johan, surprised and frightened by the appearance of the hermit, had shaken his head. "Then you'd best know," Amsel had continued amiably, "that he will die from the sun if you leave him on his back for long. To kill for food is a forgivable thing, but to kill for fun is not."

Rather to the inventor's surprise, Johan had said, "That makes sense," and rolled the turtle back into the water. It had been the beginning of a friendship. Amsel had found

Johan to be a bright lad, eager to learn and given to laughter. As he came to know him better, he found himself becoming more and more cautious with his words to the lad, for Johan was one of those very rare folk who consider and sometimes even take advice from others. It was all very well to offer advice, secure in the assumption that it would be ignored, but when Amsel realized that his words meant something to Johan, he knew he had to be careful.

He had obviously not been careful enough. His guilt was enormous, for he had aroused Johan's interest in things beyond the day-to-day farmer's existence, without assuming any responsibility for possible results. Perhaps he had been wrong to enlarge the boy's horizons—he did not know. He had always been puzzled and confused by people, had never known what to say to them. Now the young child who had trusted him was dead.

He packed a small bag and set off for the cave, crossing Greenmeadow Mesa and climbing high into the Toldenar Hills. Eventually he had to stop to catch his breath and rest for a moment. Playing mountain goat among these crags and crevices was not as easy as it had once been. He would not mind growing older, he thought ruefully, if he could believe that he was also growing at least slightly wiser.

He was about to continue when he heard a breath of whispered voices nearby, and then the settling of some dislodged gravel. He felt coldness spread suddenly over him. He debated for a moment the best course—whether to confront whoever it might be or to run and trust to his knowledge of the hills to save himself. The decision was made for him. There was a sudden scrabble of footsteps from around a rock corner, and Amsel leaped to his feet, heart pounding, to face his attackers.

Three small children stood together beside the rock, staring at him. He recognized them—they had been friends of Johan's; he had met them once. Johan had dared them to visit the crazy hermit with him, and they had come, trembling with fear at first. They had soon gotten over that; Amsel had served them sweetmeats and cider and showed them his inventions, and they had vowed to come and visit him again. They never did, and he had been somewhat relieved. His experiments and research would have stopped completely if he played host all day.

He nodded to them, not remembering their names. "What brings you here?" he asked.

"We were playing touchstone on yonder hill," the largest one, a stout brown-haired lad, said. "We saw you." He spoke fearfully, eyes wide, and Amsel thought with a flash of sorrow: No amount of sweetmeats and cider will make him like me now.

"Go ahead, ask him," said one of the others, a strident little girl. "You said you would."

The stout boy looked away from the inventor and shook his head.

"What did you want to ask me?" Amsel inquired gently. "Was it about Johan?"

The child still would not meet his eyes.

"I did not mean for the accident to happen."

"But it did," the girl said. "It did, and now Johan's dead. What are you going to do about it?"

"I don't know," Amsel said simply. "I honestly don't know." He paused. "I think I should . . . talk to some people."

"What people?" the girl asked.

"I'm not sure yet. But I have the feeling that a big reason why this happened was because some people—myself, Johan, Jondalrun—didn't talk to each other enough."

"Are you going to the Council?" the last child asked suddenly. He was a thin lad, with one arm slightly deformed. It hung uselessly at his side.

"What Council?" Amsel asked. Surely the town had had its meeting of Elders by now.

"At the Stairs," the girl said. "Everybody's going. It's a big Council, biggest ever."

Amsel blinked in astonishment. A High Council had been called! He could recall one other, born of the need to do something about the Wayyen River flood victims, years ago. According to his scrolls of the history of Fandora, there had been only five High Councils in the country's history.

It could not concern him alone. What could it possibly be? Of course, there was the possibility that it had nothing at all to do with him. Amsel doubted that; he clearly remembered Jondalrun's threats and accusations, and his final vow to make the Simbalese pay for what he believed they had done.

Amsel had a sudden awful suspicion that he understood the reason for the meeting.

"When is it being held?" he heard himself asking. His voice sounded far away, and from a distance came the answer of the girl: "In three days, at sunrise. Are you going?"

Amsel blinked, and tossed his head, as though to clear it. "Why," he said, "I hardly think I would be welcome." Then he felt a breeze sweep across the hills. "It's getting cool now, children. You'd best get back to the village."

The three children turned and ran away over the lichen-covered rocks toward Tamberly Town. Amsel watched them go. Then he looked toward the hills where the Stairs of Summer waited. "No, I won't be at all welcome," he murmured. "But I think that I must go."

•

It was dark, far too dark for it to be morning, but a blanket of clouds over the sun announced a coming storm. The Wayman sat with his back to the door of Graywood Tavern. It was early, far too early for him to be drinking, but through his one good eye he watched the rosé wine dwindle to the bottom of his glass.

It was too dark to be morning, it was too early to drink, and he was too intelligent to be a Wayman, but all three were true. Through the window of the tavern he watched the Fandorans file by in clusters of four and five. It was time for the High Council, and the people of Tamberly Town were making their way to the event. Many took blankets and leather-tops to protect themselves from the rain. They would doubtless camp out on the winding steps of Hightop Pass to await the decision of the Elders.

The Wayman smiled. The Fandorans were good people, with a sense of justice. He was a Southlander and a victim of a less noble code of ethics. He had fled to Fandora after his trading business and left eye had been ruined by a notorious band of thieves. Unable to pay his debts, he had traveled north until he had found employment as a Wayman in Fandora. It was a suitable profession for an outsider. His job was to track down runaway young men and women who had tired of the rugged life of Fandora or petty thieves who infrequently victimized the farmers and merchants of the Fandoran towns. Although the Wayman was one of the few foreigners to reside in the country, he was well-liked and respected. His experience in the Southland was invaluable in his new work, and his tall frame and broad shoulders made the solicitation of clients easier than he had expected. He kept to himself, saved his waxings, and explored the countryside in his spare time.

There were some thirty villages in Fandora, stretching over approximately fifty miles of northern and eastern coastline and about fifty square miles within those natural borders. The Wayman had visited over half of the towns and found many similarities within them. Yet with the exception of the High Council, all were relatively autonomous, with government rarely rising above a local level. Private farms and dwellings subscribed to the laws of the closest village. Elders generally negotiated problems between adjoining areas. It was a simple system, noted the Wayman, compared to the complex government of the Southland, and until now it had seemed to serve this country without any serious problems.

The Wayman rose and turned toward the door of the tavern. Across the main square he saw a group of young men and women dressed in black with white knit caps. They were the Dancers. He was watching them perform when a sharp pain shot through his eye.

It had been a difficult month for the Wayman. He had been hired to find the son of a rich merchant from far Delkeran Town, but had lost the lad twice in as many weeks. He was sure the boy was in Tamberly Town, but the cool spring weather had affected his eye, and many hours had been lost to a wet cloth and a dark room. The oratory of Jondalrun had thrown Tamberly Town into an uproar, and the past few days had been filled with rumors of war against Simbala. Every accident and injury of the past few months was being blamed on the Sim. Two children had been murdered. A windship had crashed. He had never seen the Fandorans so worried or so angry. He knew of the Simbalese, and he knew that these people were no match for either the Sim windships or their military strategy, but he also remembered that Fandora had offered him a home. If they elected to go to war, he would do what he could to help. In his heart, however, he hoped that cooler heads would prevail.

•

Amsel was on his way to the Stairs of Summer. His route was much more direct than the road taken by others, but it was also more hazardous. He leaped from rock lip to granite spire, across chasms easily seven hundred feet deep. He moved swiftly along ledges scarcely six inches wide. Though he was not as fast or as surefooted as he had been when younger, the inventor still made good time. A rainstorm was coming, and he did not want to be caught in it. He was also anxious to reach the site before the Elders, so as to position himself where he could hear them but not be seen. He worried, for it had been three days since he had learned about the meeting from the child, and much seemed to have transpired in Tamberly Town during this time. He had kept his distance from the townspeople, and from afar he had found it difficult to discover the issues at hand. He leaped from an outcropping and landed on the thin edge of a rock chimney which split the cliff face parallel to the Stairs. He descended this, back against one side and feet on the other, and arrived at last at a natural alcove in which a balcony of stone overlooked part of the amphitheater. Amsel settled himself there, his small notebook and quill pen in hand, and waited.

•

Many of the townsfolk had followed the Elders to the Stairs of Summer, for a council was a rare thing, and the subject they discussed concerned the people deeply. None but the Elders, however, were allowed to climb the Stairs to the natural amphitheater where the voting would be done. Jondalrun was the last of them to ascend. Before he did so, he turned to the men and women who had assembled outside.

"Take care you do not set foot on the Stairs," he charged them. "Remain here. You will know the results of our caucus soon enough."

"What harm would be done if we listen?" asked a tall man. "We would not interrupt the Council."

"You cannot listen," Jondalrun said with finality. "We must proceed according to the law." With that he turned and began slowly mounting the Stairs to join the other Elders.

They were not aristocratic, these Elders of Fandora. Some

still grasped the sickles and mattocks they had used to climb the rocks. Most were dressed in the simple garments of farmers. Yet their expressions were those of men who knew that their vote would affect the lives of their countrymen.

In accordance with the rules of the High Council, the Elders had previously selected from their ranks a Mandator, who would function as chairman for the meeting. Pennel had been elected. He stood on a small stone pedestal in the center of the amphitheater and stared out at the assembly, illuminated by torches. He saw tense faces, bitter faces. Pennel knew who must, by custom, speak first, and so he called the name of the Elder who had initiated the meeting.

"I call Jondalrun, Elder of Tamberly Town."

The father of Johan faced the council. He spoke with compassion and anger. His love of Fandora was as much a part of him as the voice that stirred even the hearts of Elders from distant towns who knew little about the Simbalese.

"There have been murders," Jondalrun said. "We live in a state of siege, afraid for our children's lives and our own. We search the skies for the insidious windships, and we are frightened to brave the streets at night! We struggled hard to build this land and we have endured much to remain here and work, too much to be threatened by those who are jealous of our prosperity. This is either the start of an all-out attack by madmen or the casual bloodthirstiness of sorcerers! I call for justice! I call for war!"

Jondalrun returned to his seat. For several moments none of the Elders spoke. None dared challenge the principle of bringing justice to those responsible for Johan's death. Yet there were questions, doubts that could not remain unvoiced.

Pennel called upon an Elder of Gordain Town, who told of how the Simbalese windship had crashed into the town and started several fires. Then another Elder ascended the pedestal. It was Lagow, the wheelwright. Tamark's words at dinner and his own objections forced him to make his dissension known. "Why would the Simbalese wish to attack us in the first place?" he asked the crowd. "If they live such lives of pampered ease, why would they want our land?" Lagow spoke with honesty and compassion. He did not wish to add to Jondalrun's burden, but he had even less desire to send his country to war.

"They envy our self-sufficiency, our prosperous farms and sea-fishing!" Jondalrun shouted. "From what we have learned, they are forced to do much trading with the Southland for foods."

"It seems to me," Lagow said, "that sorcerers would not have trouble finding something to eat."

"Not so!" cried Tenniel of Borgen Town. "They are ignorant of the land—they know little about farming."

"Yes!" said another. "They are hungry people. They are jealous of our full harvests and our healthy children! Everybody knows that sorcerers need victims on whom they can practice their foul craft! They would not use their children, and so they attack ours!"

When the protest subsided, Lagow returned to his seat. He was unconvinced, but he thought there was little chance of persuading the Council to agree. There seemed to be much support for the invasion of Simbala. The obstinacy was frightening, but he thought it prudent to remain quiet now. To antagonize them further would diminish his influence. He felt his time could be better spent in an effort to ensure moderation in any action the Elders proposed. In any case, he would vote against the invasion.

Tamark of Cape Bage watched Lagow, appreciating his honesty. The accusations that had been made were unproven, based on rumor and even lies. They were rushing into war without knowing what war would be. He had traveled, he knew the Simbalese by reputation, and what he had learned would be enough to scare any of them away from the thought of war. The sorcerers were geniuses at defense and experts in battle. Even women shared in their plans. Tamark regretted the death of the children, but he knew there must be another answer. He rose to challenge the Elders.

"We have come here to decide the issue of war. I say there must be no war." Tamark's voice echoed in the amphitheater.

"Fool!" came a cry from the back row. "Traitor!" echoed another. "Children have been murdered!"

The fisherman gripped his jacket defensively. His voice was filled with pity. "I too grieve for Jondalrun, but there is no proof that a windship was responsible for the tragic event. I have yet to hear a single fact that ties the Simbalese to the murder of Jondalrun's son."

"The Wing was shredded. I saw it myself," said Agron of Tamberly Town.

"Ignore Tamark," shouted an Elder from Delkeran. "He is a foolish fisherman. I call for a vote!"

"No!" Tamark reddened and smashed his left fist into his right hand. "You will all listen to what I say! I have traveled; I have seen more than you ever will! I know about these sorcerers. Their army would do us terrible harm! We *must* not go to war with them over this tragedy. Your son was killed, Jondalrun, but we do not know that he was murdered."

"Liar! He *was* murdered!" Jondalrun walked angrily toward the pedestal.

"What about the shepherd's daughter?" another Elder said. "There was no cliff for her to fall from, no hermit magician to bewitch her into the sky. It could only have been a windship!"

"You have heard how the Simbalese attacked Gordain Town," Jondalrun shouted, pressing his advantage. "Only the rains kept half the town from dying in the fires!"

"I worry for my children's safety," said an Elder of Gordain Town. "We must defend ourselves."

Many of them shouted approval of this. Amsel, tucked away in his secret spot, murmured, "This doesn't sound good at all." If this went on, the decision would be war—of that he was sure.

He stood up. He could not let them vote for war without having his say. He had to convince them that he had nothing to do with the Simbalese—that he alone bore the guilt for Johan's death.

Pennel, the Mandator, had succeeded in quieting the crowd. "Is there anyone else who wishes to speak?" he asked.

Amsel took a deep breath and stepped from his balcony onto the Stairs. "I wish to speak," he said. His voice sounded very small to him.

There were shouts of outrage as he was recognized. Jondalrun leaped to his feet. "Spy!" he shouted.

"I want to address the council," Amsel said. "It is my right to speak—"

"You have no rights, murderer!" another Elder shouted.

"You were spying! Hiding in the rocks, eavesdropping on the High Council!"

"Wait!" Amsel cried. "I wasn't—"

"He is a spy!" Jondalrun cried. "Take him!"

Several of the younger Elders, including Tenniel, ran up the stairs toward Amsel. The inventor, panicking, turned and ran ahead of them up the ancient natural steps. Beyond the first arch there was a section where the wall had collapsed. Amsel clambered nimbly up the steep slope and disappeared from view.

Once again Pennel slowly restored order. Once again he asked if there were any other voices to be heard. This time there was no response.

"Then," he said in a heavy voice, "we shall vote."

•

Amsel did not stop running after he reached the top of the slope. He kept going, bounding from crag to peak, until at last he crouched safely on a high eyrie.

From there he listened. He could see the townsfolk gathered outside the amphitheater, the children playing, the men and women waiting somberly. Then came the first echo as the vote of the High Council resonated through the walls and crannies of the hills. He heard the first "Aye," and then another, and another, spoken in determined voices. Few dissented.

Soon after, the Elders left the amphitheater. The clouds were lifting now, but the air hung more heavily than it had before the Council. Amsel sighed. "No doubt about it, no doubt at all. The vote was for war, and once again I am in part to blame. If only I had not run—but what else could I have done? Their mood was ill; they would not have listened. What could I have told them? Even I do not know what brought Johan to death."

He hung his head. "Johan, Johan," he murmured. "If they persist in this folly, you will be but the first of many."

He looked up at the gray clouds. "Someone must do something," he said, "and it looks like it must be me."

VI

The Couriers passed the word quickly. For the first time in its two-hundred-year history, Fandora would go to war.

In the main square of Tamberly Town, Jondalrun, flanked by the other Elders, addressed the people in the square. "We shall raise an army," he told them. "The Sim forests and windships will burn and their evil shall no longer spread to our shores. They shall be punished for the death they have brought to Fandora." There was a low muttering of approval. The boisterous support heard only hours ago had cooled considerably.

Tamark stood before the blacksmith's shop and watched the crowd. They have what they wanted, he thought, and now they are uncertain.

After the speech, Jondalrun was approached by the Elders Tenniel, Agron, and Lagow, who found him, grim-faced, by a well off to one side of the square. Lagow was the first to speak. "I shall abide by the decision of the High Council, and I acknowledge your appointment as the director of our army."

"You acknowledge it, but you do not approve, Lagow."

"It is out of my hands. We are still neighbors, Jondalrun, and I am still a Fandoran. Have you given any thought to how you will raise and arm your army?"

"We will make weapons," Jondalrun said. "A man knows how to fight. Our most important weapon will be the fact that we are right and that we know it."

Lagow looked at his heavy brown boots, scarred by the journey and the rain. "It will take more than enthusiasm to be victorious over the Simbalese."

"If you lack the confidence to join us, Lagow, I am sure there are others from Jelrich Town who would be eager to take your place."

Lagow looked up. "Don't be insolent with me, Jondalrun! You need all the help you can get for this fool's invasion!"

Jondalrun stepped closer to Lagow. "Is it foolish for a father to seek justice after the murder of his child?" he asked in a threatening tone.

"No," answered Lagow harshly, "but I would think you'd be more cautious about sending other men's sons off to be killed!"

Jondalrun swung his fist at Lagow. Lagow quickly ducked and leaped forward. The two grappled.

"Please!" Agron shouted. "This is no way for Elders to act! The children will see!" He made a vain attempt to separate the two. Jondalrun pushed him away and again lunged at Lagow. Lagow tripped Jondalrun; they rolled in the mud of the square.

Tenniel broke up the fight with a clumsy blow to the back of Jondalrun's head with the bucket from the well. The Elder, stunned, rolled over onto his back.

Tenniel gasped. "I think I hit him too hard!" He lowered the bucket down the well quickly and splashed water on Jondalrun after it had returned. During the process Lagow departed, after speaking briefly to Agron.

When Jondalrun had recovered, Lagow was not to be seen. "The coward," said Jondalrun.

"No," replied Agron. "He is a patriot. He has gone to send a Courier to his town with news of the High Council's decision. You must prepare yourself for opposition to the verdict, Jondalrun. No Fandoran has ever set foot in Simbala. The thought of doing battle with sorcerers is frightening to some."

"Aye," said Tenniel, "to many."

"We need something to protect us against them. We need magic of our own," said Agron. "Some sort of potent spell to protect us against any Simbalese sorcery."

"No!" Jondalrun protested, pounding the brick lip of the

well with his fist. "We shall not seek justice with their evil ways!"

"Be sensible, Jondalrun," Agron said. "This is war, and we must be prepared for anything they bring to bear against us. It does not mean that we will have to use it—simply that we should have it if the need arises."

"But where would we find such magic?" asked another Elder who had hurried to the scene of the fracas.

"I have heard of a place," Tenniel said reluctantly. "Within the Alakan Fen, according to tales, there dwells a witch—"

"No!" Jondalrun shouted. "We'll have naught to do with magic that black!"

"What is so terrible about this witch?"

"She was once an inhabitant of Tamberly Town," Agron said. "At a time when the raving fever was at its worst, she was found guilty of aiding its spread by inculcating it in rats."

"She claimed she was trying to find a way to stop its progress by feeding the rats certain foods. She might as well have attempted to stop a fire by throwing oil on it!" Jondalrun said. "A storm overturned the cages and released the rats, and several people died from their bites. After this she was banished. We'll have naught to do with her!" He glared at the others.

"According to what I have heard," Tenniel said, "she also performed many good deeds, such as producing corn with huge ears, and telling you where to sink the shaft for this very well."

"True," Agron said slowly. "This well has never run dry, even during the drought three years past."

It eventually took an impromptu gathering of the Elders and a vote to sway Jondalrun. It was decided that even though most of the Elders shared Jondalrun's objections to the woman, the risk was warranted.

•

Amsel inspected an old map of Simbala which he had bought years before from a Southland trader. His plan was born of desperation. It hinged on a successful journey across the strait to Simbala, where he hoped to confront the Simbalese and ask for their help. If they could build windships,

he reasoned, they must be an intelligent people, and if they
were an intelligent people, sorcerers or not, they would be
opposed to war. It was a desperate plan, but he had little
choice. He did not know what else to do.

"Sorcerer! Surrender!"

The door of his tree house exploded under the impact of a
heavy shoe. A moment later, three Elders, the same who had
chased him up the Stairs of Summer, appeared in the room.
"We have come to take you back to Tamberly Town to stand
trial as a murderer and a spy!" the youngest shouted.

"I'm sorry," Amsel said, "but I was just leaving." He
turned and ran. The three pursued him; one of them tripped
on a table leg and overturned a candle burning under an
alembic. It landed in a stone dish of telharna oil, which
blazed up suddenly and set fire to a stack of scrolls next to
the collection of fossilized bones.

There was barely time for the three Elders to escape to the
outside. In the confusion, Amsel slipped out a side window.
He climbed swiftly up the old tree beside his house, until he
reached the branch that was level with Greenmeadow Mesa.
Then he hid behind a hillock of grass and watched the
smoke rise. His house and his possessions were in flame—the
results of a lifetime of experiments and research, done for no
other reason than the love of knowledge, but nonetheless
precious for that. Amsel watched silently, tears running
down his cheeks. When the smoke began to subside, he
turned away from it and set out. All he had left were the
things in his pockets and his pouch—his spectacles, a
notebook, the seeds he had intended to investigate a few
days earlier, and a knife. He had lost the map of Simbala.

He made his way through the early-morning light toward
the seaside cliffs, jumping nervously at the occasional
sounds of squirrels or birds. In every shadow he thought he
saw the Elders waiting to pounce. He was hungry and tired,
and he wondered why he was trying to save these people
who wanted to imprison him, who had burned his home. He
had never harmed anyone—had, in fact, gone out of his way
to avoid people—and this was how he was thanked. Let them
reap the consequences of their folly, then! It would serve
them right if the Simbalese were sorcerers and if they
turned every Fandoran into stone!

If he had any sense at all, Amsel told himself, he would try to find a new life for himself in the Southland. But he kept walking toward the sea. Before him, in the afternoon sky, it seemed that he could see a vision of a young boy, fair-haired and laughing, shaming the birds as he soared on a device of leather and wood. And now he could see the boy falling, could see the joy on his face turn to terror. . . .

Amsel closed his eyes. He pressed the heels of his hands hard against them for a moment, until he saw luminous patterns. Then he shook his head, and kept walking toward the sea.

He did not know how or why the shepherd's daughter had died, but he knew why Johan had died, and he knew the lad deserved a better epitaph than being a reason for war.

He reached the waters of Balomar late that afternoon. Some weeks before he had moored a small skiff, with provisions and water, in a cave on the beach. To his relief, it was still there. He promptly put out to sea, rowing past the breakers and then unfurling the single sail of yithe cloth. The wind was against him, and it was necessary to tack slowly and tediously. He was nervous. He had never sailed very far from land, but he would make it, he told himself. He would make it, for Johan's sake.

VII

The first rays of morning sunlight streamed through the clouds that had shrouded Simbala for a week. Parrots, macaws, and other birds took to the air, joyous in the sun, their plumage iridescent. It was as though a rainbow had broken into brilliant shards over the towering tree canopy. For a moment they seemed to celebrate the passing of the rain—and then, in an explosion of harsh and melodious cries, they were gone. In an instant the sky was left to a single bird, high overhead, which dropped swiftly toward a rift in the sea of green.

It was a hawk. Huge, wings curved and rigid, it shot through the interwoven branches and vines that were still wet from the storm. Monkeys with orange hair chattered in fear and hugged close to tree trunks as the hawk fell past them. Squirrels dived into knotholes and peered out, blinking.

The hawk paid no attention to them. It burst through the forest roof and into the dim green light of Overwood. It flew between giant trees, over a forest floor thick with tangled wet undergrowth. Then it passed over a low wall of stone, and beyond that the grass was short-cropped, and the undergrowth was replaced by tended beds of flowers.

Here and there were individual bushes of topiary, trimmed in the shape of beasts and birds; the hawk flew past a living sculpture of itself, with wings five feet across. There were also leafy likenesses of lions, bears, and horses, as well

as the giant goats that pulled the Rayan wagons. Trees whose trunks had been tessellated with jeweled mosaics lined the paths.

The hawk flew on. The first buildings it passed were small, ivy-choked cottages and stone huts. Some of them were shabby or rundown. Occasionally one of the more massive trees had a crude door cut into it.

The hawk began to pass people now, men and women whose clothes were rough and patched. Some were miners, with the marks of digging on their hands and clothes—caked dirt on their boots and beneath their nails. They sat on benches and stools beside their homes. Others were woodwrights, tradesmen, stoneworkers. They watched the hawk wing its way past them, and some of them, miners and others, smiled and pointed as though seeing a good omen. But others scowled and turned away.

The hawk continued its flight. The dwellings became more numerous and more elegant, though they always kept an integrated feeling with the wood that surrounded them. More trees with doors, windows, and terraces were evident. Some buildings were built around the trees; others stood on their own. The architecture was rich and varied. There were mansions with peaks and gables, buildings of quarried marble, and small homes with exquisite gardens. Roofs were laid with tiles or shingles, or covered with domes of hammered brass.

The hawk passed more people on the wide flagstone paths or crossing streams by bridges made of giant tree roots. The men wore tunics of muted colors, pleated and stitched with filigree. The women wore gowns that swirled silkenly. These people also reacted in various degrees of delight or annoyance at the sight of the hawk.

The hawk did not deviate from its course, unless it was to fly around a trellis covered with sweet-smelling blossoms, or some other obstacle. It flew on until the parklike spacing of the trees grew broader still, and the dim misty green of the forest showed hints of gold and crimson from the hidden sun. Then it entered an open clearing, and there before it was what could be called the father of all trees: five hundred feet in diameter, its top lightning-riven by countless storms. In other lands, its lesser branches would have made trees to talk about. At the base of this noble giant, this oldest of living things, a flight of wide steps led to the entrance of the palace. At various levels in the trunk, terraces, balconies, and windows had been carved. The hawk flew toward a very small, narrow window high above the ground, and disappeared within.

●

Two shadowy forms brushed the darkness. The first was young, the second old, but the dim light of the staircase did not betray a difference.

"Hawkwind," said the latter, "you move too quickly for an old man to keep pace!"

The young man smiled. "You are no older than Monarch Ambalon was when he taught you how to govern Simbala."

The old man shook his head. "I am not my father, Hawkwind."

"The people say you are his equal, Monarch Ephrion."

"Nonsense."

"Even those who resent my presence in the palace do not deny it."

"Frah! They say I am an old man who no longer understands the meaning of his decisions."

The younger man laughed. "Perhaps they are correct," he said, his eyes twinkling in the darkness.

The white-haired man in the beige robe started to join him in laughter, but the sound was staccato, more like a cough than an expression of delight. "Perhaps they are correct!" he said. "How did you talk me into this excursion? I should have let you explore these back halls yourself!"

The younger man helped him down the staircase. "I shouldn't have brought you here," he said, "but there are few who know the palace as intimately as you do."

"True," said the older man. "There has been peace for so long that the Family has lost interest in secret corridors and staircases. I do not regret it."

"Nor I, Monarch Ephrion. It is just that I find it difficult to live in a place that keeps secrets from me."

"Perhaps you find the palace to be too much like yourself."

To this observation the young man did not reply. The pair quietly continued their descent toward a soft light at the bottom of the stairs.

The younger man was named Hawkwind. He was tall and

lean. His eyes, black as a starless sky, stood out starkly against a pale complexion. He was the son of a miner, and in his thirty-three years he had known both poverty and abundance. He walked with his shoulders back and head high. It was the posture of a hero, but few knew the modest heart behind the legend he had become. There were stories about him, about his bravery, and there were mysteries, too, for he had traveled to unknown lands and chased dreams that most shared only in childhood memories. His voice was deep; it inspired confidence in those who supported him and anxiety in those who did not. There was much anxiety in the Royal Family these days. He was Hawkwind, a common man, and the newly elected Monarch of Simbala.

The older man was white-haired, soft-spoken, and eighty years old. His unsteady gait betrayed the effects of a debilitating stroke, but his eyes revealed a man who had lost little, if any, of the intelligence and compassion which had earned him the love of Simbala. He was Monarch-Emeritus Ephrion, the man who had selected Hawkwind as his successor, the first Monarch in centuries to look outside the Royal Circle for a person to govern Simbala.

He gazed affectionately at Hawkwind. He remembered the first time he had seen the young man's midnight eyes, and he remembered the feeling that had welled up inside him. In Hawkwind he saw the future of Simbala, a man whose love of life and people, whose sense of honesty and justice, could take the country beyond the problems of the merchants, the poverty of the Rayan, the discontent of the Northwealdsfolk and the pretentiousness of the Royal Family to an era even more beautiful than that of his own forty years in office.

He had hoped that the opposition to Hawkwind would give way to a new excitement and a dream. His sister, Lady Graydawn, had supported Hawkwind; she alone of the Royal Family had given him wholehearted support. Ephrion had depended on the people for the approval of Hawkwind, and popular sentiment had indeed swayed the Circle. Yet the support of the citizens and the consent of his rebellious sister had not settled matters in the Family. There were still too many intrigues against the young man.

Ephrion saw the window at the bottom of the high and narrow stairway. As he did, Hawkwind smiled. The old man took delight in the way the expression dispelled the ominous cast of the younger man's features. The people should see him smile more often, he thought. It would help those who doubt my decision to understand it better.

As they reached the window near the bottom of the steps, a cry pierced the silence, and with a great flapping of wings the hawk entered and settled on Hawkwind's shoulder. The young Monarch braced himself, but showed no signs of discomfort at the bird's weight.

Ephrion arched his brow. "Uncanny. He's found you once again."

Hawkwind did not reply at first. He took a morsel of grain from a pouch in his robe and gave it to the hawk. The bird accepted it gravely, its eyes alert and unblinking.

"We move in circles, Monarch Ephrion."

The Monarch-Emeritus grasped the younger man's arm. "Do not be pretentious with me, Hawkwind."

Hawkwind smiled. "The hawk and I move in circles. We travel a path that brings us back to where we began."

Ephrion nodded. Whether or not this meant that Hawkwind would one day leave the throne and return to the mines, he did not know. At times the young man could be exasperating. Ephrion stepped forward and felt the firmness of a landing beneath his foot. Hawkwind, doing likewise, faced the wall in front of them.

"Here?" he asked Ephrion.

"Yes. Feel the temwood sill with your hand. You should find a deep incision. Meliphon, the architect of these hidden passages, designed them to be opened and closed only by those who have learned their secrets. When you find the incision, pull it to your left."

Hawkwind felt the door with his hand. He felt a thin horizontal line in the wood, and he pulled the section above it. The entire panel gave way, revealing the bright light of another room.

"Monarch Hawkwind!"

The two men entered an adviser's antechamber. In front of them stood General Vora, Minister of the Army of Simbala, a rotund, bearded whirlwind contained in a uniform of military design—silk breeches, tansel surcoat, and silver tunic. To his right was Ceria of Shar Wagon, a Rayan woman and Minister of the Interior, adviser to Hawkwind.

The room was small, but spectacular. The northern wall was a huge open window, providing Ceria, Vora, Ephrion, and Hawkwind with a view of the woods far below, where animals roamed freely behind the palace. A sweet breeze caused the curtains on each side of the window to billow gently.

Directly in front of the window, framed by the curtains and the outer view, stood a throne, raised four shallow steps above the carved floor. Walking around this, Hawkwind extended his arm out of the window and with a muscular effort "threw" the heavy bird up into the air. Then he returned, nodded to the two Ministers, and took his place on the throne.

He looked at Ceria, and fire leaped from his eyes to her face. She returned his gaze and smiled, a beautiful yet enigmatic smile. Her eyes were blue; they were not piercing like Hawkwind's, yet they seemed to see to the heart of everything. They reflected the young Monarch's dark gaze and turned it to light. To others, Ceria was a threat, an outsider. To Hawkwind, she was love.

"Sire," she said, pulling back the cowl of a simple red robe to reveal black hair curled at the sides of her head, "is it not the role of your Ministers to say when policy and rules are not in the best interest of our people?"

"It is," said Hawkwind, noticing a frown on Vora's face, "but perhaps you could explain such matters to me, Ceria, rather than to my other advisers."

"You weren't here. The General and I were simply rehearsing our respective stances, that we might be succinct for you."

"Succinct, she says!" General Vora laughed. "The day you put something succinctly, my dear, will be the day the sun rises and sets in an hour!"

The woman gently bit her lower lip. "Monarch Hawkwind, I merely maintain that it is not necessary for our troops to remain on the flooded Valian Plains, when they can return home at night. To have them do so causes needless hardship and ill will. We are not at war."

"An army is an army!" the General said. "During maneuvers it is necessary that all preparations for battle be carried out. Otherwise they will be ill-set for attacks and hardship, should they occur. Now is an excellent time to train!

Hawkwind has sent almost half of our troops to the South-land to accompany Baron Tolchin's caravan. Putting the remainder through maneuvers provides them with rigors faced by soldiers on the road."

Ceria spread her arms in protest. "They are strong enough already, Vora. It would do us well to spend more time on the soldiers' minds."

"Their minds? Meddler! This Rayan woman is insuffer-able, Hawkwind."

"Insufferable? You have the manners of a Fandoran, Vora! I am insufferable? I demand—"

Ephrion spoke quickly, as if short of breath. "This matter is trivial, Lady Ceria. Our mines are flooded from the exceptionally hard spring rains, and the safety of our miners must be ensured. It is far more important to discuss this than the intelligence of Vora's troops."

"Insufferable!" muttered Vora as he left the room.

Hawkwind sighed. "Ceria, you must learn to contain your thoughts."

"If my thoughts are correct, should I not speak them?"

"Naturally," said Ephrion, "but you must be more politic. Although our army is composed of both men and women, General Vora has too much pride to be challenged by an adviser as young as yourself. If you wish to change Vora's mind, you'd best approach it more circumspectly."

Hawkwind broke in, his quiet tone soothing the charged atmosphere. He began reviewing the day's events. "Minister Elloe will bring news of the closing of the Sindril mine. Then we shall leave the palace. Are all preparations completed for the appointment of Prince Kiorte?"

"Yes," said Ceria. "The ceremony will take place at the Dais of Beron. The Royal Family has been notified of the affair and they will all attend."

"Good. The event may charm Princess Evirae to some small degree."

"Not likely," said Ephrion, as the door to the antechamber opened to reveal General Vora, his good humor evidently restored, eating a handful of crackleberries.

"If Evirae had her way," said the General, "she'd be giving the appointment to Kiorte herself. It's no secret that Evirae wants the Ruby. Her parents would be happy to see her have it."

"General Jibron and Lady Eselle would be happy to see anybody from the Royal Family in the palace," said Ceria.

"Enough speculation!" Hawkwind rose from his chair. "General Jibron is entitled to his opinion, as is his wife. We shall see them soon enough, and you must both be cordial."

"It is not always easy," said Vora.

•

"Hold fast to those ropes!" Kiorte cried. He ran across the docking area toward the trees. All about him was shouting and disorder as men tried to seize the flailing ropes trailing from the runaway windship. The strong wind whipped at Kiorte's black hair and tore at the sleeves of his dress uniform—at times it buffeted him hard enough to make him stumble. But he did not stop.

Behind him, on the gigantic flat stumps that were the launching platforms, the other windships' balloon sails were being quickly furled. The gale had risen unexpectedly, and they were lucky, Kiorte thought, that just one craft had been torn free. Even that would not have happened if that fool groundfellow from the palace had not insisted on going aboard.

The rear anchor had not been raised, and had become entangled in a tree at the forest's edge. If not for that, the windship would have blown out over the strait, like the unmanned vessel that had vanished weeks ago. As it was, the ship hung, caught like a child's kite, sails straining, half-inflated. It could pull loose at any second.

Kiorte, Prince of Simbala, leaped up and caught the lowest branch of the tree, swung himself up and began to climb. Leaves lashed his face, and he scratched his hands on the rough bark. He could feel the tree swaying as the windship tugged against the anchoring rope. He could see it above him, the small boat beneath the giant sails, which flapped and boomed in the gale.

The anchor had caught almost fifty feet above the ground. Kiorte's brother, Thalen, and others were holding onto the other ropes; for a moment the ship hung fairly steady as the wind dropped. Kiorte reached a branch level with the anchor rope. He took a deep breath and leaped out, catching the rope. He hung there, high above them, waiting for the momentum of his leap to expend itself. The rope reacted to his weight by giving; for a heart-stopping moment he thought it might come loose from the tree. But it did not. Kiorte pulled himself quickly up, hand over hand.

His arms were trembling from the strain when he finally grasped the wood railing and pulled himself on board. The boat was canted at a steep angle. The brazier, solidly mounted and shielded against the wind, was going full blast—the buoyant gas from the Sindril jewels was pouring into the flue of the sails. Kiorte saw the groundfellow, a minor palace functionary who, he had been told, had insisted on going aboard one of the boats without supervision to check its stocks. He was now sprawled in the stern, eyes wide with fright.

"I don't know what happened," he began to babble as Kiorte slid down the steep deck toward the small cabin. "I must have accidentally touched the ignition handle on the brazier—the jewels began burning!"

Kiorte swung himself up to the cabin's low roof, where the brazier was secured. "You could not have opened the valve enough to soak the jewels like this!" he said, shielding his eyes and staring into the brazier. "What else did you do? Tell me!"

"I . . . I saw they were burning," said the official. He was a small little bantam of a man, with his braid and sash sadly askew and dirtied now. "So I . . . I tried to put the fire out!"

Kiorte glanced about. In another corner of the stern he saw an empty water cask. "You *idiot!*" he shouted. "The Sindril jewels are ignited by water, not quenched!" No wonder the ship had leaped into the wind like a stallion stung by a bee. It was only because the deck was at such a steep angle, causing most of the gas to rise outside of the flue, that the anchor rope still held. Otherwise the windship would have shot into the air, up beyond sight, until the sails exploded, and that would have been the end of an expensive ship—not to mention the groundfellow.

Kiorte dispersed the blazing jewels with a poker—the exposure to air quickly extinguished them. Then he climbed up into the rigging and tucked the ropes that opened the vents in the balloon sails. They began to deflate slowly. He returned to the deck, cut the anchor rope, and pushed the sinking windship free of the branches with a long clearing pole. Below, Thalen and the others pulled on the ropes, and slowly the windship was brought back to its mooring place.

The official clambered shamefacedly to the ground and staggered toward the forest, clutching his stomach and muttering something about the inspection being completed. The Windriders watched him leave, some laughing, some looking disgusted.

Kiorte vaulted over the railing onto the ground. As always whenever he left a ship, he felt a moment of sadness at being back on the ground. To be with the wind and clouds, to soar unhindered, above the highest trees, even over mountains—that was the beauty life held for him. He looked at the departing groundfellow with amusement. He had had an opportunity that comes to few outside the Brothers of the Wind—to fly, for even an instant.

Thalen joined him as they walked across the sparse grass and dirt of the landing field toward the barracks. Several Windriders passed them, saluting the Prince and complimenting him on the brave rescue.

"Who ordered the inspection?" asked Kiorte after they had passed.

"Monarch-Emeritus Ephrion," his brother replied with some impatience. "Perhaps there is truth to the rumors of his decline, after all. Or perhaps we should blame Hawkwind for charging him with the supervision of Simbala's naval fleet. I dread to think how the North Shore flotilla will fare under his inspectors."

They entered the barracks, a dome-shaped building divided into four compartments, each illuminated by light from a circular window latticed with fenestrals of horn. The brothers strolled toward a large cask. It was filled with kala juice, wine not being allowed to Windriders on duty. "I do not trust Monarch Hawkwind, as you know," said Kiorte, "but I credit him for keeping the Monarch-Emeritus active. A man of Ephrion's dignity must be entrusted with some affairs of state or he will simply waste away."

Thalen drew juice into a wooden cup. "I am surprised you afford Hawkwind the title of Monarch, brother." He sat down on a bench and shrugged. "I can understand Ephrion's virtual adoption of Hawkwind, as Queen Jeune died childless. But to choose a man such as Hawkwind for the palace, a miner who is not of royal blood, strikes me as the desperation of a Monarch with no legitimate heir."

"Desperation? Perhaps," Kiorte said. "Yet even I admit that the presence of Hawkwind compares favorably with the possibility of my wife on the throne. But that is damning with faint praise. Hawkwind, for all his experience, is still outside our circle, and this makes him casual with his appointments. I wonder if he intends to fill the palace with outlanders and commoners. A distressing thought! He has certainly made an auspicious effort in that direction."

"Ah!" said Thalen good-naturedly. "Now the cloud in your sky takes shape!"

"Not at all. I have nothing against the Rayan as people—but they know nothing of the complexities and nuances of government. For that reason, I think that making Ceria one of his advisers was a serious error on Hawkwind's part."

"Rumors say that she is more than adviser to him."

"I have heard. If this is true, then she is certainly in a position to see her whispered suggestions become laws. I need not tell you what those suggestions are like!"

"I know," said Thalen, placing his cup back on a shelf.

"You should! I've spoken of it in tones of dread often enough. If Hawkwind listens to her, we might very well have women in the Brothers of the Wind. It is an insufferable notion! No woman is strong enough or quick enough to sail a windship!"

His brother held up a hand, as though to stem a familiar tide. "Nevertheless," he said, "you must be careful how you air your views, for everyone knows how much Evirae desires the Ruby."

"It is not Evirae that I worry about. I worry about Simbala. I see the appointment of this miner's son, for all his good intentions, as a turning away from the regime. I know many of our people feel this way, too. He is not fully trusted yet. He may never be. If a real crisis arises, they will turn on him quickly." Kiorte straightened the collar of his uniform.

"It is an occupational hazard of monarchs," Thalen said, wiping dust from his brother's hat.

"True. But though Monarchs come and go, the Royal Family of Simbala has continued. That is what worries me, Thalen—that the Royal Family may not continue."

VIII

The voyage across the Strait of Balomar had become a nightmare. Sailing had never been more than a hobby to Amsel, and he regretted that now. He had hoped that the crossing would take only a day, even tacking against the winds, and he had taken only a few provisions from the cave where the boat had been stored.

His ignorance of the strait's conditions had undone him. He had encountered relatively calm water at first, but then, as he approached the center of the strait, where the waters of two great seas met and clashed, he realized just what folly he was attempting. Driven by wind and opposing currents, the waves clashed in every conceivable pattern. He had been swept into them before he fully realized the danger, and it was only the lightness of his small craft that had kept him from being capsized.

The small boat was tossed and spun about on the foaming sea, and Amsel was soon too seasick to do more than hang on helplessly. At first he traveled in circles; then he was seized by a strong current that pulled him northward, out of the worst of the strait's turbulent center. He was soon carried into calmer water, but he was also being pulled rapidly north. At first he tried to battle the current, but he was exhausted from the heavy waves, and he soon realized that the current was taking him far north of where he wanted to land. For the rest of the day and through the long night, he drifted, helpless in the current's grasp. As the sun set at the end of his second night at sea, it became clear that he was not going to be able to land at the northern end of Simbala—a strong wind was now offsetting the current's shoreward pull. In the evening light, Amsel could barely make out a few people on the distant beach; he waved, but received no response.

The northwesterly wind grew stronger. Amsel realized with a feeling of helpless terror that he was being blown out into the North Sea, known in legends as Dragonsea. It was not until late that night that the wind softened and the current dissipated in the open waters. In the calm he at last fell into an exhausted sleep.

When he awoke the next morning, the sky was overcast— there was no sun to give him an idea of the direction of the land. Not that it mattered much, because the air was now perfectly still. The sail lay limply against the mast.

He allowed himself a few sips of water and a mouthful of cheese. The fact that his countrymen were preparing to attack another country in a suicidal war while he floated helplessly adrift was maddening, but he sternly counseled himself not to waste energy reflecting upon it.

His musing was cut short by a strange sound—for a moment it sounded like the beating of distant breakers, and his heart leaped. Then he realized that the sound came from *above* him. Amsel stared overhead. In the gray clouds overhead it seemed, for an instant, that he could discern a strange, regular movement, like the motion of a bird's wings; but what bird, so high as to be concealed by the clouds, would be that large?

He listened intently, but the sound was gone. He blinked, and rubbed his eyes—the glimpse of movement was gone too. All was still. Amsel shook his head. "Hallucinations already—a bad sign," he murmured.

It took until midmorning for the overcast to burn away. This, Amsel told himself, was both good and bad—he could cast his course by the sun now, but he also had its heat to contend with. It reflected from the glassy surface of the sea, dazzling and enervating him with its light and heat. He was already quite hungry and thirsty again, but he realized that he would have to be stern with his rations. It might well take him days to reach land.

There was a single oar under the seat. He took this and

began to paddle slowly and laboriously toward the southeast.

•

Noon in Overwood was a time of green-golden light and drowsy, humid warmth. On the Avenue of the Vendors, open-air market stalls stood side by side. Here could be purchased dried fruits and foods from the Southlands. A few stands boasted fresh vegetables and fruits, chicken and fish, but most of the food came by small wagons from the Northweald, and by caravan fom the south. On this avenue could be found bolts of tapestry and damask, gossamer veils of spidersilk, precious carved jewels and wood—the products of a country of artisans. The length of the colonnade was being decorated with lanterns in which various oils and resins burned, hung from a complicated latticework, producing bright flames of different colors and scents that discouraged insects.

Everywhere people were gathering, waiting for the procession to begin. Rayan entertainers from the south juggled brightly painted gourds or played mandolins and flutes to earn tookas, the jeweled currency of Simbala. Miners sat wearily beneath trees; soldiers and commonfolk lined the streets. A sculptor was working feverishly on the trunk of a tree, trying to put the finishing touches to his sculpture of Lanoth, the Windrider who had used his ship to divert an avalanche and save a mine ten years before.

The air was full of the smells of baking pastries and the sounds of music, laughter, and conversation.

Two young miners sat in an open-air tavern. One of them, his mud-caked boots propped on the next bench (much to the distress of the proprietor), said to his companion, "It's not fair. Hawkwind was a miner, just like us, and now he's Monarch of Simbala."

"So you think it could happen to you?" the other miner, a woman, asked.

"I'm not saying that. Just saying I thought for a while that we had a friend, that the conditions in the mines would improve. But they haven't. The lower shafts are still flooded, and everything's damp in the Sindril caverns. Every time we swing a pick there, we chance setting fire to a lode."

"Even a Monarch can't control the weather," she replied. "The timbers and braces have been mostly replaced, and they're digging sluiceways for drainage. I think Hawkwind's doing a fine job."

"He was a miner," the other insisted.

"You won't be happy until you get to mine in a silk robe with a jeweled pickax," she said with fine sarcasm. He scowled at her and looked away.

At a stall, a young woman picked over various fruits while conversing with the vendor, also a woman. "It's the first time a woman has ever been made a Minister of the Interior," the customer said, "and I don't know that I like it. Some jobs ought to be left to men, says I. Not only that, but to appoint a Rayan woman . . ." She shuddered.

"It doesn't seem like a bad thing to me," the vendor said. "At least it was a decision," and she looked pointedly at the melons the other held in her hands.

Two little children were playing in the shadow of a stone fountain. One, a boy of twelve, had pinned a scrap of cloth around his neck in the manner of a cloak, and held in one hand a wooden hawk, carved wings spread. "I'm Monarch Hawkwind!" he cried. "And my eagle sees whatever evil you do!"

"He doesn't have an eagle," the second boy corrected. "He has a hawk."

"It is so an eagle!"

"Well, if it's an eagle, why don't they call him Eaglewind?"

The first boy was unable to counter this logic. "They can call him whatever he likes," he said. "He's a miner like my father."

The crowds gathered as the time of the procession grew near. Stories and opinions were exchanged, but all agreed on one thing: it would be a memorable occasion. On that point they were more prophetic than they knew.

•

The sounds of the gaiety came faintly to the ears of a lone traveler, deep in the woods to the north. He moved quickly and silently between the trees, avoiding crackling underbrush and open spaces with the unconsciousness of habit. His evident knowledge of the woods, and the green and brown of his clothes, together with the great bow and quiver of arrows he carried, marked him as a hunter of the

Northweald. His name was Willen. He was a handsome man, with long blond hair and a high forehead. Laughter and sport came easily to him on an ordinary day, but this was no ordinary day. His usually smiling face was set in hard lines. The turn of weather and the beauty of the forest were lost on him. Strapped to his belt was a small pouch. Occasionally his left hand would cup and caress it, then tighten into a fist.

He listened to the sounds of the distant city. Let them laugh and enjoy themselves while they can, he thought. They will have little reason for rejoicing after I have spoken my piece! The Royal Family has looked down on us for centuries, but when the Overwood has need for food, we are never pariahs. So be it; our people have not complained. We have no need for the pretensions of windships or palaces. The Northweald can take care of itself. But what happened yesterday was beyond such squabbles. Now we shall demand what is due us as rightful citizens of Simbala.

Lady Graydawn had told him of the procession. She did not intend to be there, but Willen did. What better time, after all, to present what had happened to Monarch Hawkwind?

He was nervous—he rehearsed his speech mentally, over and over. He had been to Overwood only once before in his life, as a small child, and he retained only a confused memory of sweeping marble-and-wood buildings encrusted with jewels, of people dressed in fine sparkling clothes, and of the giant tree castles. It had been beautiful, but he had never felt a desire to live there. His home was the Northweald—the steep wooded hills and valleys cut by icy streams, the scent of pines, the sound of the wind through meadows filled with crackleflowers. Better the smallest log cabin of Northweald than the finest palace of Overwood. It was his home, and he did not intend to let an attack on it go unrevenged.

His hand once again sought the pouch by his side; this time he opened it and withdrew several fragments of jagged brightly colored shells. He held them tenderly, looking at them until tears made the colors swirl and run in his vision. These fragments had been clutched in the fingers of little Kia when his son had found her crushed and broken on the beach. She had been missing for weeks—search parties had combed the area but had not found her. Only by accident had Willen's son, exploring a remote part of the beach, discovered what was left of the girl's body. She had evidently been collecting seashells when the Fandoran barbarians had attacked her. Nearby, his son had found more of the shells, shattered on the rocks—the remnants, no doubt, of some large mollusk cast up from the sea.

Of course, it had been the Fandorans that had attacked her. Who else could it have been? Certainly there were no creatures living in the barren lands near the sea. Nor was there any reason in the world for the Southland or Bundra to attack them. Simbala lived peacefully with its neighbors.

Last night, however, a small Fandoran fishing boat had been sighted in the fog of the strait, far offshore. Willen returned the shells to his pouch. The Fandorans were barbarians—that much had always been known. Now it was evident that they were murderers, too. Kia had not been his daughter, but he had known her and loved her like his own. It could as easily have been his own son killed.

The Fandorans could not be allowed to go unpunished. He would seek the help of the people of Overwood. Despite their differences with the Northweald, surely they would help.

Before him was a low stone wall on the edge of Overwood. Willen vaulted it with a leap and hurried down the path. The sounds of merriment were very close now.

•

From the broad steps of the huge tree containing the palace, along the sweeping road known as Monarch's March, the Royal Family began its procession to the Dais of Beron. People lining the street joined the march cheerfully as the Family passed by, and in a few moments it seemed that virtually the entire city had joined the casual parade.

In the forefront walked Hawkwind and Ephrion, with General Vora and Ceria. The latter glanced over her shoulder at the huge, happy throng behind them, then looked at Hawkwind and laughed. "This threatens to grow out of hand!"

"Listen to them, Hawkwind," Ephrion added, speaking as loudly as he could to be heard over the sound of music and singing. "So much for those who say you are not well-liked!"

"If you say so, Monarch Ephrion," said Hawkwind, but the General, on his other side, responded, "On the first sunny day after a week of rain, I would join a parade even if a dragon were leading it!"

Behind them, loosely arrayed, walked the rest of the Royal Family: the Lady Eselle and General-Emeritus Jibron were in the forefront. Eselle, younger sister of Ephrion and mother of Princess Evirae, was resplendent in a gown of lace and gold lamé, her beauty tempered by age but still considerable. She spoke in a penetrating whisper to her husband, Jibron. "Notice how Hawkwind and Ceria laugh and speak together so casually," she said. "I am sure they discuss more than matters of state, dear. Is it not entrancing?"

" 'Scandalous' is more the word!" General-Emeritus Jibron snorted. He was a tall man, gray-haired but unbent, in better physical condition, in his opinion, than many of the Simbalese soldiers young enough to be his sons. "This is yet another sign of the laxness of the current regime," he told his wife. "It is a comedy—the Monarch and his chief adviser are commonfolk, and like as not lovers; the General, my successor, is a fat disgrace with only the barest lineal claim to the Family, and the previous Monarch is senile. There is more theater here than in the halls of the Southland."

"Do not speak that way of Ephrion," Eselle said in a tone distinctly cool. Jibron glanced at his wife, on the verge of saying something else, but he remembered that Ephrion was her brother and thought better of his words.

Behind them walked the subject of the occasion, Prince Kiorte, obviously uncomfortable in his dress uniform. Hastily cleaned and brushed, it still showed signs of the rescue he had performed in the midst of preparations for the ceremony—the silver braid on his right shoulder was stained with pine sap, and one of his pockets was torn. The pride he projected, however, kept even the closest of friends from passing comment on it.

Besides Kiorte walked a young woman, tall and quite beautiful—taller even than her husband by virtue of her hair, which was piled in a great cone atop her head. The sunset-colored tresses were woven with strings of jewels and pearls. Her skin was pale, almost translucent, and her eyes were the green of the surrounding forest. A slightly petulant cast to her mouth gave her an adolescent beauty that many Simbalese men found entrancing. Her nails were almost as long as her fingers, and each one was painted a different color. She stared straight ahead as she walked, smiling briefly to either side as people called either her name or Kiorte's. She was Evirae, Princess of Simbala, wife of Kiorte.

She slowed her step and dropped back a pace, until she walked abreast of a young brown-haired man who wore the uniform of a palace functionary. He did not look at her as he spoke. "Smile, milady," he said softly and with a trace of cynicism. "This is a happy occasion. Your husband is being installed as the rightful head of the Brothers of the Wind. Are you not delighted?"

"Of course I am, Mesor." She smiled brilliantly, waving to the onlookers. "It is simply hard to enjoy the fact when the commendation is being given by a Monarch from the mines."

Kiorte glanced back at his wife and her adviser but said nothing. Evirae drew in her breath. "Did he hear us?"

"Not at all," Mesor said. "It is simply bad form for you not to walk by his side for more than a few moments. You know Prince Kiorte's respect for form. Did you wish to ask me something?"

She sighed. "No. Not really. I merely had to express my resentment at following *them*." The last word was almost a hiss, and accompanied by an emotional look at Hawkwind and Ceria.

"Yet follow you must—at least for the time being."

Evirae looked at Mesor and smiled. "You are subtle." The smile left her face. "I fear I am not so subtle. You have heard what they say about me—the people?"

"The people always talk," Mesor said cautiously.

"A saying of late: anyone possessed with an overriding desire is said to want it 'like Evirae wants the Ruby.'" She paused. "Am I too blatant, Mesor?"

"How could one describe the rightful heir as blatant?" Mesor countered. "But . . . it might be politic not to voice your resentment so openly. Sooner or later, the miner and the gypsy girl will prove themselves unfit for office. They are, after all, not of the blood. Your day will come, Princess Evirae. I am sure of it."

"Yes . . ." Evirae said. "But we must help."

"I always have your best interests in mind, milady. Return

now to your husband. This is not the time to start another rumor of your discontent."

Evirae nodded and stepped forward. Mesor watched her and smiled. Behind him walked Baron Tolchin and Baroness Alora, the head of the Merchants' Guild and the head of the Bursars of Simbala, respectively. They were both short, round folk, looking a great deal alike, as couples married long sometimes tend to do. The only major difference was the flowing white beard Baron Tolchin wore. They were both dressed in clothes of silk and ermine, despite the heat of the day. They strolled rather than marched, conversing amiably with each other in a singsong timbre common to the merchants of Simbala.

"The caravan should have reached the Southland border by now," Tolchin was saying. "I do not know what persuaded Hawkwind to send the troops to safeguard it, but I am glad that he did."

"The hill brigands will not be so ready to rob us this time," Alora agreed. "A very good thing, too. Our losses were adversely affecting the principal rate between our merchants and those of the Southland."

Tolchin nodded slowly, as if troubled. "It was a helpful concession, those soldiers," he said. "Our country cannot live without trade. It is time Hawkwind helped us. I had been worried since the confrontation we had over the hunting of rare birds in the Northweald. Now I am disposed to give the young man a chance, if for no other reason than out of respect for my cousin Ephrion. Do you agree, Alora?" His wife did not respond. She had noticed the familiar face of a banker in the crowd, and was speculating on a way to clear up the rumors of his illegitimate affairs.

The procession continued through the forest, which was filled with sounds of dancing, music, and singing. Those who did not walk with it crowded the streets and paths to watch, to wave, and to shout cheers, for, while the people might have mixed feelings about Hawkwind, they were of one mind about Kiorte. Word of the windship rescue had spread, added to other tales of the Prince's bravery. He was a hero this day, and many ribbons and flowers were tossed in his direction.

Not all who watched the procession cheered. From a van-

tage point in a tree near the Dais of Beron, the North-wealdsman Willen watched the people of Overwood approach. It would not be long now, he told himself. Soon both he and the adoring populace would see just what sort of Monarch Hawkwind really was. The archer was still quite nervous about the imminent confrontation, but he put that in the back of his mind as much as he could. He had come to tell Monarch Hawkwind the message of the Northweald, and if his speech was too simple for the tastes of the Simbalese, it would still be good enough for his mission.

General Vora was not taking well to the walk. "I said from the start it was an error to pick a Monarch who enjoys exercise." He groaned. "I've not seen so much of Simbala since I was a soldier in the troops, thirty years ago!"

Ephrion replied teasingly, "Think how you will fare when you reach my age, Vora! You will have to hire someone with a pushbarrow to take you about!"

"General," Ceria added with a grin, "you must set an example to your troops!"

"I do," the General said. "They've but to look at my well-fed form and fine clothes, and they'll be inspired to work their way up through the ranks to a life of luxury as I did!"

At that Hawkwind laughed suddenly—a full-bodied, gusty laugh. Ceria glanced at him in surprise. In recent days she had not heard him laugh at all.

Hawkwind was an enigma to her; even, she knew, as she was to him. They did not purposely keep secrets from each other, but privacy was their nature. Yet they had so much to share, and there was so much to learn. These days there never seemed to be enough time.

When she had first met and loved him, he had been a dark-eyed miner, full of life and laughter. Now he was Monarch of Simbala, no less loving, but often serious and silent now, and much occupied with affairs of state. He had been the first to rise from the proud ranks of those who worked in the caves to join the Royal Family of Simbala. He seemed more at home with the Family than she did. He was, after all, from the Overwood, and she was not. She was Rayan; a Simbalese woman, yes, but a child of the Valian Plains and the wagons, not the central forest. She had the talents of the Rayan, talents alien to the people around her.

There were no words in the Overwood to describe her talents, but people were aware of them nevertheless. Ceria knew that she was envied, but more than envied, she felt that she was feared. This troubled her. Resentment did not have a home among her folk. Rayan people trusted each other; they had to, because nobody else did. There was good reason for this attitude, Ceria admitted; many of the Rayan found their food and lodging through scheming and thievery. Ceria's family was honest, and she wished that she could cut herself from the Rayan thieves, but how could she? Rayan were Rayan. She had risen to the role of Minister of the Interior despite the Rayan outlaws, and she intended to keep the position. Neither the Royal Family nor the scoundrels of the Valian Plains would drive her from Overwood. She looked at Hawkwind again. They both had many years ahead of them in which things could be changed. Their blood was royal to each other, she told herself, and then laughed. It was a phrase as pompous as those she often heard around the palace.

A small girl heard her laughter and skipped up alongside Ceria and Hawkwind. "May I walk along with you?" she asked shyly. Ceria watched Hawkwind's reaction. He smiled, reached down, and without breaking stride, swept the child up and set her on his shoulders. "Walk indeed!" Hawkwind said. "Why walk when you can ride?" He carried her, laughing and shouting with delight, for a few strides before setting her down. This proved to be an error in judgment, however. Other youngsters in the parade saw the indulgence, and in short order Hawkwind was surrounded by twenty of them, each of whom waved and clamored and demanded a turn upon the royal shoulders. Hawkwind turned to Ceria with a look of such comical helplessness that she added her laughter to that of the crowd. They proceeded, Hawkwind gamely scooping up one child after another for a pace or two. He was a strong man, but it was over a mile to the Dais of Beron, most of it uphill, and Ceria laughed again when they came at last into view of it and she saw the relief in Hawkwind's eyes.

"Let that be a lesson to you," she whispered. "A Monarch cannot be selective in his favors."

Hawkwind smiled ruefully in acknowledgment.

The parade had now reached the Dais of Beron—a platform made from a gigantic tree stump fully a hundred feet across. Steps led up to it, and a railing surrounded it. In the center was a raised circular podium surrounded by a semicircle of chairs, all carved from the giant's last sprouts. The entire surface had been heavily lacquered with jewel-inlaid resins; it sparkled and shone, giving off bursts of dim color as the leaves above let in shafts of sunlight.

The crowd filled the clearing. The musicians still played their lilting instruments, and children laughed as they tossed balls to one another or ran about the perimeter of the clearing with small kites in the shape of windship sails fluttering behind them. A contingent of Windriders stood in a group, slightly apart from the rest of the people, arms folded, looking very somber in their dark uniforms, as though they considered and spoke in soft tones of matters beyond the comprehension of those around them.

Monarch Hawkwind and Prince Kiorte mounted the steps to the dais, and the cheerful noise gave way to a respectful, expectant silence. Kiorte sat down, his pale face reposed and contrasting sharply with the midnight blue of his uniform. He did not look at any of the people, including the Windriders. He kept his eyes on the sky, more out of shyness and discomfort than concern with the sky. Hawkwind stepped within the raised circular podium. He turned slowly, surveying the faces in the crowd. Ceria smiled as she watched him, noting how noble he appeared—the elegant simplicity of his robes adding to the effect. The crowd cheered and applauded—unaware that the spotlight would suddenly turn to another intruder in this section of the forest.

Hawkwind spoke carefully. The Royal Family was watching, and he wished to show an improved facility for public speech. "We are here to honor Kiorte," he said warmly, "Prince of Simbala. For five years, since the death of his father, Eilat, he has led the Brothers of the Wind, defenders of Simbala. The Brothers of the Wind patrol our shorelines and boundaries and convey vital messages the length and breadth of our land, as well as to the Southland nations. Without them, we would have no easy lines of communication. They also keep watch over our beloved forest, to warn of fires and floods and other disasters."

Some members of the Circle did not feel obligated to be silent while Hawkwind spoke. "Look at Kiorte," Baroness Alora whispered to her husband. "Even with all his self-control, he is unable to keep the color from his face." She smiled with amusement. "The dear boy is embarrassed by all the attention!"

Tolchin was less than amused. "I would not confuse anger with embarrassment. Did you hear Hawkwind's words? He describes the Windriders as messengers and watchmen of the forest! It is no surprise that Kiorte looks as he does. I would too, were I head of the Windriders."

General-Emeritus Jibron agreed. "Why does Hawkwind persist in emphasizing these attributes over the Windriders' military effectiveness?"

Monarch Ephrion, standing in front of both Jibron and Tolchin, turned to them and explained. "There have been no battles for over a century. The Windriders are no longer fighters. We should be thankful for this, Jibron. I think Hawkwind wishes only to remind the people of the Windriders' continued importance in other areas."

Jibron and Tolchin nodded, but there was an air of condescension in their response. Lady Eselle, who had been listening to her brother's words in earnest, turned to her daughter. "Although you and Hawkwind may have your disagreements, you must admit he is painting a glowing portrait of Kiorte."

Evirae whispered softly to her mother, "He is merely attempting to ingratiate himself with the Circle—as if sycophantic words could make a miner acceptable as Monarch!"

" 'Sycophantic,' is it, daughter? You take your words from Mesor's mouth these days!" Lady Eselle frowned at Evirae. The Princess returned her attention to the stage.

"In awarding Prince Kiorte our recognition for his service," Hawkwind was saying, "we recognize the continuous efforts of the valiant Brothers of the Wind in protecting the safety of Simbala." There were cheers of approval at that.

Ceria, standing in the front of the crowd, looked to either side of the stage at the green depths of the forest. She had no solid reason for doing so—nothing but a feeling of unease that associated itself with the shielding trees. She did not say anything for a moment, and after that it was too late. Above the cheers a voice, slightly tremulous, but clear and strong nonetheless, cried out, "Simbala is not safe!"

All eyes turned toward the trees to the left of the platform. They saw a man dressed in green and brown crouching on the limb of a tree that overhung the dais. Before anyone could move, he hurled what appeared to be two small gray balls toward Hawkwind and Kiorte; they drew back reflexively as the first gray ball, which was a rock, hit the polished surface of the dais with a loud crack and skittered across it, drawing a large scratch in the flawless lacquer. There was a gasp from the crowd at this. The second gray ball bounced along behind the first, tethered to it by a bit of yithe rope. It was a leather sack.

Before the rock struck the glossy surface, several crossbow quarrels from guards at the edge of the dais were in flight toward the tree. Willen drew back into the foliage and changed his position, hiding behind the tree's trunk.

Simultaneously, realizing her premonition to be correct, Ceria ran up the steps of the dais, putting herself between Hawkwind and the still-rolling rock. Had she thought about it, even for an instant, had she waited to see that the thing hurled was not a weapon, she would not have done it. But she did not wait.

She realized what she had done immediately; she did not need the collective gasp of the crowd and then the low tones of whispered conversation to tell her. The rumor that she was more than an adviser to Hawkwind was now confirmed. Not even Ephrion or the General had rushed to the Monarch's protection with such alacrity—even the palace guards were only now firing their quarrels. She and Hawkwind shared glances for a moment, and in that moment, communication flowed between them—regret and worry from her, and understanding from him.

Jibron turned to Baron Tolchin behind him and flashed a knowing smile. "I told you! They are lovers!"

Tolchin stared at the drama taking place on the dais. "Yes," he murmured. "You were right. I am sorry to admit it."

Evirae's fingers closed on Mesor's shoulder—he could feel the long nails pressing upon the fabric of his tunic. "Mesor

. . ." she hissed. "I see it, milady," he replied softly. "It is our . . . your chance."

The guards were loading a second volley of arrows when Hawkwind turned to them. "Let be!" he shouted. "It is not an attack!" He turned to the General, who had moved his mighty bulk onto the dais and picked up the pouch. He opened it, his large fingers fumbling for a moment with the drawstrings, and then removed from it a crumpled garment wadded into a small mass. He did not unfold it, but handed it instead to Hawkwind. As Hawkwind took it, the General looked at his hand. There were flakes of dried blood on his fingers.

Hawkwind quickly examined the bunched cloth. It was the tunic of a small child, ripped and torn, and so covered with dried blood that it was hard to tell what color the cloth had originally been. Again there was silence, save for a sibilance in the back of the crowd, as those too far to see were informed of the pouch's contents by those closer to the dais.

Hawkwind looked up slowly into the tree. "Show yourself!" he called. "No action will be taken. Show yourself in peace!"

Willen stepped out onto the branches again, this time completely free of the leaves. It was obvious to all that he was a Northwealdsman, and once again a low murmur of conversation began. "A Northwealdsman!" Jibron muttered to Eselle. "I should have guessed as much. Only they would be guilty of such crassness."

"What do you want, Northdweller?" Hawkwind asked.

Willen held firmly to the branches with both hands and fervently hoped that the weakness in his legs and the trembling in his arms were not too evident. It had been an enormous effort just to throw the rock the necessary distance. His voice, he noted with relief, was steady.

"You know us, Monarch Hawkwind," Willen said. "The Monarchs before you have known us. We have never asked for your help, but we ask now. We demand retribution! One of our children has been killed in an act of war!"

The crowd voiced its disbelief, then waited for the Monarch's reaction.

"Do not speak to me of war. Who are the murderers?"

Willen leaned forward and raised his voice, that all might hear. "The Fandorans!" he shouted. "They have come to our shores and killed a child!"

This time, for the first time, there was laughter in the reaction of the crowd. Not much—only a few scattered bursts—but it was enough to make the Northwealdsman angry. "Hear me!" he shouted. "I speak the truth! A Fandoran fishing boat was seen off the coast of my land yesterday morn, and hours after that, the child was found dead—killed as only barbarians would have killed!"

Shouts of ridicule came from members of the gathering.

"Is their reaction yours as well, Monarch Hawkwind? You are of the people!" Willen shouted. "Unlike the Royal Family, you know the difference between simple truth and lies. What I say is true. If you choose to laugh it off, then the Fandorans may not be the only enemy of Simbala."

This statement was tantamount to treason, and the General and Ephrion, together on the dais, looked at each other in dismay. "I had hoped that he was alone in this," the General said, "but to risk such words must mean that it is a serious matter indeed."

Ephrion shook his head sadly. "It is starting again," he murmured. "The old antipathy between the Northweald and Overwood."

"We know that the Fandoran farmers and fishers have always envied us," Baron Tolchin said doubtfully to Alora, "but they couldn't have taken their resentment to this extreme?"

"Foolishness," Alora answered. "How could they possibly think that they could war with us and win?"

Willen paid no further attention to the crowd. "Understand me, Hawkwind," he said. "We of the Northweald demand revenge against the Fandorans! We will hear your answer to the Northweald in three days' time. If there is no word of justice, you will receive no additional shipments of meat or vegetables from the Northweald!"

Tolchin clenched his fists. "They would not!"

"I think they would," his wife responded.

"We have heard your terms," Hawkwind shouted. "Will you not stay and await our decision?"

"You underestimate us again," said Willen. "We will give you no hostage. If I do not return to my companion by nightfall, he will go back to the Northweald and order the boycott to begin."

"We shall see," Hawkwind answered. Then he turned to his aides, who still stood with crossbows cocked. "Let him have safe passage back to the Northweald." To Willen he continued, "You will hear from us."

Willen nodded and disappeared quickly into the foliage, with scarcely a rustle to mark his passage.

There was silence for a moment following his departure, as everyone stared at the woods. Hawkwind still held the torn and bloody rag that had been a child's dress. He stared at it, then laid it tenderly on the edge of the podium. He turned to Kiorte and spoke quietly with him.

Talk and movement suddenly exploded within the crowd. Ceria could hear fragments of excited conversation. "The Northwealdsfolk have always been mad. . . ." "Why would the Fandorans do such a thing?" Hawkwind raised his arms. When quiet was restored, he said, "In view of the circumstances, Prince Kiorte has agreed to a curtailment of the ceremonies. He is hereby proclaimed Commander of the Windshipmen."

Kiorte quietly accepted the medal, a flawless emerald hanging from a peacock feather. Then they both left the dais, Kiorte by rope ladder from a windship that now hovered above the forest clearing.

The crowd quickly dispersed to carry the news to Simbala. Hawkwind joined the General, Ephrion, and Ceria.

"There were those who said that only woe would come of a miner's son on the throne," he said, more to himself than to them. The others were silent, not knowing what to answer. Then Hawkwind sighed, and shielded his eyes with his hand for a moment. "I will need your advice," he said. "Let us return. There will be little sleep for us in the palace tonight."

They turned away from the Dais of Beron. Ceria walked behind Hawkwind, noticing the too-straight set of his shoulders. She looked beyond him, at the deepness of the forest they approached; the afternoon sun had merged its shadows into dark depths, quite different from the happy, secure place she had left earlier.

Behind them, Evirae still stood before the dais, as the clearing gradually emptied. Mesor stood by, watching her and waiting. She stood with fingers folded, tapping her long elegant nails against each other. Then she raised her head and looked at Mesor.

"Get him," she said.

Her confidant quickly vanished into the forest.

IX

Jondalrun, Tenniel, Lagow, and Tamark rode south on horseback toward the Alakan Fen. They had been elected by the Council to visit the witch, and the fen where she lived was the better part of a day's hard ride from Tamberly Town. A dawn start saw them well on the way by full day, and Jondalrun pushed the group unmercifully, not stopping for food or rest. They ate their rations of dried fish and corn in the saddle. They drove through scraggly forest and windswept highlands, riding southward, until they reached the Opain River, which they followed to the southwest. The slope of the land was downward, and the men passed several small lakes, fed by the river and its tributaries. As the sun reached its zenith, they still rode, until the horses stumbled beneath them. "A rest!" Lagow cried. "Before my mount's heart bursts through his ribs!"

"At the fen," Jondalrun shouted, not wishing to concede anything aloud to a man who had openly opposed his proposition of war. "The horses will rest and take grass at the edge of the fen. We will walk from there." The men pushed on through dust raised by a growing wind. They would reach the tangled trees of the fen by midafternoon. Better to get there now than in darkness, thought Jondalrun. Thus they rode through a stretch of rocky ground covered with slippery lichens and moss, toward the home of the witch.

When Lagow spotted the maze of trees and vines a short time later, he dismounted. He took his horse to a nearby creek and let it drink for a moment, then led it to and fro. He said angrily to Jondalrun, "Why they did not die on their feet is a mystery to me!"

"They'll have the night to rest," said Jondalrun as he took his own horse to water.

Tamark dismounted. "There are wolves hereabouts, Jondalrun! Perhaps one of us should stand watch with the horses."

"They hunt in the mountains, Tamark; they fear the fen's quicksand. The horses will be safe here where they can graze."

The fisherman wiped the lather from his horse's flank, not totally convinced.

Tenniel watched the three other Elders in silence. He had not expected such bitterness between them. Though he had had to settle many a dispute in his time, he was still surprised. They were Elders of Fandora, not farmhands. If they fought among themselves, how could they be expected to face the Simbalese? Tenniel himself had deep regrets about the death of the inventor Amsel. He had joined the other two Elders in a moment of frenzied patriotism, but when he had seen the small, amiable man trapped in the burning tree house, he had been horrified. He had helped to kill a man—a traitor to Fandora, perhaps; but still he should have listened to Jondalrun. With all his anger and obstinacy, the old man had still wanted Amsel to have a just trial. If he had listened, Tenniel thought sadly, the inventor would still be alive.

Lagow stood by the edge of the creek. "On with it," he said with a sigh, and started toward the fen. He had volunteered to be one of the four Elders who would supervise the war effort. The invasion seemed inevitable, and he felt that as a supervisor he would be in a better position to save as many lives as possible. There was one life he was sure he would save. His son would not go to war. If Lagow had to break the boy's leg to ensure it, he would.

Tamark searched his riding pouch for the map that had been given to the group by Pennel. He too was resigned to the madness of war, and he felt that he could best help Fandora by becoming a supervisor with authority over the invasion plans. If it went as far as an invasion, he thought cynically; if the farmers crossing the strait did not drown in an hour's time. Even with his experience, the waters between Fandora and Simbala would be more treacherous than the sorcerers. He wished Dayon had returned to Cape Bage. The young man knew more about the strait than many experienced sailors, for in his naiveté he had shown the daring necessary to journey though long-uncharted waters. Yet Dayon had set out on a trip two weeks earlier and had not returned. Tamark was worried.

The Elders set out through a maze of twisted trees, reeds, rushes, and ferns, their boots occasionally sinking deep into rust-colored mire. Mist surrounded them, drifting in languorous, clammy caresses over their necks and heads. Birds would burst into sudden flight nearby, startling them, and on rare occasions they would see something large and indistinct in the mist, moving slowly away from them.

They hacked through curtains of cattails with scythes. All about them were the sounds of the fen: bubblings as noxious gases were released from beneath the stagnant water, the deep mournful croaks of frogs, and sometimes a distant bellow that would cause them to stop, knuckles white on the shafts of their crude weapons. The deeper they went into the swamp, the darker it grew, as though it was always evening there at the center. They glimpsed the cold glimmerings of foxfire on stumps. The smells increased until they felt like gagging—noisome, evil odors of corruption and death. Once in a while they would pass a bush filled with small black seed pods, and Lagow, accidentally crushing one of these between his hand and a tree trunk, was refreshed by the sharp citrus smell it gave off. Thereafter they walked with a handful of them, crushing them beneath their noses when the smells became too intense.

This was the Alakan Fen, a vast miasmic swamp which covered the low pass between the Cirdulan Mountains. It, and the mountains to either side of it, effectively prevented easy access from the Southlands into Fandora. A perilous trade route existed along the spine of the mountains, coming down eventually through Hightop Pass. Other than that, Fandora was isolated, and proud of it.

For hours, it seemed, they struggled toward the center of the swamp, slapping at mosquitoes and wiping the cold-water condensation from their necks. At one point a red adder struck at Tenniel from a log—its fangs embedded themselves in the leather of his boot, and he danced back in

shock and fear. Tamark seized him by the shoulders, then
reached down and took the adder by the neck just back of
the head, pulling it free of the boot. He flung it away from
him.

"You do not seem at all fearful," Tenniel told Tamark.

"I have done the same to poison eels that have leaped into
my boat," Tamark said. "Teeth do not frighten me."

At last the thick vegetation and morass began to thin. The
ground started to rise slightly, and eventually the four
found themselves on a dreary, open low steppe covered with
stagnant pools and brown grass. In the center of this was a
small hut made of mud and reed and a few stones. They
approached it cautiously.

A fire smoldered before the hut, and crouched beside it
was what seemed to be a bundle of rags and hair. After
staring a moment, Tenniel realized with disbelief that the
filthy, ill-smelling pile held life within it.

She stirred from her crouch and raised her head, staring at
the men. She was even worse than they had expected—
shriveled and old, her face crevassed with dirt-caked wrinkles, splotched and swollen in places with disease. She lifted
an arm that was like a stick wrapped in dead leaves and
pointed it at the men.

"What do you want?" Her tone of voice surprised them.

There was something missing—the witch was reputed to
be all-knowing, all-wise. There should have been a hint of
that in her voice—an assurance, an arrogance. Instead, it
was merely an old woman's voice, querulous, even slightly
frightened.

The four men ranged themselves before her: Tenniel and
Lagow leaning on their staffs; Tamark impassive, stern gaze
fixed elsewhere; and Jondalrun, arms folded. Ready, Lagow
did not doubt, to wring the old woman's reedy neck if he
was not given a talisman.

"Woman," Jondalrun said in a flat, hard voice, "Fandora
goes to war against Simbala. We need a token to protect our
men against the Sim warlockery. I think it is a foolishness,
myself, but the majority desires it. Give us, then, some
magical working that will ensure us victory." Briefly he
explained the situation, how the children had died. Then he
was silent, and the silence of the fen surrounded them.

The old woman lowered her head again. At first Tenniel

thought she had fallen asleep, so quiet and motionless she was. Then he was aware of a slight dry sound, like two pieces of uncured leather rubbing together, and with a start he realized that the old woman was laughing. Or crying? He was not sure.

She stared at them again, and in those eyes he could see a terrible sadness. In a dry, hissing whisper she said, "Who am I, that ye ask this thing of me? I know," and she raised one emaciated hand to forestall an answer, "I am she whom ye call the witch of the fen. I am she," she shouted suddenly, "damned to an exile of mud and mist, and the babbling of occasional fools!"

She was silent after this outburst, save for mumblings to herself. Tenniel and Lagow looked at each other uncertainly; even Tamark seemed surprised. Only Jondalrun was unmoved.

"You are she with the knowledge we need," he said bluntly. "We've no time for idle conversation. Give us what we want."

She grinned a yellow, mirthless grin. "Long I've crouched here on this desolate mound," she said slowly. "This be my only respite from the monotony—visitors like yourselves. Otherwise, I am forgotten. Do any of you even know my name?" she shouted.

Tenniel, to his great surprise, found himself pitying her. He realized suddenly that she had been young once, perhaps even comely, hard though that was to believe; she had had a past, had had parents, perhaps even love. She had delved into the mysteries of nature, and she had been punished. Perhaps she had meant no harm. Yet they had called her "witch" and banished her.

Tenniel felt a great sadness well up within him. He wanted to go and leave the old woman in peace.

"Let's let her be," he muttered, half to himself. Jondalrun looked at him, and Tenniel, surprised, noticed uncertainty in that look. Then Jondalrun turned again to the witch.

"I'm sorry, old woman," he said. "But we must have protection."

"I would lie to ye if I could," she said. "I would see your trip be for naught, but I know that would eventually bring ye back for revenge. Even such as I cling to life." She plunged a hand into the crusty folds of her robe, and with-

drew it, holding a handful of small black pods. Lagow recognized with surprise the same pods that they had been carrying to ward off the odors of the fen.

She offered the pods to Jondalrun. "These be all over the swamp," she said. "String them into wristlets, and guard them well, for they be all that will protect you from the enemy you do not suspect."

Jondalrun put them in his pouch. "What do you mean?" he asked. "How are we to know their use?"

"I will say no more," she answered. "Begone, ye men of families and homes, who would risk them on so foolish a thing as war." She settled back into her crouch, and became once more a motionless pile of rags.

The men retreated slowly and quietly. When they reentered the morass, Jondalrun paused to pick more of the magical seed pods, and gruffly instructed the others to do likewise, until oncoming dark threatened. Thereafter they made a more rapid return, following their own trail. They camped at the edge of the swamp, spending a weary, mosquito-ridden night. The next morning they collected more seed pods, until their pouches and saddlebags threatened to burst.

On the ride back to Tamberly Town, Tenniel noticed that Jondalrun was silent, as he had been for the most part on the ride to the fen, but this was a different kind of silence; almost, Tenniel thought, as though he were ashamed.

X

Near the outskirts of Overwood, a man was tied to a tree. It was Willen, the North-wealdsman; he stood trussed to a small sapling in the center of a secluded clearing bounded by carefully trimmed shrubbery. It was a bower that was meant for contemplation, where those so inclined could come for peace. Willen, however, was not feeling peaceful. He had left the dais quite proud of himself; he had delivered the ultimatum to Hawkwind in no uncertain tones, and he fancied he had left an impression. He had, in fact, been so taken with himself and the assurances he had received that his normal caution had lapsed. He had been absorbed in his prideful reflections when suddenly a net had dropped upon him from a tree and he had been taken forthwith to this place, where he had been tied for several hours. It was now late afternoon.

"I tell you once more," he said tightly to his guard, "I am here as an emissary from the Northweald! Severe trouble will be the result of this! If I do not return soon, my companion will carry word back that I have been detained!"

The guard merely shrugged. He was one of Princess Evirae's personal staff, chosen because he had the admirable quality of being able to follow orders without thinking much about them. Mesor said the Princess had wanted the Northwealdsman detained, and this had been done. Now he was content to play a game of rough-side-up with bark chips while he awaited further orders, and the imprecations of his captive bothered him not at all.

He was about to have his calmness disturbed, however, for Willen had been playing a game of his own with the rough bark. Ever since he had been tied to the tree, he had been dragging the ropes about his wrists back and forth across the surface. Now, after several hours' work, they had frayed sufficiently to snap. The first indication the guard had of this was when Willen burst his bonds and ran across the sward toward the shrubbery. Though the guard was slow of wit, he was not slow of wind. He overtook Willen, tackling the Northwealdsman just as they reached the edge of the bower. They rolled upon the grass, kicking and striking at each other. The guard's greater bulk eventually began to tell—Willen was rolled over and pinned beneath the other's body. One of the guard's hands was on his chest, the other poised in a fist over him; then there was a sudden crashing in the shrubbery. They both looked up toward the noise, and what they saw made them stop in mid-struggle, posed ludicrously.

"Release that man!" said the Princess. Evirae, astride a beautiful spotted horse, had emerged from the shrubbery. From Willen's viewpoint, her huge pile of hair seemed to reach above the treetops. The jewels interwoven in it sparkled, and small bells set there surrounded her with music. Her riding gown was a brilliant yellow, and her long sleeves were gathered by silken bows, that they might not interfere with her travels through the forest.

Behind her was a man, also on horseback. Willen had seen him next to her at the ceremony. He was Mesor, Evirae's chief aide. The two reined in, narrowly avoiding those on the ground. Evirae dramatically pointed a finger tipped with a long nail at the guard. "How dare you so treat an emissary from the Northweald!"

The guard scrambled to his feet, confused. "Your pardon, milady . . . I but did what you—"

"Silence!" Evirae cried. The horse reared slightly and snorted at her twitch of the reins, giving her order added emphasis. Mesor smiled slightly at this.

"We will deal with you later," Evirae told the guard. "Return to Overwood and await my word!"

The guard swallowed, nodded, and left. Evirae did not

watch him go. She turned instead and smiled down at Willen, who was still sprawled on the ground before her horse. "Mesor," she said, "do help our guest to his feet, and see that he is made comfortable." Mesor swung down from his horse and assisted Willen, brushing dirt and twigs from his tunic. He learned the Northwealdsman's name and passed it on to the Princess. Evirae dismounted, extending her hand to him. Willen took it, carefully avoiding the nails; he had heard tales that she painted them with poison—though, faced with her beauty, he found this hard to believe. "Please accept my apologies," she said to him, and her voice was more lilting than the first birdsong after a rain. "I had no idea that fool would forcibly restrain you. I had told him only to ask that you await me at this private place. I wish to talk to you, Willen Northwealdsman, about an urgent matter of state."

Despite his years as a hunter, the Northwealdsman was still naive to the ways of the Overwood. This woman's beauty moved his heart. He sensed a sweetness and helplessness in the Princess that made him feel protective toward her; and at the same time he was acutely aware of his lack of manners and courtly ways. She led him gracefully—it was hard to imagine her doing anything ungracefully—to the shade of the sapling. There they sat, Mesor spreading a small quilt for them. He then returned discreetly to the stallions.

Willen sat cross-legged next to Evirae, close enough to smell the various subtle perfumes she wore. He was also very much aware of his own unwashed state, and hoped that the breeze would remain in his favor.

"I need your trust, Willen," Evirae said earnestly. "I need your pledge of secrecy. What I am about to tell you could mean the future of Simbala. Do you pledge not to reveal to anyone else what you will now hear?"

Willen hesitated. "Yes?" Evirae said. "Speak frankly—this is too important a matter for protocol."

"Milady, I must say in advance that if you try to talk me into withdrawing the ultimatum I gave to Hawkwind—"

"By no means!" Evirae said. "I think the Northweald is well within its rights, for reasons I hope to make clear to you. Now, will you listen?"

"As you will," Willen said. He was intrigued by her words, and totally captivated by the storybook intrigue. "But," he added, "if I do not return to my companion by sundown, he will leave without me, and the embargo will begin."

"I will be brief. The death of the child is a tragic thing. If you were right, and it was the fault of the Fandorans—"

"My own son discovered the body near the cliffs," said Willen. He held up two rainbow-shaded fragments. "I think she was collecting seashells when the Fandorans found her."

"Then we are in grave danger," said Evirae. She looked at the fragments for a moment, then pushed them away. "I doubt if Overwood has now the leadership to see us through this crisis. The government is being subverted by those who wish to use it to their own ends."

"What do you mean?" Willen asked.

"I mean this: Hawkwind and Ceria, with the help of General Vora, intend to use Simbala for their own gains, perhaps in league with the Southland."

Willen simply stared at her in disbelief.

"Monarch Ephrion," Evirae continued, "has suffered dearly, Willen. He was ill when he selected Hawkwind. He grows senile, as all doubtless know who have heard him speak. He has no wife or children, and Lady Graydawn, his beloved younger sister, continues her self-imposed exile in the Northweald. Hawkwind realizes these things. He was honored by Ephrion for his heroism in the mines, and he seized the opportunity to ingratiate himself. Once in the castle, he and his gypsy lover, Ceria, manipulated Ephrion. The Monarch is an old sick man, Willen, and it is easy to see how he could have taken the miner for a son. How else could an outsider have come to join the Royal Family?

"Though I am a member of the Royal Family, I did not oppose Hawkwind at first, but it has become increasingly clear to me that Hawkwind is weak. He does not rule Simbala—he is a hollow man, a puppet ruler. He rarely speaks to the people. It is Ceria who pulls his strings, supported by the General. A frightening pattern has begun to emerge, Willen. Hawkwind, for example, did nothing to offset or prepare for war during previous troubles with Fandora—"

"Excuse me, milady," Willen said hesitantly. "But . . . previous troubles?"

"That is too complicated to go into now—by your own statement, we have not the time. I asked you to trust me, did

I not?" Evirae said with a disarming smile. Without waiting for an answer, she concluded, "Hawkwind is Ceria's puppet. Nobody knows her true origins, save that she is a Rayan. The Northwealdsfolk have had problems with the Rayan before, have they not?"

"Indeed they have!" Willen replied hotly. "Thieves and vagrants, all of them! Never ones for honest work when they can—"

"Exactly so," Evirae said, interrupting smoothly, "but they are canny, very canny. Ceria has ambitions which are being furthered by Hawkwind's actions, and I must learn what they are. To do that, I will need help. I will need the help of a people who are not afraid to demand what they feel is just, even from the Monarch of Simbala."

"I understand," Willen said.

"Good, good. Please keep in mind that this conversation is secret, but if you care to discuss Hawkwind's and Ceria's actions with a few people whom you trust in the Northweald, then do. I am afraid Lady Graydawn is loyal to Hawkwind, and I must solicit your pledge of secrecy regarding her."

Willen was troubled. Keep this information from Lady Graydawn? How could he possibly . . . ?

Evirae sensed Willen's discomfort and said, "After all, Hawkwind was appointed by Lady Graydawn's own brother. It would be impossible for her to protest."

Willen nodded. That made sense. The Princess spoke with such conviction, much more so than the people of Overwood he had dealt with in the past. Yet, in the back of his mind something bothered Willen. He had trouble trusting a person who seemed to have all the answers.

Evirae leaned toward him. "Remember," she said confidentially, "there are rumors about the Rayan. They are nomads. They could easily have lived in another country, years ago, could they not? Perhaps . . . Fandora?"

Willen drew back and stared at her. His mind focused on the land across the Strait of Balomar. Evirae raised her hand quickly. "Again, all of this is only conjecture. But . . . it is something to think about." She paused. "Return now and await word from me. Simbala—both Overwood and the Northweald—is in danger."

Willen nodded. He stood, turned to go, then remembered

to take her hand. She smiled at him, and under the spell of that smile he said, "You can depend on me, milady." Then he hurried away into the woods.

Evirae watched him go, keeping herself carefully in repose. There was quiet for a moment, and then the bushes rustled again and Mesor stepped into the bower. She looked at him, and now she was trembling with nervousness.

"Did you hear?" she asked him.

"For the most part," he replied. "You were very convincing."

She sighed. "I hope so. It is a difficult job, building suspicion out of such insubstantial materials. Do you think he suspects me?"

"I doubt it very much. He is only a bumpkin, remember. You used your presence very effectively. You could have told him that dragons live in the palace, and he would likely have believed you." Mesor paused a moment, then asked, "What previous dealings with the Fandorans has Hawkwind neglected to counter?"

She smiled wanly. "None, that I know of." She rose then, and went to him, putting her head on his shoulder, much like a small child in search of solace. There was nothing seductive in it at all, nor did Mesor feel any desire for her as he patted her back and made comforting sounds. It was simply another part of his office.

She said softly, "Part of me loves the intrigue, and part of me fears it. Oh, Mesor, what if he suspects, what if he talks of this to Graydawn, what if my accusations return to Hawkwind?"

"That will not happen," he said sharply. "Continue spinning your web. Soon Hawkwind and Ceria will be so thoroughly enmeshed in it that it will not matter if they learn of your workings. You will have them. You will have the palace." And, he added to himself, so will I.

•

Amsel dreamed. Asleep in the gently rocking boat, he saw again the bright claws of the fire tearing their way through his tree house, saw leaves becoming black cusps, furniture and equipment burning, containers of fluids exploding from the heat. In his nightmare he found his escape route to Greenmeadow Mesa cut off, and he was forced to continue climbing, higher and higher. The tree seemed to extend forever, and the fire spread until it engulfed the entire forest. Then he was at the top, and on the topmost branch stood Jondalrun, huge and terrible, a knife in his hand. He heard a voice crying his name, and saw Johan hovering nearby on the Wing he had invented. Amsel leaped up and out, and seized the crossbar. The Wing went into a dive, and Johan began to scream as they fell. . . .

Amsel opened his eyes, shuddering. He was still in the boat, where he had been for the last two days. The heat that had been the fire in the dream was the burning sun above, but the sun was not shining on him now.

He squinted at the dark form in the sky, then gasped as the last vestiges of sleep cleared from his mind and he saw it clearly. It could only be a windship. It was not more than twice the height of a man above him. A boatlike craft, bigger than Amsel's and intricately carved with the figurehead of a snarling bear, hung by ropes from a huge and complicated arrangement of sails. The sails were sewn in such a way that balloonlike ribbing covered them—instead of a flat surface, they were humped with gentle, rolling billows. These strained against the wind with a flexing sound, almost musical. Obviously, some sort of buoyant gas filled the ribbing of the sail, but what produced it in such quantity without weighing down the windship?

Amsel was immediately afire with scientific curiosity, but the sound of an arrow thudding into the floor of his boat quickly brought him out of the mood. He looked at it. There was a blue ribbon around the shaft.

"You are trespassing in Simbalese waters. Abandon your craft!"

Amsel looked up and saw two men, dressed in dark blue uniforms, leaning over the railing near the low cabin aboard the ship. The taller man aimed a crossbow directly at him.

"Do you understand me?" the man shouted.

"Yes," Amsel replied. The speech of the Simbalese man was similar to that of the Fandorans, but the accent made it difficult to follow.

A rope ladder suddenly dropped from the windship. "Abandon your boat," said the Windrider again.

Another arrow sank into the small wooden seat beside Amsel.

"Obviously I don't have much choice," said the inventor,

but as he rose to grasp the yithe fibers of the ladder, he realized that he was weak with hunger and exhaustion. Gulls had swept down on his boat and had taken the remaining cheese while he had slept. The perilous journey had been draining. Nevertheless, the ladder had to be climbed. With much effort Amsel seized it, and as he did, he glanced out across the strait. To his surprise and delight, land was only a few miles away. He had paddled all the previous day and until now did not know that he had evaded the current and had come so close to the Simbalese shore. The news buoyed Amsel, and he started to climb the rope ladder.

The task proved harder than it looked. Although the height was low, the ladder spun around under Amsel's weight. The inventor grew dizzy, then lost his grip and landed with a splash in the azure waters.

The two Windriders looked down in disgust. "A Fandoran," said the first.

"That explains it," said the second.

XI

Jondalrun watched as the children of Tamberly Town joined in a game of betie. They cheerfully kicked the cloth betie ball through a wooden board scalloped with eight arches of different value. It was painfully clear to Jondalrun that the children were oblivious of the preparations for war. Some would be losing their fathers and brothers, he thought sadly, and the news of those losses would bring sorrow and confusion to what were now sweet and innocent lives. The war would make them older. He sighed.

The ball bounced in his direction. Jondalrun picked it up and threw it back to the children. For a moment the Elder wished that it could all be forgotten, that Fandora could return to its regular pattern of affairs. But that was impossible. Jondalrun turned slowly from the square, unable to watch the children's faces, seeing Johan in each of them. He walked slowly toward Graywood Tavern. He was expecting Agron to join him.

Jondalrun sat silently in a booth, not drinking. An hour passed, and Agron entered the tavern.

"They have returned," he said. Moments later, two men covered with soot and cinders appeared. In their arms were scrolls, bound books, and objects unknown to Jondalrun, brought from the ruins of the hermit's house.

"Ale for these men!" shouted Agron, and he helped them bring the objects to Jondalrun's table. The three remained there, drinking from stone grogs as Jondalrun analyzed their find. He picked up a long black tube charred by the fire. Handling it gingerly, considering its undoubtedly sorcerous origins, he noticed that it was hollow, with a clear glass lens at either end. He turned it over several times and then held it up to his eye. With a startled cry he dropped it, and the clay cylinder shattered on the floor.

"What did you see?" Agron asked.

"I saw Meyan, the tavernkeeper, and that keg of ale he is tapping, as though he were a handsbreadth away!" Jondalrun said. He shuddered. "Amsel was a sorcerer—no doubt about it!"

The men looked at each other uncomfortably; they had carried these things for many miles.

Jondalrun picked up one of the scrolls—it, too, was charred and brittle. With extreme care he unrolled a portion of it. Jondalrun could read relatively well, but he could not read what was written in a fine hand on this parchment, though it had a disturbing familiarity to it. Agron said, "It seems to have been written backwards. Hold it up to a glass."

"No need," Jondalrun said with satisfaction. "The fact that he disguised his notes is proof enough. I was correct—Amsel was a spy." He opened another scroll. "Here is the final proof!" He showed a detailed map of the coastline of Simbala.

"We shall turn his works against him," Jondalrun said. "This map shall help us launch our invasion. It is only fitting that the murderer of my son should help us destroy his people." He turned to the men. "Did you find proof of his death?"

"There were a great many charred bones in the ruins," one of them said.

Jondalrun nodded. "Then he is dead," he said with a grim expression. "I would not have seen it done this way . . . but it is done. Let the people know what we have learned."

Within hours, word had spread through Tamberly Town that positive proof had been found that Amsel was a Simbalese spy, and many doubts and misgivings about the war were quieted. The Elders each returned to their respective villages to prepare their people—each village was to send a hundred men to the army.

The preparation was an incredibly difficult task. No

swords had clashed within living memory, no horses had charged over the rocky fields and heather-grown moors. There had been no reason to make war. Fandora was effectively isolated from other nations, and no civil strife had ever formed. The wild currents of the Strait of Balomar and the high cliffs which faced it had kept Simbalese and Southlanders from invading.

Finding the men willing to fight was easy enough, but finding weapons to arm them was another matter. The land was rich enough in iron ore, but there was no time to mine and refine it and cast weapons from it. Each village was expected to arm its men, any way they could.

•

"I will not let you take them!"

The old man stood, arms akimbo, at the top of the stone steps that led to his house. He was a very old man; his skin was dry parchment, his hair a fine spiderweb of white. Though rigid in his anger and indignation, he still stood stooped with age. He wore a yellow robe made from thin night-moth silk. An opalescent ring glittered on his finger, as though reflecting the anger in his eyes.

His house was a marvelous sight for Fandora; it made the homes of rich folk seem like mud-and-reed hovels. It stood on the edge of the town, near a stand of woods, and was surrounded by a high stone wall. The roof was domed with beaten bronze rather than shingled with wood. Two squat towers with windows of glazed glass flanked it, and the second floor opened onto an ornately carved wooden balcony. The old man stood in front of the closed double doors and glared down at those before him.

"We must take them!" said one of those who faced him. He was also an old man, though not so old as the one on the step. He wore clothes of rough wool and a threadbare cape. He was the Chief Elder of the town, and behind him were four other men. Three of them seemed impatient and angry; they shifted from foot to foot, while the old man harangued the Elder. Only the fourth did not fidget. He was a giant of a man, almost six feet tall and built like a barrel, with huge arms and a dull, placid face.

"Please believe me," the Elder said. "I don't want to do this, but you must understand our position."

"Your position is barbaric!" the old man shouted.

The Elder removed his cape and wiped his brow with it. He sighed impatiently. "You cannot tend crops with them! You cannot travel in them! You have no use for them! Fandora is going to war! We need that iron! We need to cast weapons from it!"

"Then melt down your rakes and harrow blades!" the old man said. "Take the rings from your fingers and the shoes from your horses and cast them into the fire! I tell you that you will not take from me what is dearer than my life!"

One of the others, a man half-bald from a scar which ran across his head, ssaid, "Why are we arguing with this old fool? We need the iron, and we don't have much time. We go and get the things, says I!"

"Try, and I'll stop you!" the old man cried.

"Please," the Elder said in a last attempt at peacemaking. "Understand . . . the war leaves us no choice—"

"There is always a choice about war! If you fools want to fight and kill each other, it will not be with weapons made from—"

"Oh, enough of this!" another man said. He was tall, and thought of himself as handsome; he wore what he considered to be an officer's uniform—a black tunic and leggings, crisscrossed with gold braid and dotted at random with epaulets. He was obviously sweltering in the hot sun, but he kept his plumed hat on and his collar resolutely buttoned. "We have no more time to waste!" he continued. Then he went around the house toward the crenellated stone wall behind it. The others followed. The Elder paused, looked apologetically back at the old man, and then went with them.

The old man hurried back into his house and slammed the doors.

The ground behind the house sloped down slightly toward the forest. The men followed the wall until they came to a massive wooden gate. It was unbolted; they pushed it open, speaking loudly to each other in encouraging tones, the way men will do when they are engaged in something they know to be bad. They entered the garden, and then stopped at the sight that met them.

There was a garden, a work of living art. Small hillocks were molded from the earth and covered with grass and flowers. They gently framed a brook which had been diverted to run through the old man's property. It formed a series of lily ponds connected by small waterfalls. Delicate stone and crystal outcroppings were scattered here and there, but the most impressive part of the garden was the sculptures.

There were twelve of them, each crowning a small hill. Each stood more than five feet tall. Some of them the intruders recognized as being the stuff of legends: there was a winged dragon in flight, and a seaworm surrounded by ocean spray. And there were other, more imaginative concepts: a creature half-horse and half-fish, and a winged stag posed with hooves uplifted in defiance. There were jewel-encrusted flowers and bat-winged demons. Some of the pieces were executed with stunning realism, to the last meticulous hair or petal. Others were roughly molded, cut with artful abandon from the metal. For they all had one thing in common: they were all wrought from iron, by the sculptors of Bundura.

The men entered the garden, treading all the more roughly because of their uncertainty. Delicate crystalline pieces were crunched underfoot with a sound of eggs breaking. Two of them seized the nearest statue, that of the winged stag, and rocked it back and forth to loosen its base from the soil. They tipped it over, lifted it, and began carrying it toward the gate.

Before they reached it, however, one of them turned suddenly, looking toward the back of the house. The Elder, engaged in freeing another statue, also looked. Framed in the rear door stood the old man. He held a weapon strange to most of them; the Elder recognized it as a crossbow.

"Put it down," the old man said to the two with the statue. They did so—the base cracked a flagstone.

"For twenty years I worked to build this house and garden," the old man said. His voice was high and cracked, his forehead shiny with sweat. "In my travels to the Far Westland, I have searched out the best artists, and paid dearly to have these sculptures brought back here. You—you would destroy them because they cannot plow a field or pull a cart? You would send them to the smithy to be melted down and reformed as weapons? Never! You don't understand—these sculptures are priceless! They were made not to serve a function, but simply to *be!* Now, go, before I kill you all!"

While the old man was talking, the Elder noticed that the

crossbow's line was not cocked. The sight of the mistake caused a surprising sadness in him. He turned to the giant and said, "Keep him inside his house until we are finished here."

The giant nodded, turned, and crossed the garden. For all his weight, he moved lightly and quickly on his feet.

"I warn you!" the old man shouted, hysteria thinning his voice. "Keep back! Leave those statues alone or I'll use this!"

The Elder shook his head. "You would not use it," he said, "even if you knew how." He motioned for the others to resume working.

The giant stood before the old man, who stared at the wooden buttons on the giant's too-small shirt. He breathed a harsh, ragged sob and lowered the weapon. The giant took him by the shoulders, turned him about gently, and pushed him into the house.

The walls of the back room were decorated with Southland feather paintings. The old man sank into a chair, and the giant sat down across the room. He stared at the old man in curiosity. He could not understand why the old man was upset. If he could speak, he would ask—but he could not. Of course, there were many things he did not understand, and he did not consider himself any worse off because of it. The world, by virtue of its very mystery, was a bright and fascinating place to him, and he was always keen to learn more about it, even if he did not understand it. He did not understand now why the old man sat hugging his bony knees, racked by sorrow. The giant looked through a window. They had removed five of the statues now. The squares of raw black dirt where their bases had been contrasted with the green hills. He looked at the remaining sculptures. He had never in his life seen such things before. They were so real, some of them, so detailed—like living things that had been frozen in metal. Why had the people responsible—his mind struggled for the word, remembered it, *artists*—why had the *artists* gone to such trouble?

Behind him, the old man watched. "You needn't worry— I'm quite sure they will take them all. Those statues represented the search of a lifetime, you know. Not that you care. Not that you could possibly comprehend the crime that's being committed. To destroy art for the sake of war—there can be no greater crime."

The giant stared at the statues being set by the gate, one by one. He watched them being lifted from their places in the garden, and as each one left its hill, he felt a stab of pain deep within him. He did not know why. The garden looked so empty without the statues in their proper places. He turned suddenly away from the window and stared down at the old man. He did not want to see what was happening out there anymore, and he did not want to hear the old man's accusations either. They caused pain within him. He made an inarticulate sound, a growl of pain and incomprehension that caused the old man to stare at him. The giant was looking at him, staring at him, with a mixture of pity and struggling understanding.

"*Do* you understand?" the old man asked in a whisper. "It would almost be worth it, if you did. It would not replace these beautiful works of art, nor the love they reveal, but it would be of some solace to know that their destruction inspired in you an appreciation of their worth. . . ."

The giant pulled the old man gently to his feet and toward the window. "No," the old man protested, struggling feebly. "No, I cannot look at them, do you not understand? It is too painful. It is too much to see the love in them deformed. Looking hurts too much."

The giant scowled and shook the old man gently, as a father might shake a recalcitrant child. He nodded again at the scene beyond the window, to each of the statues in turn. Then he held his hand before the old man's face and held up one finger.

Comprehension began to dawn in the old man. "You want me to . . . to pick one of them?" he asked in astonishment. The giant nodded. The old man looked through the window again. It was a very difficult choice. All of them held so many memories for him. The sculpture they were so callously uprooting even now, for example—that one he had been given in repayment for saving the artist's life in a tavern brawl in Dagemon-Ken, decades ago. Or others, leaning as though in loneliness now, that he had bought or bartered for simply because their beauty had haunted his nights. Decide between them? How could he? It was like being asked to choose between a son and a daughter. He could not.

Yet he had to save a work of art if he could. He let his gaze run lovingly over all of them, one last time, inspecting each of them. When he had finished, he made his choice. With tears in his eyes, he pointed toward one of the smallest of the lot—the image of a woman being born of a flower. "That one," he said. It had been a gift to him by an artist now dead, a woman he had known and loved for a time in Bundura. This part of her, at least, would live on.

The giant looked at the small sculpture in surprise—it seemed to him almost unnoticeable, compared to the others. But he had already decided that there had to be more to this than he was yet aware of, and so he nodded. He walked out into the garden and started toward the others, one of whom—the uniformed man—had approached the sculpture in order to remove it.

He looked up when the giant's shadow fell across him. The giant laid one huge hand on the statue, and with the other waved him away.

"Here, what's the matter with you?" the uniformed man said truculently. The giant ignored him. He lifted the statue with one hand, and the other quieted abruptly. The giant turned toward the house, carrying the statue.

"Where are you going?" The quiet voice of the Elder reached him. The giant hesitated, then turned to face the Elder. Still holding the statue with one hand, he nodded determinedly toward the house, where the old man stood framed in the window.

The Elder looked at the old man, then at the giant. After a long moment he slowly nodded. The giant returned to the house and watched as the old man saw the sculptures being taken away. Then the old man turned from the window and saw the sculptured woman in the flower, so odd and out of place in the giant's hand. Its dirt-caked base rested on a handwoven rug.

The old man looked up at the giant. There did not seem to be any change in his expression. It was passive, open, but quiet. The old man studied it as he would a sculpture, and the giant watched him nervously, as if he did not know what to do.

He is waiting, thought the old man. Does he know? Does he know how I feel? Or does he pity me?

The old man took the giant's hand and gently put it in his own. Then he took the giant's fingers and ran them lightly up and down the sculpture of the woman's back. "I knew her, once," said the old man. "She did not look this way, but when I touch this, I feel her."

The giant stared at him, a glimmer of understanding in his eyes. The old man started to embrace him, to thank him for what he had done, but the giant pulled away and rushed toward the door.

The old man watched from the window as the younger man ran across the lawn. Then, to a Bunduran woman he had not seen in years, the old man whispered, "My lady, I saw a tear."

•

As the general excitement and fever of the impending war spread over Fandora, people reacted to it in different ways. Oil was poured into doorlocks and latches, and tumblers creaked protestingly as bolts were closed for the first time in years. With the coming of night, the fear of a Simbalese invasion was a palpable thing—it stalked the streets of many towns like the billowing black sails of a dark windship. Children slept in their parents' arms, and adults took turns standing watch at the towns' outskirts.

Lagow, recently returned to Jelrich Town, viewed this grimly as yet another problem caused by Jondalrun's plan for war. He grudgingly admitted, however, that it did make his task of recruiting his quota of soldiers easier. The men practically queued up in their eagerness to defeat the dread enemy and protect their families.

"It is easier," Lagow told his wife, "that they're so eager to join this foolish crusade. For the soul of me, I cannot bring myself to order them to march in Jondalrun's army."

"It was the will of the High Council," his wife said, "however foolish it may seem. The responsibility's not yours any longer, Lagow. No one can fault you for doing what you're supposed to do."

"I wonder," he answered. "Can a bad be made good by a lot of old men so decreeing?" Deena sighed. "I'm afraid you already know the answer to that, my husband," and she turned over in their bed to face another sleepless night.

•

In Borgen Town there was much opposition to the war. It was a relatively wealthy town, and many of its inhabitants had no desire to chance losing what they had earned by years of hard work. Much concern was also voiced about how the women and children would fare should the men of the village not come back.

Tenniel listened to these arguments, and he could not help admitting that they were fair and just points of view. So the enlistment quota for Borgen Town did not rise rapidly. Tenniel discussed the problem with Talend and Axel, his fellow Elders.

"We must make them understand," Talend said when he learned of the problem. "If Fandora does not protect itself now, the sorcerers will commit further and more serious invasions of our land!"

In his youth, he had hunted the wild boars and buffalo of the highlands, and he knew that, if an arrow only wounded without incapacitating, the hunter was lucky indeed to escape the animal's retribution. Talend had not been so fortunate, as his crippled leg showed. Fandora had to react like a wounded animal to Simbala, Talend reasoned, and to do this, they needed men. He called a meeting in the town square and spoke at length to the people.

As a result, many more villagers were shamed and frightened into volunteering. Tenniel was impressed, and also downcast; he considered the recruiting of the men his primary responsibility, and his youthfulness and inexperience in the matter had made it necessary for Talend to take over. But the quota was still lacking. In desperation, Tenniel conceived of posting notices that any brigand, highwayman, or runaway farmhand being pursued by Waymen could find asylum in the army, and over the next few days several men with ragged clothes and a generally unwholesome attitude added themselves to the roster.

Talend disapproved of this method, but Tenniel argued that they had no choice—the quota had to be met; and it was. The next step was to transfer the contingent to Tamberly Town, where the entire army was gathering.

That, Tenniel told himself, would be easy. He had already passed through the most difficult part. He was in for a disheartening surprise.

•

The Elder of Cape Bage had a sense of the dramatic, and so he announced the decision of the High Council in a dramatic fashion. Upon returning to town, he headed straight for the bell tower at the Court of Fools.

It was midnight. The sound of the bells rang forebodingly through the streets of Cape Bage. Dreamers and drunkards alike stumbled from the inns to discover Tamark, atop the tower, shouting at the top of his lungs. "Volunteers!" he cried. "An army forms in Fandora! We need volunteers to defend our homeland!"

Those unable to comprehend his words returned to their tankards, but the majority of Cape Bage remained in the streets, wondering if the fisherman had lost his mind. Most of them had heard talk of the attack on Gordain Town, some had even seen the windships off the Simbalese shore, but few believed that Fandora would dare venture across the sea to do battle with the sorcerers in the east.

Among those who watched with alarm was Dayon, a young navigator freshly returned from a perilous journey through the strait. He waited at the foot of the tower, hoping to catch Tamark on his way outside.

Minutes later, as Tamark rushed from a small wooden door in the side of the tower, Dayon caught hold of his shoulder. Tamark looked angry, started to pull away, then recognized the young man's face. "Dayon!" He smiled. "You're safe." He reached out to embrace him.

Dayon was embarrassed by the Elder's show of affection. He had not realized that Tamark cared this much about him. "Yes, sir," he said stiffly. "I was swept out into the worst part of the currents. My boat was finally cast up upon an islet, and it took me days to repair it." He shuddered. "A terrifying experience. Now I hear you say there are more problems to come. What is this talk of war?"

Tamark frowned. "Not just talk, I'm afraid. The damn fools in Tamberly Town are driving Fandora to war."

"Tamberly, sir? That's my hometown!"

"Then you must know of Elder Jondalrun. The hot-tempered fool has the High Council on his side."

Dayon smiled. "Jondalrun is my father."

Tamark's face slackened and his throat went suddenly dry. "Your father?"

Dayon nodded. "By your description, it is definitely my father."

Tamark averted his eyes from the young man's face. "I have bad news," he whispered. "I must speak to you alone." The two men broke through the growing crowd and returned to Tamark's room behind the bake shop.

There was the sound of weeping, and the door to Tamark's room opened once again. Dayon ran across the cobblestones to a small building on the other side of the street. In his room, he quickly packed clothing and food for a day's journey. As some fishermen watched from the edge of the Court of Fools, he ran down the dark road toward Tamberly Town.

XII

On the western coast of Simbala, north of the gentle beaches, the land folded upward into cliffs. Though by no means as sheer as those of Fandora, still they were impressive, made more so by the many strange shapes and colors that the weathering years had brought to them.

On one high promontory overlooking the strait, a massive formation stood, lonely and aloof against the stars. The wind and rain had sculptured it into a shape similar to the skull of some gigantic beast—a dragon, according to popular legend. It was called Dragonhead. From the top, an unobstructed view of the Strait of Balomar could be found.

A dark horse and rider emerged from the curtain of fog that surrounded the bare rock and precipice. They came to a stop beside the skull-shaped formation, and the rider dismounted. It was Hawkwind; he wore a heavy robe, with a sword scabbarded at his belt. The hawk sat upon his caped shoulder. A moment later, three other riders joined him, the iron hooves of the horses striking sparks from the rock. The second rider, a small slight figure, tossed back her hood to reveal the beautiful features of Ceria. Hawkwind stepped to the edge of the precipice and observed the misty sea. The hawk launched through the mist with a cry, circling in the cold, wet air, voicing its harsh cry. The bird was upset, and Ceria wondered what caused it. She had noticed before that the moods of Hawkwind and the hawk seemed eerily the same at times. Hawkwind seemed distant now, as though an unseen wall separated him from others, including her. To her frustration, Ceria could fathom this change no better than she could the disposition of the hawk.

The two other riders were palace guards. The older of them, Lathan by name, now approached Hawkwind on foot, bringing a torch. Hawkwind turned away from the cliff's edge and extended a hand to Ceria. The hawk continued to circle above them, keening, as the two of them walked toward Dragonhead.

"Is there a reason why you have brought a sword?" Ceria asked Hawkwind softly. "Do you expect something, my love?"

"As of the past twenty-four hours, I expect many things," he replied.

The answer did not satisfy Ceria, but she kept close to Hawkwind as they reached the edge of the rock. In front of them was a jagged, irregular crack, black as a mine shaft. Hawkwind raised his torch, and it illuminated the damp granite walls as they entered.

"I don't know what killed the Northweald child," he said, "but from what the Northwealdsman has told us, it sounds as if the girl had been crushed and mangled—almost as though she had been hurled from the cliffs or beaten with clubs. It does not sound as though it could be the actions of a forest animal."

They edged around a corner, to be confronted by a fork in the passageway—the right way led steeply up, the left just as steeply down. Hawkwind took the left-hand passage.

"Yet," said Ceria, "you agree with me. The Fandorans could not have been responsible."

Hawkwind smiled. "Ephrion has told me often enough that a monarch should have all possibilities investigated, and, whenever possible, investigate them himself. I wanted Kiorte to order a windship out to survey the Fandoran coast, but he says that the winds that blow currently in the strait are too violent to allow it. We must see what we can see ourselves." His torch, held overhead, illuminated a shallow pool of water on the level floor they had reached. "Legacy of the rains," Hawkwind said. "It will be cold—shall I carry you?"

"Please," Ceria said warmly, "as long as you keep in mind what happened at the brook."

She was referring to an incident of well over a year ago, when they had spent a day by themselves in a secluded part of the southern woods. Having gallantly offered to carry her across a small brook, Hawkwind had slipped, and they had both been soaked in the icy water. Both had laughed about it then, but this time the memory elicited only a faint smile from Hawkwind. As he lifted her in his arms, Ceria felt a definite pang of rejection. He is distant, he is excluding me from this, she thought. I do not know why.

Once across, they paused while Hawkwind emptied his boots of the water that had poured in over the tops, and dried his feet on his cloak. Then they proceeded. The passage now wound steeply upward, and fresh cold air blew down on them, making the torch flicker.

They came out of the passageway into a vast, hollow cup of rock. They were in one of the huge eye sockets of the skull-shaped rock. Far below them, spread out in a panorama of black velvet, was the Strait of Balomar. Cottony streamers of fog and mist entwined about the cliffs' spires, and they could see occasional phosphorescent bursts of plankton in the waves, like stars exploding. The breakers sounded like faint, faraway drums. The sky overhead was clear, and the half-moon was low in the west, illuminating the distant fog-shrouded cliffs of Fandora.

"It is not the best night for viewing," Hawkwind said. "Still, we might see something." He pulled a spyglass from his belt and held it up to his eye.

"What do you see?" Ceria asked after she felt he had made her wait long enough.

"Very little. The moon is bright, but the fog is thick. I can see no sign of any activity."

"Yet the Northwealdsman insists that a Fandoran ship was seen in the waters," Ceria mused.

"Perhaps a fishing vessel, carried over by the currents and wind," Hawkwind said. "Much of this would be cleared up if there were more contact between our two lands. The strait's treacherous waters have prevented it, but still, it should be. It is something I wish to initiate."

There was a sound behind them—a footfall on stone. Hawkwind turned quickly. Ceria saw the movement. He does expect something, she thought.

A guard emerged. He was panting as though he had run

through the passages. "Monarch Hawkwind," he gasped. "Two men are passing on horseback in the woods nearby! They stopped for a moment, and I overheard them speaking. They had the accents of Northwealdsmen."

Hawkwind handed the torch to him. "Stay with the Lady Ceria," he said. "I will question them." Without waiting for an acknowledgment, he hurried down the passageway.

"But it is black as the mines in those tunnels!" the guard said to Ceria. "How will he find his way through them without his torch?"

"He will," she answered.

Hawkwind emerged from the crack in the rock, startling Lathan, who held the horses. "The Northwealdsmen—we shall catch them!" he said. "Show me their way!"

"But . . . my liege!" stammered Lathan. "They ride stallions of the Northweald—we cannot hope to overtake them!"

"We shall overtake them," Hawkwind said. His hawk circled over his head; then, as he leaped upon his horse, it flew ahead of him, toward the forest. Lathan mounted and started after Hawkwind, but the Monarch's mount seemed itself like a hawk in flight. It leaped away through the concealing wall of the forest and was gone. Lathan, clinging close to his horse's neck, feeling branches and vines lash at him in the dark, had time to wonder just how Hawkwind could ride so swiftly and surely through a forest in the black of night.

•

Willen had met his compatriot from the Northweald at their prearranged rendezvous, just at sunset. Willen said nothing of his meeting with Evirae, though her words had been tumbling about in his head constantly. He told his companion that he had been late simply because things had become more involved than he had anticipated. His companion, whose name was Tweel, pressed him about the confrontation with Hawkwind, and Willen angrily told him to leave off until he had had a chance to order his thoughts. They had ridden in stiff silence for a time after that, while the sun went down and darkness filled the woods.

The fog and ground mist thickened, shrouding the trees. After a time, Willen, feeling that he owed Tweel some word of explanation, reined up and said, "There is much news to tell. Most of it must wait until we return to the Northweald, but I can tell you this entire matter encompasses more than we had imagined. Much more."

"In that case," Tweel said, "we had better ride all night. We are near the sea now—I can hear the breakers and smell the salt on the night air. If we strike north at a steady pace, we will reach the Northweald by dawn."

They put boots to their mounts and settled into an easy canter that the horses could keep up all night. They had not done so for long, however, before Willen became aware of a strange sound rising above the regular beat of the hooves. At first he thought it was his imagination. Then he thought it the wind. It grew louder, more insistent—a high, keening sound. He looked about him as they rode. The trees rose like giant grasping fingers in the fog. Vines seemed to curl and twine like huge vipers coiled in the trees. Then suddenly there was an explosion of air about his face, and a shriek in his ears. The world tilted as his horse shied, and it was good fortune that Willen did not find himself thrown in the bushes. He hung on grimly, and managed to control the animal's panicked flight with difficulty. He saw that Tweel was in similar straits. Willen caught a glimpse of something dark, swooping against the stars. At first he thought it was a huge bat; then he realized that it was a hawk, wheeling about the horses' heads with claws extended.

At the same time, he saw a rider on a large black horse burst through the fog and forest like a slow shattering of glass. Willen caught his breath—a bandit perhaps, or a Rayan?

Then the moon illuminated the intruder's face, and the Northwealdsman gasped as he recognized the Monarch of Simbala.

The hawk flew back to circle above the oncoming rider. Willen glanced at Tweel; his companion was as pale as the fog when Hawkwind reined up. His face was like marble in the moonlight. He looked at Willen. "I gave you leave to return straightaway to the Northweald. There is a good reason, I presume, why I should not have you taken back to the prisons of Overwood."

Willen glanced at Tweel, then back at Hawkwind. Such was the Monarch's authority that Willen was on the verge of confessing why he had been delayed—but then he remem-

bered his pledge to Princess Evirae. He was not at all sure
who was to be trusted in this alien world of political intrigue, but he was a trustworthy man, a man who kept his
word.

"I had business of my own to attend to," he said, and was
relieved that his voice had once again remained steady. He
kept his eyes on Hawkwind, with no idea of what would
happen next.

At this point, Lathan joined them, and stared at the scene
before him. Though he had heard none of the dialogue, still
he could feel the tension between Hawkwind and the two
Northwealdsfolk.

Hawkwind stared at Willen; Willen swallowed, but returned the gaze steadily. Tweel was silent. He was acutely
aware that Hawkwind was within his right to have them
both imprisoned for Willen's refusal to answer.

"I will ask you again," said Hawkwind. "Why have you
remained in the forest?"

"As I said, I had business." Then, somewhat lamely Willen
added, "I was also detained by royal guards, until I convinced them that I had your guarantee of safe passage. Also,
I became lost in the woods, and had trouble meeting my
companion."

"A Northwealdsman, lost in the woods?" Hawkwind
asked skeptically. "This I find hard to believe."

"Nevertheless, that is my answer," Willen said.

For a moment the tableau held—Hawkwind, the hawk
now upon his shoulder, glaring down at Willen; the
Monarch's black steed moving restlessly about, snorting, its
hooves stamping the ground fog into tiny writhing tendrils
of mist. The moon began to impale itself on the black
silhouettes of treetops to the east. At last Hawkwind spoke.
"Very well. I will not force you to tell me. Doubtless you
have your reasons for refusing. Both of you may go."

Shocked and relieved, Tweel and Willen lost no time in
turning their mounts toward the north. As they disappeared
into the mist and the trees, Hawkwind turned to Lathan.
"Follow them," he said softly. "Even if it takes you all the
way to the Northweald. Follow and learn what you can, and
return to me by tomorrow eve."

With no further words, Hawkwind reared his horse and
rode away. Lathan watched him leave, floating through the

mist like a dark ghost, and the chill he feit was not caused entirely by the cold night air.

•

It was quite late at night, and few lights burned in the windows of Simbala's homes. In the bedchamber of the tree castle of Prince Kiorte and Princess Evirae, an oil lamp, fashioned from a huge faceted geode, sat in a niche carved from the living wall. It illuminated the bedchamber—a small and private room, reached by spiral stairwell. The bed's oiled wooden frame fitted snugly on one side of the room, its canopy covered by a green tangle of pintala vines. Occasionally one of the fragrant pods on the vines would burst with a soft sigh, adding a pleasant, subtle fragrance to the room.

Evirae lay among the furs and silks that covered the bed. She stared at Kiorte, who stood looking out of a window formed by a huge knothole. Evirae tapped her nails against each other nervously, with a sound like crackling leaves. Her hair, no longer bound up in the impressive style she wore by day, fell about her in tangled red tresses, covering as much of the bed as the furs did. She took a deep breath, as though to say something, but no words were spoken. Instead, after a moment, it was Kiorte who spoke.

"I asked you a question, Evirae," he said softly. "Why will you not tell me what you discussed with the Northwealdsman?"

Evirae said, "I intended to tell you, Kiorte." To herself she thought: Carefully, now, very carefully. He knows much, somehow.

"Did you," Kiorte said dryly. It was not a question.

"Yes, I did. I merely wanted to question him further about his problem; since you and I are members of the Royal Family, I felt we needed to know of it."

"It is admirable that you have taken such an interest in the affairs of the Northweald, Evirae. Especially since last week you professed an inability to understand why Lady Graydawn would want to live among such . . . 'animals,' I believe was the term?"

"Kiorte! How can you say such a thing? It was the death of the child that touched me."

"I was not aware that you cared for children any more than you cared for the Wealdsfolk—but we shall let that pass. I still cannot rid myself of the suspicion that if one of my windships had not chanced to pass over the bower where you had your meeting, I would have heard nothing of it from you. I know you, Evirae. Schemes come to you like eagles to an eyrie. There is something mysterious going on, and I know you have a part in it. Will you tell me, or must I find out on my own?"

Receiving no answer, he turned and looked at her. She glared at him in return and said, "If you intend to treat me like a scullery servant who has stolen the silverware, then I have nothing at all to say to you!" She turned away from him and faced the wall. Kiorte noted how she exposed one leg provocatively, as an incentive for him to forget the argument.

Kiorte sighed. Although he loved Evirae, he showed it in the same cool way that he exhibited all degrees of affection. There was no passion, no spontaneity. He knew this and viewed it not as a fault, but as befitting his position and profession. Kiorte's dedication was reserved for the Brothers of the Wind and for Simbala.

Evirae watched her husband anxiously, not daring to push her words of rejection further. She had put too many lies between them already, and she had little understanding of how to repair their marriage with truth. Trust implied a surrender of the upper hand in their relationship, and this was something Evirae could not accept. She would have to wait for him to come to her. If she could not control Simbala, then at least she would control her husband.

To Evirae's surprise, Kiorte walked across their room to the stairwell and descended it. The stairs spiraled down through a richly carved ceiling to the main hall of the tree that housed them. Kiorte took his cloak from a guard at the foot of the stairs and walked out the door.

Evirae rolled over in bed. At times like this, she regretted her long nails—they made it difficult to clench her fists. She pounded the flats of her palms against the silken sheets, and then was quiet, listening hopefully for the sound of her husband's return.

It did not come.

She was angry and upset, but more than that, she was worried. Evirae had never been sure of Kiorte's affection, had often thought that it came largely out of a feeling of pride in being wed to the Princess of Simbala. Marriage in the Overwood was a mutual decision, but in the Royal Family it was often a question of politics. As Princess, Evirae had been free to select whomever she had wanted. To the Family's surprise, it had been solemn Kiorte. The only time she had ever seen him really smile was at the helm of his windship. He was aloof from the Family and from the politics within it. That very quality had attracted her to him. She equated it with incorruptibility. Aside from Monarch Ephrion, Evirae viewed Kiorte as the only man in the Royal Family who could not be swayed by her charms. It made keeping the upper hand a challenge to her.

She lay there on the bed, feeling like a lonely child. Kiorte did not understand the importance of what she was doing! She had been denied what was rightfully hers—the Ruby of Simbala; she had been passed by in favor of a commoner! She felt the blood begin to pound in her temples at the thought of it. The indignity! The pain! To walk down one of the tree-lined lanes of Simbala and know that women laughed behind their fans at her, that men chuckled and made jokes about her status! Evirae, Princess of Simbala, denied her Queenship by a miner! She could not allow the farce to continue. She would have Hawkwind removed from the throne, she would feel the weight of the Ruby on her own forehead, and then . . . She was not sure. Things would take care of themselves. She would be the new ruler of Simbala, and she would see that everyone jumped when she spoke.

Then suddenly she sat upright, scattering the furs and silks to the floor. Through the open window she had heard the tread of boots upon the steps outside. Kiorte was returning! Hurriedly she threw a robe about herself and rushed down the stairs. She would show him how contrite she was, how much she was sorry. Then, with his masculine pride assuaged, perhaps he would forget about her conversation with the Northwealdsman until she was ready to tell him the truth.

She waved the doorman away and opened the massive door. Yet it was not Kiorte who stood there, knuckles raised to knock on the wood. She paused in astonishment, staring at a windrider who held a sealed envelope. He looked at her, disconcerted. Evirae tugged her robe tighter about her.

"Yes?" she said haughtily.

"Your pardon, lady. I have a message for Prince Kiorte . . ."

"I will accept it for him. He is . . . indisposed at the moment."

The windshipman, a young lad with tousled hair, blinked in confusion. "Beg pardon, but the captain said to give this only to the Prince."

She drew herself up, and her green eyes froze him with the glare that she did so well. "I am the *Princess* Evirae, if it has escaped your notice! Are you refusing to give the message to me?"

"No, milady, of course not." He handed it hastily to her; she tore it open and stepped inside to read it, saying, "Bide a moment," over her shoulder.

When she had finished, she stood quite still for a time, not daring to believe such luck as this had come her way. It is destiny, she said to herself. Obviously destiny. I am meant to rule Simbala—else why should so fortuitous a circumstance have put this information in my hands?

She sat down at a small writing desk and penned a note on a sheet of vellum. She sealed it with a drop of candle wax and the signet of her ring, and gave it to the messenger.

"Return this to the captain," she said. "Tell him I know of this affair. It is Prince Kiorte's wish that the Fandoran captured in the strait be transferred to the location specified."

The messenger bowed and left. Evirae tugged on a bell pull, then sat down and dipped the quill in the inkwell once more. She wrote feverishly. A moment later, an aide entered the room. Evirae sealed the letter and handed it to him.

"Take this to Baron Tolchin immediately," she said. "See that it reaches him—wake him up if you have to—and tell Mesor I wish to see him at once."

When the aide had gone, she sat hugging her knees for joy, but the joy was soured somewhat by the knowledge that her husband had not returned.

•

The troops from Borgen Town had camped for the night outside Durbac Town. A shortage of supplies had caused much dissatisfaction, especially from the scoundrels Tenniel had recruited when it seemed that Borgen Town would be short its quota.

A large brigand named Grend, with one ear missing and a

huge black beard, approached Tenniel. "Not enough food!" he complained. "We are hungry!"

"Every man was to pack what he could comfortably carry for the journey," said Tenniel. "What happened?"

The brigand smiled a toothless smile. "We had nothing to pack."

Tenniel felt he could not assail Grend for his poverty, so he looked westward to Durbac Town. "I suppose we must requisition supplies from that village, then."

Grend smiled again, as at a private joke.

Tenniel led the troops to Durbac Town. They were greeted in the main square by a crowd of women of all ages, and several old men. "What do you want here?" a tall, spare, gray-haired woman asked firmly. She wore a faded but clean shift. Tenniel hesitated—he was unsure how to begin. "Where are the Elders?" he asked finally. "I must speak with them."

"Two have gone to war," the woman replied. "Iben, the third, came down sick yesterday. I am his wife, Vila. I am in charge now."

Several of the men behind Tenniel murmured in astonishment or snickered. A woman in charge of a town? It took Tenniel a moment to comprehend this.

"We need food," he said foolishly.

"So do we," Vila replied. "You should have left with more provisions. Return to your own town and restock."

"There isn't time for that! There's a war starting!"

"Then hunt rabbits and squirrels," Vila suggested. "Dig for roots . . . forage for berries. But do not take our food, for it is all we will have until our men return."

"I do not believe this!" Tenniel shouted. "This is a prosperous town, and you refuse to feed troops that are going to war to protect you!" It was the first test of his authority, and he was acutely aware of what a ridiculous figure he cut. His voice was becoming shrill. He was being ordered about by a woman. This was not the way to gain the respect of his men.

"We are sorry to deny you," Vila said, "but we must think of ourselves and our children first."

"I say they owe us food," Grend shouted, "and I mean to have my share!" The others of his band shouted agreement, and with Grend leading them, broke away from the troops and ran down the streets, pushing the inhabitants aside roughly.

"Wait!" Tenniel shouted, but to no avail.

The raid took only a few moments. The raiders hurried back up the main street, carrying armloads of foodstuffs. But before they could escape, they were suddenly met by a hail of bricks and rocks from the rooftops. Shielding their heads with their arms and stolen goods, they took shelter in the recessed doorways, under wagons and the like. They tried to enter buildings, but all were locked.

"Keep throwing things!" Vila, the Elder's wife, shouted. She stood on a roof, throwing tiles. "If we let them get away with this, we'll not have a moment's peace until the war is over!"

"They can't do this!" Grend shouted. He picked up a stone and hurled it at Vila. She ducked, but it caught her on the shoulder, causing her to fall. She slid halfway down the roof before she caught the chimney, and only this saved her from falling to the ground. There was a moment of silence from both sides. Even the scurrilous lot that had robbed the town found it hard to believe that one of them had attacked the Chief Elder's wife. Grend glared at his fellows. "She asked for it! They all did! We're just taking what we should have! Come on!" and he charged out into the street, hunched beneath his sack of food. The others followed, but Tenniel and the rest of the Borgen Town contingent blocked the street. The raiders turned to run back in the other direction, but Tenniel had ordered men to go down a side street and trap them.

Grend was brought to face Tenniel. "I can see now that I should have listened to Talend," Tenniel said. "I should not have tried to fill the quota with the likes of you! You are no longer in the army, Grend. We will escort you and your men away from this town and release you. Thereafter, you are on your own." He raised his voice to address the others. "You will return the food immediately! Those of you who pledge never to do such a thing again may stay with the troops; the rest must go with Grend! If we continue such practices as this, we will not need the Sim to destroy our villages. If we run short of food again, we will search honestly for it ourselves!"

As the men were returning the food, Tenniel apologized profusely to Vila, and the woman offered both sympathy and provisions in return. "It is possible that we could spare enough meat and vegetables for a large kettle of stew," she said. "It would not be much per man, but it would let you all travel with full bellies this day."

Tenniel thanked her, and announced the offer to the men, who sent up a rousing cheer. Tenniel, however, remained worried. Were there other, similar incidents taking place in other towns?

XIII

Tamberly Town seemed much smaller to Dayon. A fog had blown in from the sea, shrouding the streets and houses in mist. The village had not changed very much, except for the crowds. Dayon watched the frenzy of people around him. What had happened to his old friends? He knew the answer. They had grown up, grown surly and set in their ways, and now they were the people who chased the children from the shops and scolded them for stealing berries from the marketplace. Dayon had seen one or two of his old cronies, but had not said anything to them. Not yet. It was his father, Jondalrun, that he wanted first to see. He had been told that he would find him at the Graywood Tavern, in the back room with Pennel the Elder, making plans for the war.

He hurried across the square and entered the tavern, his boots crunching the sawdust on the floor. He did not relish a confrontation with his father, but he was driven to see him by the death of Johan.

At least, Dayon told himself, he would see his mother soon. He had missed her terribly these past two years.

He knocked on the door. Jondalrun opened it with a jerk, glared at Dayon, and said loudly, "Have you come to enlist? Can you write your name?"

"I can," Dayon said quietly, realizing Jondalrun, in his haste, had not recognized him through his beard. "My name is Dayon. Son of Jondalrun."

The old man sagged back against the door, and Dayon was afraid for a moment that his attempt at the dramatic had been too much for his father. Jondalrun recovered quickly, however, and he turned to Agron and Pennel, who sat at the oaken table in the room's center. "Leave us!" he growled. "My son and I have much to discuss!" Dayon stifled a smile. His father had not changed a bit, ordering two men out of a public tavern without a thought about it. Agron was apparently moved to comment on the same thing, but Pennel laid a hand on his arm and they both left quietly. Pennel locked eyes with Dayon for a moment, and much was conveyed in that glance—welcome, sympathy, and above all, a wish of good fortune.

The door closed. The two men looked at each other for an instant of silence, neither knowing what to say. It must start somewhere, Dayon thought, and so he spoke first. "Father, I have heard about Johan. I—"

"You left your home!" Jondalrun shouted. "Now you come back seeking my forgiveness?"

"Yes," Dayon said simply. "I suppose I do. I left because I had to leave. There were things I wanted to do."

"Now you have done them," Jondalrun said, looking at Dayon closely, "and now you are no longer my son. By the looks of you, you are a fisherman of Cape Bage. I put you aside long ago. Do not ask me to take you back now."

A familiar feeling of outrage filled Dayon. "I *am* your . . ." he started to protest, but then he reflected on the scenes they had shared two years ago. What was the use? His father would never change. Dayon could only offer his sympathies and condolences, and then stay away.

"How is Mother?" he asked.

Jondalrun's face dropped, as if another son had just been felled by the sorcerers. "You do not know?" he asked. "No—of course not. You could not."

Dayon felt coldness creep over him. "What do you mean?"

"She died soon after you left," Jondalrun said gruffly.

Dayon stared out of the window. The fog had been clearing, but for a moment he thought that it had grown thicker, for the trees and houses were misting in a peculiar way. Then he admitted to himself that he was weeping.

"Are you saying that her death is my fault?" he asked harshly.

Jonda¹run was silent for a moment, and then Dayon felt his father's hand upon his shoulder. "No," the old man said in a low voice. "She died of the fever—there was nothing that could be done. I . . . did not mean to imply that." He hesitated, then said, "I am an old man—I raise my voice too much."

Dayon turned and looked at him—he had never heard his father's voice that soft before. The old man was not weeping, but his eyes were suspiciously bright. I would like to embrace him, Dayon thought, but his arms were leaden at his side.

The father and his son stood there silently once more, and it was as if the years had suddenly turned to dust at their feet.

•

In the hills above Tamberly Town, an army was gathering—an army of tired, cold, and hungry men. Twenty towns had sent a hundred men each. These were the first arrivals, from Borgen Town and Jelrich Town. They had marched long, determined to spend the night in soft warm beds, their bellies full of good meals. Over two hundred strong, carrying torches and shouting with excitement, they rushed down toward Tamberly.

The townspeople saw them coming, a great raggedy wave that poured past the fields and cattle pens and into the streets. Some women shrieked in fright and hastily barred windows and doors. Others watched with interest. Shopkeepers and merchants in the marketplace sold their fresh produce enthusiastically at first, but then they too began to panic as the supply ran low and the hungry crowd began to shout for food and lodging. There were not nearly enough beds in all of Tamberly to accommodate the new arrivals.

"Quick!" a shopkeeper told his daughter. "Tell the Elders! There'll be trouble before this night is out."

In the back room of Graywood Tavern, neither Jondalrun nor Dayon noticed the rising noise outside. They were preoccupied with each other.

"Father! You ask the impossible! I am a navigator and a fisherman, not a fighter!"

"You just asked to be called my son!" said Jondalrun. "If you are my son, you will fight at my side!"

The old argument had returned. Once again the father could see the son only in terms of himself. Once again the son could see his future only in terms of his life at sea. "How could I possibly be your second-in-arms, Father? I know nothing about war!"

My father is as stubborn as always, thought Dayon, but this time I will not walk away. "Father," he cried, "you will not even reach the Simbalese coast! It is a rare day that the strait can be crossed! The currents are wild and the ships will simply capsize in the strait! I know! I have been there!"

"Then go there again for Fandora! If you do not wish to fight, then use your skills as a navigator to help us reach Simbala!"

Dayon did not answer. A compromise from his father was as rare as a smile. Part of him felt as if he could not deny his father anything after all he had been through. Yet, at the same time, Dayon could not bring himself to agree to the plan. He had barely escaped the maelstrom on his last trip out to sea. How could he take farmers and blacksmiths into those same waters? He could not guarantee safe passage. How could he take responsibility for their lives?

Dayon thought about the Simbalese. They were sorcerers, of course. He had heard that the Monarch of Simbala could change himself into a hawk. To challenge them was madness.

Yet, if the Simbalese had killed Johan, was there any reason to think they would not kill another Fandoran?

"Elder Jondalrun!" came a cry at the window. It was a girl's voice. "We have trouble in town!"

Jondalrun turned angrily from his son, who had still given him no response. Dayon followed him. They rushed through the tavern, which was now filled with travel-dusty men demanding drinks. "Good!" Jondalrun said. "The troops from the other towns are arriving!"

Then they both stepped outside, and were shocked by what they saw.

Tamberly Town was overrun with the incoming troops. Down the main street from the hills they poured in a ragged wave, crowding into the narrow streets. Hungry and thirsty, they disregarded the orders shouted by the Elders of their villages and rushed about madly, some chasing poultry or stealing produce from farm wagons with the intent of making a meal, others taking the last few bits of food in the markets and raiding butteries for dusty jugs.

Shouts and scoldings filled the main streets, along with the sounds of distressed livestock.

Dayon and Jondalrun crossed the street from Graywood Tavern to the old stable. Dayon watched his father closely. To his surprise, he saw uncertainty in Jondalrun's face—uncertainty, and a growing fear that did not set well on the stern old features. Jondalrun looked about—at every turn there were more men.

"These are only the first arrivals!" Dayon heard him say. "There will be hundreds more!"

Dayon watched, not sure what to do. How would they feed and shelter them all?

Jondalrun sat down on a barrel. "You see how we need help!" he said to his son, his hands suddenly shaking.

Dayon nodded. For the first time, the fears behind Jondalrun's words were evident in his voice. The young man put his hand on Jondalrun's shoulder. "We will do the best we can," he said. "Come, Father, I will help you."

XIV

Beneath Overwood, the roots of the giant trees had tunneled the ground, crossing and crisscrossing, forming a gargantuan maze. Although the trees of Overwood were ancient, by Simbalese standards, eventually they did die and decay, and their roots were gnawed away by small animals and insects that populated the unbroken darkness, leaving huge tunnels.

In one of these tunnels, quiet save for the occasional dripping of water from the roots, a yellow light glimmered. It bobbed in a regular fashion, growing steadily stronger. It was a torch, a long stick made of compressed firemoss, which burned cleanly with a steady flame.

Four people moved uneasily down the tunnel, their nostrils filled with the smell of mold and their nerves frayed by the sound of a thousand rodents and nighttails, which could be heard but not seen clearly in the dark. Such were the consequences of intrigue at this untimely hour.

The torch was grasped firmly by Princess Evirae, ludicrously out of place in her long gown, ducking low at times to avoid the entanglement of her huge coiffure in the mud-caked roots overhead. Behind her walked Mesor, tight, self-contained, permitting himself a private note of amusement every now and then as the Princess caught her gown or hair.

Watching the Princess with equal parts of suspicion and anger were Baron Tolchin and Baroness Alora. By virtue of their intellect and lineage, they were among the most respected couples in the Royal Family. Their silken robes and finery would have dazzled the eyes of the richest Simbalese, yet they wore the only clothes considered suitable by Alora and Tolchin for an undertaking as filthy as that for which Evirae had summoned them.

"My dear Princess," said Baron Tolchin in an uncommonly formal tone he adopted to reflect discomfort, "with all due respect, my wife and I demand to know the reason for this escapade! To say that it is an urgent matter of state is not enough!"

"Are you questioning the wisdom of the Princess?" Mesor inquired silkily.

"Only insofar as her retaining your services," snapped Alora. "The statement by my husband was not directed at you. Do you presume to answer for the Princess?"

Mesor subsided with a slight smile. It masked the churning in his stomach. Alora's rebuke reminded him that, even with Hawkwind in the palace, there was still a large difference between the Royal Circle and the Royal Family. As an appointed adviser to Evirae, he was a member of the former, but this had neither the security nor the respectability of royal lineage. He had risen from the ranks of Alora's own Bursars, picked by the Princess herself—but one word from Tolchin or Alora, and he could be back in the Bursars again.

Princess Evirae did not reply to Baron Tolchin's query. She was trying to remember the correct turn they should take in the tunnels. Evirae was familiar with the caverns. Over the years she had used them many times: for clandestine rendezvous as a young woman, and later as a place for conspiratorial meetings with trusted members of the Circle. Still, the labyrinthine twistings confused her.

"We shall be there soon," she said, at last spying a familiar configuration of roots by the torchlight. The group came to a widening of the tunnel, and in the distance they saw a wooden door set in a curving wall. Outside, sitting on a stool, was a large man fearlessly keeping watch in the darkness. As Evirae's torch came into view, he lumbered to his feet.

Evirae motioned for the door to be opened. "Now, Tolchin, you will see the reason for my summons."

The guard took a ring of keys from his belt, and as the

sound of rattling echoed through the tunnels, he opened the door.

"I think," said Evirae with confidence, "that this is far more important than a good night's sleep."

•

Amsel turned suddenly at the sound of the key in the lock. He had been pacing back and forth in his small underground cell, feeling extremely tired but incapable of sleep. I've been in Simbala for close to a day, he thought, and I'm no closer to fulfilling my mission than when I arrived.

Amsel had been brought unconscious to the headquarters of the men who flew the windships. As a result, he had seen little of Simbala. The canopied carriage that had ferried him from the windship headquarters had provided little in the way of scenery. It had been covered in silk as dark as the cell to which he had eventually been taken.

The driver of the carriage had treated Amsel like a small boy. Perhaps this was due to the difference in their sizes, thought Amsel. Or perhaps it was due to the childlike expression of wonder on his face when he first glimpsed the gigantic trees of Simbala.

The transfer from the canopied carriage to the tunnels below these trees had afforded Amsel his only chance to observe the fabled forest. It was evening when he saw them, and the dreamy, dark verdancy, combined with the arborescent beauty of the streets, had caused Amsel to gasp in delight. It was like a paradise, alive with the fragrance of a hundred different flowers. Amsel had looked up in amazement. Within the trunks of the larger trees, the Simbalese had built places to live! High above these trees floated the windships, moving gently through the clouds.

Amsel had rubbed his eyes to make sure that he had not been dreaming. There were trees so large that entire Fandoran houses could fit within them. Through the stained-glass windows of one of these trees Amsel had seen light and color so abundant that it seemed as if all the activity of a Fandoran street brimmed inside it. Blues, primrose, yellow. How he wished to see it!

The driver of the carriage had taken his hand then, and led him quickly, far too quickly for Amsel, toward a darkened back path. In the distance, Amsel saw wide polished steps of marble next to a garden of small trees and flowers.

At the end of the patch were the roots of another large tree, and set into those roots a small round door. To one side of the door stood a torch, which the driver had lifted carefully from its cresset. He opened the door and they descended narrow steps down to a series of tunnels that twisted and turned beneath hanging roots. Not a word had been said to Amsel by his captors, and despite his repeated pleas, he had not seen anybody in Simbala of more than moderate authority.

Instead, they had taken him to the cell.

He was hungry, cold, tired, and angry beyond words. He had a message of urgent importance to deliver, and instead, he was standing in a cold damp room with a wooden stool and a heap of straw for a bed. Then he had seen the shadows beneath the crack in the door. Amsel watched anxiously as he heard the clicking of the lock. With a rush of cool air the door burst open. A streak of yellow light illuminated the chamber, and a frenzy of dust and soil clouded the air. Amsel saw four shadows enter. He heard a woman's voice. "I present to you a Fandoran spy," she said. For a moment Amsel expected to see a Fandoran spy. Then he realized that the woman was referring to him.

She was a tall woman whose huge conelike structure of hair, dusted with precious stones, forced her to stoop beneath the tangled roots in the ceiling. She was very beautiful—the torch she held seemed not as bright as her red hair. She was smiling, but somehow the expression did not reassure Amsel. He looked at her hands. She wore no rings, but the fingers were tipped with wickedly long nails painted various colors and filed lovingly to points.

The others also wore clothes of highborn finery—the silver-inlaid pouch at the portly man's waist would be worth three years' food and lodging in Fandora. He had a huge white beard. The stout woman next to him was obviously his wife. Amsel felt that, under other circumstances, he might like these people. At the moment, however, they did not look as if they had come in search of friendship.

The last member of the party he distrusted on sight: he was a foppish young man with a smug, self-satisfied air. A climber, he would be called in Fandora. Amsel reminded himself that his instinctive feelings about other people were suspect. He had been a hermit and he had not taken enough time to know the people of his own town. I'd best not judge these Simbalese too quickly, he cautioned himself.

This insecurity aside, Amsel was still angry. "I am *not* a spy!" he protested. "I am an emissary from Fandora!"

The tall woman glowered at him. "You will speak when you are spoken to, and not before, Fandoran!"

"My name is Amsel," he replied. At least, he thought, I am in the presence of a woman with authority.

"Your name does not matter," said Evirae. "You are a spy—and perhaps you are a murderer!"

This last comment, voiced with added drama, startled Amsel, who for a moment thought Jondalrun had arrived in Simbala to spread rumors against him. Suddenly dizzy with fatigue and emotion, Amsel sat down on the wooden stool.

"What is the meaning of these charges, Evirae?"

The man in the white beard was deeply agitated. His wife stood away from the others, by the door, watching Evirae. The portly man continued, "This man's accent is as barbarous as his clothes! He cannot possibly be a Fandoran soldier! If he has anything to do with the Northwealdsman's story, I suggest—"

"I am here on a mission of peace!" cried Amsel to the man.

Evirae turned toward him quickly and thrust a sharp fingernail at his throat. "There is rumor among my people," she said, "that the tips of my nails are painted with poison. Unless you wish to find out the truth, I suggest you remain quiet unless spoken to."

Amsel nodded and gulped. The woman removed her fingernail from his neck. "Very good," she said. "Now, tell me, Fandoran, is it not true that you were found off northern shores?"

"Yes" said Amsel. "I have been traveling from—"

"The 'yes' will suffice, Fandoran."

"But wait," Amsel said. "I—"

Evirae raised her finger meaningfully.

Amsel waited, angry and frightened at the same time. The woman's threat was less important to him than the fact that she seemed to enjoy it. If she was indeed a figure of authority in Simbala, then he was in for trouble.

Mesor watched Evirae's performance uneasily. If the

Princess is not careful, he thought, Alora's suspicions will be aroused. Evirae must make it clear that she has only the interests of Simbala at heart. In her quest for the Ruby, he knew how close Evirae had already come to outright treason.

Evirae continued. "You say you have invaded our shores to ask for peace, Fandoran. Why? What reason would you have to believe that there is a threat of war?"

The man in the white beard asked, "Have you come here out of fear of a trade war?"

"No," said Amsel. "I came because Fandora has declared war on Simbala." The moment the words came out, Amsel regretted his candor.

"No!" said Tolchin.

Amsel noticed a flash of excitement between the woman called Evirae and the man at her side. He did not understand it, but it troubled him more deeply than the feeling that things had just gotten out of hand.

"There is time to avert the war!" he cried in an effort to make amends. "You need only understand the reason for my people's actions! A child has been killed, and Fandora thinks that one of your windship riders is responsible."

"Absurd!" answered Alora from her position by the door.

"Lies!" said Tolchin.

"You may be put to death for such charges!" Evirae threatened. "Now, tell us the truth! You are a Fandoran spy and you have come to our shores on a mission! If you value your life, you will tell us what it is! Take heed, Fandoran! You address the Princess of Simbala!"

The Princess of Simbala! Amsel rose from the stool. He barely came up to Evirae's waist, but his voice, boosted by the urgency of his mission, filled the room. "Princess, my people are a good and simple people. They are not warriors. They are peaceful farmers. Some are jealous of Simbala. Most are just frightened of you. I do not belive Simbala is responsible for the death of the child. Ignorance has caused Fandora to declare this war! There are those who oppose it already! You must do something to prevent it! You must send an emissary to tell them you did not murder the child! You must send a windship to Fandora!"

"A trap!" shouted Evirae, overwhelming Amsel's words.

"Fandora only wishes to capture a windship and turn it against us! We have heard about the death of the child—but it was a Simbalese child, not a Fandoran!"

"No!" cried Amsel. "That is not true!"

Alora reddened. "Do not tell *us* what is true or untrue, Fandoran! Yours is a land of simpletons! We know a child has been murdered!"

"Please!" cried Amsel. "Listen to me! Fandoran boats may already be assembled for the invasion. My people are no threat to you. I have seen your windships, your soldiers! Look at me! I am barely half your height! My people cannot possibly pose a threat to you. Please help me avoid bloodshed!"

"Kiorte lost a windship in a storm only weeks ago," said Evirae to Tolchin. "Now I think I know where it has gone."

Amsel overheard her words. The windship in Gordain Town! "You don't understand," he said. "That windship came over during a storm!"

"Then you admit it is in Fandora!" said Evirae with a mixture of venom and glee. "We have ignored the Fandorans for too long! We must take action!"

The white-bearded man stepped forward. "A moment, Princess. I have a question for the spy."

Mesor nodded. She is getting to Tolchin, he thought.

Amsel looked nervously at the older man. He hoped his anxiety would not be misconstrued as guilt.

"Amsel," said Tolchin softly, "if what you tell us is true, then Fandorans may soon be coming toward our shores. Is that correct?

Amsel nodded. "Yes, but—"

"I'm sorry." Tolchin turned to Alora and said, "There is a clear and present danger of war. The Family must be notified immediately." Then he turned to the younger woman. "Evirae, you must speak to Hawkwind at once!"

Amsel said urgently, "The invasion can still be prevented! A windship can reach them! Just send an emissary to Fandora!"

"There is a pattern to his words," observed Mesor. "No doubt his mission is to confuse and delay us while they attack."

"Silence!" said Tolchin. "We know what must be done."

Then to Alora he added, "I suggest we return to the Over-wood at once."

The Baroness nodded grimly and faced Evirae. "For once, Princess, I think you may have done the proper thing."

Evirae replied sweetly, "There must be some leadership in the Family. From now on, I hope you'll always think of me in those terms."

Time to leave, thought Mesor. Evirae is starting to show her colors. "Milady," he said tactfully, "I suggest we depart."

"Wait!" cried Amsel desperately, but Baron Tolchin had already summoned the aide at the door.

"See to it that the spy gets some food," he said. Then Tolchin turned to Amsel. "I am sorry for you, young man," he said. "For you and Fandora."

The door shut, and Amsel's cell was dark again.

"Young man indeed!" groaned the inventor. "A young man would not have said the foolish things that I have said! A young man would not be responsible for a war! Oh, what have I done? What have I done?"

•

Deep in the merchants' quarter, far from the tree castles in the center of Overwood where the members of the Royal Family made their homes, was the domicile of Baron Tol-chin and Baroness Alora. The nature of their role in Sim-balese commerce dictated this location, but it was not a situation they regretted. It provided them with a unique view of the Royal Family's affairs. They were part of them, yet they were apart from them. The day-to-day business of the Family left them unaffected, and the couple's frequent tours of the Southland kept them both in blissful ignorance of the petty politics of the palace.

They had supported the appointment of Hawkwind be-cause it had been the wish of Ephrion, and they had toler-ated the outsider's intrusions on their authority because he showed more potential for the throne than any of the candi-dates from the Royal Family. Still, they did not really trust Hawkwind.

This morning's incident had further strained his position with Alora and Tolchin by virtue of the fact that both now held Evirae in higher regard. They had been impressed by

Evirae's revelation that Prince Kiorte had entrusted her with the interrogation of the Fandoran spy, and they had been surprised by the speed with which she had learned of the invasion plans. Upon their departure from the tunnels, when Evirae had petitioned them for another meeting before telling Hawkwind of what they had learned, Tolchin and Alora had consented. Had they known of Evirae's duplicity with the Northwealdsman, had they known that Kiorte was not on a mission to the west—as Evirae had told them—but was actually missing, they would have informed Hawkwind immediately. Alora and Tolchin knew none of these things, however; and so, with the aroma of Bunduran tea filling the sitting chamber, they greeted Evirae with unprecedented warmth.

"I am glad you left your shadow at home," said the Baron.

Evirae looked behind herself with concern, then realized that Tolchin was making a joke. "Yes," she said with a belated smile, "I did not wish Mesor to be present for our discussion."

"Come along, then," said Alora with less charm than her husband. "Although you have assured us that there has been no sighting of an invasion, I do not like the idea of keeping the news from the palace. I presume you have your reasons, Evirae, and I wish to hear them as soon as possible."

As an aide poured tea, Tolchin and Alora seated themselves on the featherleaf couch in the center of the floor. Evirae remained standing, her hair denting the folds of a silken canopy. She spoke with caution. "This is a difficult meeting for me. As you both know, I have been less than diplomatic in my opposition to Monarch Hawkwind in the past. In all honesty, I did not and do not feel he is qualified to be Monarch. I have come to say now that he may not even be qualified to live in Simbala."

Alora, accustomed to the circumlocutions of the Bursars, nevertheless frowned. "If you have information, make it brief and clear, Evirae! We are discussing the safety of Simbala."

It was an effort for Evirae to keep her composure. She had a feeling of being in the center of a vast, revolving pattern, such as the game of dochin, in which bets were placed on the length of time it took for a wheel made of hinged carved segments to spin and fall into place as a beautifully ordered design. She was watching that spinning now, in her mind—the pieces were coming together for her. Again she thought: It is meant that I be ruler of Simbala. The fates conspire for me.

Aloud she said softly, "Does it not seem odd to you that the news of the Fandoran invasion comes at a time when Monarch Hawkwind has halved the size of the Simbalese army?"

Alora frowned again. "Yes, it does, but there is good reason for that action—very good reason, as you may know."

Tolchin nodded. "I requested the use of our troops to escort a trade expedition to the Southland."

Evirae tapped her long nails on the perfumed wood of the wall. "Yes, yes, I know that; but Monarch Hawkwind has never agreed to any such escort mission in the past."

Tolchin sat up in his chair. "How did you know that, Evirae?"

The Princess smiled. "*Somebody* must keep an eye on the palace."

Alora put down her cup of tea. "Young lady! Monarch Ephrion is fully capable of guarding the interests of Simbala. He has done so for over forty years."

"We all grow old and tired," said Evirae. "My father had the grace to resign from the army when he no longer felt capable of supervising its affairs. Monarch Ephrion could learn from his example."

Tolchin replied, "Unthinkable, unthinkable! Ephrion is not a general, my dear; he is a Monarch."

"Hawkwind is Monarch now," said Evirae, "and that is my objection. With Hawkwind and his Rayan woman, the Royal Family has lost its grip on the palace."

"Please, Evirae," said the Baroness. "We have heard the argument many times already! If you have no further news, get yourself to the palace and inform Hawkwind of the news."

"The Family," said Evirae patiently, "must be considered. If the Fandorans do indeed attack, it will be a grave time for Simbala. Can you tell me that you actually trust the future of our country, of our Family, to the son of a miner?"

To this question, Alora and Tolchin did not reply. There had been incidents, there were rumors, but the new

Monarch had done nothing to betray Simbala. Still, if there was war—was he fit to govern? They had not asked themselves the question. Even Ephrion had no reason to consider the possibility. When Tolchin had protested the embargoes on trade imposed by Hawkwind, the old Monarch had told him, "Hawkwind needs some time to grow."

"Hawkwind listens more to the Rayan woman than he does to us," the Princess said cautiously. "We do not even know where her loyalties lie. It truly bothers me, Alora, to think that in time of battle the Overwood will be subject to the plans of a thief's daughter. Surely we should take precautions."

The Baroness poured herself another cup of tea. Tolchin rose from his seat and began to pace the floor of the chamber.

Evirae played on their patriotism. "For the safety of Simbala," she said, "could a small act of precaution hurt?"

Baron Tolchin tapped his foot on the thick rug. "Dear girl," he asked warily, "what do you have in mind?"

"A small test," answered Evirae.

"Monarch Hawkwind is not a child!" said the Baroness. "He will not stand for any tests."

"If he does not know about the test, he cannot object." Evirae seated herself.

"Simbala is in danger," said Alora. "There is no time to waste on foolish games."

"This will not take much time," Evirae answered.

Tolchin strode across the room and unwound a thin brown cord from its stay. A yellow sash curtain floated forward, covering the room's only window. "Tell us, said Tolchin suspiciously, "what you have in mind."

•

Lathan had always thought of himself as a civilized man, a reasonable and unexcitable man, and above all not the sort of man who would harbor grievances against his Monarch. Still, a strenuous day-and-night ride through the forest and then an evening spent crouching, damp and hungry, watching the Northwealdsmen dine on wild turkey and yams had certainly been enough to make a man think sour thoughts.

He had no intention of abandoning his duty, however, especially now, when it appeared that his long riding and waiting were about to reach fruition.

It was nighttime on the border of the Northweald. The air was crisp, smelling of the pines that flourished in this northern forest, and with just enough of a breeze to add to Lathan's discomfort. A scratchy-skinned lizard crawled into his boot, seeking warmth, and he had to grit his teeth to keep from crying out as the sharp scales rasped his leg. He pulled the boot off and flicked the lizard away petulantly. He deserved a medal for this, he told himself.

Lathan concentrated on the conversation that drifted through the camouflage of bushes and branches.

"What she had was more to say than good morning, I tell you!" The Northwealdsman, to Lathan's disbelief, was recounting a meeting with the Princess of Simbala herself. He and his companion had camped by an ale cache, a cold stream wherein a waterproof leather bag of wineskins had been stored. This they had consumed along with the turkey, without too much turkey. The wine had loosened Willen's tongue. He told of an encounter in the woods, of a conspiracy by Fandora against Simbala, and the Princess' accusations against Hawkwind. This was treason for sure, thought Lathan, and he was ready to return to the palace when he heard a strange rustling sound overhead.

Suddenly the dim moonlight was blotted out by a huge shadow that flowed across the ground. The two Wealdsmen looked up, as did Lathan. Overhead, the stars were blocked by the silhouette of a windship—a one-man ship, smaller than most of the fleet, but still huge and impressive. It settled slowly toward the campfire like a vast dark ghost, noiseless save for the creaking of its ropes and the subdued rustling and flapping of its sails. Willen and Tweel watched in fascination. It was too dark to identify the single figure who worked the ropes. His back was to the ruddy glow cast by the brazier beneath the sail, and the boat shielded him from the campfire.

Lathan realized he would be seen by the Windrider if he remained where he was. Accordingly, he crawled through the copse where he hid, and down a hill several yards, to take shelter in a large bluewort bush. The heavy, cloying scent of the flowers made his head spin, but at least he was sure he would not be seen.

The windship landed. Its rider threw a rope with a grappling hook into the fork of a tree as the almost-weightless ship rebounded from the ground with dreamlike slowness. Then, when it had stabilized, the Windrider stepped forward, and the campfire highlighted his features.

Lathan, now secure in the bush, gasped. It was Prince Kiorte himself! First the Princess, then the Prince! Did this fellow Willen hold the key to a Sindril mine? He strained to hear what was being said, but to his frustration realized that he was a bit too far away—the voices were a meaningless mumble.

Willen had also been amazed to see Kiorte, but he and Tweel were too drunk to be impressed. He leaned against a tree as Tweel waved his turkey leg mockingly at the Prince.

"A bite to eat, Prince?" Tweel inquired with exaggerated politeness. "No doubt you've had a long and difficult journey."

"I have," Kiorte replied flatly, "but food has not been on my mind. I have searched long and questioned many bands of your fellows to learn your location, Willen. I wish to know what words you had with my wife, Princess Evirae."

Willen cocked his head and feigned a deep sadness. "Ah, I'm deeply distressed to deny you, Prince, you being a Prince and all. But I've promised the Princess that what we discussed would go no further. I'm a man of my word."

Kiorte held his temper with an obvious effort and spoke evenly. "I am a Prince of Simbala and Evirae's husband. What she says is my affair. Her interests are my interests."

"That's all well and good, but she made no exceptions, you see. Until she tells me otherwise . . ." Willen spread his hands.

"You are a simpleton," Kiorte said in a tight, low voice, "and you are drunk. What about you?" He turned to Tweel. "Are you also going to defy an order of the Prince of Simbala?"

Tweel hesitated, looking at Willen. Then he shook his head. "Willen has told me nothing," he said to Kiorte. "Therefore, there is nothing to tell you."

For another considerable time there was silence, save for the crackling of the fire and the creaking and rustling of the windship. Kiorte studied the two impassive forms before him. He could not force them to talk. Such actions were distasteful to him, and also, at the moment, impossible to implement.

Evirae was up to something—that he knew. He had been married to her too long not to recognize that air of preoccupation. This time, however, was different from her usual schemes—he knew that, too. She was approaching it with the same naive attitude, but she was playing with something larger—larger and more dangerous. She was involving innocents this time. Of that Kiorte was sure. He had to learn all the details, but he would not learn them from these two drunken fellows. That was also obvious.

Lathan watched as the head of the Windriders disengaged the windship, which drifted slowly into the night sky. Then he stood cautiously and stretched, feeling his joints creak and pop. He had hoped to get some rest before starting back, but he knew there would be no rest tonight. He would have to inform Monarch Hawkwind of this meeting immediately.

With a sigh he limped off toward the woods, where his horse was tethered. There were times, he told himself, when it just did not pay to be conscientious.

XV

It was always midnight in the mines, thought Hawkwind. Though the noon sun had been bright when he entered the tunnel, the first turn had changed the daylight to darkness. As he descended the broad steps, his torch of firemoss in one hand, he felt as if he was returning to a reality abandoned for a long time.

He thought: It is good that I've come. I will have a chance to settle my thoughts.

The tunnel had been closed for over four years. It was in disrepair, the wooden arches and walls were mossy, the torch niches were empty, and there were creeping vapors of deterioration in the air.

This tunnel had been the site of the attack, the place where many thought Hawkwind had taken his first steps toward the palace.

Since becoming Monarch, he had had little time alone. There were always matters of state, merchants and Ministers waiting to see him. Even the time he spent with Ceria, much as he loved her, did not have the solitude he had known in his days at the mines.

This troubled Hawkwind. Alone he felt truly in harmony with himself. With Ceria, he felt in harmony with the world, as if the natural order of two beings together gave his life new meaning. Alone, however, he felt like Hawkwind: he felt like a miner's son who for five years had worked the mines, face black and dusty, arms hard from swinging a pick into the earth. Here, in the mines, he could understand his life as an extension of his dreams.

"I have gone beyond my dreams," he said aloud, as if talking to the younger man in his past, "yet I still have hopes unfulfilled." He wanted little more for himself, save perhaps marriage and a child. He was happy. His hopes were now for Simbala.

He walked slowly down the sloping floor of the tunnel. Here and there along its length were the arching entrances of side tunnels, many of which were now closed forever with bricks and mortar. He knew that some of them led to the root tunnels beneath the city proper. Lying on the bare rock before him was the rust-pitted blade of a pick. Hawkwind lifted it, looked at it, and remembered . . .

He had been the overseer of the tanium shaft, which dropped vertically at the tunnel's end, deeper than all the others. It was so deep that the air was hot and heavy, and miners sometimes fainted from foul gases that seeped from the earth. They had been mining a rich vein of tanium, a liquid metal. It was risky work—at such depths, the pressure of the earth above was such that an unwary swing by a pick might release an arc of tanium that would strike with the force of a battering ram and flood the mine.

A miner had swung his pick one day and opened, not a vein of tanium, but what seemed to be a natural cavern adjacent to the shaft. Hawkwind had been called to investigate, and had found a wonderland of stalactites and stalagmites, columns and frozen waterfalls of rock. The men, entranced, had wanted to explore, but Hawkwind had ordered the investigation to wait until the next day, when everyone was fresh.

It was quiet now as he walked along the deserted tunnel. Hawkwind was suddenly very aware of the hundreds of feet of ground above him, and the fragility of the manmade intrusion into the ancient rock. He walked more quickly—for some reason, he felt impelled to reach the shaft at the end of the tunnel.

That night, over four years ago, watchmen outside the tunnels had heard strange, shuddersome cries from the depths of the mines—howling, like the shade of a wolf. The next day, not far from one of the root tunnels' entrances, a small stone house stood open and empty. A young mother, who had lived alone since the death of her miner husband, was missing. On the floor had been found traces of muck and grime, and in one of those patches was imprinted a strange, splay-toed footprint.

Hawkwind stopped suddenly. He turned and raised the torch, letting its illumination spill back toward the tunnel's curve. He had thought he heard something—perhaps the trickling of pebbles down one of the walls—or perhaps the scrabbling of claws on the stone floor?

He hesitated, then continued. The top of the shaft was only around the next bend, and he had a very bad feeling about it now. He had to see if it were still sealed, as he had ordered it to be years before. His boots splashed in puddles of water that had seeped down from the last rain.

The shaft had been cut at a steep angle into the rock, and niched with hand- and footholds for the miners to use. There had also been a windlass and bucket for hauling up the day's take. On that day, years ago, Hawkwind and a group of miners had descended into the shaft, where the opening into the caverns had been enlarged. Armed with torches and weapons, they had gone into the caverns.

They had not gone far when they discovered the body of the young widow. A miner found it behind a rock—he staggered away from it with a pale face, for it had been mutilated and feasted upon. He had barely gasped out the horrible news to Hawkwind, when seemingly from behind every rock and column and out of every fissure and crevice had poured a horde of loathsome gaunt creatures. Their skins were a mottled dead white; they were short and squat, with barrel-shaped bodies and thickly muscled limbs. Their faces were wide and flat, with broad, thin-lipped mouths filled with fangs. Their eyes were huge, and they seemed to have no ears at all on the sides of their bald heads. They were accompanied by slinking, wolflike creatures, also with bald, corpselike skin and huge eyes.

They came toward the miners, making chattering sounds. Hawkwind and the others immediately recognized them as a horror tale come true. They were the Kuln, and the animals with them were cave wolves. Stories of them had been used to frighten many a miner's child into obedience.

Hawkwind had ordered the miners back into the shaft, but they did not retreat quickly enough to avoid a battle.

The miners were armed, but vastly outnumbered, and the Kuln and their foul pets attacked even at the expense of losing limbs of incurring wounds that would have killed a man.

Hawkwind wielded a sword that day as few men have ever wielded one; fifteen of the Kuln he defeated, and eight cave wolves as well, but they lost five miners before they reached the opening into the shaft. Even then, the miners were not out of danger, but at least they were not attacked on all sides.

"Climb up the shaft!" Hawkwind had ordered them. "A single man can hold them for a time!"

"But how will you escape?" one of the miners cried. "We will not leave you!"

"Hurry!" Hawkwind shouted again. "I order you!" The miners climbed, one man at a time, and the men remaining battled the subterranean horde, until at last Hawkwind stood before the Kuln alone. With a sword in one hand and an ax in the other, he fought until the bodies of Kuln and cave wolves all but filled the bottom of the shaft. At length the creatures blocked the opening to such an extent that they had to drag some through into the cavern before they could come at him again. Hawkwind, aching with weariness, hurled his ax and sword at them, and seizing a pick, swung it at the wall, tearing away a huge piece of rock. Nothing came of that swing, and so he did it again, embedding the point of the pick deeply into the side of the shaft. He wrenched it out; again, nothing. A scrambling behind him told him that the Kuln were coming through. Hawkwind swung the pick once more. This time he struck true: a red stream of liquid tanium, like the blood of the world, gushed forth six inches wide, faster than a crossbow quarrel. Hawkwind barely got out of the way in time—the fluid shaft tore the pick from his hands. Then it struck the first Kuln to come through the opening, picked him up and crushed him against the wall. The wall groaned and trembled as tons of the liquid metal poured out, washing the screaming Kuln and the cave wolves back into their underground lair. Already it was filling the shaft. The roar of its passage was deafening. Hawkwind reached the inclined wall with difficulty, wading through the heavy flood, and began to pull himself up. His boots were heavy with tanium;

he kicked them off and climbed on, feeling the cold metallic tide lapping at his heels. Above him, he could hear the miners shouting encouragement. The level of the tanium rose higher—it covered his legs, slowing him. In a moment, Hawkwind knew, it would cover him completely; and then, slowly, viscously, it began to subside. It had reached its level, and would rise no higher. Hawkwind pulled himself free of it and climbed out of the shaft.

He had ordered that shaft covered with a rock that had taken twenty men to move. It was impossible for the Kuln to have moved it from below, even if they had survived the flood of tanium. Why, then, did he now hurry his steps; why was he so determined suddenly to learn if the shaft were still sealed?

He turned the last corner and faced the chamber of the shaft. There was the moldering remnant of the windlass, its rope long since disintegrated, its wooden wheel and crank collapsed. Beside it was the rock that had capped the shaft. It capped it no longer. The shaft was open.

Neglect and seepage from the rains had caused part of the chamber to collapse in a mudslide, and the earth had pushed the heavy rock aside as if it had been a child's toy. The mud had dried and shrunk, and a gaping crescent, like a new moon of darkness, lay between the rock and the mud. The shaft was open. There were tracks in the mud.

Hawkwind forced himself to step forward. He raised the torch and peered into the shaft. He saw nothing—not even the wavering reflection of the light on the wall of tanium. Evidently it had slowly drained into the cavern over the years.

He examined the tracks, and exhaled slightly. It was unlikely anything could have come from the shaft without leaving tracks, and the only tracks there were those of a single cave wolf. There was no sign that a Kuln had also left the shaft. He looked behind him. The tunnel was empty. Hawkwind started back the way he had come. Somewhere in the myriad tunnels and mines, a single cave wolf was loose. It was not good—but it could have been worse. He shuddered to think how much worse it could have been. This was not the answer to the mystery of the murdered child, but he would, of course, order the shaft resealed.

The discovery of the cave wolf posed new danger, but in a

way he almost welcomed it. Unlike Evirae, the animal was everything it appeared to be—there were no questions about its true motive, no complex plans to unravel. He missed the simplicity of the mines.

He remembered the day Monarch Ephrion had presented him with a medal for his heroism there. It had been a moment of quiet victory, with Ceria at his side. There had been no pretense then, nor any worries. His immediate concerns had been himself and his friends. Now he felt the weight of the Overwood's affairs, and the responsibility was far more than he had imagined.

The young Monarch climbed the steps toward daylight. The stone was familiar, its surface gray and wet beneath his feet. It reassured him to know that some things remained the same. He could always return to the mines; there would always be a place for him in Simbala. Evirae and her petty conspiracies did not matter down here; survival was a clear and uncomplicated road. If I can face the Kuln without fear, thought Hawkwind, then I can surely face the problems of the palace.

Yet he was troubled. The new problem was beyond the politics of the Overwood. The possible murder of the girl was an attack that demanded immediate retaliation—if it had, indeed, been an attack. But the only evidence was a child's bloodied dress. As he returned to daylight, Hawkwind reviewed any possible answers. None made sense. There was no beast known to the Northweald which would attack a young child alone on the beach. Nor was there any reason for the Fandorans to commit such a terrible crime. Although he had not met any Fandorans, they had always been known as peaceful people. He remembered the days of his travels, of the lands he had seen and their inhabitants. He had never spoken of those days, not even to Ceria. They had been among the most exciting days of his life. The things he had learned had changed his dreams for the future of Overwood. Nothing that he had learned there, however, suggested a solution to the murder of the Northwealdsman's daughter.

Sunlight flooded his face as he emerged from the mines. He untied his horse from a nearby tree, and was surprised to note that lately in thinking about the palace, he felt more and more as if it was his home.

XVI

Far to the north of Fandora and Simbala, beyond the Northern Sea, was a land of spires and monoliths, of lunar plains, and mountains so steep and icy that few living things dared them. Here creatures lived; gigantic creatures, suited to the vast scale of this land—and here they perished.

It was the end of the Age of Dragons.

The length of that age was such that the stars themselves might have marked it. Continents had risen and sunk during the course of it, and lesser species had been born and vanished. Yet the end these creatures shared in common with others was slowly approaching, and they were afraid.

Deep in this land a spire of stone rose above the white glaciers and black basalt. Within it, a labyrinth of tunnels and caves had been gnawed from the rock. These were the lairs of the coldrakes. They had lived here far beyond the memory of man. The centuries' passage of great scaled bellies over stone had worn vermicular grooves in the bare rock. The mist and steam that rose from the hot springs and geysers at the spire's base shrouded a bleached forest of bones. It had been their home for centuries, long past the time the others had left—but it would not be their home much longer.

Above the spire circled a single coldrake. He was larger than the others, and his scales were gleaming black rather than mottled gray. His vast ribbed wings lowered, and he felt the cold wind strike them, slowing his descent. The chill brought a hiss of pain and helpless anger from him. The struggle against the bitter wind, against the biting snow, was a part of him now—a pain that would not go away. He was tortured by rage, and its darker sister, fear.

The night was approaching—the long, cold night. The sunset tinted crimson the ivory-and-ebony landscape. The coldrake, a darkling silhouette, settled on the spire's tip, wings spread for balance. From this vantage point he could see in all directions. It was a view befitting his stature among the coldrakes. He was respected by the others willingly, by the dim realization of their brute minds that his intelligence was superior to their own. He was stronger and swifter, this coldrake, and he was different in other ways as well, ways that they did not know.

The wind rose, buffeting him, and he stretched his long neck into it, hissing his fury. Below, in their darksome caverns, the rest of the coldrakes shivered. The storm of his rage—the hissing, like the strike of lightning, and the thunderous booming of his wings—frightened them. They did not understand his anger. They did not know of the tale the Guardian had brought to him, many nights ago, from her appointed task in the south. They did not know what the humans had done, what a menace they now represented. They only knew that the Darkling, the strongest among them, was afraid—and so the danger must be large indeed.

The Darkling had brooded long over what the Guardian had said. She had told him that the humans could fly, even as they could. What they had done proved beyond doubt that they were dangerous and hostile. The Darkling raised his horned head and shrieked rage and helplessness—a sound like a mountain being riven. At that moment he envied those below him for the simplicity they possessed. They could not understand the magnitude of the problems that beset them. The cold that increased yearly, the scarcity of food—these things frightened them, but they could not forecast from them the end of their kind. They did not have the awful clear light burning in their minds, as the Darkling did; the light that illuminated their approaching fate so cruelly, but did not show him how to prevent it.

If he was to be governed by his fury, he would take them now to the warm land in the south, to war against the humans. However, he was compelled by something stronger

to wait. Although the Guardian's tale had proven the humans to be dangerous, migration to the land of the humans had been forbidden by another, whose authority he had never dared to challenge. The coldrakes had been barred from the warm southern lands by the dragons long before the Darkling had been born.

The rage he felt was like a virulent breath; it descended from him to those below. Their shrieks and snarls filled the air. Several launched themselves from the jagged crannies below and caught the wind, rising like vast bats in the bloody light. A large coldrake soared close to the Darkling, and filled with the contagious rage, snapped at his tail without realizing whom he attacked. The Darkling could not control his reaction—his head shot out in a flickering strike, and teeth ripped the other's wing, crunching the fragile bone. With a reverberating cry of pain, the wounded one tumbled toward the rocks far below. Simultaneously, the Darkling launched himself after the injured creature. That part of his brain blessed—or cursed—with reason had seen the consequences of his action, but had been too late to prevent the bestial part of him from retaliating. He must now repair the harm he had done; their numbers were far too few to risk deaths in the battles of despair.

Wings flat, slipping into the wind, he swooped underneath the panicked coldrake, breaking his fall in midair and slowing him until the wounded one was able to regain control and catch the air currents, safely gliding to a ledge. When he saw this had been done, the Darkling returned to his eyrie.

He knew that he must not lose control again. He was responsible for them. In their dwindling numbers there was still some strength. Without him to direct their hunts, to apportion the take fairly, they would all starve, including the Darkling. They needed him, and he needed them.

He brooded upon his perch, and his demeanor gradually had its effect upon the others. Their cries lessened, and gradually, one by one, they returned to their warrens.

The Darkling knew that something had to be done. The cold encroached steadily; they seemed unable to resist it as they had in the past. The warmth from the hot springs and geysers could no longer hold it back. They could not remain here to starve and freeze.

The Darkling would search the caverns to the north of the sea again, for any sign of life.

The Last Dragon had disappeared long ago—the last of its race that had vanished in the ice of the coming cold. But the coldrakes would not violate the edict as long as there was a chance that the Last Dragon was still alive. But if the dragon could not be found, then it would be time to test the humans, to find out how dangerous they really were. The land to the south, the warm and golden land, awaited.

The Darkling took to the cold air and flew southward.

XVII

chain of a thousand torches made its way through the Fandoran hills. It wound its way through small towns, toward the cliffs of Cape Bage.

"Elder Jondalrun!" came a call from the Tamberly contingent. "The men ask for a moment's relief!"

"No!" went back the word. "Those that cannot make the trip to the shore are unfit for the invasion!"

Jondalrun marched at the head of his army. He too was tired and hungry, but he of all the men could not complain. "They march for Johan," he told Dayon, at his side. "They march for Analinna and all the children of Fandora."

His son nodded silently, dreading the voyage to come.

•

The armada, if such it could be called, was built slowly and laboriously, from every skiff, every dinghy, every carrack and coracle available. In Cape Bage, every owner was automatically made a captain. The army began to arrive about noon, and it was soon apparent that the boats could not ferry them all. Additional boats and rafts were being built, it having been decided that two crossings would demoralize that part of the army left on the beach of a hostile country. The building of additional boats and rafts took the better part of two days. Fortunately, there was a convenient stand of trees nearby, which provided timber. Nevertheless, Jondalrun's earlier apprehensions were justified. The food supply was low, and with it his army's passion for the invasion.

The four Elders had regrouped in the midst of the activity. Barrels of pitch were bubbling over fires, and small gangs of men were desultorily applying the calk to wounded ships. Dayon, late of Cape Bage but now a member of his father's contingent, directed the rebuilding of the rudder of a large fishing ship.

"Winners all!" said Tamark sardonically as he slapped a dilapidated boat and felt the wooden hull fall apart beneath his hand.

"Not this fellow," said Lagow. "This skiff will not even reach water!"

"This boat is not even among the worst," said Tamark. "The currents will do more damage than Jondalrun expects." He watched as the Elder of Tamberly Town conferred with Tenniel about supplies.

Lagow leaned uneasily on the skiff's lee side. "Tell me, Tamark; you were so opposed to the war before it was discussed in council. How did you allow yourself to get involved as deeply as you have?"

Tamark picked a splinter from his hand. "I can ask you that same question, Lagow. Was it not you who leaped to my defense?"

. "Aye."

"Yet you also accompanied Jondalrun and Tenniel on the trip to the Alakan Fen. I am convinced you had the same motive as I did at heart."

"That being?"

Tamark raised his brows, as if to announce a message of utmost importance. "When a man is at sea and he feels the wind buck up and the waves hurl forward like the head of a dragon, he knows how foolish it is to resist. The best he can do is cover himself, protect his ship, and pray."

Lagow nodded. "You saw no way to stop the war, so you chose a path that would allow you to protect Fandora."

"Precisely," said Tamark. "And you have done the same thing. By directing the invasion, we can perhaps prevent disaster."

Lagow frowned. "But I would still turn back tomorrow. I fear you would not."

Tamark took a step away from the vessel. "A decision has

been made. I question its wisdom but not the emotion behind it. Fandora must be protected. Perhaps we are incorrect. But perhaps the Simbalese do plan to extend their influence across the strait. I do not think that is true, but to surrender before we start, and then discover that Jondalrun was correct, would be intolerable. The sentiments of Fandora should not be ignored, as much as we disagree with them."

"The people of Fandora are frightened, Tamark. They do not know the meaning of war. I would still like to reason with them."

The fisherman surprised Lagow with a deep laugh. "Look around you! Cape Bage is filled with 'soldiers'! It is their grand adventure! A trip to lands unknown! A confrontation with sorcerers! There's a boy in every man out there, crying to get out! You think an ounce of reason will hold them back now?"

Lagow knitted his brow. "Not reason, perhaps, but I hope hunger and impatience will do the trick."

The fisherman flashed a bitter grin. "The strait will do it," he said.

●

In his small underground cell, Amsel sat and considered his circumstances. Obviously, the people who had questioned him had no intention of releasing him.

Amsel remembered that the Baron had spoken of a man named Hawkwind in terms that indicated a high place in the Simbalese echelon. Perhaps he had some authority over the woman named Evirae. Perhaps he could find this Hawkwind. At any rate, he was not aiding Fandora or Simbala, let alone himself, by remaining in the cell. "There's no other way about it," he said. "I shall have to escape."

Amsel methodically went through his pouch and pockets. There was little there—the Windriders had confiscated most of his things, including his notebook (he felt a pang of loss at that) and his net and knife. In the bottom of one of his pockets he found his spectacles, and also the pungent seed pods he had plucked from his garden patch. That seemed a year ago to him now. None of these things would help him escape.

Amsel contemplated the ceiling of the cell. It was a tangled mass of root ends and spiderwebs. Contact with the air had withered the root ends, causing their outer layers to peel away in brown strips. Amsel stepped onto the stool, stretched his arms over his head, and found he could barely reach the roots. He peeled off several strips; they were dry and crumbled in his hands to a dry powder. They would burn very easily, he reflected. He dug his hands into the roots, trying to ignore the shuddersome feeling of tiny spiders and insects scurrying along his fingers. He pulled himself up into the thick latticework, and found that he could cling there, although not very comfortably.

"Very good," he said, and dropped back to the floor. He collected several strips from the larger roots and began crumbling them into powder and filling the small pouch he had removed from his belt.

XVIII

So," said Ceria, "the Princess strikes again."

She sat next to Hawkwind, her hand on his shoulder, in the private suite of the Monarch of Simbala. It was a round room, cloaked in light blue silks that complemented the dark polished walls of the palace. They sat upon a large gray causeuse studded with pearls. It was the most comfortable piece in the room, an antique that dated back to the days of Monarch Ambalon.

"Lathan looked as if he were ready to join Evirae, did he not?" Hawkwind smiled. His visit to the mines had been helpful. Despite the threat of the cave wolf, it had given him an opportunity to quietly contemplate the problems that had arisen in the past two days. Although the news from the Northweald was disturbing, he had resolved to deal with it calmly.

"I have never seen a man so exhausted by a ride," Ceria said. "I can imagine the state of his horse!"

"He is a good man," said Hawkwind. "I do not blame him for wanting a fortnight's rest. It was a difficult mission."

Ceria nodded. She was pleased to see Hawkwind at ease. It was rare that they had any time together alone, and it felt good to share each other's love. She toyed with the diadem and jewel that had been deposited casually on an arm of the causeuse. "You must be careful with the Ruby," she scolded. "It is proof of your position in Simbala. Evirae would give all the windships in Kiorte's charge to have it."

"No," answered Hawkwind, "Evirae is a spoiled child, but she is not a traitor."

The comment took Ceria by surprise. "Surely you do not believe that now! Not after Lathan's message! Evirae's meeting with the Northwealdsman was treason. Her accusations were treason! What must the Princess do to convince you? Kidnap me?"

"That"—Hawkwind grinned—"would not be treason. That would be charity!"

"Charity!" Laughing, Ceria threw the jewel by its diadem across the room to Hawkwind's bed. *"Charity!* I should leave you to the Princess! Then Evirae would have both the Ruby and the palace!"

Hawkwind smiled broadly and pulled Ceria closer. "Now, *that* would be treason!"

They both laughed then, and Ceria nestled tightly in his arms. "I think you take Evirae too lightly," she whispered. "At the very least, what she is doing can throw doubt upon the integrity of your name. At the worst, her intrigue could make serious trouble for you. Many people believe the rumors of war. The murder of a child has not been taken lightly, Hawkwind, and the windship which vanished has left many concerned."

Hawkwind stroked Ceria's cheek. "You worry, as always, my love. I am aware of those problems. According to Kiorte, the windship blew away in a storm. The ship was unmanned, and it is very unlikely that it could reach the Fandoran shores. As for the child, that matter troubles me deeply. I have no explanation. Perhaps Kiorte shares my concern. That would explain why Lathan saw him in the north."

"You believe the Prince was investigating the attack on the child?"

"I would hope so. I certainly do not believe that Kiorte has decided to do Evirae's bidding."

"True," said Ceria. "Kiorte is not under her spell . . . but there are many others who would do Evirae's bidding in exchange for the friendship of the Royal Family. That young Bursar, for example . . ."

"Mesor."

"Do not trust him."

"I don't," said Hawkwind, "but now is not the time to discuss matters of state."

Ceria frowned. "You put me off again," she said. "You have avoided discussing this since the ride to Dragonhead. Do you fear what I have to say? Or do you no longer respect my opinions?"

"Do not jest," he answered. "It is just that I do not wish this moment soured by talk of politics."

"Then do not make your lover Minister of the Interior! What I have to say should not wait any longer. I am worried, Hawkwind."

He kissed her. "You know very well that intrigue is common in the palace. It does not exist among the miners or the Rayan because they are too busy earning their keep. The Royal Family members are different. Food and shelter are available to them without work. As a result, some spend time plotting against each other. Evirae has no cause to champion, no important responsibilities. Her silly plot against me is the result of envy and boredom. She sees no other outlet for her energies. There is no time to worry about her distractions. The fate of the child demands our attention."

Ceria did not smile. "Evirae wishes to do more than distract you," she said. "Her cause is your removal from the palace. Treat this lightly if you will, but you shall regret it. I feel things that you do not, Hawkwind. You know this to be true. You have always known it. Please do not turn your back on me now! There is something happening that neither you nor I understand ... something more than Evirae. Whatever it is, it is growing and moving toward the Overwood. Rumors spread like wildfire, and the North-weald is consumed with grief. A fire burns toward the palace, my love. Do not get caught in the flames."

Ceria rose and walked toward the canopied bed on the other side of the room. "Now, come," she whispered as her cape dropped slowly from her shoulders to the floor. "There are other words I have waited too long to say."

•

Circling the massive central tree of the palace at the heart of Overwood were giant trunks of relatively smaller proportion, each the home of various dignitaries and Royal

Family members. The larger the tree, the more important its inhabitants to the government of Simbala.

Outside this circle, the royal grounds ended, but the homes beyond them were among the most spectacular in Simbala. Many of them were integrated with the trees, and their colors—from shimmering copper and silver to the dusky red of iron-rich stone—harmonized with the beauty of the forest. Some rooftops were dusted with sparkling jewels. Others, covered with flowering vines and shrubs, caused many a traveler to walk the curved broad streets with eyes uplifted.

Between these streets and the busy central squares of Simbala, the Kamene River emptied into a stately blue lake. The lake was shared by miners and merchants, who used it for relief from the heat of the day. Tonight, however, two figures who strolled on the walkway around it were from neither the merchants' quarter nor the mines.

"I will confront him tomorrow," said Princess Evirae.

Her adviser looked surprised. "Confront him? Then Hawkwind has accepted?"

Coyly Evirae replied, "Mesor, you surprise me. Hawkwind has not been told." Evirae stroked a small brown tree bear that sat docilely upon her shoulder. It watched the surface of the lake as Evirae and Mesor strolled in the shadow of a domed coach. The driver was deaf; Evirae had taken pains to find him.

"Pardon," said Mesor, "but how can Monarch Hawkwind attend a meeting in the merchants' quarter if he is not aware of it?"

Evirae smiled confidently. "*You* will inform him of it in the morning, of course. I want you to tell Hawkwind that I request his presence on an urgent matter of state."

Mesor did not respond. She was moving far too quickly, he thought. She had practically accused Hawkwind of being in league with the Fandorans already. Now she planned to challenge him in public! If Hawkwind had heard anything about the presence of the spy, Evirae's entire plan would collapse in full view of Overwood!

He had to convince her to wait. He sought to change the subject so that he could possibly return to it later when the plan might appear in a less favorable light.

"Milady," he said, "is there any word from Prince Kiorte?"

"Of course!" Evirae snapped unconvincingly. "Thalen has just informed me of his return from the coast. Kiorte has been surveying the shore for signs of Fandoran ships."

The Princess was lying. Mesor knew it. There was a layer of fog over the shore that would keep even the most experienced Windrider away. Prince Kiorte was still missing—and Evirae did not know where he had gone.

"Perhaps it would be best to wait for your husband's return before taking further action," Mesor suggested carefully.

"There is no time!" said Evirae. Then she whispered, "Tolchin and Alora have been swayed. They have doubts about Hawkwind. I must move quickly before Hawkwind learns of the spy. I must win the support of the people in the merchants' quarter. If they suspect Hawkwind, as the Northwealdsfolk must already, then only the miners shall remain as his defenders. I am sure they can be convinced to change."

Mesor was worried. Her plan was too blatant, much too blatant! This was far worse than anything she had planned in the past. He had never realized how fully consuming her designs on the throne had become. He had to convince Evirae to—

"*Mesor!*"

The adviser looked up, startled. The small tree bear had jumped from Evirae's shoulder to the path below. It was now scampering toward the pond.

"Quickly!" Evirae shrieked. "Catch her before she reaches the water!"

Mesor rushed forward and seized the tree bear gently. As he did, he spied Evirae's reflection in the lake. It was grotesque, pulled by the ripples of the water into a giant mouth and tiny eyes.

"Come, my pet," said the reflection, and Mesor wondered if the phrase referred to him. He handed the small animal back to Evirae. "Thank you," she said. "Now it is time for you to return, to prepare your speech for Hawkwind." She smiled at Mesor. "The driver will take you home."

Mesor forced a smile. Over the years he had developed a certain fatalism, and he knew that for the moment he could not dissuade the Princess from her course. He would simply have to wait and do Evirae's bidding until she was once again open to his thoughts. Things could be worse, he reasoned. At least I am privy to her plans. Should Evirae actually reach the throne, I would profit more than most. He started back toward the coach, but as he extended his arm for Evirae to join him, she shook her head. "No," she said. "I would like to walk back."

Mesor was disturbed. The Princess, usually so predictable to him, was continually surprising him of late, and he did not like that.

"Very well," he said reluctantly. "I will see Hawkwind in the morning," and he mounted the coach.

Evirae listened to the sound of diminishing hoofbeats. The Bursar is a fool, she thought. He seeks my favor, but he is blind to the consequences of his ambition. If my plot is discovered, I will lay the blame on him. A Bursar's word will not be taken over that of a Princess, even if that Bursar is the Princess's adviser. Mesor thinks me hotheaded and irrational. Little does he realize that tomorrow's meeting is without danger to me.

She tapped two long nails together and looked at her reflection in the now-placid water. An old aphorism came to her mind. Smiling, she said, "A woman's beauty is the best refuge for the truth."

●

In the old tunnels under the forest, a large portly guard sat on a chair beside a locked chamber. He had been ordered by the Princess Evirae to guard the Fandoran spy, and this was what he was doing. Still, he thought, there could be no harm in catching a few moments' rest. The cell was securely locked, and he was going to close his eyes, not sleep. He had been slumbering peacefully for over an hour when he was suddenly awakened by the sound of coughing—loud and hacking, as though someone were choking—from within the cell.

"Guard, help!"

The guard came ponderously to his feet. He put his ear to the door. The prisoner's coughing fit had stopped; all was silent inside the cell. He eyed the door suspiciously. Since Evirae had ordered the prisoner guarded, it followed that she wanted no harm to come to him. The guard unlocked the door and peered inside.

The Fandoran was nowhere in sight!

The guard stared about for a moment. A trick? Perhaps the fellow was hiding behind the door. He stepped into the cell. . . .

"Hello," a voice said from directly above him.

The guard looked up, and a cloud of fine dust dropped into his eyes. Blinded, he stumbled backward, tripped over the stool, and fell heavily, half onto the straw. He heard something hit the floor lightly beside him . . . quick footsteps . . . then the slamming of the door.

The Princess, he realized, would not be pleased.

•

Amsel paused for a moment outside in the corridor, considering his route. He recalled that Evirae and the others had gone to the left after leaving his cell; therefore, he went to the right. He hurried down the tunnel, at first running as fast as he could, then with more restraint. The floor was covered with a thin film of slippery mud. He was very tired; he had not realized how much so until he had started to run. He had been through quite a bit in the last few days; in fact, he was amazed that he had held up so well.

I hope the guard was not hurt, he thought to himself as he ran. He had clung with his feet and one hand to the interwoven roots near the roof, and when the guard had entered, attracted by the coughing, Amsel had dumped a pouchful of freshly powdered root fiber into his eyes. That, and the locked door, would hopefully give him time to get away.

Now he had to decide where to run. He knew nothing about Simbala. He had heard of the man named Hawkwind, but he did not know who he was or where to find him. It does not matter right now, thought Amsel; first I must find a way back to the surface.

Suddenly, far behind him, there was a sound like an explosion—its echoes reverberated about him, then chased each other down the tunnel. Amsel was mystified for a moment; then he realized it was the sound of the guard kicking open the cell door. A moment later he heard heavy running behind him, drawing closer. The guard was pursuing him!

Amsel tried to run faster, but his weariness made it impossible. Roots slapped into his face, disorienting him. The guard was rapidly gaining. Amsel came to forks in the tunnel, dimly lit by torches, and ran down them at random, hoping to lose his pursuer, but the guard was close enough to see him now. Amsel saw a small hole in the wall just ahead; if he could reach that, he would be safe; the guard would never be able to squeeze his massive bulk through it. He gritted his teeth and tried to put on a final burst of speed, but his exhausted body would not obey him. A heavy hand fell on his shoulder. Amsel twisted away. His foot slipped in a patch of mud and he half-fell. The guard also slipped and fell with him. Amsel, staggering away from him, saw the guard grab a tree root hanging from the ceiling in an effort to save his balance. The root gave way before the guard's massive weight, and then there was a strange rumbling sound that filled the tunnel. Amsel looked up and saw the ceiling caving in on him, a cascade of mud, roots, and dirt. He tried to leap to safety, but a large rock struck his shoulder. He heard the guard cry out for help. Then the sound of the cave-in deafened him, the world turned the color of mud, and there was darkness all about him.

●

A sudden gust of wind caught one of the boats being lowered down the cliffs of Cape Bage. It dangled by three ropes halfway down, and the wind now swung it dangerously close to the rocks. Its passengers, several black-and-white-garbed Dancers, gripped the gunwales as the swaying boat slowly settled again.

On a tiny strip of beach below, Jondalrun and Dayon stood watching as five boats were lowered slowly into the water by the windlasses. On the cliff, beyond their sight, were many other boats waiting to enter the water—all of them hastily repaired or knocked together from old wagons and carts, calked against the sea with hasty daubs of pitch.

Dayon shook his head. "I never would have believed it," he said.

"It will save time," Jondalrun said. "Time is what we need. It would take a day to carry these boats down to the beach—and the beach is already overcrowded with the men being apportioned into the other boats. This way, we will have them all in the water by dawn."

Lagow also stood there watching. "What good will that be," he asked, "if all the men are killed in the process?" He looked belligerently at Jondalrun, and Dayon tensed, ex-

pecting his father to explode into one of his famous rages. Instead, Jondalrun did not acknowledge the question at all. He turned away and crossed to Tamark, who was shouting orders to the men at the top of the cliff.

Lagow stared after him, then looked at Dayon. "Your father is a stubborn man."

"Stubbornness gets things done." Dayon felt compelled to defend his father, although he too was not looking forward to this crossing. The thought of venturing out into the heavy, wind-tossed seas of the strait again, so soon after his last experience, was terrifying.

"Lower the prow!" Tamark bellowed as Jondalrun joined him. "It's dropping too fast . . ." He broke off and shook his head as the straining snapped one of the ropes. The boat turned over, spilling its passengers and all their supplies into the water twenty feet below. A moment later the boat fell in with a loud splash that reached Jondalrun's ears a moment after he saw the impact. He saw the young men bob to the surface and swim for the craft, which had luckily landed upright. A Dancer's cap was rescued from the water by one of them.

Tamark looked at Jondalrun, and Jondalrun, as usual, felt vaguely disturbed by those black eyes. He had the distinct feeling that Tamark was laughing at him, even though the fisherman's face was grim. Jondalrun looked back at the boat. "Perhaps," he said uneasily, "it will go smoother with the larger ships."

"Perhaps," Tamark said.

Jondalrun glared at him. Something about the single word stung him to rage. He did not like Tamark—the man was too cynical, too silently disapproving. "Have you a better way?" Jondalrun demanded loudly.

"None," said Tamark. He turned away and looked up at the fishermen who stood on the edge of the cliffs. "Next boat!" he shouted.

On the top of the cliff, Tenniel stood staring down. He had helped lower the first boat, and he had watched in horror as it fell. He was vastly relieved that no one had been hurt. But how long before someone *was* hurt? It seemed so absurd to have a casualty before they even met the Sim. It was not right, all of this fumbling and uncertainty, all these problems that bothered them. If they were so plagued now, why should he expect it to be any different on the battlefield?

It will be, he reassured himself. It must be. After all, these problems were to be expected, were no doubt due in part to the eagerness of everyone to come face to face with the enemy. Tenniel glanced behind him at the crowd of men waiting to be lowered over the cliffs. In their faces he saw some apathy, and much nervousness and fear. He saw nothing he could call eagerness. He turned to the next boat and began to prepare it for lowering. Battle will transform them, he thought. But he did not look back again.

Through the night the extra boats were lowered from the cliffs. The men worked without food or sleep, and when the first rays of dawn broke over the misty horizon of Simbala, they sailed to join the main fleet, which had been launched from the beaches.

The Fandoran army was now at sea—over a thousand men and boys with patchwork weapons, floating in boats made from rafts, flatbed wagons, and fishing vessels, powered by oars or paddles or sails patched with grain bags, setting forth on Fandora's war with Simbala. Few were aware of how ludicrous they would have appeared to the Simbalese. They were a militia of bakers, tinkers, farmers, and fishers. Their outlook ranged from despair to a feeling of adventure. However, it was a grim determination to seek justice for the murder of the children, and the threat it posed to the very existence of Fandora, which almost masked their pathetic appearance. Naive and unprepared as they were, they nevertheless had a cause—they were responding to a threat with courage. Not all armies, not all wars, had such. Children were one of the very few comforts and blessings of Fandora—tangible proof that life would continue.

Stubbornly, then, with much fouling of courses and shouted instructions and imprecations, the army of Fandora began its voyage toward the east.

●

The northern winds blew constantly, bringing snow which covered the cliffs. The Darkling threshed the air with his enormous wings. Soaring high above the icy river, he flew south toward the fabled caverns where the dragons once lived.

Long before the Darkling's birth, in an age when the frost

had not fully covered their land, the dragons had flown south to the glowing place within the cliffs. The coldrakes had remained behind them, fighting the cold winds for survival. They were swift in flight and they learned to be hunters. Living in the caves near the hot springs, they had survived for ages.

As the dragons vanished from the glowing caverns, the coldrakes grew frightened, for it seemed as though their land too would be safe no longer.

The coldrakes respected the dragons, for the dragons had protected them in an earlier age. They feared them too, for the dragons possessed the secret of the flame.

The Darkling shrieked as he flew above the icy river that flowed south toward the glowing caverns. He knew the dragons' strength. Though he had searched for the dragons time and time again without success, he knew their secret still. It was in part his own. He had been born of coldrake and dragon, the forbidden child of a dragon who had returned to the hot springs in hope of survival. It had not survived, but the Darkling had been born; the other coldrakes knew not of his existence then, but as the cold winds grew, he had emerged smarter and swifter than them all. As the dragons perished, he became the coldrakes' protector.

The pain that burned within him had driven him many times to the caverns in the south, but always he had found the same thing. In those glowing caverns that had not been covered by rocks and falling snow existed only the frightening remains of the noble creatures who had once dwelled there.

The last age of the dragons had passed and the coldrakes were alone. He was the most alone of all, neither coldrake nor dragon, living with creatures who implicitly felt that the dragons would rescue them from the growing cold.

To ensure their survival, he had to convince them that the dragons were gone. Only then would the coldrakes defy the edict of the dragons and respect his own. Only then would they dare to leave their warrens and fly south to live in the land of the humans, the land from which the dragons had barred them long ago.

The last search had come. The Darkling flew swiftly through a narrow pass between icy cliffs and flapped toward a wall of ice and snow beside the river. He would search one last time for any evidence of the dragons, would look inside the glowing caverns for any proof that they would return.

There had been none, and he expected none now, but he would search carefully, for what he would ask the others to do required his own conviction.

If they were to learn that the dragons were truly gone, if they were to fly to a warm land where the Guardian could watch without fear, if they were to war with man to seize a place where the northern winds did not blow, then he would have to be sure that no dragon had survived.

He swooped through a break in the gray fog toward the cliffs where the openings to the caverns could be found. Some were covered with thick blue ice or had vanished in the fallen rock and snow. He would fly into those that were free. If a dragon still survived, it would not lie trapped within the others; its pride would not allow it.

As he glided down to a familiar ledge where one of the glowing caverns waited, the Darkling saw within the ice the form of an old dragon, neck extended and wings out, as if it had been frozen in the act of flying. Or falling.

This sight always brought anger, for he did not wish to perish as that dragon had a long time ago.

He screamed, but the sound was buried by the freezing winds.

The hours passed as the Darkling explored what had been the home of the dragons. He could find no trace of any of the creatures in the open caverns. As the search grew, so did his anger. He confirmed again what he already had known. These tunnels had not changed; the last age of the dragons had passed.

Shrieking as he soared out of an icy cliff, the Darkling flew back toward the warrens.

The coldrakes would be told. He would prepare for the journey south. He would bring them here. He would also send a scout to the land of the humans. There was much about them that he wanted to know.

XIX

Evirae had selected a large marketplace at the edge of the Merchants' Quarter for her confrontation with Hawkwind. It was bordered on the east by a small hill. At the foot of the hill was a stone podium, and it was from this forum that the people of Simbala would witness a most extraordinary meeting.

Two hours before the arrival of the Monarch and the Princess, the area started to fill with people from all parts of the Overwood. There was much tension and speculation within the crowd, especially among the discontented merchants whose trade had been curtailed by Hawkwind in recent months. All were anxious to hear the reason for this sudden meeting.

Hawkwind arrived, flanked by aides, the hawk on his shoulder. To his left walked Ephrion. There were shouts of approval as they made their way to the hill, but both men agreed that the sounds were less enthusiastic than they had been at the Dais of Beron.

As Hawkwind and Ephrion awaited Evirae's arrival, the older man once again cautioned his successor. "You must be careful of her, Hawkwind. She has a sly and clever tongue and she will twist your words."

Hawkwind looked up impatiently at the hill. "I have heard the Princess's arguments before," he answered softly, "and I am not impressed."

Ephrion argued angrily. "You *must* be careful!" He

leaned heavily on a walking stick. "She is of the Family and she has had experience in matters of politics that you have not. You must not underestimate her influence with the people."

Hawkwind frowned, lifted his arm, and watched as the hawk took flight. First Ceria, now Ephrion, he thought. They do not believe that I take the Princess seriously. He nodded to supporters as he and Ephrion reached the flight of stairs behind the hill.

"There is nothing Evirae can do in the face of the truth," he said. "It is my most valuable defense. There is nothing that I have done that is in opposition to the interests of our people. I refuse to let either the Family or Evirae force my hand on matters concerning Simbala. This meeting is just another excuse for Evirae to intimidate me. She will be disappointed."

Ephrion squeezed the young man's arm. "She is coming," he said. "Please remember her position. Now is not the time to antagonize the Family."

"The Family cares little for my opinions," Hawkwind replied grimly, "as Evirae is quick to remind us."

A few moments later he turned and ascended the steps to await the Princess. As he did, he spied her silk-draped palanquin, carried by four aides. There was respectful applause from the crowd as it approached the hill.

•

Down in the marketplace, Mesor was worried. He walked uneasily next to the palanquin, awaiting a message from Evirae. He still had no idea if Hawkwind had learned about the Fandoran spy. Evirae's demand for the public meeting had already angered Hawkwind, and if the Monarch had any evidence against Evirae, she and Mesor would both be subject to arrest.

The palanquin started to turn from him then, cutting a path through the crowd. As it did, Mesor glimpsed Evirae's long nails holding back a curtain on one side. He hurried closer. "Take care of the men," Evirae whispered, "and watch carefully for any evidence of my husband's agents." Mesor nodded, and the palanquin bobbed toward the back steps of the hill.

Hawkwind turned to the crowd. Evirae would be joining him shortly. He did not have to raise his voice to call for attention. There was a silence of anticipation in the square already.

Despite his efforts to remain calm, Hawkwind viewed this latest stunt by Evirae with growing anger. It had no purpose but to agitate the people of Overwood just when he most needed their support. There were problems enough already—the murder of the child, the flooding of the mines—he had no time to spend on petty rivalry between Princess and Monarch. Yet it was for that purpose that he was here, for he knew he dared not leave Evirae to address the merchants alone with whatever plot she had planned. The charges of the Northwealdsman had done enough damage. Hawkwind could use this meeting as an opportunity to reassure the citizens of Simbala on that score, at least.

Evirae mounted the steps at the back of the hill. He acknowledged her with a formal smile. She would have the first opportunity to speak. In that way, he could answer any claims she would make to the crowd.

Hawkwind extended his arm, as if to give Evirae right of passage. She ignored him and walked quickly to the podium.

Hawkwind sighed. There is nothing, he told himself again, that she can do to change the truth.

Evirae looked out over the crowd. Her long painted nails glistened in the sunlight. She did not smile. "My people," she said dramatically, "I bring news of importance to all of Simbala."

Hawkwind arched his brow and waited.

"Our forest is in danger!" she said. "The Northwealdsman spoke the truth at the Dais of Beron. The murder of the child will not be the last unless measures are quickly taken to protect us—measures which Hawkwind refuses to consider!"

A gasp went up from the crowd.

"The Fandorans are attacking!" Evirae shouted. "War has been declared against Simbala! We must act now to defend ourselves!"

Evirae glanced back to get Hawkwind's reaction, but he had turned in anger to Ephrion at the foot of the stairs. "She would not dare!" Hawkwind whispered.

From Ephrion came the answer: "She already has."

Hawkwind started forward to challenge Evirae, but she

waved an arm imperiously in his direction. "Wait," she said grandly; "your turn will come."

Before he could answer, Evirae resumed her speech to the crowd.

"Hawkwind knows that Simbala is in danger. He has known this since the Wealdsman's tragedy was told at the Dais of Beron. Yet he has done little since. Why, I do not know, but his attitudes and background are, after all, somewhat . . . different. In this time of emergency we cannot afford the subtleties of political maneuvering. We must rush to action. I have risked both my title and position in the Family to speak to you now. I do so out of love for Simbala. Listen not to the miner or his maiden! Trust those who have governed for centuries! Trust the Royal Family to protect Simbala!"

Hawkwind could wait no longer. She is mad, he thought. This is treason!

Sensing Hawkwind's anger, Evirae hurried. "We must defend ourselves from any attack by the Fandorans! You must trust Prince Kiorte. We stand together on this matter of state."

No! cried Mesor to himself. She is cutting her own throat and mine as well!

The crowd was beset with speculation. Evirae's husband supports her plan? Could that possibly be true?

Hawkwind pushed forward, his plans for diplomatic composure all but forgotten.

"People of Simbala!" he shouted. "Silence! You must hear what I have to say!"

The people ceased their gossip, but a whisper of suspicion continued to distract them.

Hawkwind scanned the sea of faces, seeing anxiety and concern. He spoke quietly, but with authority. "You must understand the real meaning of Evirae's words! I have heard the same rumors as you have, and I have gone to pains to learn the truth. We have no evidence that the Fandorans are attacking. For two centuries they have not disturbed us. Why should this suddenly change? I have viewed the seas from Dragonhead. They are empty! No army approaches! The winds and currents are fierce this time of year. Only fools would launch an armada now—and even fools would be hard-pressed to cross the strait in safety."

He studied the crowd again and saw hope arise in the expressions of concern. These people did not want war. His words were having an effect.

"Go back to your homes!" he continued. "Go back to your children! They are safe! I do not yet know what murdered the Northweald child, but it was not the work of the Fandorans! Please go home in peace! We will find the murderer!"

Evirae, face crimson, hurried down the stairs. "My people," she said, "I also wish to see our country at peace—but I am not a fool! Monarch Hawkwind refuses to see the truth, and so I ask that the matter be decided by you!"

Mesor put his hand to his head. Five pairs of eyes caught the signal.

Hawkwind faced Evirae. "The people's will is clear. There is no need for further speeches!"

Evirae glared at him. "I call for a Senate meeting!" She faced the crowd. "Is there a person here who objects?"

"A Senate!" shouted a Northwealdsman in the square. "Yes!" said another. "A Senate!" The cry was picked up by the crowd. Soon it was obvious that a majority had spoken, and the crowd fell silent, awaiting a response from the podium.

Hawkwind watched in anger. The first men to speak had all been Northwealdsfolk. This was more than coincidence; it had to be Evirae's plotting. Hawkwind was sure of it, just as he was sure that Mesor's presence was more than a simple show of support. He faced Evirae. There could be no alternative to calling the meeting now; to oppose it could arouse suspicion. If there was to be a Senate, however, Evirae would be unable to use it for her plan. He would call for a meeting on his own terms.

"We shall have peace," he said into the silence. "I declare a meeting of the families to be called for tomorrow morn! Princess Evirae, you may leave!"

Evirae was furious at the dismissal, but Hawkwind's expression was such that she stepped quietly from the platform and ascended the stairs. There would be time later, she thought, when the crowd will hear me alone.

Hawkwind watched her. Proper protocol required Evirae to leave the hill, but she waited stubbornly at the top of the stairs. Her flagrant disregard for him could no longer be tolerated! Although he had little interest in many of the formalities of the Family, he could not ignore the fact that, from her point of view, she was willfully ridiculing him in front of the people.

Hawkwind turned his back to the crowd and addressed Evirae. His words were spoken loudly; he wanted the people to hear them. "I have been lenient with you for too long, Princess Evirae. If you wish to play games with me in public, then you will learn what it is like to lose! Leave this meeting! I must address the people!"

Evirae waited a moment, just long enough to register her defiance. Then she faced the back stairs of the hill and descended.

Hawkwind talked to the crowd. "We will meet to discuss the protection of the peace tomorrow. Return now to your families and summon those who will cast the crystals. The meeting will convene in the Cavern of the Falls. Speak carefully until then. Rumors will not bring back the child. We must work together!"

He departed, cape swirling, to join Monarch Ephrion, and told his aides to bring up the horses. He was upset with himself for his outburst at Evirae. It had been foolish, for she would now think that she could provoke him at whim.

Ephrion had been correct. Evirae was more dangerous than he had thought. In the future, he would guard himself against her words.

The question of peace would now be settled by the people. This is as it should be, he thought; the truth will be a deciding factor. Yet Hawkwind was troubled. Truth and the Princess had been adversaries far longer than he had been ruler of Simbala.

Ephrion pulled back on the reins of his horse. "My son," he asked, "why did you not expose her scheme? You knew that Evirae was intriguing with the Northwealdsman."

Hawkwind swung himself into the saddle. "That would be Evirae's tactic," he answered. "I will not stoop to accusations. I will win against Evirae through the law."

Ephrion smiled. "Good," he said, "but perhaps it would help if I spoke to Lady Eselle. She still has some influence over her daughter."

"No!" Hawkwind extended his arm for the hawk. "You selected me over Evirae. If I am worthy of the position, I must prove to the people that Evirae does not have their interests at heart, and I must do it in a way that does not divide the Family. If you plead with Lady Eselle, I will not earn her respect."

Ephrion nodded with fatherly pride and said, "The hero is becoming a statesman."

●

Evirae watched from behind the podium as the dark stallion vanished into the woods. The miner knows nothing of the spy, she said to herself, and nothing of Kiorte's disappearance. It has gone smoothly, more smoothly than I had expected.

Mesor gave her his arm and Evirae left the podium regally, paying no attention to his words of praise as they returned to her palanquin. I have planted doubts in the minds of the merchants, she thought, and those who already mistrust Hawkwind will now think him a traitor. I must find Kiorte, she said to herself as she waved to the crowd, and I must return to the spy. There must be much he can tell us about Fandora.

●

Far below the palace, in another part of the caverns, Amsel stirred and opened his eyes. The first thing he noticed was a throbbing pain in his back. He tried to turn his head, and felt it held by a rock in a strained position. He tried to lift his hands, but they would not move. As sensation returned, he realized that he was buried up to his neck in cold and clammy mud. He was lying on his back. The pain was intense, but not enough to make him fear that it had been broken.

He opened his mud-caked eyes with an effort that did him little good—he could see nothing. The tunnel was perfectly dark. The last two fingers of his right hand were free; he used them to dig feebly at the mud surrounding the rest of his hand.

It took a long time. He felt like cheering when he finally pulled his right hand and arm free of the clinging muck. He pulled the rock away from his head, and the pain in his back was relieved. Amsel rested a moment, then started to struggle out of the mud.

Eventually he extricated himself, although he was coated

shoulders to feet with grime. He walked briskly back and forth, and the ache in his back subsided.

He felt over the slope of mud that filled the tunnel, but could find no trace of the guard. The man had either been buried completely or was on the other side of the cave-in. "At any rate, there is nothing I can do for him now," Amsel said regretfully. He began to make his way down the pitch-black tunnel, feeling his way cautiously, one hand touching the wall. He was still bone weary, and had to stop every few minutes to rest, but the act of walking soon took away his stiffness.

The tunnel's length was indeterminable—it seemed that he walked for days. He could not tell if he was following a broad curve or a straight path. The slope seemed to be steadily upward, however, and the sound of his footsteps soon changed. The mud and clay had given way to rock. Amsel smiled. He was nearing the surface.

How long had it been since he left Fandora? He was not sure—the days in the boat blurred together in a dream of sun and waves—but he knew that the entire trip had lasted at least a week. Could Fandora mobilize an army in that time? It was possible, with sufficient motivation, and Amsel knew all too well the effect Johan's death had had on Fandora. Which meant that an armada could be on their way to Simbala's shores.

"That must not be!" he said aloud, and the words came back to haunt him. The echo was almost frightening. Amsel felt lost and lonely, but he had no choice except to explore the tunnel and pray. "Johan, no more will die!" he said softly, and kept walking. Sometime later, he stopped to rest. The echoes of his passage faded, and all was silent. Then, far behind him, Amsel heard a tick-tick-ticking sound. For a moment it confused him; then, with a cold chill, he realized that it was the sound of claws hitting the bare rock.

Something was following him.

XX

Dayon stood in the prow of the lead ship, a small fishing boat that carried twenty men. It was dangerously overcrowded, and constantly shipping water in the choppy sea. The Strait of Balomar was over fifty miles long and less than twenty wide, and, save for the relatively calm fjords and inlets along the coasts of Fandora and Simbala, every one of those miles was dangerous. The clash of two seas filled the strait with a myriad currents. Also, the warm air from the Southern Sea and the cold air of the northern Dragonsea met here and fought. The combination of wind and currents produced towering whitecapped waves and strong undertows. On the calmest and sunniest of days the strait was inhospitable; on bad days, it could be a maelstrom.

On this day it was neither at its best nor at its worst, and so the armada stood some small chance of reaching the opposite shore. Dayon had ordered the boats to hug the coast for the greater part of the day, until they were near an area of the strait where the waters were the shallowest and the turbulence less. He knew that the winds and waves were capable of swamping ships much more seaworthy than these. He stared ahead at the whitecapped waves. He did not allow himself to think about all the men who would be directly affected by any decision that he made. He knew that if he did that, he would panic.

Jondalrun was also in the lead boat, and he stared in awe at the waves, some of them ten and twelve feet high, which appeared at random all about the ships, lashed into whitecaps by the winds. "I did not know it was like this," he shouted to Dayon.

"There are so few who do," Dayon shouted back. He kept his eyes on the waves as the armada moved slowly forward. His knuckles were white on the gunwales.

"Can you get us through?" Jondalrun asked.

"I can try," Dayon said. "We'll seldom have a better time. The moon is down, so it's low tide, and the winds are relatively calm. Of course, that means the fog is bad, but we're not likely to run into anything out here. If we can cross this stretch of open water, the opposite side should be as calm as the one we left."

"How wide is this barrier of waves?"

"It varies from day to day. Sometimes only a mile or two—sometimes as much as ten. There's only one real way to find out. We'll have to go through it. Once we start, there's no turning back."

"Then let's get on with it," said his father.

Dayon gave instructions, which were relayed from ship to ship. All the men in the boats were to anchor themselves to whatever security they could—masts, oarlocks, benches, and remain that way until further orders were given. He ordered the boats to spread out as much as possible to avoid being hurled into one another, and to follow his lead as well as wind and waves would allow. Anxiously he watched the flotilla prepare. "Sails up!" Dayon said soon thereafter and he hoped that his terror was not visible to his father.

The configuration of the strait was remarkable. The shapes of the two facing peninsulas resembled two crescent moons. Each had a northern and southern promontory, which made the waters within relatively calm, though filled with strong eddies and currents. In the middle of the strait, where the oceans clashed with nothing to temper them, were the heavy seas that the armada now had to cross.

Those vessels with sails now unfurled them, and the wind hurled them forward, as though eager to test them against the sea. The others rowed feverishly, trying to keep up with their wind-powered countrymen, but to no avail. The seas quickly grew mountainous, and the waves seemed to come from every direction, with no rhyme or reason to them. The ships were lifted and dropped with a force that terrified the landbound majority of the crews. Dayon stood, steadying himself against a forward mast, studying the strait. Despite the worried shouts and cries of those in the boat, Dayon knew that it was one of the more favorable days. Nevertheless, he was frightened. Many of the ships were overloaded with men and supplies. Though he did not speak of this to Jondalrun, he was sure they would lose many ships. He looked at his father, sitting behind him, bailing steadily with a bucket as the waves broke over the side. More than anyone else, Jondalrun was responsible for putting these men in this position. Quite a few would drown before the crossing was made. Would his father be held accountable?

It had been each man's decision to come—they had not been ordered into this army. They were here because they felt the mission was in the best interests of Fandora, Dayon told himself. He returned his attention to the waves.

Even as he did, however, over the roar of wind and water he heard the sound of cracking timber, and screams. He looked to his left—a raft, riding higher in the waves than the boat next to it, had been lifted up and dropped squarely on top of the boat, breaking it in half. Four men, shouting in fear, went into the water. Peering back, Dayon saw three come up, to be pulled into other boats. Dayon turned his gaze away quickly. He could not allow himself to feel responsible for them—he could not even allow himself to feel fear. He had time to think of only one thing—the distant Simbalese shore. As he had told Jondalrun, there could be no turning back.

●

In a small dinghy Jurgan and Steph took turns rowing and bailing. Despite their best efforts, they, among several others, were falling steadily behind the main body of the fleet. The mountainous waves had made them seasick at first, but once they had emptied their stomachs, they had felt marginally better.

Jurgan dumped a load of water from the nutshell he used for bailing, and stared at Steph. Steph, as he rowed, was constantly craning his neck, looking up into the cloudy sky.

"You've been staring out like that ever since we reached the strait," said Jurgan. "I'd like to know why."

"I'm looking for windships," Steph said.

Jurgan snorted in disbelief. "As if we ain't got enough

trouble! Floating every which way in these waves, falling behind the rest of the fleet, and you're looking for windships!"

"I can't help it," Steph said, and sniffled. "I'm scared."

"Look," Jurgan said. "It's hard enough keeping this leaky washtub afloat in these waves. So if you're gonna cry, do it over the side."

Steph made no reply to that, and Jurgan saw that his companion was really quite scared. "Well," he said, "we're not doing this for ourselves, Steph. It's for Fandora."

"You're a fine man to talk! Was you who had second thoughts in the first place!"

"True enough, but that was just sore back and ax blisters talking. Listen, we can't let these Sim come swooping down on us without even an if-you-please. We got to show them what's what!"

"Let Jondalrun show them what's what," Steph said. "Me, I'm turning this boat around!" He began to scud with one oar. A large wave caught them broadside and nearly overturned them, despite the lightness of the craft.

Jurgan seized the oars. "You can't do that, Steph! It's treason!"

"It's good common sense!" Steph glowered at Jurgan. "All right, then," he said, "I'm swimming home!"

"You're crazy, too! You think swimming in this mess is like paddling across Mossybottom Pond? You wouldn't last a minute! I'd be eating a puney fish someday and find that wooden ring of yours breaking my teeth! Now, sit down and start bailing! The way out of this is straight ahead!"

Steph hesitated, then seized the nutshell and began bailing sullenly. Jurgan slipped the oars into the water. The waves had turned the boat, and in the fog, he now had no idea which way to go. The last of the other boats had passed them. Jurgan began to row determinedly in the direction he hoped was correct.

•

"Evirae . . ." said Kiorte.

His wife turned on the stairs outside their tree castle. She blinked in amazement. "My dearest Kiorte!" she cried. "You've returned!" She hurried down the stairwell toward the garden where he stood, not far from a large pillow plant. She was genuinely excited. Then she saw his face.

He knows! He knows everything! she thought. She slowly crossed the patio and waited for her husband to speak.

He did not speak. Instead he studied her, looking through her beautiful face and full figure, oblivious of the scent of orchids and the glint of sunlight in her auburn hair.

"Kiorte, darling!" she said at last, desperate with anxiety. "So many things have happened since your departure! Come inside where we may discuss them alone!"

Prince Kiorte frowned, and the sight of that expression, coupled with his silence, was more frightening to Evirae than any threat she had ever heard.

"My darling," she asked shakily, "are you ill?"

Again Kiorte did not reply. Confused now, and frightened by the thought of what her husband might know, Evirae adopted a more arduous tone. "Kiorte!" she said. "Talk to me. I have not seen you for so long."

Kiorte at last replied, but his words burned like the fire of a Sindril jewel. "You have lost me forever," he said. "You have dared to misuse my name and besmirch my honor in an attempt to win support for your plans. You and I are—"

"No!" Evirae screamed. It was a cry that came from the depths of her soul. Tears filled her eyes, and she found it difficult to speak. "You must tell me what you know, my darling! You cannot possibly understand what I have done!" The obvious sincerity of her cry unnerved Kiorte. He had not expected such emotion. With deliberation he responded in a softer voice, "I know you have used my name to conspire against Hawkwind. The Overwood is filled with the news of your confrontation. I know, too, that you have slandered Hawkwind to the Northwealdsman Willen. Yet these things are minor compared to the union of my name with your call for war!"

What he said relieved Evirae slightly. There is a chance, she thought, that he does not yet know about the spy. She cried again, this time with more theatrics than emotion, "You have not been told the entire truth, my husband!"

Kiorte stared at her. "I have had enough of your truths, Evirae. My journey to the Northweald has cured me of your lies. I will never endure them again!"

Kiorte walked past Evirae toward their home. "I will stay with Thalen until the Senate," he said. "I suggest you prepare for it. My speech may lack the flourish of your words, but I guarantee it will be remembered."

Evirae placed her long nails on his shoulder. "Darling," she pleaded, wiping tears from her eyes. "I tell the truth! There is an invasion! There *is* a war! I have learned of these things from a Fandoran spy."

The Prince turned. "A spy?" he asked.

She brightened. "The Fandoran! Surely your 'sources' have told you of the spy."

"No games!" said Kiorte. "I have no more patience for games."

Evirae answered quickly. "When you left, a message came concerning a Fandoran captured in the strait. I interrogated the spy myself, in the presence of Tolchin and Alora. He told us of the Fandoran plans for an invasion. I rushed with the news to Hawkwind, but he refused to take action. He dismissed it as a mad accusation in a plot to remove him from the palace. I was very worried. You were missing. So I called for the public meeting. The Overwood had to be told of the threat to Simbala, my darling. In your absence, what else could I do?"

Kiorte frowned. "This spy—where is he?"

"In the tunnels. I can take you there now."

"If this is a trick," said Kiorte, "I will—"

"It is the truth," said Evirae. "I will show you myself!"

●

The coldrakes' warrens were filled with howling as the creatures flew about them in confusion and fright. The Darkling had taken the coldrakes to the icy cliffs, where they had seen the frozen dragon and the glowing caverns. Within them, they had seen the ruins and the bones of dragons, and the sight, coupled with their growing hunger and desperation, caused many to shriek in fear. The Darkling knew then that they could be compelled to defy the dragons' edict.

Even those who thought the dragons would return could not deny what the others had seen. Those who would still obey the edict could be driven by the cold to abandon the warrens.

The Darkling crouched on a peak and brooded over his next decision.

Their panic would pass, he knew. They would turn to him. Having seen the caverns, few would challenge his plans. He spread his wings against the cold wind, secure in that thought. The frost numbed him, reached deep into him, seemed to penetrate and chill even his innermost being, and the secret that burned there. He was tempted to reveal that to them, the secret of his birth, to tell them that the race of dragons had not vanished entirely; that the secret lived on within him. But he did not dare. It was something no coldrake had ever possessed; they might not comprehend how he came to have it. It was better to keep it hidden.

Arching his neck, the Darkling made a piercing sound. In response, a coldrake rose from the mists below and approached the Darkling. He was huge, even for his race.

The Darkling spoke with him. The Guardian had reported seeing a human fly. This situation had to be confirmed. If all humans could indeed fly, then a major advantage was lost to the coldrakes.

The creature circled slowly about the peak, listening to the Darkling's instructions. Then he flew away toward the east, to search for mountain goats and other game. He would need energy for the long flight to the south.

The Darkling remained upon his lonely pinnacle, watching the coldrake disappear into the clouds. He thought about the humans. Few coldrakes had seen them. They were so small, so insignificant in appearance, but they were dangerous. They would have to be dealt with cautiously. The Darkling had told the others what the Guardian had discovered. A fury against the humans had been aroused and would not soon fade. He could afford to act slowly now, to ensure the coldrakes' survival.

●

That evening in Simbala, the Northwealdsfolk, informed by windship of the Senate, made preparations for the heads of their families to journey south. These were grim preparations, and there was little doubt as to which way they would vote. Each felt a responsibility to the family of the child.

Representatives of the miners' families also made ready to appear in the underground cavern where the voting would take place. These people, smudged with the black dirt of the mines, their casual jewelry startlingly bright and colorful against their pale skin, were supporters of Hawkwind, but some had their doubts . Strange things were happening in Simbala these days. There was also much talk about Ceria, the mysterious Rayan woman who was more than Hawkwind's closest adviser.

●

The exterior of the house of Baron Tolchin and Baroness Alora was eclectic and individual. The Baron had designed it himself, incorporating the features of many buildings he had seen in his travels. A hanging roof garden, filled with scented flowers, touched the breezes with ginger and jasmine. The building itself was low and open, with an atrium and fountains. Its windows and entrances were of ivory and elkwood, heavily carved with friezes depicting caravans en route. Connected to the building was the large tree in which could be found both the parlor where Evirae had been entertained and the boudoir in which Tolchin and Alora now prepared themselves for the Senate meeting.

Members of the Royal Family were not allowed to vote during these meetings. They were designed for the citizens of Simbala alone. Each citizen's family, a term encompassing all the branches stemming from a specific ancestry in the ancient days of Simbala, was to send a representative. The representatives were distinguished by their matriarchal or patriarchal robes, which functioned both as the escutcheon on which the family flanche was embroidered and as the required garb for the meeting.

As he dressed, Tolchin speculated on the outcome of the Senate. "Hawkwind is in trouble," he said.

Alora reviewed a multicolored selection of fans for a complement to her attire. "Do you really think the people in Overwood view him as a traitor?" she asked.

"Some do," Tolchin replied, "although not one-tenth of the number that must feel that way in the Northweald." He buttoned a beige doublet around his midriff with difficulty. "There are many reasons to view Hawkwind with disfavor, my dear. There are many in Simbala who would profit from his removal."

Alora sighed. "After twenty years in the Bursars," she said, "I think there is more to profit than tookas in the treasury. Hawkwind cannot be removed from office for economic reasons. For the Family to act, there must be proof of a traitorous act. For all her charges, Evirae is without evidence."

"She will use the spy," said Tolchin.

Alora shook her head. "No proof of any misdeed there, Tolchin. Evirae can dispose of Hawkwind only if Monarch Ephrion decides to remove him from office, and there is no reason to think that Ephrion would give that suggestion a moment's thought."

"You seem almost pleased, my dear." Tolchin lifted his coat from the bed. "Hawkwind's removal would do much to cure the dissent he has caused in the Family."

Alora held a wide silk ribbon in the air. "Ah! The blue snood, don't you think?"

"Don't ignore me!" said Tolchin.

His wife smiled. "I am not ignoring you, dear. It is just that I have reservations about any plan of Evirae's. Certainly you can understand that."

Tolchin adopted a conciliatory tone. "I must tell you, Alora, that it would be a lot easier for Hawkwind without that Rayan woman. What business does she have in the palace?"

"They love each other," Alora said, and her face softened as she thought of it. "It's so obvious, darling. It is a type of love I have not seen in years."

Tolchin snorted. "Aye, and that also worries me. Can you imagine a marriage between Hawkwind and Ceria? The Royal Family would burn down the palace!"

Alora laughed, and remembered her own days of youth.

●

In the caverns below the palace the door to the empty cell stood open, its lock dangling from the splintered wood. Evirae stood before it, eyes wide, palms pressed against her cheeks.

"Where is your Fandoran, Evirae?" asked Kiorte. His voice was not mocking. Obviously, somebody had been there.

"He was right there, locked within this cell, and a guard sat on that chair!"

"He must have been quite powerful, to burst the door open like this," Kiorte said, examining the ruined jamb.

Evirae stammered, "He was half your height! There is no way he could have done this!"

Kiorte looked at her closely. She was quite pale, and obviously distressed. He held his torch low to the corridor's floor and looked in both directions.

"There," he said, "and there as well. Small footprints, and the larger ones of the guard. Come, Evirae."

They followed the tracks. The footprints led down forks and side passages seemingly at random, until Evirae admitted to being unsure of where they were.

"We had better go back and get help," Kiorte said. "The Senate will convene soon, and we must not be late." He started to leave, but Evirae did not follow.

"Just a few yards more," she said. Then she tried to take the torch from his hand. Kiorte would not relinquish it, however, and she stepped forward without it, peering down the corridor.

"Kiorte!" she cried. "Look! I think I see the guard—there has been a cave-in in the tunnel!"

Together they hurried down the corridor. The cave-in filled it. The guard's body lay half-buried in mud. He was breathing shallowly. Kiorte soaked a handkerchief in muddy water and massaged the guard's wrists and neck. After a few moments the man regained consciousness. Kiorte dug the mud away from his legs and pulled him free. As he did, there were several ominous rumbles and trickles of mud from the sagging ceiling. The guard looked at Evirae. "Your pardon, milady—the prisoner escaped me." In a hoarse tone he explained how it had occurred.

"The spy has no doubt been trapped on the other side of this mound," Evirae said. "Don't stand gaping! I can't dig, but you two certainly can! We must find him!"

"There's still danger here," said the guard, looking up apprehensively. "Perhaps we should go—"

"Don't be presumptuous!" This was a disaster she could ill afford, and she intended someone to bear the brunt of her rage. "We must find him!"

"The guard is correct," Kiorte said. "As long as we stand here, we are in danger of another cave-in. We must return immediately."

"Neither of you understands the urgency of the situation!" Evirae shouted. "We do not have enough time!" She bent and seized the fat white column of a root, suppressing a shudder at its cold sliminess, and pulled. The root dislodged a rock; the rock released a trickle of mud, which, with a roar, swiftly grew into an avalanche. The three barely had time to duck before a second section of the tunnel roof collapsed above them.

XXI

The sun rose unclouded that morning, but in the western sky an angry gray wave of storm clouds was gathering. At the entrance to the Cavern of the Falls, the representatives of the families of Simbala were gathering. The heads of the clans and the officials of various merchant groups were there, dressed in their finest gowns. All talked of the land to the west, and the possibility of an invasion launched from the shores of Fandora.

In attendance were prominent members of the Royal Family, including General Jibron and Lady Eselle, the Baron and the Baroness, various Ministers of the Circle, and Monarch Ephrion, who pursued the defense of Hawkwind with much fervor.

Present also was Mesor, who waited silently for the arrival of the Princess Evirae. He was worried; it was not her nature to be late for such an important confrontation. Although she could not vote, her very presence would be enough to sway opinion. If she did not appear soon, it would be too late. Already it was close to the striking of the third hour, when the doors would be opened for the descent into the underground voting chamber. Mesor looked past the crowd anxiously, hoping to see Evirae in the distance. Instead, he glimpsed Hawkwind quickly approaching from the main entrance of the palace. Ceria was at his side.

"There are moments when I would rather face a cave-in than a public meeting," Hawkwind said softly.

"There is no reason to worry," Ceria answered. "You have defended yourself admirably against Evirae's charges. The miners stand behind you, my love, as do the loyal supporters of Monarch Ephrion."

"I know, Ceria, but there has been much sympathy for the Northwealdsfolk since Evirae's speech in the merchants' quarter. It is difficult for me to echo the sentiment and at the same time take issue with the—"

The melodious sound of a gong interrupted him; it was time for the Senate meeting. Hawkwind approached the representatives.

"We shall convene the Senate meeting," he said simply, and with a ponderous creaking, the doors behind them were opened. Hawkwind led the crowd down the wide stone steps inside. As he descended, Hawkwind felt the eyes of the people upon him. In opposition to Monarch Ephrion's advice, Ceria had remained at his side. Many, including Baron Tolchin, viewed this as an affront to the Family itself. Evirae's supporters whispered their disapproval at a level just loud enough to reach Hawkwind's ears.

Outside, Mesor was one of the last to enter the palace. He had waited in hope that Evirae would arrive at the last minute, but there had been no sign of her. What could have prevented her from coming? His mind conjured up all sorts of disasters, not the least of which was that Hawkwind had somehow discovered her actions and ordered her confined.

He was not the last to enter, however; that dubious honor belonged to General Vora. The portly soldier came huffing up just before the doors were closed. Mesor watched him approach, wondering if his tardiness had anything to do with Evirae's absence, but the General paid him no attention. Vora merely passed and hurried down the wide torch-lit steps.

Mesor shrugged and followed. He tried to be philosophical about it—until he had more information, there was no use being worried. Unfortunately, his stomach did not agree.

•

Seven hundred feet above the western shore of Simbala, a windship rode the morning air. Beneath the balloon sails, two Windriders sat near the brazier, for despite the sun, the air was cold.

The older man squinted at the white disk of the sun, which slipped in and out of the clouds, and said, "The meeting must be under way by now."

"I wish I could be there," the younger man said. "My mother's representing my family. This would be the first time I'd be old enough to watch. They say it's a beautiful sight."

"That may be," said the other, "but it's not held to decide a beautiful matter."

The first Windrider shook his head in disgust. "The Fandoran rumors! If it wasn't for the Princess, we'd be back sitting around a warm hearth."

"Then pray that the vote goes against war, or you'll see a lot more duty," his companion said. "Myself, I wonder . . ." He noticed that the first Windrider was not listening. Instead, he had leaned over the railing to view the water below.

"Bayis," he said to the second Windrider in a choked voice, "I think I may be dreaming."

Bayis stepped quickly across the narrow deck and joined his friend. Both stared in disbelief. Below the windship, emerging from a curtain of fog, was a sight at once ludicrous and frightening. A patchwork armada of fishing boats, rafts, and virtually anything that would float, all filled to overflowing with men, was approaching the beach. The Windriders could see that they carried crude weapons, farming tools, and even clubs and rocks. They kept coming out of the mist. That was what was so frightening—the boats kept coming out of the mist.

"They haven't seen us," Bayis said in a tense whisper. "Put about! Head back to the forest!"

●

Centuries earlier, the roof of a large tunnel in Overwood had collapsed, diverting part of the Kamene River underground. The water flowed along the tunnel until it reached the large cavern now used for the meeting. It fell almost fifty feet, forming a deep pool and a subterranean stream. Before this pool were gathered Hawkwind and the Senate of the families of Simbala. The few spectators allowed within for one reason or another filled the cavern, from the stairs to the walls. Some crowded under a dolmen; others stood on rocks to see. The heads of the families stood in lines facing front, waiting to hear Hawkwind speak. Each held in his or her hand two uncut gemstones—one wine-dark, one clear crystal.

Hawkwind stood on a rock dais in front of the stairs. Silently he watched the representatives before him. He tried to judge their attitude, but the emotions he read on their faces were so diverse that he took no further guesses at what the vote might be. He sensed their expectation, however, and he hoped that his words would be enough to sway them from war. He also noted Evirae's absence, and this troubled him. There was no reason for her to miss the meeting, unless, he speculated, she thought it would convince the crowd that he was somehow responsible for her absence. Yet there was no time to worry. Hawkwind stepped forward to address the families.

The acoustics of the cavern were such that the sound of the nearby waterfall was only a gentle murmur.

"You come in peace," he said solemnly, "to vote on a matter which may result in war." He scanned the rows of men and women. "I ask only that you think of the welfare of Simbala, not the affairs of the palace or the Family."

Baron Tolchin leaned toward his wife. "A bad choice of words," he grumbled.

Hawkwind continued. "This council has been called because a child was killed in the Northweald. This is the gravest of all matters. Our children are our future. We must protect them at all costs, but there is no reason to attack a poor and ignorant people."

At these words, a murmur ran through the crowd.

Mesor, having worked his way forward to the Royal Family, stood next to Baron Tolchin. "A prideless day," he said softly, "when a Monarch pleads for the acceptance of terrorism."

Tolchin answered with a glare worthy of Evirae, but Mesor thought he saw a flicker of doubt in the Baron's face. He decided not to press the matter any further.

Hawkwind sensed the crowd's anxiety, and he observed Ephrion's admonition to keep his plea both simple and short. "There must not be war," he said. "I will do everything possible to discover the reason why the child was killed. Until the truth is known, we must work together to resolve the problems caused by the flooding of the mines. I have sent word to the Southland for our troops to return. When they arrive, they will stand guard in the Northweald to protect our children. Others will work in the mines to help our families in meeting their quotas. Do not worry about an invasion. The Fandorans dare not attack Simbala! Our forest is protected! Our people are strong!"

These last words pleased General Vora, and he nodded enthusiastically as Hawkwind called for the vote. There was no discussion in the crowd.

The first row of representatives approached the waterfall. Each would cast either the dark or clear gemstone into the pool, and the rushing water would reveal their decision. The gemstones were similar to the Sindril jewels, but instead of igniting when wet, their organic composition caused a color change in the liquid's color. A majority of dark stones would stain water red—a sign of war. The light stones would cause the river to run deep blue.

Hawkwind cast the opening stone—this was a custom acknowledging his willingness to let the people decide. The stone, a flawless diamond, flew through the mist raised by the falls and sank into the pool. Hawkwind stepped down, and the voting started.

Row by row, the family representatives tossed stones indicating their vote. The first to be thrown was cast by a man from the Northweald. He stood, and without hesitation hurled a dark stone into the pool. It sank, and a stain of blood color rose from it.

Next was a representative of a miners' clan. His stone was clear, and the red tint was lightened momentarily by blue. More dark stones fell, to be followed by light ones, then dark again. Ceria, Ephrion, and the General watched the subtle gradations of color in the pool. The vote was close, too close. The pool continued to change. It ran red, then blue, then red again. Yet when the final stone was cast, the water ran slowly, almost surprisingly, *blue*.

Ceria smiled radiantly and gazed at Hawkwind. Through the mist of the waterfall, she could see the relief on his face. There would be peace, although not by a large margin. The rumblings of the crowd made that abundantly clear.

Ceria joined Hawkwind and, together with Ephrion and Vora, they prepared to leave the cavern.

Hawkwind strode quickly from the steps, with much

pride and a sense of vindication. Ceria was relieved. The apprehensions she had felt but not voiced earlier had been dispelled. They started back toward the doors.

Behind them, representatives spoke heatedly about the outcome of the Senate meeting. Hawkwind's supporters were delighted. It had been his first major test as Monarch, and he had survived. Many approached with words of encouragement, and he received them warmly with a handshake and an uncharacteristically broad smile.

Minutes later, the doors were pushed back and the crowd emerged into the light of day.

Their jubilation turned suddenly to surprise as people saw five Brothers of the Wind on the steps outside the tunnel. Thalen, the second-in-command, stepped forward. His face was drawn and tense.

With a growing sense of danger, Hawkwind said, "What brings you here?"

Thalen answered slowly, as though the words caused him pain. "An armada from Fandora was sighted not long ago. By now it has landed on our shores."

Shock was evident on Hawkwind's face. "How many ships?"

"The report says over two hundred."

The words fell upon Ceria like stones. She watched Hawkwind confer with General Vora. Then she heard the ripple of silence flow down the stairs to those in the Senate who had heard Thalen's words.

Then, flowing back like a raging tide, came the condemnation.

"He has lied to us! We are unprepared for war!"

The crowd pushed forward quickly. Hawkwind, Vora, and Ephrion headed toward the entrance to the palace. The heads of the families swarmed out behind them. There were many expressions of sorrow and anger. Representatives hurried off in all directions to warn their families that war was imminent.

Mesor had already emerged from the tunnel when he heard the news. He wanted to run to Evirae's side, tell her what had happened, but Evirae had vanished. He had to find her! He spied Tolchin and Alora in the crowd and rushed toward them.

The Baron saw Mesor approach and quickly turned away, but the Bursar called out behind him, "Wait! It is urgent!"

Tolchin sighed. "We are caught," he whispered.

Mesor arrived, out of breath but determined to speak. "I . . . I know something has happened to Evirae. We must find her."

Tolchin saw that the fellow was genuinely disturbed. The sycophant could ill afford the disappearance of his sole protector, he thought.

"She would never miss the Senate," Mesor insisted. "Nor would Prince Kiorte. I fear Hawkwind has taken some action against Evirae!"

Tolchin frowned. He had thought Evirae's absence might be part of her plan, but the Bursar's anxiety was evidence against it.

Mesor's last charge had also provoked Alora. She said, "Hawkwind has no use for Evirae. Something must have happened. Evirae would not miss such an important meeting."

The Baron nodded. "Alora, I suggest we proceed to their mansion immediately."

The couple moved swiftly away from the crowd, leaving Mesor to hurry ignominiously behind them.

XXII

Forward!"

Two hundred men already stood on the foggy shore. Behind them, in the water, the ragged armada waited. Some boats had already been pulled onto the beach. The sea was relatively calm; nevertheless, several ships had already collided in the breakers and capsized. Few among the Fandorans knew how to coordinate a landing so large, with the result that a part of the army found itself swimming—or trying to swim—to shore.

The sea air was filled with shouts of confusion and fear. Many men, exhausted by the crossing, had cast themselves on the cold sand, seeking a moment's rest. Others, under the direction of the Elders, waded in the shallow water, pulling on the boats' ropes, in an attempt to beach them without further incident.

Dayon stood in the cold salt water and stared for a moment at the boats offshore. "I brought them through," he said to himself. He had spoken softly, but his father had heard him. The old man put a hand on Dayon's shoulder. "That you did," he said. "I know nothing about the sea, but I could see that was a masterful work. I am proud of you."

Dayon nodded. He was proud of himself. He had conquered his fear of the Strait of Balomar, had run the gauntlet that had haunted him.

Jondalrun returned to the rescue mission. "Pull now!" he shouted to the others, as if he had spent his life on the shores of Cape Bage. "There are ill and injured out there! We must get them to shore!"

Dayon, his clothes soaked, took up another rope. Tenniel stepped behind him, feet placed firmly in the sand, and they pulled in unison on a rope. A small boat surged through the breakers.

"We have it!" Tenniel grunted. "Once more, Dayon!"

When the boat was beached, the two young men waded through the evening tide looking for other boats that were having difficulty landing. In the distance they could hear the complaints of the Fandoran army, rising above the sullen breakers. Then Dayon heard his father's stentorian tones. "Silence! Would you betray us to the sorcerers?"

This possibility brought an uneasy quiet to the confused, cold, and hungry farmers. Some men watched the fog for windships. Others pulled grimly on ropes. As others reached shore, they joined their fellow townsfolk in informal groups on the beach.

From out of the mist, another ship loomed before Dayon and Tenniel. The young fisherman recognized it—an old barge he had helped repair for the journey.

"Strange," said Tenniel as they approached it. "It looks empty."

"It's taking on water," said Dayon. "Look at the stern; it's far too low."

They waded out and pulled themselves on board. At first glance the wide deck seemed empty. There were signs of confusion; ropes and tools had been scattered about, as though dropped in haste. A barrelful of limes rolled slowly with the rocking of the waves. The repetitive sound made them aware of the lack of human voices or movement; when a gull keened overhead, both of them started.

Tenniel touched Dayon's arm. "Look," he said. Dayon turned and saw a man in the shadow of the hull's lee side. He was an old man, and he seemed asleep, curled up in a ball. Dayon approached him, saying gently, "Come along, old fellow. The crossing's completed. Where is your crew?"

The old man did not move. Dayon nudged him, then pulled him upright. His eyes were open and unfocused, his face pale. His mouth was slack. Dayon was suddenly aware of the cold sea air.

"What's wrong with him?" Tenniel asked.

"Shock." Dayon looked around the deck. Could the voyage alone have caused it?

"I don't like this," Tenniel said. "This ship's deserted, save for him . . ."

"I'm not convinced," Dayon said. "I remember this barge was boarded by men of Jelrich Town, which is inland. It is doubtful they knew how to swim." He stood and faced the low cabin in the stern. "I think we should have a look in there."

The two men approached the cabin. Within it, they could hear water sloshing with the waves.

"I don't like this," Tenniel repeated.

Dayon motioned him to silence. "Do you hear that?"

"Of course," the Borgen Town Elder said. "Do you think I'm deaf? This barge is sinking."

"Not the water. Something else."

Tenniel listened. There was another sound: a thrashing, unlike the lapping of the waves; more rhythmic and severe—and somehow savage. "I don't like *that,* either," he said. "I think we should leave. This lady's deserted."

"Not until we check the cabin," Dayon replied. He pulled the latch, but the door would not budge.

From inside the cabin there came again the thrashing, louder this time—a disturbing sound, like the slapping of wet flesh.

The wherry shifted beneath them. Tenniel was nervous. "Dayon, it's going down fast! I say we take the old man and get ashore."

"Help me with this door," said Dayon. Tenniel sighed and seized the latch. Before they set their muscles to it, they both heard a moan from inside the cabin. The thrashing increased.

"Pull!" shouted Dayon. "There's a man in there!"

They heard the snapping of wood. The door ripped open, revealing the interior of the cabin.

Neither Dayon nor Tenniel was prepared for the sight.

A stench of wet decay accompanied the sight of at least twenty bodies floating in the flooded cabin. The small table and benches had been overturned and splintered and several of the bunks ripped open. In the rear wall was a ragged three-foot hole, and in that hole was a ten-foot-long eellike beast with a fringe of writhing tentacles that sprouted from behind its head, and a wide snapping mouth. Spines along its back had caught on the ragged edges of the hole, and it hung there, trapped. A severed arm was caught in its teeth. Blood streaked the water.

Dayon and Tenniel stared in horror. Judging by the bloated appearance of the corpses, the attack had happened many hours ago. Most of the bodies were beyond the marta's reach. By now the amphibious beast had to be mad with hunger.

Another moan brought their attention to a bunk in the wall near the hole. A boy was crouched there, staring with wide eyes at Dayon and Tenniel. Several more were unconscious. The marta's tentacles could not quite reach into the bunk to drag them out, but effectively prevented them from reaching the door.

"Help the boy!" shouted Dayon.

Tenniel did not move. The marta thrashed, snapping its jaws.

"Tenniel!" Dayon said urgently.

Tenniel shook his head slowly. A tentacle lashed near him, and he retreated with a cry.

Dayon examined the cabin. The beast's struggles had knocked several smaller holes in the stern; waves were pumping water in slowly and steadily. Soon the marta would be supported and able to struggle inside the ship. He and Tenniel would have to act quickly to save them all.

He seized a broken length of plank floating nearby and hurled it at the beast. The tentacles seized it instinctively and dragged it toward the needle teeth. Dayon leaped into the middle of the cabin and extended his hand to the boy in the bunk. "Come on!" he shouted. The boy half-leaped, half-fell into the water, and Dayon grabbed his hand, pulling him toward Tenniel. Tenniel stepped forward, eyes on the marta, and seized the boy under his arms, dragging him from the cabin as Dayon pulled another out of the bunk.

Tenniel had not retreated beyond the reach of the marta's tentacles when the beast wrapped one about his leg, suckers fastening around his breeches. With a cry of disgust Tenniel ripped free. Moments later, he and the boy were outside the cabin.

Dayon and Tenniel laid the two boys beside the old man on deck. They were not much more than fourteen or fifteen years old. The boy nearest to Dayon struggled to talk. "My brother . . ."

Dayon nodded. "We'll get him out."

Tenniel looked toward the fog-covered beach. "I'm sorry, Dayon," he whispered. "I can't face that thing again."

"Tenniel!"

Tenniel refused to meet his gaze. "It's just too . . . I don't know what happened in there, but I've never been frightened by anything like that! I'm sorry. I just . . ."

"All right," Dayon said softly. "Return to my father and warn him."

"Warn him?"

"If there is one marta here, there may be twenty out there! Tell him to make sure there are no wounded men in the water. Blood will attract the martas."

"More martas? Are you sure?"

"No, but we mustn't take a chance." Dayon hurried back to the cabin. "Hurry! There are many lives at stake!"

He heard the splash as Tenniel leaped into the water. He did not know how many people in the cabin he could rescue before the room filled with water, but he hoped to have a chance to save them all.

The marta would be waiting. He did not know how badly his maneuver had affected it, but he knew it would continue to attack.

Dayon braced himself for the sight of the beast and stepped inside the cabin again.

At the other end of the cabin, the water rushed loudly through the hole in the stern. The water had risen too quickly. The hole was empty. The marta had escaped!

"Dayon!"

Dayon gasped. It was Tenniel's voice. The son of Jondal-run rushed back to the deck, looked over the lee side, and saw Tenniel standing in the shallows about twelve feet away. A shadow was swimming in a circle around him.

"Don't move!" Dayon shouted.

The circle was growing smaller. Attracted by the blood from the cabin on Tenniel's clothes, the marta was ready to attack.

"Dayon, help me!"

Dayon rushed back to the cabin. He would ask forgiveness later for what he was about to do.

He plunged into the choking atmosphere of the cabin and seized one of the corpses. The clammy flesh against his hands made him feel ill, but he did not hesitate; he dragged it on deck, carefully avoiding any glance at its face, and tumbled it into the sea. The splash blinded him for a moment.

He heard Tenniel scream—then silence.

Dayon rubbed the water from his eyes and looked fearfully into the water. A long black shape with a red-stained burden in its mouth was moving toward the open sea.

In the shallow water next to the barge stood Tenniel, silently watching the trail of foam and blood.

"Say a prayer," shouted Dayon, "then get yourself to my father. Everybody must be warned!"

•

Much later, the Fandoran army would take count and learn that only a miraculous twenty out of a thousand were known to have drowned or were unaccounted for in the chaotic crossing. Now the men camped, shivering and damp. Even Jondalrun, who had continued to supervise the landing of the boats, agreed that the men would get little done until they were dry, recovered, and fed. Eventually a few small fires were started and food was apportioned.

The beach sloped gradually up to the east, toward a series of low craggy hills. Beyond that, they could not see. Jondalrun and his assistants prowled among the men, helping and talking down outbursts of rebellion.

In the morning hours, Lagow found Jondalrun seated on a large piece of driftwood. The old farmer sat straight-backed, hand gripping his staff. In his wet clothes and with a strand of seaweed woven into his tangled white beard, he looked to Lagow like some absurd old man of the sea.

Lagow sat down beside him, marveling at the Elder's stamina. Lagow had had no sleep for two nights, and felt ready to drop. Jondalrun was twenty years his senior, but appeared cast of iron.

"We must move soon, Jondalrun," he said.

Jondalrun started slightly, and looked in surprise at

Lagow. Lagow, also surprised, realized that Jondalrun had been sleeping with his eyes open.

"Yes," Jondalrun said. He got to his feet slowly, aiding himself with his staff.

At Jondalrun's orders, the men grouped into straggling ranks. Those who retained their weapons carried them; others armed themselves with sticks or pouchfuls of rocks. Many walked with their hands empty. Slowly, with grumblings of hunger and concern, the ragged defenders of Fandora headed toward the hills.

Tenniel walked at the head of the Borgen Town contingent. He was tired. The encounter with the marta was fresh in his memory, but he attempted to convince himself that his enthusiasm for the invasion had not been dampened. Nevertheless, he continued to reach the same conclusion no matter what explanation he made. This had to be the most poorly managed excuse for a war that he had ever seen. He had thought much about the fate of Amsel, which he had been partially responsible for, and wondered if this invasion would be just retribution.

He had lost hold of his vision of war as a glorious enterprise. Now—he admitted to himself—he was thoroughly frightened and appalled at what they had done.

●

"I still do not understand," said General Vora. "Even with troops in the Southland, our windships are more than enough to defend us against the Fandorans. How could they possibly expect to win?"

In a large conference hall at the rear of the palace, the Royal Family had assembled to discuss the matters of war. Although the weather was cool, Hawkwind had directed the satin curtains of the hall to be pulled back, and from their seats the Family was able to see a magnificent view of the surrounding forest.

There was a sense of urgency at the meeting, and a sense of resentment. Hawkwind was seated at the head of a large wooden table. To his left sat Ephrion. To his right was Ceria. Positioned around the table were Lady Eselle, Lady Tenor, Thalen, and six Ministers of Simbala. Across from him stood a tall white-haired man—General-Emeritus Jibron.

"Where is my daughter? I demand to know what has happened to my daughter!" Jibron looked accusingly at Hawkwind.

Hawkwind rose calmly from his seat. Ephrion watched him nervously. The young man could not afford to lose the support of Simbala's former General.

"I regret I have no news of Evirae's situation," Hawkwind told Jibron. "Both she and her husband have been missing since the morning."

Jibron responded quickly. "That is impossible! There must be a reason for Evirae's absence from the Senate!"

Hawkwind nodded. "There is a rumor concerning Evirae's concealment of a Fandoran spy."

"A *spy?*" said Jibron. "Are you accusing my daughter of being in league with the Fandorans?"

Ephrion could not tolerate this exchange. Jibron was playing politics while the country's future was at stake! "No!" he said from his seat. "Hawkwind merely means that a Fandoran spy may have been taken prisoner by your daughter."

"This troubles you?" asked Jibron. "Is it not meritorious behavior?"

"Quite possibly," said Hawkwind, "except that I had not been told of the spy's presence. I have just learned of the rumor through Thalen."

"Is this true?" asked Lady Eselle. She faced Kiorte's brother. Thalen nodded. "A young captain has told me of a Fandoran fisherman brought in while Kiorte was on an exploratory mission. According to this captain, the fisherman was taken to Evirae's aides by her own request. There have been rumors that this man is not a fisherman, that he is actually a Fandoran spy. That is all we know, for the Fandoran has disappeared."

Another Minister rose from her seat. "There seems to be a danger to the Circle," she said calmly. "As we all know, Baron Tolchin and Baroness Alora are also missing. Could this Fandoran have been sent on a mission of subversion against the Family?"

"How could that be?" Hawkwind answered. "The Fandorans know little about our land, and even less about the Family. The forest hides the secrets of Simbala, and the forest has been protected. The Family is safe! I have ordered the returning Senate members to warn their families of the invasion. The army is being assembled at various stations throughout the forest."

General Vora agreed. "Our men are positioned throughout the forest and around the palace. There is no reason for concern."

General-Emeritus Jibron frowned. "It is not your daughter who is missing, Vora. You and Hawkwind were quick to dismiss the possibility of invasion at the Senate. You showed little concern at that time also."

Vora pounded the tabletop. "That is unfair, Jibron! Had you been in my position, you would have also voted against the war! The Fandorans are known to be ill-equipped for any attack. They are farmers. There is no reason, there was no reason, to suspect an invasion."

"Only a fool lacks caution, Vora. A threat of war should never have been ignored. My daughter warned Hawkwind hours before the Fandorans were discovered."

"Then it is obvious she knew something we did not know," said Hawkwind. "Have you considered why?"

Jibron's face reddened. "Do not taunt me, miner! I have given you a chance to prove yourself worthy of Ephrion's trust. I need not have you accuse my daughter of traitorous acts!"

"I do not accuse her," said Hawkwind. "I just seek an answer to the mystery of this invasion!"

"Then seek it within your own circle! The Rayan has abilities, does she not? Ask her about the Fandoran! Tell your trusted aides to find the Fandoran spy. Perhaps then they will also find my daughter!"

Ceria waited angrily for Hawkwind's response. He ignored Jibron's taunts and returned to his seat to initiate a discussion of the defense of the forest. Ceria pushed her feelings away. Once again the Family had used her to antagonize Hawkwind. She knew his feelings about this and watched in admiration as he exhibited a statesman's control.

"A small fleet of windships will be directed to fly close to the Kameran Valley," said Hawkwind. "The ships will observe the Fandorans and determine their plans. Then they will attempt to frighten the invaders. These men are not soldiers. We are convinced they can be defeated without danger to our men."

"Without danger?" asked Lady Tenor skeptically. "Is it not dangerous to send a few windships against the entire Fandoran army?"

"Yes," answered a young Minister of Finance. "Just as it was dangerous sending half of our troops to the Southland!"

Hawkwind was losing patience. They were blaming him for ideas that were not even his! Ephrion had taught him to ignore royalist sentiment, but it was not always easy.

"The Fandorans are *not* soldiers," he insisted. "There is no reason to plan any—"

Before Hawkwind could complete his sentence, a distant scream was heard through the hall. It was followed by several others, and sounds of panic and confusion. Then a high-pitched sound, alien to the forest and chilling in its effect, echoed in the courtyard. The members of the Family looked at each other in shock.

"Is it the Fandorans?" Lady Tenor whispered.

The shriek came again, louder. The hawk lifted itself from its perch, as if answering the hideous sound, and quickly flew out the arch.

Hawkwind rushed to the front of the hall. Behind him hurried Ceria and Vora, followed closely by the other members of the Family.

In the distance they could see a small dark cloud, moving quickly, too quickly for a cloud, toward the center of the forest.

In the courtyard, small animals ran to safety. Guards leaped for cover as their horses ran out of control.

Ceria watched the cloud as it grew larger. She could sense a feeling, borne as if on the wind. She felt pain, a hidden warmth, and then suddenly, coldness.

She looked up. The cloud was no longer a cloud. Two giant wings brushed the top of the palace. A horned head opened its mouth and shrieked a sound like a thousand nightmares. Ceria screamed. A body ten times that of a man cast its shadow across the palace hall.

A legend had come to life.

To those members of the Family who stood transfixed at the edge of the archway, the creature seemed to move quite slowly. All had time to observe the huge wings, the long tail, and the head, larger than a windship craft and full of gleaming teeth. The dragon raised its head and shrieked again.

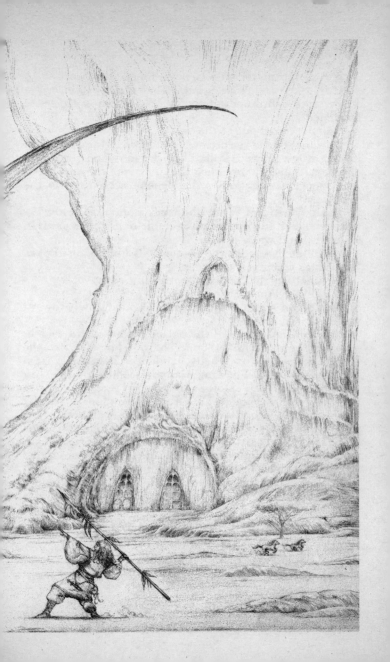

"It is a nightmare!" said General-Emeritus Jibron.

"It is real," said Hawkwind. "Thalen! Dispatch a messenger to the Brothers of the Wind. All ships are to be grounded!"

Thalen hurried out of the hall.

Ephrion stared at the creature, studying its long neck and its two massive legs. It had to be a dragon—and yet, it was different. It had not breathed fire; it had not the attitude of intelligence, of gentleness that legend accredited to the dragons.

"Look!" General Vora shouted, pointing below. A watchman had run out from the stable in the courtyard. In his right hand was a javelin.

"Back!" he shouted to the dragon, as if addressing a horse. "Return to wherever you came!"

"I cannot watch!" said Eselle, turning away.

"Back!" the young man repeated.

The dragon stared at him, then descended slowly toward the courtyard.

"You will not threaten the palace!" shouted the watchman, and he stood his ground. The watchman hurled the javelin at the creature's belly. It glanced harmlessly from the armored scales. The dragon almost seemed to smile. In a motion unbelievably fast for a creature so large, it swept one huge taloned foot against the foolish watchman, batting him away like a bothersome insect. The watchman flew through the air, rolled over, and staggered to his feet, one arm dangling uselessly. As several other guards rushed out to help him, the dragon took to the air again. The wind from its huge wings ravaged several small trees and a garden as it rose past the palace, shrieking in triumph at the tiny beings within the giant tree.

Hawkwind and the Family watched as the creature sailed over the trees in a northwesterly direction.

"What is it?" said Lady Eselle. "What could it want in Simbala?"

"Can there be any doubt?" the General said harshly. "This is obviously why the Fandorans have attacked. Somehow, they control the dragon!"

•

Baron Tolchin pressed his fingers lightly to the inside of Evirae's wrist. "She's alive," he said with relief. Mesor stood near the recumbent forms, half-buried in mud, of the Prince and Princess. "She has apparently fainted from lack of air," he said, "as did Kiorte and the guard." A third figure rested in the mud not far from Evirae.

Tolchin paced quickly in front of the mound of dirt. He, Alora, and the Bursar had entered the cave-in area through a small opening in the tunnel. "From the look of things," he said, "this crack opened as the mud settled, but it did not open soon enough to keep them from losing consciousness. We are fortunate to have found them. Mesor, you must fetch some aides to carry them out! Alora and I will find a physician to take . . ." Tolchin looked up suddenly at the tunnel roof. "Listen. Do you hear it?"

The Bursar and the Baroness listened. Very, very faintly, filtered through several feet of dirt, they heard a scream. A moment later, a vibration rippled through the cavern, as though something heavy had just crashed to the ground. A thin trickle of earth dropped from the ceiling of the tunnel.

"The attack has started already," Tolchin said bitterly.

"That is not possible," Alora protested. "The Fandorans have just landed!"

Tolchin paced nervously. "How are we to know if the ships seen by the Windriders were the first to arrive?"

"It does not matter. No band of farmers could penetrate the forest!" Alora wiped dust from Kiorte's face.

"This is Hawkwind's fault," said Tolchin. "Evirae was correct."

•

Caught in a maze, Amsel stumbled through the lightless tunnels. He was weary to the point of collapse, yet he could not stop, for every time he did, he could hear the rapid footsteps of the thing that stalked him.

The pattern was always the same. He would wait, and as the echoes of his passage diminished, he would hear the tick-tick-tick of the thing's claws upon the rocks. Then, sensing that Amsel had stopped, it too would be silent, waiting for the inventor to start again. It was watching him, wearing him down, waiting until it sensed that he was too weak to resist its attack.

He could not elude it; to defeat the creature, he would have to outwit it or outrun it. Amsel checked his pockets; only his spectacles and the seed pods from the Spindeline

Wood remained. He hurried forward, determined to get as far ahead of the creature as he could. To his disappointment, the tunnel took on a downward slope; he was going away from the surface again.

If only he had a light! The horrible, smothering darkness was the worst of it. The stalker was a phantom; the tunnel twisted and turned without warning. If only he could see!

Amsel gasped. He searched his pockets frantically, and his hand closed on his spectacles. He had ground the lenses himself, but the metal for the frames had been purchased from a Southland merchant. The metal was steel. The tunnels were full of crystal and quartz deposits. Amsel crouched and began feeling about the tunnel floor for what he knew had to be there.

He heard the sound of claws on rock approaching. He searched faster, picking up pieces of rock, hitting each stone against the frame of his spectacles and then discarding it for another.

The creature was coming closer. He could hear it breathing! Then suddenly there was silence again. Amsel panicked, picked up another rock, and threw it in the direction of the creature. He heard it hit flesh. There was a growl, and then the swift sound of the creature's charge.

Amsel leaped to one side. His foot slipped on a loose rock, and he fell, throwing his hands out to keep his balance. The hand that held his spectacles skidded across the surface of a long flat rock with a scraping around. A shower of sparks dazzled him. *Flint!*

In his moment of sight, Amsel glimpsed a large, hideously white creature, like a wolf but hairless, with two large red-rimmed eyes. The creature howled in shock at the brilliant sparks, then turned and fled, its claws skittering on the stone. Amsel heard it turn left and disappear. He lay prone for a minute, gasping in relief. He did not know what had attacked him, but it obviously did not like the light.

When he felt relaxed enough, Amsel moved forward. A few moments later, his questing hand found a corner. Another tunnel crossed this passage. The creature had run off to the left. "Therefore," Amsel told himself, "I shall go to the right. No animal that flees from a few sparks would escape toward daylight!"

He hurried down the new tunnel and soon felt it sloping

upward. "At last!" he whispered to himself. "Congratulations, Amsel. You may yet find an answer to Johan's murder." Then he nodded with determination. "I will, I will find an answer." He hurried up the tunnel.

•

Alone in the library of the palace stood Ceria. She hugged herself tightly, for the room was cold. There were no windows. On the high curved walls was shelf after shelf of books and documents about Simbalese history. These had always impressed Ceria; she had had little formal education, and the physical presence of so much knowledge was at once imposing and intriguing.

Although she wished to find the secret to the madness she had seen, she longed for the familiarity of her home, for the freedom of the plains. The threat of war troubled her deeply, and she wished the Family would listen more closely to the voices of reason, to Hawkwind, and Ephrion, and the others who were not driven by ambition or pride in their attitude toward the Fandorans.

Hawkwind had departed the palace with General Vora to make additional preparations for the defense of the forest. Since the arrival of the dragon, both he and Vora had agreed that it would be best to continue the withdrawal of as many windships from the sky as possible. Thalen had been dispatched to the Northweald to get reinforcements for the army. With the exception of his ships and the ships which would soon be assigned the mission of confronting the Fandorans in the hills, all others would be confined to the ground.

In the place of the windships, the army would be responsible for the defense of the forest. Yet the threat of the dragon had made even ground troops wary of war.

The appearance of the dragon disturbed and confused Ceria. She had been told stories about dragons when she was a child; the legends of the friendly and noble creatures were known to all Simbalese. But the animal they had seen was neither friendly nor noble. It was, however, very real.

The Family viewed the dragon as a tool of the Fandorans. Ceria thought differently. How could farmers control a creature larger than a windship? More was happening here than she understood. Ceria remembered a feeling she had had the moment before the dragon had appeared; a desperation, a sadness that went beyond any tragedy she had known. It had been frightening. In the silence of the library she again sensed the cold, heard the cry, felt a distant terror that seemed to envelop her like a mist. She ran toward the door, but when she opened it, she saw not the palace corridor, but icy cliffs and a leaden sky above her. She could feel the jagged rocks and the freezing grip of the wind. She screamed.

Minutes later, footsteps sounded in the hall. Two aides entered and found the young woman on the library's floor.

"Tell Monarch Ephrion!" the first aide shouted. "Hurry! It is Lady Ceria!"

•

At the cavern entrance, several aides carried Kiorte and the guard out. Evirae was on a stretcher made of tanselweb. Tolchin, Alora, and a physician followed. They reached the surface near the palace grounds and stepped into chaos. People were running through the streets, some carrying weapons, all appearing terrified or outraged. The Baron looked aghast, but as he was about to speak, Evirae feebly beckoned to him. He stood close to her. Her face was pale, and the streaks of mud on her cheeks were quite dark by contrast.

"Tolchin . . ." she whispered.

"I am here," said the Baron.

"The Fandoran . . . escaped . . . all Hawkwind's doing . . . Fandoran may cause . . . harm . . . stop him . . . stop . . . Hawkwind . . ."

Her hand fell limply to her side, and her eyes closed again. The physician felt the pulse at her throat and nodded in relief. "She must have rest," he said.

Tolchin looked up at the crowds in the square. Evirae opened one eye a slit to watch him, then quickly closed it again.

Tolchin caught the arm of a young man dashing by, brandishing a heavy brass candlestick. "What has happened?" the Baron demanded. "Have the Fandorans reached Overwood already?"

"No, but their demons have!"

"Demons?" Alora asked incredulously.

"Aye! The city has been attacked by a dragon! The Fandorans have magic and legendry on their side! The city must be defended!" He wrestled free of Tolchin's grasp and was gone through a hedge.

Tolchin called after him, uselessly. He observed the confusion in the street with growing anger. "The miner is responsible for this!" he said. "If Hawkwind had listened to Evirae's warning, the people would have been prepared for the invasion. Dragons indeed! His inexperience has caused this panic!"

Tolchin took his wife's arm and started toward the ordinarily quiet plaza. "Where are you going?" she asked.

"To speak with the rest of the Family. Hawkwind must not be trusted with the affairs of war!"

"I will stay here," Alora replied. "Evirae and Kiorte must be taken back to the palace grounds."

"The physician will see to it!" said Tolchin. People had started to gather around the Prince and Princess. He did not wish to be caught in the crowd.

"I wish to see to it myself," Alora answered.

Sensing his wife's inflexibility, Tolchin rubbed his chin and then frowned, nodded, and rushed off alone.

XXIII

On the plains of Simbala, large flat meadowlands dotted with small groups of trees, the Fandoran army had gathered. Jondalrun stood, oblivious of the cold, and surveyed the distant forest. Dayon, Lagow, Tenniel, and Tamark stood beside him. The Fandoran army had traveled over the hills from shore without as much as a fence in their way.

"They wait for us," Jondalrun said. His voice was throaty from continuously shouting orders and encouragement. "There." He focused on the dark forest in the distance. The noon sun was obscured by the clouds. The light made the trees look foreboding.

"I see no soldiers," Lagow said. "Nor any windships. This has not the look of a land bent on war. I tell you, Jondalrun—"

"Spare me, Lagow," Jondalrun said. "I know your opinion by now. I still say that the Sim wait for us, hoping we will enter the forest. Then their woodsmen and archers and magicians will fall upon us. No, we will not fight them in their forest. We will wait them out on these plains, under these stands of trees. Here we are prepared for them, and we are protected from their windships. Here we will wait."

To Jondalrun's surprise, the wheelwright agreed. "I admit we have an advantageous position here. We should hold it for now." Perhaps, he thought, nothing will happen.

The night will be cold and the men may become anxious to leave. Then we can return home.

"I am not sure," said Tenniel in an unnaturally somber tone. "As Elder of Borgen Town, I am weary of all these delays. My men grow tired. Without food they will soon be too weak to face the Simbalese."

"The Borgen men are fat," said Tamark impatiently. "Do not worry about their endurance!"

"We will wait, Tenniel," Jondalrun said softly. "Tomorrow we can discuss further plans."

There was no disagreement. Tenniel reluctantly went off to tell his men of the decision. Lagow did the same, but with relief. It was not too late to hope for an early end to all this foolishness.

●

The tunnel sloped steadily upward. At times it was steep enough to force Amsel to climb with the help of his hands. "It cannot be long now," he kept telling himself. As he scrambled forward feverishly, it seemed as though he could hear Johan's voice encouraging him, urging him forward. "I will find out the truth!" he shouted, and the words echoed back in the silent passageway. "I will!" It was growing faintly lighter, and he was able to see a large boulder ahead of him. He pulled himself over it and lowered his small legs into the darkness beyond it, but as he did, the tunnel floor seemed to disappear. Amsel toppled precariously on the edge of the precipice and then dropped, with a startled scream, into darker and unknown depths.

●

"Fool, you'll leave the forest open to their entire army!"

"It is not an army! It is a band of buffoons! Jibron, you are no longer General! Do not meddle in my affairs!"

"I am not meddling, Vora, and these are not your affairs! They are the affairs of Simbala. As a member of the Royal Family, they deeply concern me!"

Hawkwind, Vora, and Jibron were in a high room of the palace not far from the windship station on the eastern wing. There was a huge glass window in the sloping wall of the room, and through it poured amber light. There was little time for speculation now; the main troops of Simbala, composed of miners and other young men and women from

Overwood, would join with the incoming troops from the
Northweald and the advance troops outside the forest. In
recruiting the men and women of the northern woods,
Hawkwind hoped to compensate for the missing troops who
were still in the Southland.

Hawkwind was worried. His original resistance to the
Baron's trade mission had been correct. He should have
argued with Tolchin; the army was not meant to be used for
caravans. A contingent of guards should have been sent to
the Southland, not the hundreds of men and women who
had gone. They needed these troops now, needed them to
protect Simbala.

Hawkwind was angered by his own inexperience. Evirae
and Kiorte were still missing, but his agents had found no
evidence of the Fandoran spy. Rumors were spreading of his
complicity in their disappearance. It was madness! First the
war, then the spy, then the dragon! He had not caused any of
the problems, but he was being blamed for them all! It was
as Ephrion had warned. If a man coughs in Simbala, it is the
monarch who is responsible for the cold.

"Hawkwind! What do you think of this matter?"

It was Vora. Hawkwind blinked nervously. He had not
been listening.

"What matter, General?"

Jibron scowled. "Dream not of the Rayan now! There's a
battle afoot!"

Hawkwind paced toward the wall opposite the window.
There was a large map engraved in the wall showing the
land of Simbala. In the center of the Overwood, a giant
circular field. To the west of the forest were the woods,
scattered trees, and bushes which preceded the larger trees
of the city to the east. Then came the Kameran Valley, a
narrow grassy plain that by now had become wet and covered with fog from the spring rains. Farther west were the
rolling Kameran Hills, and beyond them, the Simbalese
shore.

Colored strings indicated the path of the Fandorans as
relayed by Simbalese sentries. Hawkwind examined them
again, noting the irregular but generally accurate route the
Fandorans had taken through the hills toward Overwood.
The Fandorans had paused before entering the valley. If

they continued their drive, they would be in Overwood by evening.

"There is no reason to change our plans," said Hawkwind.

"Good," answered Vora.

Jibron shook his head. "The Fandorans will not be scared by the windships. They have come too far to be turned back by a few colorful sails."

"It is an opening tactic," said Vora. "There is nothing to be lost by attempting the safest plan first. The Fandorans are hardly a threat."

"You know not their reason for invading," Jibron replied. "Any people with a dragon on their side must—"

Hawkwind interrupted. "You are correct, General Jibron. We were caught unaware by the Fandorans, but the error will not be repeated. We are cautious. If Thalen's advance fleet does not push the Fandorans back toward the shore, our troops will guard the forest from both man and dragon."

As Hawkwind spoke, there were footsteps on the curved staircase outside the room. "Monarch Hawkwind!" came an aide's nervous call. "Baron Tolchin! He insists on seeing you!"

Hawkwind nodded. "Send the Baron up!"

"Good!" said Jibron. "Another man of experience."

Hawkwind folded his arms over his chest and waited. He had wondered about the Baron's absence from the conference hall earlier. He and Alora would not have missed the meeting without an urgent reason. Hawkwind sighed.

"Good morning, Baron," said General-Emeritus Jibron as the Baron walked into the meeting room.

" 'Morning," said Vora, nodding suspiciously.

The Baron did not acknowledge them. He approached Hawkwind. "I have been with Evirae," he said.

Hawkwind looked at Tolchin with surprise. "The Princess? Then you have found her?"

"My daughter!" Jibron said anxiously. "Where is she?"

"Evirae is being returned to her mansion with the Prince," said Tolchin. "There has been an accident."

"An accident?" asked Jibron.

"She is safe," answered Tolchin. "It is Simbala that is not safe!" He stared at Hawkwind. "You knew, didn't you?"

Hawkwind looked at Tolchin in amazement. "I know nothing of Evirae's accident!"

"Not the accident, miner. The invasion! You knew beforehand of the invasion!"

Hawkwind turned away from Tolchin in shock. He did not understand the Baron's accusation. He walked quickly toward the window on the other side of the room. Tolchin stared at Hawkwind, his indignation growing.

Hawkwind pressed his palms into the slope of the curved wooden wall. In front of him was the circular window from which he could see troops running through the palace courtyard. He struggled to suppress his anger. He had seen Evirae's persuasiveness in his own dealings with her, but he had never seen it affect the Baron. If Tolchin readily agreed to Evirae's accusation, then Tolchin no longer trusted him. Hawkwind knew that there was information he had not yet heard, but there was nothing that would betray his loyalty to Simbala. How could Alora's husband side with the Princess?

There was no time to refute the charge. Despite Ephrion's admonitions to avoid a confrontation with the Family at all costs, Hawkwind viewed this as a time for action. Jibron considered him to be a fool, and now Tolchin believed him a traitor—how could he stand by silently when they challenged him? He would compromise, but he would not lose his self-respect. Simbala was at war. He had to regain the peace. He would not be a tool of the Family.

He faced Tolchin silently, fury darkening his face. He lifted his left hand and removed the jewel by its diadem from his head; then, in a gesture of defiance he tossed it in the Baron's direction.

Tolchin jerked away for a moment, then belatedly caught it. Hawkwind walked toward him.

"I did not ask for the job of Monarch," said Hawkwind, "and I need no jewel of the Family to prove who I am." He looked intently at the Baron. "I am a miner's son. I was appointed by Monarch Ephrion to this office, and here I shall remain, until he no longer wishes me to pursue the destinies of Simbala!" He turned abruptly and started toward the door. "I had hoped to have the support of a man as intelligent as you, Tolchin, but if you wish to help fulfill the shallow ambitions of a Princess who cares nothing for her people, then I will oppose you."

With that statement Hawkwind turned quickly and left the room.

Tolchin stared in astonishment as Jibron closed the chamber's door. The sound of Hawkwind's footsteps faded on the old steps outside.

"Hawkwind is a fool," said Jibron. "He seeks to defy the Family! He insults my daughter! Does he not understand what we can do to him?"

Tolchin paced uneasily. "I had not expected this," he said. "Hawkwind has forced my hand. I am surprised."

Vora watched him. "How could you be surprised?" he said. "You have both forced his hand too many times! Hawkwind is a proud man. He will not submit any longer to your petty condemnations."

"Petty condemnations? You would be smart to watch your words, Vora!" General-Emeritus Jibron turned toward the door. "A fool will not take our troops into battle! If Hawkwind will not listen to the Family, then he will be Monarch no longer!" He motioned to the Baron. "Come, Tolchin. I must speak to my daughter." The two men departed together.

"Beware!" shouted Vora as they headed down the stairs. "Those that challenge Hawkwind also challenge me!"

The General heard the echo of his words outside the room. They sounded foolish, like the bravado of a young man, but he meant them. If the Family wanted a confrontation, they would get a confrontation, but it would not be with the Fandorans.

•

In the air above Simbala, an armada of thirty windships rode the cloudy skies, returning from the Northweald with volunteers for the army. More Northwealdsfolk rode on swift horses southward through the woods below, but the windships far outpaced them. Ten to a craft there were, the balloon sails filled to bursting with gas enough for the heavy cargo. The greens and browns of the Northweald garb contrasted sharply with the black and silver of the Windriders' uniforms. The demarcation was quite noticeable, for, unless necessary to perform the functions of the ships and to maintain balance in the air, the two factions did not mingle.

On one of the ships stood Willen, his knuckles white on the wooden railing that surrounded the craft. His face was a very faint echo of the green of his tunic. Nevertheless, he held his shoulders straight and did not let his nervousness show. Though he floated higher than the tallest tree, he would be as brave as the smug and efficient Windriders.

Thalen glanced at Willen with amusement. Like many in Overwood, he was condescending toward North-wealdsfolk, but he was impressed with the stolid attempts by most of them to mask their ground-fellow fears. Moved by this toward a gesture of friendliness, he stepped nearer Willen and said, "We do not fly so high this day; the extra weight holds us close to the ground."

"We are sorry to inconvenience your method of travel," Willen said stiffly.

Thalen raised an eyebrow. "That was not what I meant," he said, still wanting to make conversation. "I simply wished to reassure you that there is little danger of sudden high winds and shifting air currents at this altitude. You need not grip the railing so desperately."

Willen's suppressed nervousness turned quickly to anger. Before he could think better of it, he snapped, "I'm aware that we groundfolk seem cowardly to the Brothers of the Wind. But there are dangers we face on the ground that are far more threatening than any in the air, especially in time of war. Climb down from your safe heights then and fight alongside us, and we will see who is braver!"

Thalen drew back at the rebuff. He had enough worry with Kiorte's disappearance. He walked quickly toward the stern to inspect a pulley and line. Willen felt his face burning in the cold breeze. His loud words had caused what little conversation there was around him to cease, but the words had been said, and his pride would not allow them to be taken back.

He sighed and stared straight ahead, trying not to look down. It was too easy to imagine himself impaled on leafy needles below the ship.

●

Blackness and cold rushed up at Amsel. The fall seemed endless; then suddenly he was gripped in an icy whirlwind. His body felt numb, his chest tightened like a fist. He had landed in an underground river! Fortunately, he had hit it feetfirst. Amsel forced his legs to kick, and swam upward with maddening slowness.

A few moments later he surfaced. There was a roaring in his ears as he gasped and coughed until his lungs were filled with sweet air. The current was quite strong. Amsel hit a rock with his back, and as the river dragged him, he hugged it with both arms and refused to release it. He had no feeling in his fingers, but he pressed his arms as hard as he could against the smooth surface of the boulder. The river tugged at him, but he stubbornly maintained his grip.

He forced himself to breathe slowly, calming his pounding heart. He did not know how far he had fallen, but he did not think it was very far. He could not see at all, and though he kicked out with his legs in all directions, he could not find any indication of a left or right bank, or of a shallow area. He dared not lose his grip, for he did not know if the river would take him farther underground.

Amsel thought for a moment of the warmth and solitude of his tree house in Fandora. Then a cold slap hit him and he was once again tossed into the currents. He struggled to keep his head above water, bobbing, stroking, and treading, until, in a relatively tranquil interlude, he floated feetfirst, on his back. He kept moving his arms and legs to keep them from becoming chilled, and then he realized that he could see the cavern roof above him. A dim light suffused the underground river. He felt like cheering—the river was taking him toward the surface!

A moment later he floated into the daylight, which, dim and gray though it was, nevertheless hurt his eyes. He saw trees arching in a canopy overhead, and through them patches of clouds. He passed beneath a tree root that also functioned as a bridge. The river, once it had emerged from the underground channel, widened into a peaceful flow. Amsel forced his weary arms to paddle toward shore. He seized the grassy bank and pulled himself onto it, shivering. "Well," he said through chattering teeth, "I suppose there's some good in everything—at least I've washed away the mud. Now, I must find something to eat."

He lifted his head and spied a magnificent tree across the river, but as he did, a sharp spear was thrust into his field of vision.

"Do not move!"

For a moment Amsel was sure that he had been retaken prisoner. Then he looked at the spear and realized that its head was not made of metal. He touched it curiously, and it bent beneath his probing finger. Amsel turned and discovered a tall boy, perhaps eight or nine years of age.

"You're my prisoner!" the lad said loudly. Behind him stood an even younger girl.

Amsel smiled. "It appears that I am." He rubbed himself briskly. His wet garments were not drying rapidly—the air was humid, heavy with the suggestion of rain.

The girl wore a beautiful red cloak. "Are you cold?" she asked Amsel.

"Very much so."

"Here." The girl took off her cloak. "You can dry yourself with this, but please give it back. My mother made it. It's just like Lady Ceria's."

Amsel accepted it gratefully. "Lady Ceria, you say? Does she wear a cloak like this?"

"Of course she does," the lad with the spear said. "Everybody knows she wears it. At least, everybody who likes her. Where are you from, anyway? You talk funny."

"I'm . . . not from around here." Amsel finished drying himself as best he could and carefully hung the cloak on a nearby branch to dry. "Thank you," he added.

"Is your father a miner?" the boy asked. "I never saw you in Overwood. Where do you live?"

They think I am a child because of my size, thought Amsel. Shortness can be an advantage. He looked around him. He was standing on the edge of a flagstone walkway that curved through an arch formed of blooming bushes. On the other side of the arch was a small park. Beside him were several steps leading to what seemed to be an outdoor portico. Amsel realized that he had to be careful; if he were seen, he would surely be recognized as a Fandoran.

This area he was in seemed quite tranquil; perhaps it was a play area for children. There were few sounds besides those of the river, the gentle wind, and a few birds. Perhaps there was still time to find Hawkwind before hostilities started.

He wondered who the woman was, the woman called Lady Ceria.

"You didn't answer my question," the lad said. "How old are you, anyway? You have to be at least six to play with us."

"He looks older than six," the young girl said.

"I am," Amsel agreed. Then he asked quickly, "Who is Lady Ceria?"

"Don't you know anything?" the boy said. "Everybody's been talking about her. She's in love with Hawkwind."

"Monarch Hawkwind? Do you know a lot about him?"

"He's going to defeat the Fandorans," the boy said proudly.

"The Fandorans?" Amsel sat down on the step. He felt like crying, but instead he whispered, "Johan, I must not give up hope!"

The girl overheard him. "Johan?" she asked. "Does he live near here?"

Amsel shook his head. "He was a friend of mine from far away."

At that, the boy looked worried.

"Where do you live?" he asked again, this time with more suspicion than friendship.

●

The chamber was silent, save for the sound of Hawkwind's footsteps. He no longer wore the familiar blue robes of the monarchy. A chain-mail shield covered his chest, and on his arms were the heavy cloth-and-copper sleeves of Simbala's infantry. Hawkwind's hair was combed back freely, no longer restrained by diadem or jewel. In the darkness of Ceria's chamber he appeared to be a shadow, swiftly moving to a hiding place away from the light.

He crouched at her bedside, beneath a large tapestry of silk. Ceria was sleeping, still resting from the vision that had rendered her unconscious not long ago. Hawkwind touched her with tenderness.

"My love," he whispered, "I shall return while you are still dreaming. There shall be no bloodshed, for the farmers will learn the foolishness of war."

She lay still beneath him, unaware of his words.

"Ceria," he continued softly, "I know not how you tolerate the feelings of the Family toward you. When I return, you shall no longer bear the burden of their prejudice."

He gently kissed her on the cheek. "May you have dreams of peace," he whispered.

Then he vanished, to descend the stairs of the palace, to meet General Vora and begin the long ride to the edge of the forest.

•

The coldrake returned to the spire and reported what he had learned to the Darkling. The Guardian's claims were true. He had flown over a warm valley in the land of the humans, and there he had seen humans flying. Then he had approached the spire of the humans, the highest tree in the forest, and as he did, he saw closely another of the silent beasts in which the humans flew.

The Darkling shrieked, for he understood that the humans had made these flying craft. They were most frighteningly clever, and they were certainly hostile. The thought of what they had done once again made the Darkling want to lift his head and shriek out his rage, but he did not. He felt the burning within him. He summoned another coldrake, telling him in their hissing speech that he wished to inspect a human creature at close range with one of their flying craft. He had to learn exactly how dangerous they were. Despite their size, the Guardian had said they were many—and the strength of the coldrakes had been diminished by the cold.

The emissary returned to his warren, to feed on the sparse meal he had found. Then he rested near the bottom of the spire, close to the steam and heat of the hot springs, preparing for the long, cold flight over the sea.

The Darkling remained perched on the top of the spire. In a way that he did not entirely understand, he welcomed the cold and the pain it brought. It seemed fitting for him to be isolated this way—he who was neither dragon nor coldrake, with the blood of both within him. He had been raised in isolation. If either dragon or coldrake had known of his existence, he would have been banished or killed. He had always been alone. Nothing would change that now.

The Darkling flapped his wings and shrieked in anguish. The coldrakes echoed the sound from their warrens, knowing but not understanding his pain. Never understanding.

XXIV

There were nine of them gathered in the bedroom of Prince Kiorte and Princess Evirae. Four stood near a large wooden dresser distinguished by its sweeping curves and luminescent wood. They were members of the Royal Family—General Jibron, Lady Eselle, Baroness Alora, and her husband, Tolchin. Near the door of the room stood Mesor, and next to him a trusted guard of the mansion. In a bed at the north end lay Evirae, still recovering from the effects of the tunnel's collapse, while beside her, Kiorte, in a robe, stood watching his wife enigmatically.

On the edge of the bed sat the young physician who had accompanied them back from the mines. He had just prescribed rest for both, but the scene remained far from tranquil.

"You say I am not seriously injured," Evirae complained, "but you insist I confine myself to our bed. It makes no sense! Suggest to me a physic and get back to those who need you." She sat upright in the bed.

The physician made a valiant effort to explain. "You may feel alert now, but fatigue can set in later. Medicine is an art, not a trade. Please do not argue with me."

"Nonsense!" insisted Evirae. "How can you know what is best for me? You are no older than I am! Look at me! Do I look ill? Do I appear fatigued? Am I on the verge of physical collapse?"

The physician looked at the Princess. Her long hair,

which was usually woven tightly on top of her head, cascaded in tangles down her back and shoulders. Her right cheek had been scratched by the jagged edge of a falling rock, and her splendid clothing had been replaced by a brown silk robe. Despite a generous application of soap, water, and cologne, her pale skin still retained the odor of the tunnel mud.

"You are as beautiful as ever," said the physician. He wearily lifted a small silk bag from the side of the bed. "Now I must leave."

Evirae smiled playfully. "Perhaps I have been too quick to dismiss your opinions," she said. "I thank you for your advice."

With a look of mild impatience the physician nodded and then headed toward the door. When he had reached the staircase outside, Evirae turned to her father and said, "What is of such urgency that you and Tolchin have rushed back from the palace? Has our miner invited the Fandorans to tea?"

"Do not jest," said her father. "He has—"

"Wait," said Kiorte. "This is a matter for the Family, not the Circle."

All heads turned to Mesor.

"I shall wait outside," the Bursar said.

"Downstairs," suggested Tolchin.

The Bursar nodded. "Of course. I will chat with a tree bear in the garden."

Jibron waited as Mesor made his way down the stairs. When the footsteps could no longer be heard, he said, "Why do you keep that man at your side, Evirae?"

"My wife has many plans these days," Kiorte interjected. "She cannot always depend on my approval. Mesor provides her support when I do not."

"Mesor is merely an adviser," Evirae answered softly. "The threat of the Fandoran army weighs heavily on my mind. It is you whom I trust in matters of state, my darling."

"The matter has gone from bad to worse," said Jibron. "The Fandorans have reached the hills that face the forest!"

Kiorte shook his head and walked slowly toward Tolchin. "Surely my brother has ordered the windships to push back the invaders!"

"Thalen has been told to do otherwise by Hawkwind. The

miner has openly defied both the General and myself!" As he turned to face the other members of the Family, Tolchin removed the diadem and jewel from a pocket in his doublet. "Perhaps this will convince you!"

Lady Eselle gasped. "You hold the Ruby!"

Alora watched her husband. "What are you doing with it, Tolchin?"

"Hawkwind sees no need to wear it. He is a renegade and a traitor."

"I find that very difficult to accept," said Kiorte as he took the jewel in his hand. "Hawkwind is loyal to Ephrion, if not to us. For what reason could he possibly risk his position by rejecting—"

"He resents the opinions of the Family!" said Jibron. "He and Vora feel they can run the affairs of Overwood without us. They have ordered Thalen to prepare a small fleet of windships to frighten off the Fandoran army in the hills. Should this prove ineffective, they will attack the Fandorans in the Kameran Valley."

Kiorte frowned. "Hawkwind plans only to use a small fleet? That is a foolish way to face them. This is a matter of war!" Kiorte wrapped one hand tightly around the jewel.

"Hawkwind wishes to protect the windships. He feels their presence in the sky will be a lure to the dragon!"

"The *dragon?* What nonsense is this? Surely you do not take a legend for truth?"

Jibron shook his head. "The dragon is more than a legend, Kiorte. I have seen it myself!"

Kiorte looked shocked. "A *dragon?* In Simbala?"

Tolchin nodded. "I think there is no longer any reason to doubt it. Vora and the others think the creature to be controlled by the Fandorans. Why else would they risk an invasion?"

"Fandorans or no Fandorans, a creature of the sky should be faced by the Brothers of the Wind!" Kiorte reached a dressing booth near the guard and said, "I must see this madness myself. How long has it been since Thalen's fleet departed for the valley?"

"Before we confronted Hawkwind," said Tolchin. "I do not think you're in any condition to overtake him."

"Darling," said Evirae from the bed, "listen to Tolchin! You need to—"

"Do not argue with me, Evirae!" Kiorte vanished behind an ornate wooden door.

Evirae tapped her nails together gently. My husband is determined to reach them, she thought. Soon we will see how long the miner can defy the Family.

"What plans does Hawkwind have for the remainder of the fleet?" Kiorte asked from the booth.

Tolchin answered. "They will remain grounded until the truth can be learned about the dragon." He continued to pace nervously in the front of the room.

"We are a match for any dragon!" said Kiorte. "Thalen would not agree to such a plan until he had conferred with me."

"Thalen thinks you missing still," said Jibron. "He has not been to the palace since you and Evirae returned to the surface. Hawkwind had sent him to the Northweald on a mission to bring back recruits."

"Recruits from the Northweald? Ruffians?"

"It meets with Vora's approval."

"It is a foolish plan."

Jibron nodded. "Hawkwind's General is a foolish man."

Evirae got up from the bed. "It seems that what we say matters little to Hawkwind. His mind is open only to Ephrion and the Rayan."

"That is why we have returned," said Tolchin. "Hawkwind must not be allowed to take Simbala into war! He knows nothing of battle!"

"He is Monarch," said Evirae. "It is his right by office."

"Then he must not be Monarch," said Tolchin gravely. "On this your father and I agree."

They looked at Kiorte as he reappeared in the uniform of the Brothers of the Wind. The Prince shook his head. "I wish to see the situation for myself first."

"There is no time!" warned Tolchin. "You of all the members of the family must understand the urgency of our action! Surely you do not favor the plan of Hawkwind and General Vora!"

"I do not," answered Kiorte, "but I will not call for their removal blindly. That is not the issue. The issue is our defense."

Jibron could barely restrain his anger. "Listen to Tolchin," he said. "It is senseless to confront the miner! He has thrown away the Ruby, he has ignored the advice of both the Baron and myself! Renounce him now! There is still time to prevent bloodshed!"

Kiorte observed the Family. He knew Jibron and Eselle favored the removal of Hawkwind. Tolchin was angry, but Kiorte had seen him angry many times. He knew Tolchin had been embarrassed by his request for the troops to the Southland. His rejection of Hawkwind could be attributed in no small measure to his own error.

Kiorte looked at Tolchin's wife, Alora. Did she agree with her husband? Although they were very close, they often argued, for between them they represented on the one hand, the interests of the merchants, and on the other, the Bursars of Simbala.

To Kiorte's surprise, he found Alora watching him. "Are you in agreement with the Family?" he inquired.

Alora smiled impartially, in the manner common to the Bursars. "A Monarch may only be removed by unanimous vote of the Family," she said, "or at the request of his predecessor. Ephrion has no interest in asking for the latter, and you reject the former. My opinion matters not."

Kiorte studied the Baroness's expression. Alora was testing him. She wanted to know if he would change his position to sway her. He would not. He glanced at Tolchin and noticed the disapproval on his face.

"Alora," Tolchin said solemnly, "whatever romantic notions you have of Hawkwind must not endanger the safety of the forest."

Alora replied placidly, "I am as worried as you are, my husband, but raising the question of Hawkwind's removal is a decision we must all consider seriously. You know there can be no vote against any Monarch unless there is evidence of treason. There is no evidence of treason concerning Hawkwind or his aides."

"What of the spy?" said Jibron. "Hawkwind did nothing about Evirae's discovery of the spy! Is that not treason?"

Alora looked at Evirae. "I believe Hawkwind never learned of the spy," she said.

Evirae reddened.

"Is that not true?" asked Alora.

"Hawkwind knew," said Evirae anxiously. "I dispatched Mesor to see Hawkwind."

Alora shook her head and addressed the others. "It does not matter. Hawkwind's inaction is no proof of treason. The spy's words could not be proven before the invasion, especially if Hawkwind had not heard them himself. If Hawkwind ignored Evirae's warning, then he was foolish, but not a traitor. He is young and inexperienced. There must be proof if I am to consider charges against him."

Alora smiled condescendingly at the Princess and said, "You may wish to find the missing spy before planning to redecorate the palace."

•

> *Fair Simbala*
> *   On battle's eve I cry,*
> *Fair Simbala*
> *   With your windships in the sky,*
> *Fair Simbala*
> *   With your forests and your sights*
> *Fair Simbala*
> *   I wish you safety through this plight.*

Willen, walking through the trees on the edge of the clearing where the ground soldiery awaited Monarch Hawkwind, had heard a strange, plaintive sound nearby. He approached it warily, thinking at first it was some forest animal, hurt and howling its misery. Then he peered from behind a tree and beheld Tweel, sitting cross-legged on the damp ground by a crackleberry bush. It was he who was responsible for that horrible sound. He had been singing and strumming a penorcon, a delicately fretted instrument constructed of paper-light strips of wood.

Other members of the Northweald contingent had also come to learn the source of the painful notes. Tweel looked up and saw Willen. He smiled broadly. "How do you like it?" he asked. "I composed it myself, as a gesture of comradeship to our allies of the Overwood!"

Willen put a finger in one ear and shook it vigorously. Then he grinned and said, "In all honesty, I think it could be considered a righteous cause of war by itself!"

Tweel's smile took on the lines of his mustache and became a grimace of disappointment. The other Northweald soldiers watched, laughing. Willen reminded himself that he was the leader of the contingent, and, as such, should keep his dignity, but he too could not help but laugh.

"You do not like my singing?" Tweel asked mournfully.

"I did not say that," Willen replied. "It would be fine were this, say, a turkey hunt. As a war song, however, it leaves everything to be desired. My friend, the way you torture that penorcon! I would sooner hear the cry of a windship's sails."

Tweel gazed sadly at the instrument. "I must find a way to coax more pleasing sounds from it."

Willen nodded. "You must indeed."

Tweel rose slowly to his feet. "Perhaps you can help me, Willen."

"*Me?*"

Tweel flashed a grin and smashed the body of the penorcon against Willen's head. There was a cracking sound as the light wooden frame shattered harmlessly.

"There!" Tweel shouted, over the laughter of those watching. "That is a more pleasant sound indeed!"

The commotion brought a red-faced captain of the Simbalese army to the scene, just in time to witness Willen seizing Tweel's tunic and spinning him about to receive a boot in the backside.

The captain stared in shock. "Cease this!" he shouted. "Monarch Hawkwind is due to arrive!"

But the laughter of the Northweald soldiers drowned out his orders, and Willen and Tweel continued their half-mock, half-serious struggle. It ended with both tripping and falling into a sizable mud puddle, much to their annoyance and to that of those about them, who were splattered by flying grime.

The captain was livid. "Bring those men to me!" he shouted as he wiped mud from his armor. "I'll see that they're—"

Whatever punishment the captain had in mind was not voiced, for at that moment, heralding horns sounded in the forest depths beyond the clearing. Willen and Tweel were forgotten as four hundred men and women of the Overwood fell quickly into ranks for the arrival of Hawkwind, Vora, and the Simbalese cavalry. They stood at attention, motionless, while officers prowled among them looking for some individual upon whom to pounce.

The Northwealdsfolk had stationed themselves to one side; they looked at the Simbalese divisions with mingled amusement and uneasiness. Rows of gleaming helmets, breastplates, and jambs caught the dim streaks of sunshine through the scattered trees. The Northwealdsfolk, wearing durable and camouflaging leather cuirasses and leggings, thought this pomp and finery ridiculous, but they had been cautioned against mocking the Overwood soldiers. Simbala could not afford animosity among the troops.

The brazen call of the horns came again, louder and nearer. In the silence that followed, the sound of horses galloping could be heard and felt. Wealdsfolk and soldiers alike watched at the edge of the clearing. A moment later a horse, dark as a shadow save for silver saddle and chamfron, charged through the woods.

Hawkwind sat tall and straight in the saddle. He wore silver armor and a cape of midnight blue. His face, despite the long ride, was pale and composed. All there were familiar with that face, and yet all felt there was a puzzling, indefinable difference about it. Then, as he rode closer, gasps of shock were heard. Hawkwind was no longer wearing the Ruby!

Those who realized this had little time to reflect upon it, however, for close behind Hawkwind came the members of the cavalry and Vora's entourage. The General brought his horse to a stop to the right and slightly behind Hawkwind, as was proper. Some of the Wealdsfolk watched Hawkwind with suspicion. He had, after all, rejected their demands of war with Fandora when Willen had informed him of the murder of their child. It had taken an invasion to change his mind. Others, however, had decided to trust Hawkwind. Even Willen viewed the decision to recruit Northwealdsfolk as a gesture of respect, such as had never been made by the Royal Family. Willen did not know why Hawkwind had forgone the Ruby, but it seemed to him a gesture of independence, which he liked.

Hawkwind reined in his snorting horse on a small rise and surveyed the troops before him. The Simbalese forces had been diminished, and his lieutenants had no real estimate of the invaders' strength, save for the number of ships that had landed. Many viewed the Fandorans as simple peasants, no longer content to be envious of the wealth and beauty of Simbala, but Hawkwind was sure that there had been a different reason for war. He could not accept the possibility that they somehow controlled the dragon and that it was the sole reason for their attack.

He had sent Thalen and three windships to the Kameran Valley. They would try to frighten the Fandorans out of the hills and into the valley, where they could be surrounded and then driven back to shore.

It was risky, of course—it exposed the windships to attack if the dragon returned—but it offered the possibility of ending the war quickly and with a minimum of bloodshed.

The troops watched him quietly. He knew they were awaiting a performance. Certain roles were expected of a monarch. Hawkwind raised his right hand for silence.

"We face an invasion of farmers and fishermen!" he shouted. "They stand no chance of reanhing the forest. This war will be over before morning." He described briefly the purpose of the windships. "We will meet the routed Fandorans in the valley and imprison all who do not flee toward shore!"

There were some cheers at this, but a young soldier, loyal to Evirae, shouted angrily, "What of the dragons? You send us against monsters with no defense!"

Hawkwind shouted back, "We have seen one dragon! We have no reason to believe that there are more. We will be prepared if it attacks again! A fleet of windships carrying Simbalese archers will be more than a match for any dragon!"

This time the cheers resounded through the clearing. Hawkwind gestured toward Vora. "General Vora will confer with the division captains. We ride now to the edge of the forest to await the completion of Thalen's maneuvers!" Hawkwind reared his horse and started toward the west as the captains of the troops came forward to receive their orders.

Willen also hurried forward, brushing the mud from his tunic. He had as much right to hear Vora's words as any captain of the army. The lives of the Wealdsfolk were also at stake. Indeed, one life had already been lost.

•

Fog, the color of despair, shrouded the Kameran Valley. On a bluff overlooking the valley and the darkened forest beyond stood the Elders of Fandora. Jondalrun, tired but alert, studied Overwood. Lagow rested uneasily against an old butterwood tree. Near him stood Tamark and Pennel.

"There is sufficient food here for the evening," said Tamark.

"True, but there are other things that frighten the men," Pennel said.

"The darkness?"

"Less the darkness than the quiet—the waiting. It is strange; not a windship in the sky, though we have seen a dozen from Fandora."

Tamark nodded philosophically. "I am sure we will see more than enough Sim before long."

Dayon joined the group, holding a small colorful lizard in his hand. "Look," he said, "if you touch its stomach, it changes colors!" He was about to demonstrate, but Jondalrun stopped him. "Drop it!" he shouted. " 'Tis a trick!"

Dayon blinked in surprise. "Father, it is but a lizard."

"Perhaps," Jondalrun said, "or perhaps it is a Sim sorcerer in disguise. Drop it."

Dayon shook his head in resignation and released the lizard, which slithered under a rock.

"You must be wary of every creature in a land of sorcerers," Jondalrun lectured sternly.

Dayon nodded, turned, and stepped away a few paces to find Lagow. "I think this land is deserted," he said.

"If you do," the wheelwright answered, "then perhaps you can convince your father that it is time to return home."

Dayon shook his head. "My father will never return home until he feels the debt is settled for my brother's murder."

Lagow frowned and looked out over the grassy hills flanked by stone precipices to the north. "There was a time when you would argue with your father, Dayon. Has the heady air of authority changed your mind, or have you been caught up in the fever of the war?"

"I stand by my father, Lagow! We must all stand by him. He's not out for glory—only justice."

"Justice," asked Lagow, "or vengeance? They are two different things. The first protects you, the second consumes you. I fear your father seeks vengeance, young man. I fear we have taken steps that will do little to protect our land or our country."

Dayon did not reply.

•

As the youngest Elder, Tenniel of Borgen Town had been given the thankless task of supervising the arrival of the remaining Fandorans from the hills to the scattered woods at the edge of the Kameran Valley. It was a difficult task, for these men were the injured, the young, and the old. Although Tenniel had lost his enthusiasm for the war, he realized the necessity of keeping the men in tight, organized ranks. He dreaded the approaching confrontation, but he took pride in the fact that he was responsible for the protection of these men.

Suddenly there was a shout from the west. Tenniel glanced quickly through the fog. There was shouting on the other side of a nearby hill. He ran quickly up it, dreading the possibility of an attack so soon by the Simbalese.

He reached the top of the hill and saw, to his surprise, a young man clad in black and white, posing in a graceful posture before a group of applauding men.

"What are you doing?" Tenniel shouted.

The young man smiled, did two pirouettes, and stopped within a foot of Tenniel. "Dancing!" he replied spritely.

Tenniel frowned. "You are distracting the men."

"Nonsense! I am uplifting their spirits!"

Tenniel squinted at the man's white makeup and mask. He was one of the few Dancers that had joined the army. Tenniel had seen the troupe from Tamberly Town board a ship together. The Dancers traveled and performed in groups, yet this fellow seemed to be alone.

"I don't remember you," said Tenniel.

"Nor I you," answered the young man.

"Are you from Borgen Town?"

"I am from Fandora."

Tenniel frowned. Several of the men watching snickered,

which did nothing to improve his temper. "See here," he said sternly, "we approach a confrontation with the Simbalese. There is no room for fools or braggarts in this army. You can be sent back to the shore!"

"I am needed here!" said the young man. He did a short leap away from Tenniel. "Your soldiers are as sad as orphans. My work provides a moment's diversion."

Tenniel was growing angry. It was not the first time he had been defied during the course of this war, but he intended it to be the last. "We need dancing even less than we need this fog!" he said.

"We need this fog," the Dancer retorted. "It hides us from the Simbalese."

"Do not tell me about the Simbalese! I am an Elder of Borgen Town!"

The Dancer grinned. "A man as young as you is an Elder?" he teased. "Tra-la!" Spinning away, he broke into a dash for the bottom of the hill.

"Catch him!" Tenniel shouted. Several men tried to grab the running figure, but the Dancer eluded them easily and disappeared into the fog.

Tenniel grumbled angrily and hurried back toward the top of the hill. As he reached it, he gazed out over the Simbalese forest. In the fog, it looked like a strange green sea. He shuddered. He hoped Jondalrun would not order them to enter there for the night.

Tenniel headed down quickly toward his contingent, but as he did, he glimpsed a rippling in the fog over the trees. There was something in the sky, something large, moving slowly toward the valley. There was a moment of recognition, and then terror.

Tenniel turned toward his men and shouted, "Take cover! A windship approaches!"

•

Six hundred men watched from the mist below them. Thalen had sent up flags signaling the other two craft to circle around the hills. He planned to fly his one-man ship directly over the Fandorans. Looking down, he could see a ragged band of farmers and fishermen hiding on the edge of the hill. They are frightened, he thought. Perhaps Hawkwind's plan would work.

•

Jondalrun stared nervously at the windships, their colorful sails jutting brightly through the fog. "We were smart to
order the men back into the hills," he said. "If they are
unable to see us, we will be safe from attack."

Tamark shook his head. "They will attempt to drive us out
into the open, Jondalrun. Then they will attack."

"That is my thought, too," said Lagow. "We are easy
targets."

Jondalrun glared at him for a moment; then a slight,
almost rueful smile creased his rumpled face. "We will not
strike the first blow," he said. "Nor will we rush back to the
shore in defeat." He looked at Dayon, ordering a few
stragglers behind the cover of a granite ridge. "We have
come this far, and now will wait them out."

The windships continued their approach, separating to
surround the Fandorans. They seemed serenely indifferent,
as though those who flew them were superior to the
ground-locked humans hidden in the hills. Onward they
came, their prows scudding through the mist like boats
parting the ocean's foam.

Mutterings and shouts of fear broke out among the Fandorans. "Stay where you are!" Pennel shouted, and the other
Elders echoed his order. "Their magic cannot harm us—we
carry the protection of the witch!"

Yet, when faced with the terrifying sight of the airborne
ships, not all of the men were able to put their faith in the
tiny wristlets. Thalen's windship passed over them at a
height of thirty feet, and a wavering cry of fear broke from a
cluster of soldiers on the hill below. Jondalrun looked toward the forest again. Through the fog he saw another,
smaller windship appear across the valley. "Caution the
men!" he shouted. "Remain hidden. Do not attack!"

●

Kiorte's windship flew swiftly above the forest. The wind
and the freedom invigorated him; the frustrating confrontations with Evirae and the Family had made him ready for
adventure. He had no doubt of Thalen's ability to lead the
troops; still, he was their commander, and it was right that
he be in the forefront of the fighting.

For all his eagerness to arrive, however, he flew cautiously, and close to the treetops. He could no longer take

the rumors of the dragon as unsubstantiated—too many people said they had seen it. But even if the Fandorans somehow commanded such a beast, it would not change the battle's outcome. Kiorte could see the valley through the mist now. Hovering over the hills on the far side were three windships. As he sailed closer, Kiorte could see men—short, barbarously clad men, with primitive weapons—moving about in disorganized panic. Kiorte gave a short, disdainful laugh. These tatterdemalions were the threat to Simbala? They would be swimming home before darkness fell! He watched them milling about, obviously panicked by Thalen's small fleet. The battle would be over quickly, and with a minimum of casualties. Then there would be time for a reckoning with Hawkwind. The miner had had no right to order the grounding of the Brothers of the Wind without consulting him first. Jibron and Tolchin were correct. Hawkwind would not defy the Family without consequence.

•

The word spread quickly from patches of brush under which Steph and Jurgan hid, to a butternut tree where the Wayman leaned patiently. Through his good eye he spied the three ships over the valley. In the center was the smallest, manned by a single rider, and it headed straight toward the hills. The other two veered off, one ship to the north, one ship to the south, most likely to drive them back from three directions.

All about him, there was panic. The Elders had succeeded in keeping the men from dashing back toward the shore, and ordered most of them to take cover in the ravines and copses around them.

A burly man dashed past the Wayman, who put out a foot almost casually and tripped him. The man rolled over, shouting, and the Wayman pulled him to his feet.

"If you run out into the open, the Simbalese will find you," he warned, and he pushed the man into the shadow of the tree.

The man nodded nervously, and did his best to imitate the gnarled trunk. The Wayman turned his one good eye back to the sky. The small windship was almost directly overhead.

•

Tenniel and his small band had not reached the main encampment when the windships appeared. Uninformed of Jondalrun's plan to wait, they hid quickly on the far side of the hills, with little more than fog for cover. They cowered as the windship passed overhead. It seemed to be coming lower. There was no question but that its occupant could see them. Tenniel gripped his ax, listening to the moans of fear from those about him. He was responsible for these men. They were too old, too young, or too injured to face an attack of a windship. Something had to be done. He stared up at the windship looming out of the gray fog above them. Why had not Jondalrun ordered an attack by now?

He lifted the ax. "Someone has to begin it," he whispered out loud. Then, with all his strength, he cast the ax at the windship above him.

The men about him watched as the weapon hurtled through the mist and the ship's foresail and vanished from view. For a long moment there was no sound. The dark shape drifted silently onward. Then, suddenly, from the deck, there was a burst of orange flame.

Several men shouted in panic, convinced that the Simbalese were casting fire from the windship. Then the mist cleared, and they saw flame climbing rapidly up the sails. Tenniel shouted in relief. The ship was burning! He had struck the first blow, and it had been effective. At last, he would be a hero!

•

"Thalen!" Kiorte cried uselessly, as he saw the forward balloon sail of Thalen's ship billow and collapse. A drift of fog hid the scene for a moment, and when it cleared he could see flames climbing quickly up the sail and across the ropes to other sails. An arrow, a spear, an ax—something—had ripped open a sail, and the sagging material had come in contact with the Sindril brazier. The windship, its buoyancy fading as the ribbed sections deflated, began to drop toward the ground.

There was the sound of the troops below him, charging across the valley. As long as the ship was in the air, Thalen could still be rescued by windship. Even a crash would not keep him from his brother. Nor a thousand Fandorans. Nor a dragon. Not while Thalen was still alive.

•

Hawkwind looked grimly at the distant orange trail fading in the mist. Thalen could be injured, or worse. They had to rescue the ship.

He had hoped to defeat the farmers without battle, but the Fandorans were apparently set on war. They had made the first assault, and had done so without warning.

Hawkwind reared his horse and faced the men and women in the clearing behind him. "Give the order," he shouted to Vora. "Summon the captains! We shall rescue Corporal Thalen!"

Troubled by the knowledge of what bloodshed would bring, the dark-eyed miner rode quickly toward the hills beyond the valley.

•

From the hills the Fandoran army stared at the threat moving toward them through the valley. It would be only minutes before the Simbalese army reached the hills.

"How shall we protect ourselves?" Lagow said angrily. "They are sending soldiers on horseback! This is your fault, Jondalrun. Tenniel should never have been left alone with those men!"

Jondalrun turned to the wheelwright and said, "Silence! You must help!"

"Help? This is madness. We should retreat through the cover of the fog while there is still a chance."

Jondalrun shook his head. "No! They must be shown that we are not frightened by their windships or their army."

"At the cost of our lives?"

"No!" said Jondalrun. He clutched Dayon's arm. "Pass the word to the men. Tell them to stay hidden in the woods as we had planned." He faced Lagow again. "To kill us, the Simbalese must find us. We have lost the chance to surprise them, but we are still blessed with cover."

The words had reason, but they had come too late.

From the top of the hill they heard a call to arms, and then suddenly a panicked section of the Fandoran army charged forward.

"There's no stopping them!" said Pennel. "They are frightened and hungry. They have journeyed far."

Jondalrun nodded angrily. "We have little alternative.

They rally for justice and the security of our land. Give the order: we advance!"

"No order is necessary!" Tamark replied. "We must hurry after them to give them what orders we can!"

•

Followed by the boy and the girl, Amsel ducked through an archway of the small park. The children were becoming a problem! Although they still thought him to be a child, their suspicion was growing. The boy, whose name was Willow, had repeatedly asked Amsel where he lived. Only by keeping in motion had Amsel continued to evade the question. The girl, on the other hand, had proved to be a good source of information. From her he had learned not only the location of the palace but also more about Hawkwind and the woman known as Ceria.

At the edge of the park Amsel noticed a low stone ledge. Four feet below it was a marble pathway that headed back toward the river. If the young girl was correct, it would connect with a path to a broad walk lined with enormous trees. If he followed these trees to the east, he would be back near the center of the forest.

"Tell us where you live!" said Willow, leaping in front of Amsel. "I want to know now!" He aimed the spear in Amsel's path.

Woni pushed it away. "Where are you going?" she asked Amsel sweetly. "Why won't you tell us who you are?"

Amsel hopped quickly from the stone ledge to a marble pathway four feet below it.

"Wait!" the boy cried.

Amsel looked back at them sternly. "My friends are in danger!" he warned. "I must be going!"

"Don't go that way!" Willow shouted. "That's the way the dragon went!"

Dragon? thought Amsel. The child must be younger than he looks, to still believe in dragons.

"Why won't you tell us your name?" asked Willow again.

"I don't have the time," Amsel said. "I must be leaving." He turned and hurried down the path.

Willow watched Amsel depart. "Do you know what I think?" he said to Woni.

"What?"

"I think that's the person the guards wanted to find."

"The guards in the plaza? They're looking for a Fandoran, Willow!"

The boy nodded cautiously. "I know. I think that's him."

The girl looked keenly at Amsel as he turned a corner on the ledge. "I don't think so," she said softly. "He's just a boy."

Willow shook his head and replied, "When did you ever see a boy with wrinkles? I think we ought to tell my grandfather about him."

•

The Simbalese advanced quickly. The fog was quite thick in places now; a white ground mist was everywhere. The flaming windship was a dull orange glow in the fog; then it burst through the low-hanging clouds. Hawkwind, riding at the vanguard of his charging troops, could see that Thalen had thrown the anchor rope over the side. The hooks dragged along the ground, ripping up rocks and grass, and then caught in a small bush. Thalen swung quickly out onto the rope and began letting himself down, hand over hand. The craft itself was burning now—in a moment, the rope would catch fire. The Fandorans hurried forward, shouting and whooping. They meant to take the Windrider prisoner—or worse, Hawkwind thought. "We cannot let him fall into their hands!" he shouted, spurring his horse forward. But he knew he could not reach the windship in time.

•

The other windships were moving back toward Thalen's craft, but they were going slowly, having to tack against the wind at their higher altitude. But Kiorte was going with the wind, and his was a lighter craft. Though he had a farther distance to go, he nevertheless reached Thalen's ship before any of the Simbalese.

He fitted a bolt in his crossbow and sighted down at the Fandorans below. Through swirling patches of fog he could see Thalen climbing down the length of the anchor rope, while the burning windship settled. It was a mass of flame now, a yellow-and-red pyre. The rope was burning as well, but Thalen reached the ground safely.

The nearest Fandoran was less than a hundred yards away. Already Kiorte could see arrows beginning to fly toward his brother.

"They shall not have you, Thalen," he murmured, and released the trigger.

Tenniel was foremost in the charge toward the fallen windship. He was shouting, a wordless cry of exuberance. His action had precipitated the fighting, and now, at last, things were going as they should. Now battle was joined, and the glorious dreams he had had in what seemed like another life might still be real. He ran forward, leaping from rock to grassy hillock, dodging trees, leading his men into battle, as it should be. Now there was no more question about who was right and who was wrong.

The burning windship he glimpsed as he passed it. No longer an awesome thing of sorcery, an unconquerable behemoth of the air, it crumbled to smoldering embers. Ahead was its pilot. The misty ground was too dotted with trees and copses for an arrow shot to bring him down; he dodged from tree to rock to gully, not presenting a clear target. But it did not matter—he would not reach the safety of the Simbalese army. He, Tenniel, would overtake him and finish the job he had started.

He drew his knife and held it like a sword as he gained on the fleeing Sim. And then pain burst like flame in his right shoulder. His knife fell from a suddenly nerveless grasp, and he fell too, rolling over onto his shoulder. The pain was unbearable from the start, and falling onto it made it infinitely worse. It hurt more than anything else had ever hurt him, even the time when his leg had been caught between the spokes of his father's cartwheel and broken like a twig. Tenniel screamed. The rolling and the fall and the pain seemed to go on forever. Eventually the world steadied beneath him. He felt with his left hand; an arrow protruded from his shoulder. He had barely realized this when a fresh burst of pain in his side tore another scream from him. At first he thought he had been shot again; then he realized he had been kicked by a boot. Men were running past him, all about him, not noticing him in the ground mist, anxious to reach the enemy. Another stepped on his lower back, and another tripped and stumbled across his wounded arm. Tenniel screamed again, and began to pull himself forward with his good arm. Through the mist, a few feet away, a large rock loomed. Toward this he dragged himself, his wounded arm trailing uselessly. It seemed to take an eternity before he reached the mossy shelter of the overhanging rock. There he crouched, feeling cold water drip upon him. Red drums of pain beat in his ears, through them he could faintly hear the clangor of weapons and the shouts and cries of war. The two armies had met. The battle had finally begun, he thought bitterly, and already he was out of it.

"It's not fair," he whimpered as the last of the men ran past him into the fog. Then he was alone, save for the sounds of the battle—and the pain.

●

From his vantage point, Kiorte could see that fog covered the entire western end of the valley, and an eddying tendril of it was threatening to obscure the coming clash. He was finding it hard to keep Thalen and the Fandorans in sight. He had been firing arrows steadily at the latter, but had hit only a few men. Still, that had been enough to cause local pockets of confusion that had slowed the charge as a whole. But not enough—Thalen would still be overtaken before he reached safety. Kiorte turned his windship into the wind, tacking against it, following his brother's course. He was perhaps twenty feet from the ground, just above the gray layer of fog, when a long rift opened, and below him was Thalen, running. Not fifty feet behind him came a young Fandoran soldier, with mattock upraised. Kiorte tossed a rope overboard. "Thalen!" he shouted. Thalen looked up as the windship passed over him, the rope dangling from it. He put on a burst of speed and leaped. The mist closed in at that moment, but Kiorte could tell by the way the rope stiffened that his brother was climbing it. A moment later, Thalen burst through the mist, climbing steadily, hand over hand. Kiorte reached over the side and grabbed him by the arms. The craft tilted dangerously as he pulled his brother aboard.

"Close, by all counts!" Thalen gasped. He collapsed against the low cabin, breathing heavily, his arms and side muscles trembling.

"Close," Kiorte agreed. "But you are safe now."

"Those vermin," Thalen whispered. "They destroyed my ship—part of my life. I built her myself."

"I know," Kiorte said softly. The love of a Windrider for his craft was something impossible to explain to a groundfellow—but no words were necessary between the two of them. "I shall return behind the lines," Kiorte said after a moment. "Our Brothers will take over now." He watched the other two windships coming in behind him.

"Little good they can do in this fog," Thalen said. "Also, there is the dragon to be considered, Kiorte. If it appears—"

"Again this talk of a dragon! I have heard hysterical fragments in Overwood of it."

"It is true," Thalen said. "I saw it! A monster with a wingspan twice the width of our sails!"

"Might there not be some more rational explanation? Perhaps the Fandorans are not so primitive as we thought . . . perhaps they have flying craft as well—"

"Kiorte, this creature was alive—make no mistake. I saw its muscles flexing its wings, and I saw the awful fire of its eyes. It was a dragon!"

Kiorte looked at his brother. Tired and upset as Thalen was, Kiorte knew that he was not lying.

"Very well, then," he said. "Raise the flags—tell the other ships to resume their waiting position among the trees. We can do no good out here now."

"What of us?"

"We are going down behind the lines," Kiorte said grimly. "I must have words with Hawkwind."

●

Amsel hurried along the narrow marble walkway by the river. The children suspect something, he thought. The Princess must have sent Waymen to find me by now.

He shielded his eyes from the afternoon sun and looked down the luminescent walkway. Large orange berries from the bushes overhead had stained the marble. Amsel scooped up a ripe-looking sample.

Hookberries, he thought, but unlike any color I have seen!

He tasted one of them; it was succulent and filled with seeds. "These can hold me for a while," he murmured, "at least until I can reach the palace."

He recalled his mission and somehow kept moving, eating as he walked. Soon he was at the end of the marble path. It stopped at a winding flight of stone steps that climbed a hill. Up them he went, but slowly, for the steps were steep, and he was exhausted. The stairs were lined with thick, heavily scented bushes, and the perfumed air made his head spin. He stopped for a moment to rest. As he sat on the steps, he suddenly heard the sound of footsteps from the top of the stairs. The winding route of the staircase and the thick bushes prevented him from seeing who was coming, but the rattle and clank of trappings and armor told him plainly.

"Oh, no!" he moaned. "Waymen!" He looked back and realized there was no place to hide. The stairs ran in clear view to the marble path, and the marble path ran next to the river. He was *not* returning to the river.

"I don't know what the fuss is with this spy!" echoed a voice from the top of the stairs. "The farmers will be no match for the army! This fool can do little to upset things in Overwood."

"The Princess is obsessed with finding him," said another. "Something tells me he's worth more than the reward she's offered."

"No matter," said the first, "it's better than following Hawkwind into the valley. I've no taste for battle, even with the Fandorans!"

Amsel listened closely. If these men were correct, then the battle might not have started yet. There could still be time.

"Come this way!" said the first voice. "We'd better check the river."

They came into view—two large soldiers with scabbarded swords by their sides, wearing helmets and hauberks that gleamed dully in the cloudy daylight. They saw Amsel the same time he saw them, and they both stopped, surprised into immobility for a moment.

Amsel did the only thing he could think of to disconcert them. He ran straight in their direction. There's a reward on me, he thought. They wouldn't hurt me. I hope!

He dodged around the first soldier, but by then the other one had drawn his word, which was almost as long as Amsel. A second later the rasp of metal sounded behind him as well.

"Come peacefully," the guard in front of him said, "or you will look even shorter without your head."

Amsel nodded. "You can put that away," he said. "I'm a reasonable man."

The first guard grunted. "That's better," he said, but he did not sheathe his sword. Amsel felt a sharp jab in his back. "Move!" said the guard behind him. "The Princess wants to see you."

They started up the stairs again, Amsel between the two

guards. This may have its merits, thought Amsel; at least I'll have an escort back to the palace grounds.

The guards in front of him hurried over the top of the staircase and headed toward a path shadowed by large trees.

"If they take me within sight of the palace," Amsel murmured, "all I will have to do is escape them and find that fellow Hawkwind." He looked ahead at the giant guard and realized that was easier said than done.

The stairs led to another walkway, which wound through small wooden buildings and large trees into which had been built homes and markets. Children wearing ragged clothes played in the streets, watched by men and women who were too old to be their parents.

Their fathers are off to war, Amsel thought, and their mothers as well. How strange! A land where the women are also responsible for defense.

He saw the meager furnishings through the windows of the tree homes, and remembered their opulent counterparts in the center of the forest. This, it seemed, was a poorer section of Simbala.

This area soon gave way to a larger street, which was lined with shops and open-air market stalls. Evidently there had once been a gathering or procession of considerable size here, for there were banners and colorful strips of thin paper on the trees. Most of the marketplaces were closed now, and those that were open were largely empty of shoppers. Across the width of the street, from tree to tree, had been strung a complicated network of tansel, from which lanterns and other banners swung gently in the wind.

Amsel stared up at the crisscrossings of rope they were passing under, his gaze tracing the complicated patterns. Then suddenly he saw another sight beyond them. In the distance, partly obscured by the trees that lined this avenue, and the other, larger trees in view, Amsel glimpsed the center of Overwood, and in their midst, the giant tree that was the palace! He knew which way to go now, but how was he to escape from these guards?

A possible answer occurred to him. He looked again at the ropes above them. Despite their complexity, they seemed to be anchored only at two major points, doubtless to facilitate removal of the lanterns and banners. Amsel frowned, trying to trace out the anchor points before they passed beneath the huge web.

There! He had it! The second point was roped securely to a large oak, ahead and to the left.

He had no time to lose. He suddenly doubled up, grabbing his knees and tucking his head in, making himself as small as possible. The guard following him did not realize what had happened until he had stumbled over Amsel, staggering forward with a cry. Amsel grabbed the dagger from the guard's belt, turned, and ran toward the oak.

"Get up, you butter-handed oaf!" the first guard shouted to the second. "He's getting away!" The first guard ran after Amsel. Fortunately, the inventor did not have far to go, or he would have been overtaken almost immediately. He reached the tree, and with a slash of the dagger cut loose the thin yet strong tansel line that held half of the supporting lines in place. The ropes overhead collapsed, entangling both of the guards as they ran toward him. Shouts of rage and crashes of shattering clay lanterns reached Amsel's ears as he slipped the dagger into the sheath at his belt and climbed quickly into the tree. He did not stop to look back, but kept climbing until the foliage hid him from the ground below.

Heart pounding, he looked about, and saw that the trees grew so closely together that the branches were interwoven. For the first time in a long trial, Amsel felt at home. He could proceed with relative safety and much less chance of being caught through the canopy, and travel almost as fast as he would have on the winding paths below.

He could still hear the guards faintly as they shouted instructions and imprecations to each other. He smiled wryly. "If only I could be that clever all the time," he murmured, "then perhaps I wouldn't find myself so often in situations where I need to be."

He began moving with quickness and agility through the branches, toward the center of the forest.

●

Hawkwind had split the army into three divisions. The first, the infantry, would meet the Fandoran attack head-on. The second, the cavalry, divided under the lead of Vora and himself, would circle about and attack from the rear. The third, composed of Wealdsfolk and volunteers, would remain near the forest, to hold against any Fandorans who were able to get through the lines.

The Simbalese infantry advanced swiftly in orderly ranks, viewing with contempt the wild, undisciplined approach of the Fandorans, but as the fog closed in, they realized that, undisciplined or not, the Fandorans were definitely a threat. They had considered the demise of the windship as evidence that they were immune to the magic they thought their opponents wielded. Now they were venting all the pent-up frustration that had accumulated over the weeks—the torture of the crossing, the misery and discomfort. Now, at last, they had something tangible and human to strike out against.

That first wild chaos lasted only a short time. Hawkwind and Vora, completing the encircling movement, found themselves plunged into a sea of howling men, holding all manner of weapons, clad in piecemeal armor and protected by skin-and-wood shields, attacking without rhyme or reason. There was slight hesitation on the part of some of the Fandorans when they realized that Simbalese women, as well as men, faced them, but the battle fever ran too high for that to matter long. Hawkwind's battle-trained horse did not falter as the fighting closed about them. A Fandoran soldier struck at Hawkwind, wielding a mattock; the horse reared and kicked the makeshift weapon from the farmer's hands with its front hooves. Another man, wearing a blacksmith's apron, leaped upon the rear of the saddle, trying to stab Hawkwind. Hawkwind struck him in the face, loosening his grip, and his horse bucked, throwing the Fandoran to the ground. Hawkwind leaped the horse over him; the noble beast responded so well and so quickly to his commands that they seemed to be joined together as a single creature. But there were others to continue the attack, and the miner's sword was red more than once.

The fighting moved back and forth across the narrow width of the valley, neither side gaining ground for more than a short time. The fighting was primarily hand-to-hand; there was neither time nor room to load and wind the crossbows. The Northwealdsfolk scorned the complicated weapons, preferring the longbow, but the fog, obscuring vision and wetting the bowstrings, made them useless as well. And so the battle raged with swords, pikes, knives, and axes, fiercely and without quarter.

Hawkwind turned his horse and saw a group of Fandorans besieging a smaller detachment of Simbalese. The Fandorans were led by a fierce old man with flowing white hair and beard now spattered with red. "For Fandora!" he shouted, wielding a sword. "For Johan!" Hawkwind spurred his horse toward him. Jondalrun saw him coming, and realized by his fine armor that this man must be a leader among the enemy. He raised his sword and struck at Hawkwind. Hawkwind parried the blow, amazed at the old man's strength. For an instant they stared into each other's eyes, Hawkwind seeing the inexplicable fury that drove Jondalrun, and Jondalrun, even in that fury, wondering why he saw no malice in Hawkwind's gaze, but only surprise and puzzlement. Then a new wave of fighting soldiers surged between them, separating and masking them in the fog.

The fog was thickening rapidly now. It was difficult to tell just when the Fandorans abandoned their attack. No formal retreat was sounded; but, by that mysterious telepathy common to mobs, the majority of the Fandorans were soon running instead of fighting. That first madness had run its course, and they suddenly realized that they were surrounded by soldiers far superior to them. Rage was replaced by panic, and what little organization there had been vanished as they ran.

The fog aided their retreat. The encircling cavalry could not contain them; in small groups they slipped between the horses, beneath the swords, crouching low and running through the thick ground mist that hid them. Hawkwind reined his horse up next to Vora's as he realized what was happening.

"We must regroup!" Vora shouted. "This fog has taken them from us!"

"You are right," Hawkwind replied. "Have the bugler sound the orders! Ready a contingent to march what prisoners we have back across the valley to the forest!"

He turned his horse then, and plunged into the gathering mist. He could still hear the sound of swords ringing on scythes and harrow blades, as the fighting continued here and there. As long as there was battle, he owed it to his soldiers to be among them.

•

Dayon had convinced Jondalrun to retreat when the rout
had begun. The old farmer sat now on a log, not far from the
hills. The fog wreathed him in gray. He had been injured: a
bolt from a Simbalese crossbow had grazed the palm of his
right hand. Dayon sat beside him, bandaging the wound.
Pennel sat on the other side of him. Other wounded lay all
about. Several physicians were doing their best to tend
them, sprinkling balms of crushed herbs on the wounds and
setting broken limbs with splints made of sticks and vines.
Groans of agony filled the air. Jondalrun pulled his hand
from Dayon.

"I can finish wrapping this myself," he growled. "Surely
there are others who need tending more."

"Not at the moment," Dayon replied, "although I expect
more to appear at any time."

Jondalrun stared into the fog, listening to the ominous
silence. "What happens now?" he said softly, as though to
himself.

"The Simbalese will regroup," Pennel replied. "They will
sweep the valley, picking off our men as they find them. Our
only chance is to retreat to the hills and hope that the rest of
the men do so as well."

"Perhaps we should regroup as well," Jondalrun mused.
"The fog shields us. If we could break through their line—"

"Our men are lost in the fog!" Dayon cried. "How could
we regroup them? We have no buglers to rally them. We
have no choice but to retreat! If we are to fight at all, we
must take advantage of the fog and return to the hills!"

Jondalrun put one hand to his head, and for a moment
Dayon and Pennel were afraid he was going to faint. "None
of this is going right," Jondalrun said. "I think now that
none of us ever really believed in the possibility of dying
here." He raised his head and looked about at the wounded,
strewn over the field, mist rising about them like souls
struggling to be free.

Dayon looked too. "This is the price of revenge," he said
softly. "Your revenge. For your son and my brother."

After a long silence, Jondalrun said, so softly that they
could barely hear him, "How can it be stopped?"

"It cannot," Pennel said. "Not now. We have attacked, and
we must either win or be slaughtered. But we will not win

this way. We must retreat to the hills and regroup. There we can hold them off."

Jondalrun rose slowly to his feet. "You are right," he said gruffly. "I did not want to leave the hills in the first place. Cursed be that fool that struck down the windship, whoever he may be!" He looked at them. "Come—let us gather what men we can, to carry the wounded. We are returning to the hills."

He will not even use the word "retreat," Dayon thought. No matter. We are retreating—that is all that is important.

•

Groups of soldiers from both sides moved warily through the fog, gripping their weapons, both hoping for and dreading the appearance of the enemy in the mist. One such group was being led by Tamark. The fog had confused his sense of direction; he hoped he was leading his men back toward the hills. Like many other Elders, he was attempting to salvage as many soldiers as he could from the aftermath of the berserker attack.

He led them through the fog as slowly and silently as possible. He was not looking for another battle. His plan was to return to the relative safety of the hills. After that, they would discuss what had to be done. For now, he was looking no further than the retreat he was leading, and hoping it would pass without incident.

His hopes were soon dashed, however. Suddenly, through the fog before him loomed a line of figures, dressed in fine armor, crossing his path at right angles. The two groups of soldiers heard and saw each other simultaneously. Tamark heard excited shouts and the sound of swords leaving scabbards.

They had no choice but to fight, he realized. He drew his sword and shouted, "For Fandora!" But the battle cry sounded false to him. I may die in the next few minutes, he thought, and I am not even sure what it will be for.

Then the Simbalese charged toward them, and the two groups joined in battle.

•

The group Tamark had stumbled across was led by General Vora, and was marching prisoners back toward the forest. They had no particular desire to encounter more Fandorans, but when Vora saw the raggedy band emerge from the mist, he knew he had to attack first. Their only chance was to overcome this new obstacle before the prisoners realized a chance of rescue had come their way.

But the Fandoran who led this band was more intelligent than the howling berserkers that had attacked the Simbalese at first. A huge bald-headed man, he drew his sword quickly, rallying his men with a cry, and leaped forward to meet Vora's attack. Vora, mindful of Hawkwind's orders to take prisoners whenever possible, sought to disarm Tamark. But his foot slipped in a patch of mud, and he stumbled. Instantly the Fandoran was upon him, knocking aside his blade and thrusting for his throat. Vora ducked beneath the outstretched sword and tackled the Fandoran. They fell over together, rolling amid the shouting, cursing soldiers who battled about them. Vora drove his knee into the bald one's stomach, knocking the wind out of him. He was gasping for breath himself—it had been many years since he had gone through this kind of exertion. They were fighting in a very dense area of fog; the Fandoran was half-concealed by the ground mist. Vora broke free and heaved himself to his feet. As he did so, another Fandoran soldier appeared out of the fog, brandishing a knife. Vora turned, but a moment too late; he felt a sharp pain in his side as the soldier hurtled against him, knocking him off balance. Vora fell. Momentarily dazed, he watched the second soldier tug at the bald one, lifting the latter to his knees. Then they both stumbled away into the fog.

Vora looked about him. The ground was covered with men and women, wounded or dead. Shouts came from all about him. A Simbalese soldier appeared by his side and helped him to his feet.

"You are bleeding, General!" she said. "I will make a bandage."

"Let it be," Vora growled. "Why do you think I carry such a generous surplus of fat? It takes a long sword to reach my vitals." He held his hand over the shallow wound.

"The prisoners attacked us from behind, sir," the soldier said. "We were caught between the two groups. We lost all but one prisoner."

Vora looked about him. Everywhere was the fog, masking both friend and enemy. "I see," he said, and sighed. "I will have that bandage," he told her. He stared into the mist. The battle continues out there, he thought. And now I begin to fear its outcome.

•

Many of the main streets of Simbala were deserted as a result of the dragon and the war. The royal coach reached the riverbank quickly. Two small children and a tall elderly man were waiting there, along with several guards.

Evirae looked at the children as the coach pulled up. She smiled. They looked so young and free of guile—their very appearance was refreshing to her. "The children saw the Fandoran?" she asked.

Tolchin nodded. "They told the boy's grandfather of the incident, but he was not present at the time. They are the only witnesses."

Evirae smiled and clapped her hands. The curtain of the coach slid back, and she carefully descended. She wore a long purple dress, blue cape, and silver tiara.

At the edge of the park, Woni watched in wonder. "It's the Princess!" she said. "She looks so beautiful!"

Willow nervously stabbed at the grass with his spear's rubber tip. "She looks funny," he said. "Why is her hair all piled up like that?"

"Hush!" his grandfather whispered. As Evirae stopped before them, he continued nervously, "Good afternoon, Princess. I hope we can be of help."

Evirae nodded to him and smiled at the children. She put out a hand to pat Woni's head. The girl instinctively recoiled from the gleaming nails, and Evirae withdrew the gesture, biting her lip. "You are lovely children," she said cheerfully.

"I'm a boy," Willow said. "I'm not lovely."

Evirae nodded consolingly. "I only meant it as an expression of affection."

The boy blushed and mumbled, "What do you want to know?"

"You saw the Fandoran spy," Evirae replied. "What did he look like?"

The grandfather held Willow at his side. "From what he told me, Princess, the fellow he saw was as small as a boy, but with the face of a man."

"He had hair like cotton!" said Woni. "Like a cotton ball!"

Evirae nodded enthusiastically. "That is he!"

Willow, unwilling to be upstaged by his friend, said, "He went down the path to the stairs. He told us not to follow him!"

Evirae mused, "He is no doubt on his way to spy on the palace. I will have to alert the guards."

Woni tugged on Evirae's gown and said, "He told us he had to help his friends."

"I'm sure he did," said Evirae, "but *you* have helped Simbala." She faced Willow's grandfather. "How may I thank you for what you have done?"

The man smiled. "I wish little, Princess. Ask the children. It is they who have helped you."

Evirae turned back to Woni and Willow. "Tell me," she whispered, "what would you like if you could have anything in Simbala?"

The boy beamed excitedly. "A javelin! Like the ones used by the palace guards!"

Evirae shook her head. "Those are too dangerous for a boy as young as you, but I will see that you have a toy javelin more beautiful than any you have seen." She turned to look at Woni. "What about you, my little princess? What would you desire?"

Woni grinned shyly. "More than *anything* else?"

Evirae laughed. "Name it and it is yours!"

Woni leaned her head against Willow's grandfather and in a small voice said, "Can I meet Lady Ceria?"

The warm color drained from Evirae's cheeks. Softly, with more pain than anger, she turned away from the children, walking stiffly back to the coach without another word.

Woni called after Evirae in confusion, but Willow's grandfather put his hand on her shoulder and said, "Sometimes a Princess is a hard person to understand."

Evirae entered the coach and addressed the driver in a sharp tone. Alora glanced at her. "You seemed to be enjoying yourself," she said. "What happened?"

Evirae lifted her chin and stared out the window at Willow and Woni. "They were children," she said. "I only attempted to overcome their fear of speaking to royalty. According to what they have told me, the Fandoran is already on his way to the palace!"

Tolchin looked alarmed. "We'd best hurry back."

Evirae nodded. "Yes. Perhaps it would be better if I watched the roads myself."

●

In the highest reaches of the palace, Monarch Ephrion waited for word of Hawkwind's encounter with the Fandorans. His rooms, on the inner rim of a wide circular hallway, were not far from the small private chamber of Lady Ceria.

Decorated with long pastel tapestries, the corridor wound through the hardened trunk of the palace tree. It was silent, for the hour touched on early morning and the sentries who guarded the upper floors had been called upon to join in the defense of the forest. The task of keeping vigil over the remaining occupants of the palace had fallen to a handful of guards on the lower levels.

It was for this reason that Ephrion rose with concern at the sound of tapping outside his door. Cautiously he opened the door a crack and peered out.

In the muted light of the corridor outside, he saw Lady Ceria struggling past a large beige tapestry in his direction. Even as he opened the door, she put a hand to her head and swayed. Ephrion rushed forward and caught her, supporting the weight of her body with difficulty.

"You should not have risen!" he scolded softly. "Not after what happened to you in the library hall! You have been unconscious for the better part of a day!"

The Minister of the Interior shook her head sleepily and whispered, "A dream—I have had a most disturbing dream. It is urgent that I tell you and Hawkwind about it."

"Hawkwind has gone to the battlefront," said Ephrion.

Ceria looked astonished. "He left without summoning me?"

"You were unconscious, my lady."

Ceria nodded weakly. "We must talk," she said. Ephrion helped her step inside, nudging the door closed with his shoulder. By the time they crossed the front chamber, Ceria had recovered sufficiently to walk by herself.

As Ephrion escorted her into his study, she gasped at the beauty of the high circular room. It was illuminated by a dozen candles, which threw wavering shadows across the walls and furniture. In one corner was a broad rosewood desk, piled high with books and scrolls. On the floor were ancient maps carefully arranged by location. Candleholders sat upon their curling edges. Pages of notes had been attached by sealing wax to the wall, to make their reading easier.

Ephrion helped her to a large pillow-strewn couch. She sank gratefully into the cushions, "I am sorry for distracting you from your studies," she whispered, "but I must talk of what I have seen. First, however, tell me—has there been any word from Hawkwind?"

Ephrion sat beside her and shook his head. "None."

Ceria's face took on a concerned expression.

"You spoke of a dream," Ephrion said gently.

"Yes, a dream. A feeling. I know not how to describe it in a way that you would fully understand. Words fall short of the experience."

Ephrion seated himself in a small brown chair with arms like wings. "There is no question that you experience things in a way I do not, Ceria. It is common to the Rayan. You must share that gift with me now, for the sake of Simbala—for the sake of Hawkwind. Support for Evirae's challenge has grown. If Hawkwind should survive the confrontation with the Fandorans . . ."

"If he should survive?" exclaimed Ceria. "There can be no doubt!"

Ephrion smiled, "In war, confidence is tempered quickly by the fragile realities of life. Violence breeds violence. I pray for peace, I trust our men, but I can only hope that they all will survive."

Ceria nodded. "I could not bear the thought of losing him."

"Then do not think of it now," answered Ephrion. "Tell me of your dream as best you can."

Ceria observed a burning candle across the room. "There," she murmured. "Witness the smoke as it rises from the flame. Such is the substance of my dream." Her eyes seemed distant, as if fixed on another place and time. "In my dream," she said slowly, "I was a child again, living in the wagons of my tribe. It was a cold evening, and snowing. I felt an inexplicable fear as I lay beneath my quilt. I rose from my bed to find Zurka, the woman who raised me—but she was gone from her bed. I hurried outside, shivering. The dark woods surrounding the wagons scared me. There

seemed to be cold, glowing eyes in their depths. In the moonlight I saw an unfamiliar wagon in our camp. Its door was ajar and I glanced within. On a small velvet cushion there was a smooth and globular jewel. It had the cloudiness of a pearl, but swirled with rainbow colors, as though light were imprisoned within it. It was large—as large as two clasped hands. I felt that it was necessary to see it more closely. But as I reached within and touched it, it burst like a bubble. From it sprang a dragon—tiny at first, but it grew, became gigantic. Its eyes were dark blue, like the night. Its face . . ." Ceria closed her eyes for a moment. "It was sad," she whispered. "There was such sorrow within it."

She looked at the elder Monarch. "Ephrion, it did not look like the creature we saw from the palace. That creature had yellow eyes and two legs. This dragon had four. You are familiar with the legends; what meaning do you find in what I have told you?"

Ephrion stood and went to the rosewood desk in silence. Ceria heard the dry rustling of scrolls and texts and waited. Ephrion returned with a small scroll in his hand.

"This," he said, "is what you saw."

Ceria sat up and took the scroll from him. "Handle it gently," he cautioned her. "It is older than the palace."

To Ceria the paper seemed more delicate than a butterfly's wing. She looked intently at the faded picture drawn on the parchment. It was exactly what she had seen in her dream—a sphere filled with colors that had long ago faded with the scroll's age.

"It is one of the legendary stones of the dragons," Ephrion said. "Perhaps it is even a Dragonpearl. The picture is too faded to tell."

"Legendary?" asked Ceria. "Then it does not exist?"

Ephrion smiled. "If the legendary dragon exists, might not other legends exist, too?"

"Yes," said Ceria. "That makes sense. But why do I have no memory of it during my time in Shar Wagon? When I was a child, Zurka told me and my half-sister Balia the legends. I remember the dragons clearly, and what noble, gentle creatures they were. Yet I do not remember anything called a Dragonpearl."

"Nor did I," replied Ephrion, "until I examined these ancient writings." He nodded toward the desk. "They have sat in the palace library untouched for decades. My predecessors believed them to be nothing more than fairy stories and legends. Now, with the dragon's appearance, I view them differently. I believe that much of what had been thought to be legends is indeed the history of the uncharted northern lands."

"We must discover if they are true!"

Ephrion nodded and took the scroll from her. Placing it carefully on a small end table, he continued: "The stones of the dragons are repositories of knowledge, Ceria. They grow within the head of a dragon, as a pearl grows. The memories, the history, and the secrets of the dragons are contained within those spheres."

"What a wondrous thing!" Ceria exclaimed. "If the legends are true, then the dragons' history can be learned from these stones!"

Ephrion nodded. "Yes, for each dragon, such a stone exists. Yet, according to the legends, there are only eight Dragonpearls. There is a difference between them. The Dragonpearl is a stone which has grown in the head of a ruler of the dragons. According to legend, there have been eight dragon rulers in the past. By now there may have been more. The stones contain only the memories and feelings of individual dragons, but the eight Dragonpearls contain that, and more—the history and knowledge of the dragons' civilization. They are repositories of the past, Ceria, and the eight of them are responsive to human thought. Through them we can learn not only the history of the dragons but also the nature of their present existence."

"How can that be, Monarch Ephrion? Are not the Dragonpearls older than the palace?"

"Yes," replied Ephrion, "that is true of the eight which we know exist. If there is a head of the dragons now, however, the eight Dragonpearls will not be dormant. Much of their information is linked. Thoughts of the existing head of the dragons could be discovered with any of the Dragonpearls."

Ephrion looked at the scroll. "We must learn if your dream has any truth to it, Ceria. If it does, the stone must be found and brought here. If it is a Dragonpearl, it may have the information we need to help end this war. There is a reason for the appearance of the dragon—and why it does not appear to be a dragon of legend. The Dragonpearl may tell us; according to legend, it will respond to the thoughts of a human with your gift."

Ephrion rose again and went to a cabinet near the arched entrance. He poured liquid from a decanter. "You need a revitalizing elixir," he suggested. "There must be no time lost. You have sensed the danger we face—and you know already how Evirae's plans have jeopardized Hawkwind's. You must go to . . ."

Ephrion turned, and left the sentence unfinished, for he saw that Ceria had left the couch and was standing by the desk looking at the maps.

"Do not disturb their order!" he warned.

Ceria smiled. "I won't. I am merely looking for a map of the Valian Plains. It has been a long time since I journeyed home, and my trip must be as swift as possible."

She accepted the elixir from Ephrion and raised the glass in a toast.

"To finding the Dragonpearl!" she said.

"To peace," Ephrion responded quietly.

Ceria nodded, and drained the glass. Then she clutched her red cape about her, and with a respectful gesture of farewell, departed Ephrion's rooms to make preparations for her journey.

XXV

S ounds of surprise burst forth from the people in the streets near Monarch's March, as the ebony coach of the Royal Family passed. Atop the driver's seat was a sight rarely seen by any citizen of Simbala. Next to the driver sat the Princess herself, peering anxiously through the crowds for the sight of a small man with fluffy white hair.

"A dozen men," she cried, "a dozen I charge with the task of finding the Fandoran, and none succeed!" She tilted her head back and stared at the trees above them. "We must find the Fandoran before he reaches the palace!"

The guard nodded eagerly and cracked a whip, his enthusiasm for the Princess's plan ensured no doubt by the fact that he was deaf.

In the coach behind him, Baron Tolchin dabbed sweat from his forehead with a small blue foulard. He scowled. "All this time wasted on the Fandoran! We should be dealing with Hawkwind!"

Alora sighed. "I don't like it. She pursues the Fandoran as if he was the Ruby itself."

Tolchin nodded. "With reason! You have set him up as an obstacle to the throne!"

"*Me?*" Alora attempted an air of surprise.

"Do you not remember your own words to her? 'Twould be best to find the spy before redecorating the palace!' "

Alora shook her head. "I merely meant to show the young

woman that too many matters were still unresolved. There is
no reason to seek Hawkwind's removal on such slight evidence
as Hawkwind's disregard for the warning of a spy."

"Evirae has little interest in the subtlety of your warning,
darling. She wishes only to sit in the palace and tell people
what to do."

Alora stroked her forehead, as if to relieve a sudden pain.
"I thought you favored Hawkwind's removal. Now you
speak against Evirae?"

"I favor Hawkwind's removal and the presence of the
Royal Family on the throne. The Princess, for all her faults,
can be controlled."

Alora looked reproachfully at her husband. "You do not
know Evirae. She will run Simbala as she runs her own life.
She will be stubborn and childish. There will be chaos and
petty rivalry throughout the land if Evirae replaces
Hawkwind."

Tolchin pulled back the curtain at Alora's side. "Look
around you!" he argued. "The army is at war! The Northweald accuses us of ignoring its demands! The Fandorans
wait on the hills near the forest . . . and a dragon has appeared in the courtyard of the palace! Are things so desir-
able with the miner that you would not risk his replacement
by a woman of the Family?

"I do not trust her, Tolchin. There shall be no concession
from me unless there is proof of treason."

"Proof!" Tolchin exclaimed. "If you are as familiar with
Evirae as you say, then surely you know she will find proof,
if she has to make it herself!"

"Is that the morality that befits a queen?"

"She will be a queen in name only. It is the Family who
will govern Simbala."

•

"There goes another," Amsel said softly. He looked down
through the red leaves of a yuana tree at the guard walking
below him. It was the fifth he had seen in as many minutes.
If he had kept to the ground after escaping the palace
guards, he would probably have been recaptured long ago.
He wondered if the two men had been able to reach the
Princess before him, but he knew also that there was no
reason to dwell on it. He simply had to get word through to

Hawkwind or the woman called Ceria. He would risk whatever safety he had left to do it.

He had made good time and distance, considering that he was quite exhausted from his trials. For the most part he had been able to proceed in a straight line through the lower canopy across interwoven limbs or hand over hand along vines. Occasionally he would find himself in a tree whose hollow interior contained a house; these often had upper porches and walkways that led across open spaces to more trees.

But closer to the palace grounds the trees were espaliered in uniform rows. More and more he was forced to make precarious leaps across open space, reminding him not only of the danger of the mission but also of his age.

Amsel hurried forward in exhaustion for a few hundred yards more, but the gaps between the trees grew even wider. Although the upper levels of what seemed to be the back of the palace were clearly visible to him now, he realized he would have to reach the structure on foot.

Catching hold of a long, leafless vine, Amsel observed the ground below him. There were small trees, providing some cover in their shadows. There was a small wooden building guarded by two men, both of whom appeared to be asleep. From inside, the sounds of horses could be heard. Amsel suspected that it was a stable. To the west of it was a small stone footbridge. If he could get past the eastern side of the building, he would be able to reach a pathway toward the palace grounds.

Amsel tugged on the vine. It was shiny and relatively smooth. Good, he thought. I will slide down to the lower trees and jump from there.

"It will not be long now, Johan!" he murmured, and with a gulp of air he swung down between the branches.

As he did, he glimpsed a most unexpected sight. A beautiful Simbalese woman, cloaked in red, was rushing quickly up the pathway toward the stable!

"Lady Ceria!" Amsel exclaimed involuntarily, and to his shock, the young woman looked up. She saw what she thought was a child swing precariously from a high tree to a low branch, and then vanish in the long, thin leaves of a silkbough tree. She ran quickly toward it.

In the smaller tree, Amsel swiftly grabbed a branch. He took a deep breath and pulled the threadlike leaves away from his face. She has seen me, he thought, and she will find me in a moment! He knew not whether to reveal himself or run. The woman could be one of a thousand in Simbala to carry a cloak of red. But they were near the palace, and she had looked up at the mention of . . .

"Come down from there, young fellow!"

Amsel peeked out between the leaves and saw the woman, with hands on hips, staring angrily up at the tree.

"I am in a hurry!" she shouted. "Come down now or I will get you myself!"

Amsel stared at her. From what he could see, the woman fit exactly the description given to him by the child. Using the leaves for a screen, he decided to take a chance. "Are you Lady Ceria?"

The Rayan's eyes widened in surprise. "Yes!" she shouted. "Who are you?"

Amsel smiled. "Success at last!" he murmured. Quickly he climbed down the trunk of the tree.

Ceria saw the tuft of white hair pop out between the lowest branches. The boy's strange accent and the appearance of a child in this area suddenly made sense. He was not a child at all!

Amsel hit the ground in front of her.

"You are the spy," said Ceria softly. "Do not move." In her hand was a small knife.

"No!" Amsel cried. "There has been a grave misunderstanding!"

"Yes," Ceria replied. "Fandora is at war with Simbala. As we speak, your troops are facing ours in the Kameran Valley. That is a grave misunderstanding for us all."

Amsel sighed. "Then what I have to say is more urgent than ever! If you are Lady Ceria, you must help me get word to Monarch Hawkwind!"

The Rayan regarded him silently. This was the man the Fandorans had sent to spy on Overwood? The urgency in his voice made her suddenly unsure.

"I must get a message to Hawkwind!" Amsel insisted. "The Princess held me captive in your caverns! I have news that will end the war!"

Ceria lowered her knife and stepped closer to the Fandoran.

"The Princess? She kept you from getting a message to Monarch Hawkwind?"

"Yes! Yes! A message to stop the war! You must take me to him now!"

"Turn your back to me," Ceria said, "and lean against the trunk of the tree. I must be sure you carry no weapons."

Amsel complied. Ceria searched him. Outside of the knife he had taken from the guard, which she confiscated, he had no weapons. She considered momentarily taking the seed pods she found in his pouch, but decided they were harmless. "We must get you away from here," she said. "Come with me."

They hurried along a flower-lined path. "Evirae's guards are everywhere!" said Ceria. "Even in that stable where I keep my horse! We must reach the palace guardhouse. The sentry there is loyal to Hawkwind."

Amsel nodded. "The Princess and Monarch Hawkwind are enemies?"

Ceria nodded. "She wishes to be queen."

They ran quickly toward a wide, winding road. This was Monarch's March, and straight ahead, no more than two hundred yards away, was the back entrance to the palace grounds.

"*Hurry!*" said Ceria. "We must reach the sentry!"

Amsel struggled valiantly to keep up with the young woman, but he could not. He had gone too far and too long without ample food or sleep, and his legs were much shorter than hers. "Just one moment's rest!" he implored, but the Rayan shook her head.

"I have to leave Overwood on urgent business!" she insisted. "Your delay comes at a most inopportune time!"

"I'm sorry," said Amsel, wheezing and coughing, "but I need rest, if even for a moment."

"It is not safe here!" she replied. "I must have the sentry take you to Monarch Ephrion!"

"Ephrion?" said Amsel, startled. "What about Hawkwind?"

"Hawkwind is at war! Ephrion is his predecessor! Don't you know these things? You are supposed to be a spy!"

"I am Amsel!" he said. "I am not a spy! I have come—"

He was cut off by the distant clopping of hoofbeats on the flagstone. Somewhere behind them a coach was approaching!

Ceria took Amsel's hand and hurried forward, almost dragging the weary inventor.

"What is it?" he asked.

"Trouble," she replied. "Whoever it is must not see us." She waved frantically in the direction of the sentry post, and Amsel saw a short round man come outside and wave back.

Ceria glanced over her shoulder. The coach was about to turn the last bend before the palace. When it did, they would be seen!

"This way!" she shouted, and she tugged Amsel toward the side of the road. Yet as she did, they both caught a glimpse of the sight down the road. An ebony coach was coming directly toward them. Atop it, next to the private coachman, rode Princess Evirae!

She saw them immediately and screamed, "The spy! It is the Rayan and the spy! After them!"

Upon hearing those words, Amsel discovered a hidden store of energy in his legs, and together with Ceria he dived for the cover of the bushes at the side of the road.

"Alora! Tolchin!" shouted Evirae from the coach. "Take heed! The Rayan conspires with the spy!"

From the bushes Ceria spotted the Baron peeking out through an uncovered window of the coach. She grabbed Amsel's hand again, but he pulled away.

"No more of that!" he said. "Where are we going? The coach has already passed us and is on the way to the palace!"

Ceria nodded. "The gardeners use the footpath behind us to reach the palace. There's a gate at the end. I've already warned the sentry. Watch!"

As they hurried down the unpaved footpath through the bushes, Amsel saw the coach jolt to a stop outside the palace gate. The sentry stepped forward to greet it, but he appeared to take no action toward opening the gate. Instead, he seemed to be gesticulating and nodding apologetically to the Princess.

A minute later, Ceria fumbled with the latch on the gardener's entrance. Beyond it lay the lush back lawn of the palace tree.

"We've made it!" said Amsel.

"Not yet," answered Ceria. "He won't be able to keep the Princess out for long."

Sure enough, the moment Amsel and Ceria were spotted on the verdant grounds, the gate behind them was opened.

Evirae rushed through, followed by Tolchin and Alora, screaming, "Stop them! Guard! Stop them before they reach the palace!" The sentry obeyed at the speed of a man twice his age.

Crossing the lawn in one swift dash, Ceria and Amsel climbed a short path framed by row after row of honeycup and sanicle. Seconds later they were at the tall, columnated archway, face to face with two guards still out of range of the Princess's shouting.

"Sentry!" said Ceria. "The Princess has ordered this poor fellow to be taken prisoner! You must stop her! He is under the protection of Monarch Hawkwind!"

The sentry saluted. The two rushed inside just as Evirae came into view behind them.

"He will delay her for a moment," whispered Ceria. "But the Princess will overrule my order. Follow me!"

Amsel merely nodded—he had no breath for words. He also had no time to gape at the beauty of Simbala's palace. The columns of the entrance were of polished wood, easily fifty feet high, and they did not constitute a fraction of the size of the tree itself. The floor of the grand hallway they had entered from the rear was of marble inlaid with topaz at the juncture of every tile. They hurried on beneath a high vaulted ceiling from which hung gigantic cloth tapestries depicting Simbala's history. All this, Amsel marveled, at the rear entrance! Ceria rushed ahead, oblivious, but Amsel, tired and frightened as he was, nonetheless mourned the fact that he could not see it all.

They ran up toward a tall narrow staircase on the eastern wall. As they reached the landing above, Evirae, Tolchin, and the guards burst into the hallway. "Up there!" she cried. "After them!"

Ceria and Amsel reached the second level, which was a mezzanine. More guards appeared in the corridor, responding to the echo of Evirae's words. They found the Minister and the spy headed in their direction and promptly cut the two off. Ceria and Amsel ran through a side doorway that opened into one of the smaller libraries of the palace. It wrenched Amsel's heart to hurry through the large oval room, walls covered with shelves stacked with books, scrolls, and maps. What he would not give for the time and circumstances in which to browse through this repository of knowledge!

They ran beneath a fretted archway and down a curving corridor, guards close upon their heels. The few remaining chamberlains and courtiers stared, stunned by the sight of one of the Monarch's advisers being chased by the palace guards. A tall man, ahead of the others, closed in and lunged at Ceria, catching her cloak. She slipped neatly out of his grip and let him fall to the wood floor. She forestalled the rest of them by pulling down a large tapestry in their path. Amsel and Ceria rushed down another flight of stairs, which eventually brought them to the lower levels containing the vast kitchen of the palace.

Here were the bakeries, with their tantalizing scents, the buttery, and storerooms by the dozen. The hallway they were in was filled with distant noise—the clamor of pans and pots, and many chefs shouting back and forth. Behind them were the kitchens, and from that direction came periodic waves of heat and smell.

"We have a moment before they find us," Ceria gasped. "You had best tell me the words you have for Hawkwind."

Amsel took several deep breaths and nodded. "I am here on my own behalf," he said, "but it is my hope that what I know will profit both Simbala and Fandora. My people blame your people for a mysterious attack upon their children."

"An attack upon a Fandoran child?" Ceria exclaimed. "Why, it is a child of the Northweald that has been murdered!"

Before Amsel could voice his surprise, there were the sounds of footsteps on the stairs.

"Hurry!" said Ceria. "They have found us!" They rushed through two heavy wooden doors and into a room full of confusion. They were in one of the kitchens, and the heat from the large stone oven was overwhelming. Aproned figures scurried about with tureens and baker's pans. Ceria paid them no mind, though they stared as she moved quickly through them, red among white, with what seemed like an urchin in tow.

Overwhelmed by the abundance around him, Amsel hovered for a moment over a dozen freshly baked rolls. But Ceria pulled him away, and he followed, reluctantly, grateful for at least the aroma. They walked quickly across the slippery floor, out another set of doors, and into a small stockroom. Ceria closed the door behind them. The room was lit by a single candle.

"Are we to wait here until the guards have passed?" Amsel asked.

"No," answered Ceria, "you must go on without me. Monarch Ephrion must know of your tale."

"How am I to reach him?" asked Amsel. "The guards will be downstairs at any moment!"

Ceria smiled. "Watch, but do not speak." She faced the wall behind him and started to lift a long shelf filled with earthenware jars. "Help me," she said, "this is heavy."

Puzzled, Amsel lent his support. It was heavy, but they managed to lower it to the floor. As they did, however, they heard the sounds of the guards in the kitchen outside, followed by Evirae's voice shouting loudly at the bakers.

"They're coming," said Amsel.

"Listen to me!" said Ceria. She pulled back a wooden board to reveal an opening behind the shelf. A dim light filtered into the storeroom, and Amsel glimpsed a narrow flight of stairs cut into the wood beyond it. "I have learned of this route from Hawkwind," she whispered, "for he has long been intrigued with the secret passages of the palace. You will take those stairs to the eighth level of the palace and then bear left down the passage you will find. From there go to the third door, the third door, Amsel, and you will arrive in the private chamber of Monarch Ephrion." Ceria was interrupted by a pounding on the door.

"Take this!" she said, and slipped a ring of peridot stone from her hand. "It will identify you to Monarch Ephrion. Tell him all you have told me. Trust him, Amsel. He can help you, perhaps more than Hawkwind and I combined."

"Surrender!" Evirae shouted above the pounding of the guards. "Surrender, Rayan, or face me in prison!"

"Hurry!" said Ceria. "They'll have the door down in an instant!"

"What about you?" said Amsel. "How can I leave you here to face the Princess alone?"

"Do not worry about me. I have faced Evirae many times. Now, go!"

She pushed the small inventor into the dark opening and slid the board back into place over it.

As she reached for the shelf on the floor, however, there was a cracking sound. With a screech, the wooden door burst open, revealing three sentries and an angry Princess.

Evirae pushed them aside and entered the storeroom. She looked at Ceria, then quickly around the interior. Her face tightened in fury as she realized the spy was gone.

Ceria calmly folded her arms. "Princess Evirae," she said, inclining her head. "You wished to speak to me?"

•

Amsel hurried up the stairwell, hearing the sounds of Ceria's capture fade in the darkness below him. "She knows more about the situation than I do," he reassured himself. "Still, I hope that long-nailed fury doesn't hurt her."

He rested momentarily on the fifth-floor landing. His legs were knotted with fatigue, and he was sneezing, for the ancient stairwell was thick with dust and cobwebs. Occasional vents cut through a solid wall of wood supplied a bit of light and air. "Not long now," he sniffled. He continued up the remaining stairs of the secret passage, keeping track of the floors as he passed them. At last he reached the eighth level and turned left. He spied a succession of short square doors in the low-vaulted passage way and headed toward the third. It was jammed. He pushed against it, and finally it began to swing open. Amsel carefully stepped forward. There was a ledge no longer than a foot in front of him. Looking out, he saw that the door of the secret passage was cleverly concealed in the design of a large mural. He was high above a large candlelit chamber filled with comfortable velvet-backed chairs and tables of wood and marble. Books and scrolls were scattered about. On the other side of the room he could see the white hair and silken robe of a man, surrounded by more books.

"That must be Ephrion," Amsel whispered. Without hesitation, he jumped down to a couch below him.

The noise startled Ephrion, and he looked up.

"I have been sent to you by Lady Ceria!" Amsel said. "The Princess has taken her hostage!"

•

In the shelter of the fog, the fighting had rapidly disintegrated into a series of guerrilla encounters. The Fandoran Elders had ordered their men to work their way back to the hills, taking whatever advantage they could of the terrain and the fog, and there regroup.

But the fog was beginning to lift slightly. A wind had begun to blow from the south, tearing the omnipresent mist into long patches and streamers that streaked the valley. It still provided ample concealment, however, along with the rocks and trees and copses.

The Simbalese troops were also slowly regrouping, planning to sweep the valley with columns of soldiers. Hawkwind, riding through the fog with an uncanny sureness of direction, had managed to find and guide many soldiers back to the main body of the army. He sat now on horseback, next to General Vora, as the Captains formed the army once again into ranks.

"We need more troops," the General said. "So far, circumstances have favored the Fandorans. Much more of this, and our soldiers will become demoralized—"

Shouts from the columns behind them interrupted him. Several of the soldiers pointed at the sky. Hawkwind and Vora looked up, to see Kiorte's windship slowly and precisely lowering onto a small level area nearby. Soldiers caught the ropes and pulled the windship safely to its berth. Before it had landed completely, Kiorte and Thalen leaped out. At Thalen's request a physician applied an unguent to his hands, which had been burned and blistered on the ropes. Kiorte strode toward Hawkwind and Vora.

"Welcome, Prince Kiorte!" Hawkwind said. "Your rescue of your brother was a masterful job!"

Kiorte ignored the compliment. He stood before Hawkwind, arms folded. "This battle is going badly," he said. "The fog is clearing now. We must bring in a fleet of windships and put an end to this."

"We cannot," Hawkwind said. He was about to continue, but Kiorte interrupted him angrily.

"Why not? Because a fortunate strike brought my brother's windship down? That will not happen if we approach properly, instead of skimming low enough to count the lice in their hair!"

Vora looked shocked at this outburst.

Hawkwind said quietly, "We cannot, because there is more than fog in the air. Incredible as it sounds, there is also the menace of a dragon." He was about to speak further, but was cut off by a shout from one of the aides.

"Look you, sirs! It comes again!"

The man was pointing in terror toward the north. They all looked.

In the mist, something vast loomed. It approached swiftly, a ripple of darkness across the sky that resolved itself into a giant bat-winged shape.

"By the clouds!" Kiorte swore. "It cannot be!"

Hawkwind turned toward the ranks. "Take cover!" he cried. "The dragon has returned!"

Lagow had attempted to remain in the background during that first insane burst of fighting. He had tried to keep sense in the men he was responsible for, but they would not listen to reason, and many of them had died. He had done his best to take care of the wounded, but he could only do so much.

He was feeling old, and growing older by the moment, he thought bitterly. Now he crouched behind a rock in the mist, listening. There had been no sound of fighting for some time, but still he did not move. He had come upon this rock as he wandered in search of the hills. It was a solitary gray finger in a world of mist, and so far no one else had come near it. But he knew that was only a matter of chance; sooner or later, he would be discovered.

He could go around to the other side of the rock, beneath the overhang, and not be quite so visible. He was tired of this conflict, of this madness. Lagow thought of his family, his wife and children. He had at least left them a comfortable legacy. And he had kept his son from this lunacy. Of that he was proud. It was not much of an epitaph, but it was the best he had.

He was cold and miserable—the more so since the wind had begun to blow. Lagow squinted upward, noticing that the fog was beginning to dissipate. Now he heard something—a slow pulsing of wind, almost like breathing, or canvas flapping. It was coming from the north. At first, in his apathy, he ignored it, but its slow, ominous regularity at last made him push himself away from the rock and walk around it, looking upward toward the sound.

The sound increased. Lagow stopped beneath the overhang, staring up at the fog. His eyes widened in fear; above him, indistinct in the mist, something gigantic and winged passed over him, a dreadnought of the sky. Lagow backed up in panic—and felt his boot tread on something soft and yielding, something that was not part of the ground. He looked down quickly. Beneath his boot was a hand, and it belonged to Tenniel. The young Elder lay on his back, quite still, his eyes closed and his face pale, a Simbalese arrow protruding from his shoulder.

●

"I'm done for, ain't I?" Steph asked weakly.

"Quiet down," Jurgan growled. "If I don't tie this bandage proper, you will be, sure enough."

Steph lay on his back in a grassy gully near a bush of sweetleaf. He was pale and trembling. A wound in his thigh steamed slightly in the cold air, leaking blood in a slow, steady flow.

Jurgan crouched over him, tying a strip of cloth from his tunic about the wound. It was large, right enough, but shallow—the Simbalese sword that had made it had cut through Steph's leather breeches and shaved a slice of flesh off his thigh. Jurgan had killed the Simbalese with a blow from his ax, but not before getting the flat of that same blade against his head. There was a large purple welt just above his ear now, and as he worked, he shook his head occasionally from dizziness. He could not keep his eyes focused.

"I wonder if we're winning," Steph said.

"Hard telling. For all we know, the war's been called off, but there's still some fools out there fighting it."

"I told you these seeds wouldn't do us any good," Steph said. He looked at the wristlet of black pods on his left arm, and tore it loose in disgust, tossing it away.

"Here, now!" Jurgan said. "That's rash, ain't it? How d'you know those seeds ain't all been keeping you alive? Myself, I'm leaving them on till I'm safe back at home in my own bed, and maybe I'll keep 'em on then. They ain't in my way." He tied the bandage and sat back, blinking. "We'd best look for shelter now—this wind's getting awful cold." He shook his head. "Is the fog getting thicker?"

"No," Steph said. "It's clearing."

"Then it's my eyes. That lousy Sim knocked 'em out of whack. I'd best find a safe place to stretch out for a while—I don't know as I can walk very far." He touched the welt gingerly. "Think I'm hearing things, too. Sounds like waves . . ."

"I hear that," Steph said. "Like a smith's bellows, getting louder. Over there . . ." He pointed toward the north, then clutched Jurgan and screamed. *"Look!"*

Sky showed for a moment through a rift in the mist, framing the creature that hurtled over them. Steph clung to Jurgan in terror, babbling. "It's a monster, Jurgan! What do we do now, what do we do?"

Jurgan watched the huge apparition disappear overhead, its wings creating slow thunder. "For starters," he said slowly, "I think you'd better find those seed pods you threw away."

●

Jondalrun, Pennel, and Dayon watched the creature approaching, the fog clearing before it, almost as though its mighty wings drove the mist away. All about them, the Fandorans were raising a clamor of terror, for the behemoth was coming straight toward them, evidently bent on attacking.

"Take cover!" Jondalrun shouted, though he himself stood in the open, raising a spear he had seized in a grand and ridiculous gesture. Dayon pulled the spear from his grasp and pushed him toward the shelter of a tree.

"There are some things you cannot fight, Father!" he shouted.

Men still in the open ran in all directions as the coldrake swooped lower. The backwash from its wings sent some of them sprawling. From beneath a bush, Pennel watched it as it followed a weaving course. It almost seems to be looking for something, he thought.

Despite its erratic course, it was still coming toward the Fandorans. Jondalrun watched it approach, grinding his teeth in fury. "At last, they bring their magic to play against us!" he said. "It will not stop us!" Before Dayon could stop him, he had stepped from the shelter of the tree, directly into the coldrake's path.

"Do your worst against us!" he shouted, shaking his fist at the oncoming beast. "It will not be enough!"

"Father!" Dayon shouted, expecting to see him snatched up by the huge claws, but to his astonishment, the monster abruptly changed course, banking sharply away from the hills, almost as though frightened of something. It winged across the valley toward the Simbalese.

Jondalrun watched it go. "Did you see?" Jondalrun shouted to Dayon and Pennel. "Did you see how it fled from us? Tenniel was right—the witch's magic works! We have repulsed the Sims' greatest weapon!"

"So it would seem," Pennel said cautiously, but privately he felt that nothing in this war was what it seemed.

●

The riders of the other two windships had seen Thalen's craft brought down, and had also seen Kiorte rescue his brother. They had continued to cruise over the hills, looking for Fandorans to attack from above, but the fog had become too thick for that to be very effective. They had been isolated above a white sea of mist from which rose sounds of fighting. And so they had followed Kiorte's ship as it returned to the regrouping Simbalese troops. Since they had been farther away, however, they were still in the air when the wind began to blow, and it had driven them to the southern end of the long, narrow Kameran Valley. They had been returning slowly, tacking against the wind, when they saw the terror coming from the north.

On the ground, Willen and Tweel, hidden beneath bushes, saw the creature they thought of as a dragon approach. From their point of view it appeared to come through the fog over the hills where the Fandorans hid. "By the Northweald stag!" Willen swore. "Do you see that, Tweel? It's like they herded it our way!"

"The rumors must be true," Tweel said. "The Fandorans do somehow control a dragon!"

"If this is the same dragon that attacked Overwood," Willen said, "and not still another. Look!" He pointed to the south. Through the clearing fog could be seen the dim outlines of the approaching windships.

Tweel gasped. "It sees them! Willen, the dragon sees them!"

The coldrake approached the Simbalese troops, who, like the Fandorans, scattered for whatever cover they could find. Then it changed course once again as it saw the windships. It turned toward them, rising to meet them. An alert Windrider saw the gigantic shape rising out of the mist below him. Its size dwarfed the one-man craft. The rider banked the Sindril fire and furled the sails in an attempt to drop to the ground, but the wind and the gusts from the coldrake's wings caused the craft to yaw and pitch. The rider saw the talons, each as long as his arm, as the coldrake rose above the windship and attempted to seize the balloon sails. He screamed as the delicate material ripped apart. Gas exploded out; the rider was almost thrown over the side as the ship tilted, but instead of falling, it rose, momentarily. He realized that the monster was pulling the ship upward. But the sails, unaided by the Sindril gas, could not support the craft's weight. The ship tore free, leaving dangling shreds in the coldrake's talons. The rider felt a moment of weightlessness as he and his ruined ship plunged toward the ground. The last thing he saw was the coldrake turning toward the other windship.

The second windship was in a more favorable position; the coldrake had to circle to approach it. As the beast did so, the side of its body passed before the ship. The rider of that ship raised his crossbow and fired twice.

He saw one arrow hit, burying itself in a haunch. Another tore through the thin membrane of a wing. The coldrake hissed in pain, then dropped and passed beneath the ship.

It swooped low over the Simbalese troops. Then it rose toward the top of the trees swiftly in the direction of the center of the forest. It shrieked in pain as it did, frightening those scattered soldiers and citizens traveling between the Simbalese line and the heart of Overwood.

At the forest's edge, Thalen leaped onto a horse and spurred it quickly toward the downed windship. He had little hope that the rider was alive. The ship had not drifted down, as his had; it had been hurled to the ground like a child's toy. "It is clearly in league with the Fandorans!" General Vora shouted. "They ordered it to attack the windships, and now it is approaching Overwood!"

"It seemed to be trying to carry the ship away," Hawkwind said. "I have seen my hawk do the same with a rabbit."

"For the same purpose, no doubt!" Kiorte cried. "I demand the right to follow that dragon!"

As he spoke, the soldiers helped dock the second windship. Nearby two soldiers stood guard by the single Fandoran prisoner. He was a sullen, burly man, this Fandoran—a smith of Borgen Town. They had bound him with rawhide thongs, but they had underestimated his strength. The Fandoran had tested the thongs about his wrist and knew he could burst them when the time came. It appeared that it would come soon—the confusion about him would help his plan. He looked toward the windship.

XXVI

Ephrion faced Amsel, who sat, gratefully, across from him on the blue silk couch. "If what you say is true," the bearded man whispered, "then we must get some word to this Jondalrun and to Hawkwind at once!"

Amsel's voice quavered. "At last. I have found somebody who can help! Monarch Ephrion, this will mean the end of the war!"

The old man shook his head grimly. "No, I am afraid it will only be a step."

"I have given you the truth!" Amsel protested. "My people did not attack your child! They have gone to war for the same reason as Simbala! Obviously, somebody has attacked the children of both our lands. I cannot understand it, but the knowledge at least should prevent Fandora and Simbala from murdering each other!"

"Ah, if things were so easy, Amsel, there would have been no war. I will get word to Hawkwind," Ephrion said, "but I fear the answer to the murder of the child cannot be found within the world we know."

These words puzzled Amsel; he cocked his head sideways in the manner of a small child.

"Come with me," said Ephrion, "and I will explain."

Amsel followed Ephrion toward the rosewood desk on the other side of the chamber, from which Ephrion pulled a large brown book studded with jewels.

"The battle is beyond our control, because of this," he said.

Amsel took the book and opened it to the page held back by a yellow band. He squinted, regretting that his reading spectacles had been scratched beyond use. To his surprise, there was a large painting of a creature, with two wings, a ferocious face, and enormous black talons.

"It is a dragon!" said Amsel.

"No," replied Ephrion. "It is a coldrake."

"A coldrake? I have read many legends, but I have never heard of a coldrake."

"I am not surprised. Fandora is a young country, Amsel, and though Simbala is older, it is still far from the Southland in age. These legends date back to a time before our countries were born."

"That may be true," said Amsel, "but surely a legend is not the reason for the war."

"It is not a legend. I have seen the coldrake, as have many of the people of the forest."

Amsel looked at Ephrion, in astonishment as the elder statesman continued.

"I believe that many of the legends of the Southland are not legends at all, but the actual history of the land to the north."

"The land to the north of Dragonsea?"

"Yes," said Ephrion, "Lady Ceria has also been told of this. Although she knows not of the coldrakes, she had departed on a mission to find proof of the legends in the area known as the Valian Plains. There may be a jewel there, a jewel containing history of the dragons."

Amsel returned the book to the rosewood desk. "The dragons of legend were peaceful creatures," he murmured. "I presume these coldrakes are not."

"A coldrake attacked a watchman in Overwood," said Ephrion, "but I do not know why it has appeared."

For a moment Amsel remembered the days he had spent adrift in the Strait of Balomar, when reality and hallucinations brought on by hunger had merged in his fevered brain—or so he had thought. Had there not been a time back then during which he had heard the sound of gigantic wings, flapping, and seen something large and indistinct passing through the clouds?

Slowly he said, "A child I met when I escaped the tunnels spoke of a dragon, but I thought it to be no more than his imagination."

"It is real, and it threatens both our lands. The coldrake is like a cousin to the dragons, but it possesses neither their intelligence nor nobility nor size. Nor can a coldrake breathe fire."

Amsel looked preoccupied, his mind fixed on a moment that seemed long ago.

Then he asked, "Why have the coldrakes not appeared until now?"

"According to the legends I have most recently discovered, the coldrakes had always obeyed the orders of the dragons. They were forbidden by the dragons to have any contact with human life."

Amsel looked at the picture. "I can understand why. This creature has the features of a predator. If it is as large as it looks, it could endanger many people."

Ephrion removed the book from Amsel's hand. "That," he said sternly, "is why you must journey to the land of the dragons."

"To the land of the dragons?" Amsel grasped the desk tightly, feeling suddenly dizzy.

"If Ceria has been captured, then she will be unable to complete her mission. You are our hope now, Amsel—and Fandora's hope, too. You must learn why the coldrakes have attacked. You must learn their secret and bring word back to us! You alone will be trusted by both Simbalese and Fandoran."

"My people think me to be a spy!"

"You will be a hero," said Ephrion.

"I don't want to be a hero!" said Amsel. "I want peace! I wish to learn the truth about Johan's murder! It is for those things that I feel responsible!"

"Then you must accept this mission. For only by discovering the truth about the coldrakes will the murder of the children be put fully to rest!"

"I am very tired," Amsel responded. "I have traveled for days with little food and almost no sleep. I have been chased, attacked, taken prisoner, questioned, hunted, buried alive, soaked, and now you want me to become a hero?"

Ephrion smiled. "You have no choice, Amsel of Fandora.

You must go. You must find out why the coldrake has appeared!"

Amsel watched the Monarch as he spoke. Ephrion's face was worn with age and fatigue; he too had faced a long struggle. Amsel responded that the task of deciphering the secrets of the books and maps around them had been a tremendous undertaking, yet Ephrion had discovered a vital fragment of the legends in mere days.

"If you remain here," the Monarch warned, "the Princess will take you prisoner before night descends on the forest." He reached for a scroll on the far corner of the rosewood desk. "You must journey to the north, to learn why the coldrakes have violated the orders of the dragons. You can rest along the way but you must get away from the palace first. You must learn why the dragons themselves did not prevent the murder of our children."

Amsel nodded softly. "For Johan, I must go. My conscience could permit nothing less."

Ephrion smiled. "Yes," he whispered, "and when you return to us with the answer, your conscience will be free once more."

"No," said Amsel. "A child has been murdered due to my thoughtless ways. I shall never be free of that!"

"Then you will be at peace in the knowledge that you have saved a thousand others." Ephrion slipped the scroll he was holding into the lining of his robe. "Now, step back," he said. "The guards may arrive at any moment."

Amsel watched as Ephrion pulled a bell cord near the desk.

There was a rumbling, as of counterweights shifting in the wall behind it. Then Ephrion drew aside an arras, to reveal a dark opening in the wall. The entire palace was evidently riddled with secret passageways, Amsel thought, and he wondered at the intrigue that must have taken place over the centuries.

Ephrion caught his look and smiled. "Most of these ways are rarely used," he said, "as you must have noticed from the dust, but it is better to have them and not need them than to need them and not have them, yes?" He thrust a torch of firemoss into a candleflame, then stooped and entered the small opening, Amsel following upright.

To the Fandoran's bewilderment, however, instead of a tunnel or stairwell, he found himself in a small wooden room. "I think you will find this mode of travel slightly less tiresome," Ephrion said. He gave the torch to Amsel and slowly turned a wheel on the wall of the small room. Amsel once again heard the groaning of counterweights, but faintly, as from a distance, coming closer. Simultaneously, the opening slid down and disappeared beneath the floor! After a moment of disorientation, Amsel realized with delight that the small room was moving rapidly up a shaft in the center of the tree, lifted, no doubt, by a concealed system of weights and pulleys.

"This is ingenious!" he exclaimed. "A brilliant application of a simple concept!"

"Also a method of travel much easier on an old man's limbs," Ephrion said. After a moment, he turned the wheel again, and the moving wall before them seemed to slow down. Ephrion stopped the lift level with another door, which he pushed open cautiously. Amsel saw part of a vast chamber, the high ceiling of which was supported by columns. Flames in wall cressets illuminated the room. It was largely empty, save for stacks of barrels, large bolts of cloths, and coils of rope that were set along the walls. From one end, beyond Amsel's vision, came the dull gray light of a cloudy sky.

"Step softly!" cautioned Ephrion. "We are approaching the launching chamber for the palace windship."

"Windship?" asked Amsel. "Surely you do not expect me to travel by windship!"

"There is simply no other way for you to reach your destination in time." Ephrion motioned for silence. "I shall distract the guard while you get aboard."

"Monarch Ephrion, I have little idea of how a windship operates! I've only been a passenger once—and blindfolded for most of the time at that!"

Ephrion smiled. "You are an inventive fellow. If you can build something as exceptional as the gliding Wing you described to me earlier, then certainly you will be able to understand the operation of a windship."

As they stepped out of the lift, Amsel peered between the folds in Ephrion's robe and saw a sight that set his heart pounding. The room was larger than the Tamberly town square and it faced the sky itself! An entire wall was missing!

An arch in the trunk of the tree curved down to the floor. Framed in this arch was a windship. It was smaller than the craft Amsel had seen as a prisoner, and its sails were flaccid. Yet, with its intricate design and brightly painted sails, it was an impressive sight. A single guard stood nearby.

"Hide behind me, now," said Ephrion, and Amsel took refuge between the robe and the wall.

"Sentry!" Ephrion shouted. "Come quickly! I have seen the Fandoran spy on this level!"

The guard rushed from his post toward Ephrion. "Quickly!" the Monarch shouted. "Check the hall!"

The guard passed them without hesitation. As soon as the door closed behind him, they ran toward the windship. Moments later, at the foot of the hull, they used a small rope ladder to climb aboard.

Ephrion hurried to the middle of the craft and Amsel saw a concave metal container filled with jewels.

"Now, watch," said Ephrion. He started to spray the brazier with water from a small leather sack. As it squirted on the blue Sindril crystals, they hissed and steamed.

Amsel watched in amazement as the sails above began to fill. The jewels were producing an incredible amount of gas. Soon it would be enough to fill the windship's sails.

"I must go," said Ephrion. "Continue this until the sails are full. The sheets function in a manner similar to a sailboat. There are simple levers at the back of the ship to control them. It is an understanding of the wind that is most crucial. From your other exploits, tacking should not be too difficult for you to do."

Ephrion glanced back at the station door. "We are fortunate," he said, "that most of the palace guards have been recruited for war. I will delay the remaining sentry as long as I can."

Amsel nodded and continued to stoke the fire. "I must have directions!" he said. "I know far too little of Overwood to go north blindly. And what about food and water?"

Ephrion nodded and took the scroll from the lining of his robe. "This is an old map of a respected Windrider. His name was Eilat." He placed it on the roof of the low cabin.

"Supplies are in the cabin," he continued, and then pulled a long pole from a rack on the hull. "When the sails are full, use this to free the ropes of the moorings." Returning the pole to its berth, Ephrion extended his hand to the inventor and said, "You will return, Amsel of Fandora. You will return in peace."

Amsel grasped the Monarch's hand.

"Remember the legends you heard as a child," said Ephrion, "for from my experience of the past few days, they may have more truth than we had ever imagined."

He looked up and saw the sails filling quickly. "I must leave you now," he said. He descended the rope ladder. "A safe voyage, Amsel!"

Amsel waved silently and then started to free the ropes of the windship.

"A safe voyage!" he muttered as the old man's footsteps faded. "I'm off to face man-eating creatures, and he wishes me a safe voyage!"

When he had detached all but a few crucial ropes, Amsel hurried back to the jewels to spray them again. Then, picking up the map, he went to the bow of the windship. He wanted to make sure he was familiar with both his plans and the operation of the craft before leaving, and he observed with fascination the intricate riggings and billowing sails above him.

He did not have nearly as much time as he would have liked. The door at the far end suddenly opened again, and two guards entered. Amsel presumed they were under orders from Evirae, for as soon as they saw the windship hovering slightly above the floor of the station, they ran forward, shouting at him to give up.

"It's time to leave," Amsel murmured, "but I wish I had had a chance to practice!"

He cast the last rope from the ship, and pushed against the sloping dock with the pole. The sails were not completely filled—the craft rocked dangerously beneath him, throwing him off his feet. The guards cast spears after him, which fell short. Amsel struggled to his feet. He glanced over the side and immediately decided that he should have stayed close to the controls. The top of the palace, and the forest around it, were already beneath him. There was evidently too much gas in the forward sails, for the deck was tilted at a

steep angle. Amsel trimmed the flow of gas, seized the steering levers, and began cautiously to pilot the ship. To his relief, he soon found the proper adjustment to steady the craft. The sails firmed. He returned to the center of the windship and picked up Ephrion's map to chart a course toward Dragonsea.

The low clouds were starting to clear, he noticed. Far away, across the green roof of the forest, sunlight poured. Amsel watched a flock of dark birds wing through it. Up here, things were so peaceful. It was hard to believe that people carried on such foolish things as war and intrigue in such a beautiful land.

The thought of the war brought back thoughts of Johan and the Wing, and so he set to work, securing the ropes of the windship. There would be little time for enjoyment of the scenery. The ship was still rising, and was now danger-ously close to the north-blowing winds. Above, Amsel could see the higher layers of clouds breaking up under their currents. Then he noticed the flock of birds in the distance was coming toward him. Or so it seemed. As the clouds cleared, he could see that it was a single bird. Odd, Amsel thought, how the lack of perspective in the sky could fool him.

Then, with a chill as cold as the subterranean river, Amsel realized that the winged shape was much, much too large to be a bird. He stared at it, watching it come closer and closer.

It was not a bird. Not a flock of birds. It was a coldrake.

Amsel gripped the rail in fear. The creature's giant wings propelled it faster than the wind filling the windship's sails. Its yellow eyes, each as big as Amsel's head, were fixed on him with a singular determination. It swooped toward him, its talons extended toward the windship. Such talons could rend the sails to shreds.

Or rend a Wing, ridden by a laughing child . . .

Amsel began to shudder. He had not had much time to think about Ephrion's words. The startling statement that dragons and coldrakes existed had so many implications that he had put it in the back of his mind until the craft had left the skies of Simbala. Yet now, in the instant that he stood watching the creature, a myriad bits and pieces of previously unrelated information fitted together in his mind. What Ephrion hinted at was true! He had never seen the wreckage of his glider or Johan's body, but he had heard Jondalrun's description. The Wing had been shredded, and Johan savagely mauled and broken, in a way that no fall could explain. The Shepherd's daughter had been snatched into the sky and similarly treated. Jondalrun had blamed a Simbalese Windrider—and indeed, how else could it have possibly happened?

How else, indeed, save by those cruel talons and teeth now approaching?

Amsel leaped backward and opened the flue of the brazier. The windship leaped upward in response, and rocked as the coldrake passed beneath it, stirring the air. He watched it turn slowly, almost leisurely in the air. It came by again, quite close this time, but made no attempt to attack. Then it had passed him and was continuing north, rising higher and higher.

Amsel stoked the brazier again, and the windship also rose. He had to keep the creature in view! Above it, he could see the clouds being torn by the northerly winds. If he rose much higher, he would be in the grip of their currents. Already the lower fringes of the wind were plucking at the tops of the sails. It reminded him of the forces that had pulled his boat out into the North Sea, where he had sighted the coldrake and thought it a dream.

"Johan," he murmured, "was that yellow eye the last thing you saw in life?"

The coldrake turned again, swept toward him, circled the windship, then continued on its flight to the north. Its actions were eminently clear—it wanted Amsel to follow! It was not attacking—at least, not yet.

Amsel looked at it. "Are you the reason they fight?" he said softly. "Are you behind this war?"

He thrust the brazier lever firmly down. The windship rose quickly upward, into the grip of the northerly winds. There would be no turning back now. He was caught in the currents that would take him out over Dragonsea, to the unknown land where a legend was legend no more.

●

"At this hour tomorrow, I shall be Queen!" Evirae's words were like a dagger to Ceria's heart. "Hawkwind will be impeached, my dear. On that matter the Family will be united."

The Princess faced Ceria in a small room in her mansion. It was a guest chamber, opulently furnished, with a round bed and a dresser beneath a fenestrella window. But Ceria knew she was far from a guest. She had been taken prisoner in the kitchen of the palace, then transported quickly away, before guards loyal to Hawkwind could rescue her. Evirae's actions had been supported by the Baron.

"Hawkwind will soon no longer be Monarch," the Princess said again, "and you, my gypsy miss, are the instrument of his deposition!"

Ceria gave no sign to acknowledge the sudden fear within her. She had never seen Evirae this sure of herself. The vacuous, petty-minded Princess was gone, and in her place was a woman attempting to be sinister and deadly. Though her cruelty seemed overdone, her cloak of villainy faintly absurd, still Ceria could almost believe that those long nails were really poison-coated.

"You see," Evirae continued, "conspiring with an enemy spy is a traitorous act. Several guards and many of the palace personnel saw you attempt to save that Fandoran spy from arrest. As Minister of the Interior, as an adviser closer to Hawkwind than the Family itself, your actions are attributable to him! We have little alternative but to presume that he knows what you have been doing." She lifted a hand to her chest in a gesture that made mockery of Ceria's plight. "It is a sad day when a Rayan seeks to aid an enemy of Simbala!"

Again Ceria was silent. She could not bear the thought that the Princess would use her against Hawkwind. They had fought too long for acceptance, she had waited too long to bring a Rayan voice to Simbala's affairs to be defeated now.

"I believe you have not yet found the spy," Ceria said softly to the Princess. "Perhaps I can help."

Evirae's eyes widened as if she were a child seeing a toy for the first time. "You wish to make a confession?"

Ceria did not gaze at Evirae directly, focusing instead on the dresser behind her. "I do not know," she answered. "Perhaps if there were some *reason* for me to talk . . . It has been so long since I have visited my family . . ."

Evirae smiled. "I am loyal to those who help me, my dear. Certainly, a sudden departure could be arranged if you fully confess Hawkwind's role in this affair. I am less worried about the spy. There is no way he can leave the palace grounds undetected."

"There is so much to tell, Princess. I know not where to start." Ceria stared at the door near the dresser. "I must be assured that we speak in *total* confidence. I am very confused."

"Why, we are alone, my dear." Evirae glanced nervously around the guest chamber.

"No," answered Ceria. "I sense there is someone outside the door."

The Princess softly spun about, pulled the knob behind her, and spotted Mesor in the hall walking quickly away. "Come back!" she shouted. Then she slipped her head back into the guest chamber. "I will be only a moment, Ceria. . . .

"Mesor!" she whispered. "The Rayan wishes to confess! Make sure this hall goes unattended until you hear further from me."

Mesor sighed. "Are you sure, Princess? She might attempt—"

"She insists on privacy!"

"How could it hurt if one sentry remains—"

"You know she senses things! Now, hurry! Leave! Tell the others before she changes her mind!"

Mesor nodded reluctantly and hurried down the small landing. Evirae closed the door of the guest chamber and smiled.

"Now," she said, turning, "what did you have to say to me, Ceria?"

Ceria picked up a spiceball from a dish on the dresser and turned it over and over in her hands. "I don't know what to say," she said, approaching Evirae. "My life is coming apart—like this!"

She quickly thrust the spiceball beneath Evirae's nose and squeezed. The dry aromatic ball disintegrated; Evirae gasped in surprise, then sneezed as the powder filled her nose. Ceria lifted a small statue sculptured of talc from the fenestrella's ledge and swung it, striking Evirae at the base of her head, below the cushioning pile of hair. Evirae dropped to her knees with a cry. Ceria leaped to the small window of the chamber.

"As long as I am alive, you shall never be Queen!" she shouted, and then disappeared.

"Mesor!" cried the Princess. "The Rayan is escaping!"

The door burst open a moment later to reveal both the Bursar and a guard.

"She's gone!" Mesor cried. He lifted Evirae to her feet.

"That filthy Rayan!" Evirae sneezed again. "Oh, Mesor, my head is shattered! Is there blood? Tell me there isn't—it will ruin my gown! Oh, I'll have her endungeoned for this!"

"She won't get far," Mesor said. "She leaped from the window. It is a two-story drop—she must have broken her legs."

"She did not," said the guard, who was peering through the window.

Evirae and Mesor looked out in bewilderment. There was no sign of Ceria on the patio.

Hidden by the bushes of Evirae's garden, Ceria ran stealthily toward a neighboring mansion. She had landed squarely on the broad, cushioning leaves of a pillow plant below the guest chamber's window, and was now running to a horse tied to a nearby tree.

"There!" shouted Mesor. "The Rayan is headed toward the house of Lady Tenor. Get her!" he shouted to the guard.

The guard started toward the door, but as he did, the Princess stopped him.

"Wait," she murmured, her nails digging gently into his shoulder. "Stay here."

Mesor stared at her in shock. "Are you mad? After all we—you—have done? The Rayan is the key to your plan!"

Evirae nodded. "You are correct, Mesor. Her actions are crucial."

"Then why do you stand by as she escapes?"

"If Ceria escapes, she cannot be questioned. If she cannot be questioned, then the Baroness will be unable to challenge any of my accusations against her. She too saw Ceria take the spy across the palace lawn. That, and the traitorous actions which followed, are more than enough to win the vote of the Family."

Mesor shook his head. "You are too confident. Ceria will reach Hawkwind and warn him."

"You are too nervous!" snapped Evirae. "Ceria will go

south to rejoin the Rayan camp. They are thieves and liars, despite their talent. Hawkwind is of no use to her any longer. She will look for her fortune elsewhere! I do not think we will see Ceria again."

Evirae turned toward the window once more. From it she could see a small red figure on horseback rushing toward a gap on the edge of the palace grounds.

"Summon the Family," she said calmly. "I wish to discuss the miner's status."

"We should at least alert the guards between here and the Kameran Valley," said Mesor. "If Ceria attempts to reach Hawkwind, then they—"

"It does not matter," said Evirae calmly, "if she is found in the miner's arms."

●

As the Princess watched, so did another.

In a small chamber high above the courtyard, Ephrion was soothed by the sight of a black horse leaping a narrow row of bushes on the edge of the palace grounds.

"She's worthy of you, Hawkwind," he murmured. "We have lost time, but we have not lost hope. The Fandoran pursues the dragons as Ceria pursues their past."

He rose slowly to prepare for his departure from the palace. There was a message whose delivery he would trust only to an old and loyal friend.

●

The fog had finally lifted, for the most part, in the Kameran Valley. This, however, had been accompanied by a rising of the winds, and so using the windships was still rather risky.

The Fandorans had now returned to the hills, and the Simbalese had regrouped on the opposite side of the valley, near the forest. Hawkwind had delayed the order to charge toward the hills, because of the possibility of another attack by the dragon.

"We can surround the hills and wait them out," the General said to Hawkwind, "but there are plenty of fruit trees and small game in those hills—they could last for days."

"And the dragon could return at any time," Hawkwind commented.

General Vora shrugged. "We need more troops to make a successful assault into the hills."

Willen was standing nearby when this remark was made. He turned to the General and said, "We could win this war for you, General Vora. My people can go through brush and forest quicker than you go through a good meal, and a good deal quieter. We could penetrate the hills and flush the Fandorans out for you."

"You are insubordinate," Vora snapped, "and that is precisely the reason I refuse to consider such a move! Your people are too hotheaded! This is a war, not a personal vendetta!"

Willen turned and walked away angrily. Thalen said to Hawkwind, "My brother and I must return to Overwood, to lead the Windriders against that dragon!"

"Very well," Hawkwind said. "I agree; you will be of more service there. Go, then, and quickly!"

The two Windriders, most skilled of all their elite corps, ran toward the ships. Kiorte swung himself onto the deck of his ship and began spraying the Sindril brazier. Thalen watched him as he boarded the other windship. He felt a pang of envy and loss. Kiorte was aboard his own ship, a craft he had built himself, and loved almost as a parent loves a child. Thalen would ride a stranger this time—his own ship, the pride of his life, was a broken and charred ruin in the middle of the valley. He put such thoughts out of his mind with an effort, and began raising the sails. There was no time to think of his loss now. The safety of Overwood came first, much as he would have liked to sail again against the Fandoran soldiers who had brought his ship down.

The prisoner watched as the two windships were readied for launch. He knew he would have to make his move now. He was quite frightened, but he was even more frightened of remaining a captive of the Simbalese. So far, they had not treated him ill, only asked him a few questions about the battle plans of the Fandoran army. He had refused to answer—not out of any particular loyalty, but because he simply did not know. He was still afraid that they would work some terrible magic on him, though they had shown no inclination so far to do so. Still, he knew that he had to escape before they did.

Suddenly, he had his chance. As the two windships left the ground, an errant burst of wind caused one of the ropes still dangling from Kiorte's ship to whip about, threatening

a group of men and women, who ran to get clear of its
lashing end. His guards' attention was focused on that. He
took a deep breath and put his strength against the rawhide
loops. They cut into his skin; then they snapped, and he was
free. Before his guards were aware of it, he had seized one of
them and hurled him into the other. Then he turned and ran
toward the other windship, to which no one was paying any
attention.

A number of soldiers saw him running. They shouted and
gave pursuit, but none were close enough. The Fandoran
leaped up and seized one of the trailing ropes of Thalen's
ship. He clambered quickly up it, hand over hand.

Tweel heard the shouting, and saw what was happening.
Quickly he seized a crossbow and fired a bolt at the Fando-
ran. The wildly swinging rope, however, made him miss.
Then the Fandoran was on the ship.

The first intimation that Thalen had of him was when the
craft lurched from the sudden extra weight. The Windrider
was thrown off balance. By the time he had scrambled to his
feet, the Fandoran was on board, and leaping toward him.
He grappled with Thalen, lifting him with the intent of
hurling him overboard. Thalen boxed the other's ears painfully, causing the Fandoran's grip to loosen. They struggled
about, their shifting weights causing the craft to spin about.

Tweel raised his crossbow again and sighted. Hawkwind
saw the action and shouted, but too late; the bolt whistled
through the air. When Tweel had fired, the Fandoran's back
had been toward him. But the struggles of the two men
turned them about.

Kiorte, watching helplessly from his own ship, cried out
in horror as an arrow suddenly blossomed from his brother's
back. The force of the striking bolt threw both men off
balance; they staggered three steps, and the Fandoran's
back hit the railing. They both toppled over, to hit the
ground.

Kiorte brought his windship down quickly. When it was
close to the ground, he leaped from it, swinging down a
rope. Leaving others to catch the lines and bring the ship
down safely, he ran to his brother.

Hawkwind ran also, as did everyone not occupied in
bringing in Kiorte's windship or chasing the slowly descending other ship. Kiorte reached the bodies first. He

knelt and gently removed Thalen's broken form from the dead grip of the Fandoran. Then he turned, cradling his brother's body, and looked at Hawkwind. Hawkwind stopped; the hatred in Kiorte's eyes struck him like a fist.

"He is dead," Kiorte said.

Hawkwind said nothing. Neither did anyone else. Kiorte stood slowly, trembling. He took a step toward Hawkwind. Two soldiers stepped forward quickly, swords half-drawn to protect their Monarch. Hawkwind touched them on the shoulder gently, motioning them to step aside. He faced Kiorte.

"Thalen is dead," Kiorte said again, "and you, Hawkwind, I hold to be responsible!" He half-shouted, half-sobbed, "You sent the troops to the Southland! This ridiculous battle would have been over by now had you not!" He turned, his eyes wild and shining with unshed tears; turned about wildly, staring at the faces before him. Among them was Tweel, the crossbow still in his shocked grasp. When Kiorte saw him, he made an inarticulate noise and leaped toward him, hands outstretched for Tweel's neck. It took Willen and several others to restrain him. Kiorte raged in their grip for a moment, then, with an obvious effort, regained control of himself. Soldiers turned away, uncomfortable at the sight of the self-contained Prince exhibiting such emotion. Kiorte looked at Hawkwind again.

"I think perhaps Evirae is right," he said. Then he stooped, gathered Thalen's body in his arms, and walked to his windship. He laid his brother tenderly on the deck, and lifted the windship into the air again.

Everyone watched him sail swiftly away toward Overwood. Vora put a hand on Hawkwind's shoulder. "You are not responsible," he said softly. "Kiorte's grief spoke."

Still Hawkwind said nothing. He watched until the windship disappeared into the clouds. Then he turned slowly and stared toward the mist-shrouded hills where the Fandoran army hid.

●

The northerly winds carried the windship quickly. In little more than an hour's sailing, Amsel had already flown over the forest of the Northweald. "I guess I'm a better navigator than I imagined," he murmured. "Then, again, I've had little to decide in the grip of these winds."

Soon he spied the low cliffs and beaches of Simbala's northern shore. The craft was over them in a moment, and Amsel gasped as the gray flatness of the water came into view.

"Dragonsea," he whispered. "From here on, it is all new to me."

He turned toward the bow of the ship and saw in the clouds ahead a black shape bobbing slowly up and down. The coldrake flew ahead of him, and Amsel was sure it would continue to do so until they had reached their destination, whatever it might be.

He scurried forward and secured a jib sheet that had come loose under the force of the wind.

"What was it that Ephrion said?" he asked himself. Then he nodded. " 'Remember the legends you heard as a child; they may have more truth to them than we ever imagined.' "

He thought about the phrase for a moment, and then checked the cleats on the windward side.

"All secure," he said in relief. "I guess it would be safe to have a quick look at the cabin."

As he hurried toward the stairs, he thought about the war and the young woman who had sacrificed her freedom for his safety. There were many to whom he owed his life now, and Amsel realized with a mixture of determination and sadness that his days of solitude, of experimentation and planting, of inventing and construction, would not soon be seen again. He had always thought of himself as a man who bothered nobody and was unbothered in return. But then he had befriended Johan and . . . he shook his head. There was nothing to be gained in reliving that moment again!

He opened the door of the cabin. He found it to be an ingeniously designed area, making good use of space. Wooden cabinets were everywhere, and the polish of the chrome and quartz handles glistened like stars in the sky. Four hammocks of tanselweb were hung across the walls at the opposite side of the cabin. Behind them was a row of small glass portals.

Amsel opened the first cabinet and jumped back in fright. Then he laughed as he realized the furry masses were blankets for the crew.

He opened a second and third cabinet, finding nothing

but ropes and sail patches. When he opened the last cabinet, however, he smiled with delight. On a shelf, protected from the air by white gauze, were a dozen loaves of bread.

Famished, and feeling weak after all that he had been through, Amsel made a meal of a small loaf. He could not identify the grain. The bread was light and faintly sweet. He assumed, correctly, that it had been baked especially for Windriders to sustain them on their rigorous voyages.

As he ate, Amsel listened to the steady howling of the wind. He noticed that it did not lessen or vary, and he recalled watching high wisps of clouds from Greenmeadow Mesa scudding along at a constant pace. He wondered if such winds as this blew continually in the bleak upper reaches of the sky. What a convenient way to travel long distances—assuming, of course, that there were other such air currents going in different directions.

As he finished the bread, he began to feel quite sleepy. "No," he said. "I must stay awake!" He took a blanket from the shelf, and wrapped it about him, then returned to the chill winds of the upper deck. He sat down on a small ledge set within the bow and gazed out sleepily through the mists. He saw once again, above the northern sea, the familiar flapping of the coldrake's wings, and continued to do so as the windship floated gently into a large gray cloud. After a while the sound of the rushing wind and the unbroken movement of the creature's wings took on a hypnotic effect. Amsel felt himself growing sleepy again, and this time he could not resist.

He awoke with a shock. The windship was keeling wildly and losing height. "What a fool I am!" Amsel shouted, and he jumped quickly from the bow to grab hold of a leadline snapping against the folds of a sail.

As he did, the fur blanket dropped to the deck. "I'll get it when I come back," he muttered, but a moment later he realized that the weather was freezing cold.

He snatched up the fur and peeked over the hull. There was still nothing but sea. In the distance, an occasional inlet dotted the turbulent waters. He glanced north, and for a moment he thought he could see the silhouette of a shoreline, but it vanished in the fog.

Amsel hurried back to the task of securing the leadline. He had no idea how long he had slept—an hour, or a day. The gray light was the same.

"My friend still flies ahead of me," he murmured, as the ship plunged through a cottony cloud.

He ran toward the intricate rigging at the stern of the windship. The craft was starting to rock turbulently, for the side force of the wind had become much stronger than the forward thrust.

From his short voyages in the strait, Amsel knew that he would have to use these currents to balance the ship and keep it on its course to the north.

Taking the sheets of the mainsails in hand, Amsel raised his face to the bitter winds. "Good. Both winds are constant." He pulled in gently on the sheets. His strategy now was to use the largest sail to effect a falling-off in the force of the eastern wind which pressured it, blowing north behind the windship. This, in turn, would change the effect of the wind blowing north behind him.

"It has been a long time," said Amsel, "but if I remember correctly, this sail"—he pulled in hard on the large windward sail—"will do it."

It took a moment for the sail to respond, but after a brief interval of even luffing and falling off, the windship started to regain its balance, sailing forward in a northerly direction. Amsel sighed in relief. Ephrion had been correct—he *could* fly a windship!

Much later, he was still heading north. He could no longer see below the windship, for the clouds had grown more frequent and denser as the flight progressed. He thought he was no longer over the sea.

Amsel felt most alone and small. He wished—he, Amsel the hermit!—for a companion, another human being with whom he could speak. The feeling was uncommon to him. He had never known loneliness, for he had always lived alone. Yet there had been a time when a small child brought love and laughter into his world.

Amsel listened to the sounds around him, to the song of the sails, the whistling of the icy wind, and the distant flapping of the coldrake's wings.

What did he remember about dragons?

Over the years he had not paid special attention to the

writings about them. After all, dragons were considered creatures of fantasy, and his interests were of a more scientific nature. As a child he had read the most common tales of the dragons, in which they were noble creatures, friendly to man, living in the glowing caverns of gigantic cliffs. In these fairy stories, children of the Southland would be rewarded for acts of goodness by being taken for long adventures on a dragon's back. He remembered ancient pictures of children happily clinging tightly to a dragon's horns as it flew above the southern sea.

As he grew older, his contact with the legends was less frequent. In his readings he would sometimes find references to and descriptions of dragons in the literature of other lands. In retrospect, he realized how exceptionally consistent the descriptions of the creatures had been. He had attributed it then to a common origin of the stories in the Southland, but now he thought that there might be a more startling explanation.

The foreign legends were more extensive than those told by Fandorans to their children. He remembered a Bunduran author who wrote page after page about the glowing caverns, words that seemed as bright as the moon itself. There was another brief poetic mention of the treasure of the dragons, fabled stones with the secrets of the creatures hidden inside them.

Throughout the tales the dragons had remained consistent in their appearance. They had four legs, eyes of dark blue, beautiful wings, and the ability to breathe fire. Amsel contrasted this description with that of the coldrake, which had only two legs, eyes of bright yellow, and gave no indication at all of an ability to breathe flame.

Although he was grateful for that apparent lack of talent in the creature, it puzzled him. If it was a coldrake, a "cousin" to the dragons, as Ephrion had explained, then why did it not also breathe flame? Perhaps it did, Amsel mused, but had had no reason to do so. He admonished himself not to provoke it in order to find out. There were times when scientific inquiry could be fatal.

Coldrake or dragon, he thought, where are you taking me? To the glowing caverns? To a forgotten land? How much of your legend is not legend at all?

Hours later, he learned the answer.

He had been traveling in a cloud driven by the wind for some time, when it at last broke apart. The setting sun revealed that there was a shore not far ahead. It was a shore unlike any in Fandora or Simbala.

He passed quickly through another cloud, and when his view had cleared, he saw the terrain beyond the shore.

It was a bleak land, a blasted land, a land of sharp edges and needle spires—loneliness and desperation given cold embodiment. It was a land of darkness, a land that denied human life. A river wound its way through shores that were slabs of lava. Beyond them were weathered, angular piles of rock, as though tossed casually by a giant's child. The colors of the rocks were blacks, browns, and iron red, and the wind swept defiantly through them with a sound that made Amsel cover his ears in pain. Beyond the rocks, mountains rose that dwarfed the peaks of Simbala. Proud and defiant, some sheeted in ice, most too steep for snow, they continued beyond the river as far as Amsel could clearly see. On the periphery to the north, he could see a vast, glittering wall of white.

"It is not what I expected," said Amsel, "but I did not really have any expectations at all." He wondered where the coldrake was taking him. There would be no chance of the windship surviving a landing in those sawtooth peaks.

As though propelled by his thought, the creature began to bear slightly to the east. Amsel shifted the steering levers and followed. At the same time, he decreased the flow of Sindril gas, bringing the windship down out of the wind's fiercer stratum. The coldrake was flying slower now. He did not wish to deal with the consequences of overtaking it.

Slowly, then, he proceeded north. His hands remained firmly on the steering levers. The landscape remained distressingly consistent, until Amsel spotted in the distance a tall slender peak of black basalt. Its base was wreathed in mist, which he assumed emanated from hot springs—this was definitely a volcanic land. Its top was obscured by clouds. The coldrake swooped up toward it; this, Amsel was sure, was the creature's destination. As it approached, Amsel thought he detected movement in the mists. The windship passed into the tepid vapors, and its Sindril jewels glowed brighter as the humidity increased. Then, suddenly, the fog cleared. As the craft passed quickly through it,

Amsel looked down. What he saw was a land no legend had ever revealed.

The huge peak was riddled with cave openings, and in seemingly every one of them was the serpentine body of a coldrake. A hissing, like a snake's nest, came faintly to him as he drew closer; he was not sure whether the sound was made by the hot springs or by the hundreds of coldrakes who appeared to be watching. It was a scene to inspire madness. Some crouched upon ledges, tearing at the carcasses of animals. Others flapped slowly through the mist, croaking mournfully at each other.

Amsel had known no sight more frightening; it was a nightmare too horrible for any dream. He shuddered at the thought of a plunge into their depths, but forced himself to watch.

The hissing grew louder. Proudly, as if in silent communication, the coldrakes raised their heads. Then a hundred wings unfolded, and their mottled gray bodies emerged from the cliffs in a huge swarm.

Amsel screamed. The creatures were above him, shrieking with a murderous sound that mocked the wind. He watched in terror as they started to circle the windship, but as they did, he saw another, distant sight beyond them. As the fog rose above the spire, another coldrake, twice the size of the others, was perched upon its slender tip. Its yellow eyes were fixed directly on him.

Amsel watched those eyes, paralyzed with fear. This coldrake, black as the spire, was unlike the others in more than its size. It seemed to be observing him with an intelligence that was lacking in the others. He suspected that the dark coldrake held domination over those circling the windship. He listened as it shrieked to the others below it. The cry was echoed by the circling monsters, and Amsel started to weep as a circle of dark wings came closer and closer to the windship's sails.

Then suddenly the shrieking stopped as the larger creature took to the sky. Its wings were longer and darker than its brothers', and as it wheeled away from the spire, the other coldrakes returned to their warren.

As they did, Amsel leaped for the steering lever; the motion of their wings had sent the windship keeling. He wanted to turn the ship back, and he tried to tack, but the sails were trapped in the updraft of the hot spring below it.

Amsel gazed up. The sky seemed suddenly empty, but there was a faint whistling in the air. Then, from a height concealed by the windship's sails, the huge coldrake attacked. Its claws cut swiftly into the delicate ribbing of a balloon sail, and the gas exploded from within it.

Amsel screamed as the ship fell. The coldrake swooped down again, slashing the other large sail. As it ripped, Amsel caught hold of its sheet. He swung outward, past the hull, then back, just missing the mast as he did. The windship began to spiral downward, and the sheet tore free of the steering mechanism. Amsel, still holding it, sailed out beyond the fog. He suddenly felt heat against his skin, and he realized that if he landed in the hot springs below, he would be boiled alive.

He glanced downward and saw a jagged rock coming into view through the fog. He tried to shift his body away, but as he did, there was an unexpected thrust of cool air against his back. A black shadow appeared in the fog above him. Seconds later, huge talons clutched his vest.

Amsel screamed again, and the yellow eyes of the coldrake peered at him through the swirling mist.

XXVII

Monarch Ephrion stepped carefully onto the bridge. It was very old, and the elements had taken their toll of its construction.

He grasped the woven railing tightly and began to cross. In the pocket of his robe of state was a written message, which revealed what he had told Ceria, and in brief terms recounted his instructions to Amsel, the Fandoran. With this knowledge, Ephrion hoped Hawkwind would be able to quickly resolve the conflict in the Kameran Valley.

He walked slowly, knowing that any sudden move might break through the delicate floor of the bridge. He had decided upon this path because of its relative isolation. He could not afford to be seen leaving the center of Overwood alone. He would transfer the message to an old and trusted friend who could get it to Hawkwind without suspicion.

He rested for a moment at the center of the bridge. Looking down, he could see the river winding out of the forest. Then he looked ahead, and was startled by the appearance of two children running toward the bridge from a connecting tree. He waved his cane at them, hoping to ward them off, but they ran straight ahead. They were playing at war; both brandished wooden swords, the second yelling loudly as he pursued the first.

"I'll kill you, Fandoran!" he shouted.

What terrible words! thought Ephrion. We must put an end to this war. He tensed as the first child hopped

carelessly over a hole in the bridge. It quivered under their weight. "Slow down!" Ephrion cautioned them, but they ignored him and were quickly gone from the bridge.

Ephrion continued, again treading softly until he had reached solid ground. He rested a moment, then walked quickly through an archway toward a little-used path. This would take him back to the main road, a safe distance from Evirae's guards.

"Monarch Ephrion!" a voice said suddenly behind him. "Monarch Ephrion! Do you need help?"

Ephrion sighed. He needed only to get away from whoever was calling. He looked back and recognized a tall sentry from the lower floors of the palace. "No," he replied. "I am quite all right."

The sentry approached him, smiling. "Surely I can be of assistance, sir! You should not be walking unescorted in these parts. A spy is still missing in the forest!"

"I am merely taking a short stroll," said Ephrion.

The sentry was persistent. "Then may I have the honor of walking with you?"

Ephrion shook his head. "You have my thanks, but I would prefer to walk alone."

"I do not think I should leave you alone," said the sentry, who now stood only a few feet away.

Ephrion glared angrily at him. "How dare you object to my privacy!"

The sentry continued to smile, but in his eyes Ephrion could readily see a threat. The man was not merely concerned for the welfare of an old Monarch. He was one of Evirae's agents. "A Family meeting is to occur shortly," he said. "The Princess requests your presence there. What shall I tell her, Monarch Ephrion? I have been following you for a while now, not knowing when to interrupt. I did not dream you would be walking so far from the palace."

The meaning of the sentry's statement was obvious to Ephrion. The sentry knew he had departed on some sort of mission. If Ephrion did not attend the meeting, Evirae would suspect a plot to aid Hawkwind.

Ephrion stared angrily at the fellow. He would not be threatened by an ambitious sentry! The Princess could suspect whatever she wished! He had governed Simbala for over forty years, and in Hawkwind's absence he would do it again.

"In that case, fellow, you can indeed be of help to me," he said. "Return to the Princess and inform her that no Family meeting will be held until I return."

"Will you not accompany me, Monarch Ephrion?" The tone was still mockingly respectful, but there was an edge to it now.

"I will not," Ephrion said. "I have other concerns. Please return without me."

The sentry looked at Ephrion anxiously. He had not expected this.

"Are you refusing an order from the Monarch-Emeritus?" asked Ephrion. "Why do you wait?"

The guard looked puzzled, then turned and went back toward the palace. Ephrion sighed. *Evirae grows bolder by the hour,* he thought. The sentry's report would not favor him, but he had no alternative. Hawkwind had to be alerted as quickly and as safely as possible.

●

It was dark in the wooded hills that bounded the Kameran Valley. The full moon's radiance did not penetrate the foliage. A few small, carefully shielded fires burned here and there, and huddled around them were the remnants of the Fandoran army, sleeping the sleep of exhaustion.

Lagow stood in the darkness on the edge of one of the small clearings. His mind was full of images of Jelrich Town, of his wife, his son, and his daughter. Normally at this time of year, business would be picking up—people would want repairs done on wagons and farm tools, and the selling of spring crops would encourage some to order new furniture built. Instead of balancing a wheel or polishing a chair, he was here, with all these others, facing dragons and warriors in the dark. He looked around him at the men rolled up in blankets. He had come to know many of them, and he was shocked by their worn and tired appearance, compared to that festive night in Tamberly Town. It seemed so long ago now! It would be longer still before this madness would end. He hoped peace would come soon.

There were others, as well, who could not sleep. Dayon sat beside Tenniel, who groaned and muttered in his sleep, feeling pain as an endless succession of nightmares. The son of Jondalrun stared into the embers of a fire. He had not known what to expect from their foes, but he had thought about the possibility of some horrible, supernatural doom. Had not a dragon appeared? True, the beast had not attacked them, but this inexplicable fact was in itself sinister. Were the Simbalese toying with them? Dayon shook his head. He shook his wrist; the dry rattle of the seed pods was loud in the silence.

Dayon stared at the glowing coals. There was a slight sound nearby, and he turned to see Pennel, staring at Tenniel.

"He does not sleep well," Pennel said softly.

"Few among us do," Dayon replied.

Pennel looked up at the few stars visible through the black weaving of branches. "Here, at least, we are safe from the windships and the dragon," he said.

"Or here we are trapped by them."

"Do you think that the Simbalese have summoned the dragon, Dayon?"

"It seems likely."

"I wonder," Pennel replied. He stirred the embers with the toe of his boot. "There is more happening in this war than your father expected. He has said little about the dragon since it flew into the forest."

"Where did the dragon come from, then, in your opinion?"

Pennel shook his head. "I do not know. I can think of only one person knowledgeable enough to shed some light on the subject." He glanced sadly at Tenniel.

"You refer to Amsel the hermit?" Dayon asked. "Was he not a traitor?"

"I wish now that we had listened to him further." Pennel sighed. "Things are happening that we do not understand. I wonder if the Simbalese are not the least of our worries."

He walked off then, away from the feeble firelight, leaving Dayon alone with thoughts about a man he had known only through the words of others. "Amsel," he murmured, "was accused of plotting my brother's murder." He shook his head. "I shall never know if that is true, I guess. The hermit's body lies beneath the wreckage of his tree house."

●

Word reached Hawkwind after darkness, but it was a different message than Ephrion had originally written.

Hawkwind held the vellum scroll on an angle to the full moon in a clearing between the forest and the valley. To his left stood General Vora, scowling as he tried to read it over Hawkwind's taller shoulder. "What does it say?" he asked.

"The Princess has found evidence of treason," Hawkwind replied. "She seeks to have me removed from the palace."

"Impossible!" said Vora. "You have been here all the time! What evidence of treason could there be?"

"It seems that Evirae has implicated Ceria in the activities of the long-lost Fandoran spy."

"Nonsense!"

Hawkwind shook his head. "This is a serious charge. According to Ephrion, Ceria took the spy into the palace in full view of Evirae and Baron Tolchin."

"Is the Rayan mad?" Vora reached for the scroll. Hawkwind turned the vellum so that the General could read it. "According to Monarch Ephrion, my lady acted in the best interests of Simbala. The spy claims that Fandora has acted to avenge the murder of a child—a murder much like that of the child in the Northweald. Evirae has found a way to use the spy's encounter with Ceria as evidence of an alliance between the Fandorans and me. As a result, Monarch Ephrion suspects that Evirae will call a vote of the Family on the matter of my deposition."

"Surely it will not succeed. There will be dissension! Not all the Family will vote against you! Without a unanimous decision, the meeting will have little effect."

Hawkwind rolled the scroll back into the tube in which it arrived. "Who will stand by me? Certainly not Kiorte."

"Monarch Ephrion will support you."

"Yes," Hawkwind answered, "but he elected me to succeed him. He may defend me or call for my removal, but he may not vote on the matter."

"Then the Baroness will support you! You have spoken of her with admiration; she is not foolish enough to fall for Evirae's plan."

"Alora and Tolchin both saw Ceria take the spy into the palace. Will they ignore evidence that they themselves have seen? To do so would be tantamount to treason."

General Vora nodded in dawning realization. Jibron and

Eselle would back their daughter, as would the petty Ministers and other Family members who had more to gain with the Princess as Queen than with a miner in the palace. "There must be a way to prove your innocence," he insisted.

Hawkwind nodded. "How long will it take to ride to the southern plains?"

Vora was shocked. "You cannot be thinking of escape!"

"No, General, but I must use what Monarch Ephrion has told me. Ceria has escaped from Evirae to complete a mission for Monarch Ephrion. She seeks a jewel known as the Dragonpearl, which may be hidden in the Rayan camp of her childhood. It contains evidence of the dragons' affairs and may explain the reason for their actions against us. I must find Ceria and the Dragonpearl! It is imperative that we learn the truth about the dragons. They are as unfathomable as this war—and more dangerous than the Fandorans."

"You cannot abandon the army!"

"I will do nothing of the sort, Vora. In going south, I will be able to rally the Southland troops on their way back to the forest. With our men united, the Fandorans will run toward shore like a tree bear from a fire."

"I do not like it," Vora grumbled. "There is no telling what the Princess will do in your absence."

"Perhaps," answered Hawkwind, "but we know exactly what she will do if I remain." He smiled ruefully at the General. "Any man convicted of traitorous acts will immediately be imprisoned. Which appears worse to you? A missing hero or a Monarch in chains?"

Vora did not reply.

Hawkwind mounted and raised his arm, whistled, and the hawk streaked down from the sky. Perched on Hawkwind's shoulder, it watched silently as he turned his horse eastward. He would slip unseen into the forest and then ride toward the Valian Plains.

•

Ceria rode hard and fast, pushing Lady Tenor's horse with a relentlessness the beast had never known. She did not like to treat it so, but she could waste no time. Her mission was urgent, and she knew not if Evirae had sent agents to find her.

It was evening now. The sky was clearing. To her right,

the sun was beneath the horizon, and the clouds about it were russet and amber. The air was clean and fresh, the ground moist, but Ceria had no time to notice the beauty about her as she might have in earlier years.

If indeed she had seen the Dragonpearl hidden in the camp as a child, then it had to be jealously guarded. If it is such a treasure, Ceria thought, it will be difficult to convince them to give it to me.

True, she was the foster daughter of Zurka, the head of Shar Wagon tribe, but she had been a foundling, discovered by and raised as a woman of Shar Wagon. She had always felt a faint degree of difference in the way she had been treated by the other Rayan, but she hoped that the mystery of her past would not work against her now. She knew Zurka's daughter, Balia, had never thought of her as a true member of the wagons. Balia was not without influence.

She rode on over the gently rolling hills toward that area of the Valian Plains where the tribe would be camped at this time of the year. Near a crossroads, she passed the ashes and mounds of buried trash that indicated a recent encampment. She knew it had to be the caravan, escorted by the rest of the Simbalese troops. For a moment she was tempted to turn and ride after them, to tell them that they were needed in the defense of the forest in Overwood. She could easily overtake their slow and circuitous route home, but she knew that her quest for the Dragonpearl had been delayed far too long already.

It was late by the time she approached the huge semicircle of the wagons. She could smell the embers of the cooking fires and the rank scent of the giant goats that pulled the wagons. As she reined in her gasping horse, stiff-backed dogs sidled out from beneath the wagons, growling and sniffing warily. Ceria swung down from her horse, speaking to them softly, and though it had been years since they heard the sound of her voice, they licked her hands as she stepped over a wagon yoke.

Her horse would have to be walked and rubbed down immediately. The wagons were dark. She assumed the camp was sleeping. Then a shadow moved suddenly across a wheel. She started, then relaxed as she spotted Boblan, a mute dwarf, her mother's personal aide. He came toward her, smiling. "It is I, Boblan," she said, *"Tabushka*—I have come back. Tend to my horse, please—I must speak to my mother."

The dwarf nodded and hobbled off. Ceria turned toward the wagons, but as she did, a familiar voice called her name.

Ceria saw a woman step out of a wagon into the moonlight. She was the same age as Ceria; her hair was a dark, curly cascade, falling past her waist, and she wore an ankle-length dress covered with baubles and chains. It whispered as she walked.

"Balia," Ceria said softly. "Hello, my sister."

The other looked at her and said, "Do not address me as such. We are not sisters." Moonlight made her expression even colder than the words.

"Not by blood," Ceria answered, "but I have always loved you as such."

Balia folded her arms. She thinks me a traitor for leaving, Ceria thought. In her eyes I am no longer of the Rayan. Ceria felt sadness at this, but no surprise. She had known for years that Balia was envious of her. Ceria started to defend herself, then changed her mind. She had no time for the reconciliation of old rivalries. She had already made her feelings clear.

"I have come for the Dragonpearl," she said. "It is urgently needed by Monarch Ephrion."

Balia's eyes widened at the mention of the Dragonpearl, but she denied any understanding of what Ceria had said. "It is odd that you rush here on a mission for Overwood, Ceria, but ignore the people you claim to love."

These words puzzled the young Rayan, but before she could speak, Balia continued. "I am head of the camp now. Mother is ill. She has been confined to the wagon."

"I did not know."

"Of course," snapped Balia. "You were too busy with your lover." She wrapped a chain around one finger. "A Monarch is quite a coup, sister, but it means little to Shar Wagon. Leave now. You are not welcome here. We do not have what you seek."

"You are lying," Ceria said with calm assurance. "Do not forget that I have the sight. I know the pearl is here, and I must have it. Fandora has declared war on Simbala, and it may aid us in the battle. Let me see Mother. She will understand the urgency of my task."

Balia glared at her. "*I* am Queen here, and I do not take orders and insults from a miner's courtesan!" She turned and came toward Ceria, hands outstretched. "Begone, ere I have you driven forth!"

Surprise immobilized Ceria for a moment—she had not realized how deeply her sister's envy had taken hold. Balia's hand pushed her backward, away from the wagons. Ceria was suddenly angry. There was no time for such petty squabbles! She saw lights go on in some of the wagons as she tried to dodge past Balia. Her sister grappled with her. As she struggled to free herself, Ceria saw Boblan run past them. He knocked on the door of another wagon. Ceria pushed Balia away. At the same time, the wagon door opened, and the yellow light of an oil lamp spilled across the camp. The sisters looked up and saw an old woman watching.

"Mother," Ceria whispered, and ran up the stairs to the waiting embrace.

An hour later, when the faintest touch of dawn began to pale the stars, Ceria finished explaining the circumstances of the war, and how Ephrion had sent her for the Dragonpearl. "I must know if it is real," she said to Zurka.

There was no discussion among Zurka and the other Elders of the camp—only meditation. Balia watched Ceria, evidently desiring to speak, but the custom was to allow the Elders their say first.

The Elders discussed the matter in low tones. Ceria shook her head to keep her eyes open; despite her anxiety, she wanted to sleep. She had not yet rested from the journey south.

Zurka at last said, "Any opinion I give on this matter will be only opinion, as I no longer bear the burden of the camp. The decision must be Balia's." She paused. "You did see a Dragonpearl as a child, Ceria. It was not just a dream. Those of us who have had the sight have tried to probe its secrets. It has revealed some lore to us, but by no means all. The dragons did exist in olden times, but what became of them, I do not know."

Zurka rose slowly and went toward her wagon. Ceria watched anxiously as she climbed the worn, wooden steps. When Zurka reappeared, it was as though she had plucked the full moon from the heavens and carried it in her hands.

Ceria stared at the great shining globe as Zurka resumed her seat. It was as she remembered it in her dream—a smooth, glowing, opalescent sphere that contained clouds tinted with rainbow hues. They rolled and shifted, almost hypnotically. Ceria, staring at the stone, seemed to hear the faintest tinkling, as of wind chimes, deep within her mind. Excitement seized her, making her forget her fatigue momentarily. She took her gaze from the jewel with an effort, and looked at Balia. The hostility evident in her face brought Ceria back to reality like a dash of cold water.

Zurka was saying, "It is known that Ceria's talent is exceptional. It has been since childhood. Perhaps she is best suited to probe the mysteries of the Dragonpearl."

"Shall we give such a treasure to a woman who has renounced her heritage?" Balia asked. "Shall she take it and once again vanish for years? I will not permit it! If she feels she can succeed where the rest of us failed, let her attempt to help Simbala here and now. By my decree, the Dragonpearl shall not leave Shar Wagon tribe until Ceria proves herself worthy of it!"

Ceria looked at the other faces. They nodded assent. She looked at Balia. She knows I am exhausted, she thought; she wishes to see me fail and be humiliated. That way, she does not have to refuse me directly.

Zurka said, "I am sorry, but Balia is right to demand this. We have held the Dragonpearl for years—we have a right to know what secrets it holds before we send it away."

Ceria looked at the Dragonpearl. She had ridden all day and most of the night. She was exhausted, and now she faced a critical test unlike any she had known.

●

It was afternoon when sunlight at last broke through the clouds above Overwood. In the mansion of Kiorte and Evirae there was much commotion, for a meeting of the Family had been called and the Princess was actively preparing for her role. Monarch Ephrion would be there, she knew, with a plan to defend Hawkwind.

Tapping her long nails on the door of the dressing closet, Evirae called anxiously to Mesor on the other side. "My gown!" she shouted. "Where is my gown?"

"It is coming, Princess. The dressmaker is on her way."

"There is no time!" Evirae replied. "Get downstairs and bring it up yourself!"

"It will be here in a moment," Mesor said reassuringly. "Please be patient."

"Patient! How can I be patient when—"

The door of the bedchamber swung open. "Is that her?"

The Bursar turned and gaped at the sight framed by the doorway. "Princess," he whispered, "come out."

"I'm not dressed!" she called. "Is it the dressmaker? Tell her to hand the gown to me." Evirae's arm poked out of a crack in the closet doorway, and as it did, she heard her husband's voice.

"Kiorte!" she cried. The door swung back, and Evirae rushed out. She was clothed in only a petticoat and corset. A blanket of russet curls fell over her delicate shoulders.

Mesor left quickly. Evirae stood, staring in shock at her husband.

His uniform was torn and muddy. Evirae feared that he had been wounded, then realized with relief that he was not. "What has happened?" she cried.

Kiorte sat down on the bed, heedless of the blood and dirt on his uniform. "Thalen has been murdered," he replied. "Shot by a careless Wealdsman in battle."

Evirae was stunned. For a terrible moment she felt directly responsible, and the enormity of that guilt was more than she could bear. Up until now, the conflict had been abstract to her—an event that had advanced her plot against Hawkwind. She shuddered now, close to hysteria.

If it had not been for her scheming, there might not have been a war, and Thalen would be alive. Even as these thoughts tortured her, another part of her, a part that she could never fully control, began casting about for ways to use this tragedy to her best advantage. Kiorte would now be susceptible to her accusations against Hawkwind. She felt a surge of anger at her own heartlessness, but she felt unable to stop the thoughts. The war existed now, she told herself, whether her fault or not—and surely it was not entirely her fault, because Hawkwind was unfit to serve as Monarch. No matter what she had done, she still believed that to be true.

She realized that Kiorte was speaking; she heard his voice as though from far away. "Hawkwind must be removed," he said. "He does not know how to lead an army. There must be no more like Thalen." He stretched out on the silken bedcover, tears filling his angry gray eyes.

Evirae approached him, wondering why she felt no satisfaction from Kiorte's decision.

"Be calm, husband," she murmured. "Know that this evening there will be a meeting of the Royal Family. After that meeting, Hawkwind will no longer rule Simbala."

If Kiorte heard his wife, he gave no indication. His eyes were closed. She gently removed his boots, frowning slightly at she touched the mud and grime. As she sat on the bed beside him and unclasped his shirt, he lifted one hand and stroked her back. She stopped and looked at him. Her face, in that moment, was that of a very different Evirae, a woman many would have been surprised to see. In that moment, the love that lived so deeply within her, chained by ambition, was free. In that moment, conspiracies and confrontations were entirely forgotten. In that moment.

XXVIII

The sound of flapping wings and the faint odor of burning tansel awakened Amsel. He coughed, blinked his eyes, and gazed out sleepily through the mist.

Somehow he was still alive, and he was grateful for it. He glanced down and saw that he was on a warm, damp rock. He stood up carefully and stepped forward. As he did, he remembered what had happened.

He had been carried here by the black coldrake! He looked around quickly and saw a dank and ancient cavern. Its stark walls extended roughly fifty feet to a large irregular opening framing the mist. On the floor were strewn the skeletons of goats and other mountain creatures. He was not quite sure where he was; he wiped perspiration from his forehead and cheeks; then, with a gulp of humid air, he cautiously peered out over the edge of the opening.

Below him were the riddled cliffs that held many of the coldrakes' warrens. The drop was not sheer, but the climb down and the destination itself would frighten even the bravest explorers. The coldrake would surely see him. He looked up. Through a curtain of fog he saw the tip of the giant spire above him. From the strategic position of the cavern, thought Amsel, this could be the warren of the giant coldrake itself!

He gulped and looked down again, past the cliffs, and saw the flat rocks and rushing river far below. Through clouds of steam he glimpsed the scattered ruins of the windship. I guess I am to be another legend, he thought. The fool who found the coldrakes but lost the means by which he could leave them.

Amsel shuddered as a coldrake flew past the cavern. He stared down once again at the wreckage of the windship. Two or three of the creatures were searching the craft for any sign of life or food. As he watched, two rose from the mist with the broken mast of the windship in their claws. They flew high above him with it, even above the spire, and then, with a shriek, they dropped it. The mast plummeted toward the ground, barely missing a third coldrake who was flying off with a piece of the hull between its teeth.

Amsel anxiously patted the pouch at his side, and was relieved to find the bread he had stored there earlier. He took it out and ate it quickly. Though he had little appetite, he knew he would need his strength. The howling wind, the hissing, and the distant sight of the coldrakes below made him feel like a prisoner of this nightmare land.

The mist cleared somewhat below him, and about a hundred yards away from the shattered hull of the windship Amsel glimpsed a small fire. A section of the main balloon sail was draped over the edge of an enormous boulder; it was burning, and a smoky curtain rose above it. Amsel stared at the dark blue cloud and thought for a moment that there was another, larger shape behind it. Then he gasped as the cloud swirled away suddenly, and two yellow eyes peered out behind it. The black coldrake's wings swept the sky above the fire. The creature was circling the burning sail.

Amsel remembered the distinct feeling of intelligence he had gotten from the coldrake as it had approached the windship earlier. There was a mind behind those yellow eyes—different from a human mind, certainly, but nevertheless capable of awareness, of comparing situations and acting upon what it saw. Might it not be possible for him to communicate with such a creature?

It was a faint hope. At the sight of the Darkling above the flame, the other coldrakes began shrieking once again. The fire was to them a symbol of the dragons, the higher race to which they had been obedient long before the icy winds had touched these cliffs. Their reaction to fire was more than respect—they feared it. They would not approach the boulder as long as the balloon sail burned. The Darkling was different. He knew the dragon's fire in a way the other creatures did not. He no longer feared it. Although he regarded the balloon sail with caution, he kept his distance from it only because he knew he risked the wrath of the others if he did not. To him the fire was proof of the humans' hidden strength. Not only could they fly, but they also possessed the secret of fire. The wisdom of the dragons' edict was clear to him now. The humans were dangerous. The coldrakes were weak, their number diminished by the killing frost. The dragons no longer stood between them and the land of the humans. The balance, he thought, had been lost. The coldrakes were vulnerable to their cloud ships. To protect themselves, they would have to attack the land of the humans.

The Darkling shrieked and soared higher. He would return to the human he had left in the warren. He would learn how it used the secret of flame; then he would decide how best to attack. The coldrakes would hunt and feast, building their strength for the long journey south.

Amsel watched as the Darkling flew toward him. He had few alternatives. He could attempt to communicate with the giant creature, a highly appealing idea to a scientist—or a fool—or he could attempt to escape into the dark tunnel behind him. Either action could be fatal. The coldrake was swift, and Amsel assumed that its yellow eyes could see far better in the dark tunnels than his own.

Amsel decided to hide and wait. After all, if the coldrake had wanted him for supper, he could have eaten him long ago. There had to be a reason for leaving him here.

Then, as Amsel slipped behind the cover of a large rock, he heard the sound of flapping wings behind him.

The black coldrake's body blocked the light of the portal. In the sudden darkness Amsel heard the hissing and the slithering of the enormous black body over the damp cavern floor. There was a deafening shriek, and a sickening odor hit him. It was the scent of the coldrake. Amsel covered his ears and pressed himself farther into the shadows behind the rock. He could hide no longer. The creature was above him, its yellow eyes staring over the edge of the rock. Amsel screamed, but the sound was lost in the reverberations of the creature's shrieking. The Darkling slashed the air, and Amsel felt a talon as thick as his arm rip through his vest again.

Then, before he could grasp what had happened, Amsel found himself flying through the air. For a moment he thought he was about to hit the ceiling of the cavern, but the coldrake's claw dropped suddenly, and as Amsel looked out, he saw the creature's grinning jaws.

The Darkling cocked his head and observed the human. The idea that a thousand of these tiny creatures were more dangerous than even the frost made him shriek in anger. His blood would not suffer the same fate as the dragons!

Dangling before the coldrake's mouth, Amsel screamed desperately, "Do not hurt me! I have come from far away on a matter that concerns us all!"

The Darkling lifted him higher. The human's high-pitched chittering echoed in the warren. The Darkling could not understand it, but he was sure that no flame could burst from a creature so small. The humans held the secret of fire, but possessed no flame themselves. The dragon's edict could be defied if the coldrakes attacked swiftly and did not allow the humans to protect themselves in groups. Without flame, they were too small to be dangerous alone.

As for this human, he had served his purpose. There was nothing more to be gained from watching him. The creatures would be punished for their murderous acts. Soon the coldrakes would dwell in the warm land to the south. The Darkling opened his jaws.

In panic, Amsel searched for something, anything, he could use as a defense against the coldrake. Instinctively he reached into his pouch, but all that remained there was the handful of seed pods from his garden.

The coldrake screeched and lowered Amsel toward its mouth.

Amsel grasped the seed pods tightly. Then, as he felt his vest slipping from the creature's talon, he hurled the seed pods toward the long, sharp teeth. He felt himself falling after them. A second more, and he knew there would be no feeling at all.

The second did not come. What seemed to be an explosion flung him suddenly through the air away from the coldrake's teeth. Fortunately, he was able to roll with his fall.

As he hit, he glimpsed the coldrake's head reeling wildly above him. Then another explosion echoed in the cavern. Amsel gasped.

The coldrake was sneezing!

Amsel rubbed the arm that had been bruised in the fall and stood up quickly. The coldrake was still shaking its head and clawing at its mouth, evidently affected by the seed pods. It flung its head back again and screamed, a sound that almost burst Amsel's eardrums. He glanced quickly around the cavern for an escape route while the creature was still distracted. Large rocks blocked the cavern on either side, and so Amsel ran in the only direction left open to him—between the coldrake's wide-bowed legs, ducking his head to avoid the smooth belly. The creature screamed with rage again, and Amsel saw the huge tail whipping toward him. He leaped high in the air, letting it pass beneath him. He continued toward the edge of the cliff, and as he did, the coldrake, still sneezing, pursued him.

He reached the edge of the cliff, and realized there was no place left to run. A hundred coldrakes waited in the warren below him and behind him, and the angered Darkling was almost upon him.

He glanced back for a second, saw a black talon in the mist, and gasped. There was no alternative. He jumped.

The cliff dropped sheer for fifty feet or more, then curved gradually outward. It was wet from the mist, and Amsel found himself sliding down it at breakneck speed. His size and the fog would conceal him for the moment, but he expected the coldrake to appear at any second.

The surface grew rougher, slowing his descent and bruising him painfully. Amsel thrust his legs against projecting spires and knobs, then was at last able to hold onto a large rock before the slope ended in another steep cliff. His arms ached from the sudden strain, but he had no time for the pain; above him, through the mist, he could see the black shadow of the coldrake coming toward him. Amsel swung himself over the lip of the cliff, not knowing what was beneath him, and released his grip. He fell several feet, and landed on a wide ledge. He managed to keep his balance this time. The narrow overhang wound downward about the spire. Amsel descended it carefully, limping slightly, leaping over gaps. He passed the entrance to another warren, and a stench swept over him. Amsel ducked as the surprised creature within slashed at him through the mist. Then he was safely past, and still descending.

A screech sounded loudly, and a sudden wind buffeted him; he grasped a boulder tightly to avoid being swept from the ledge. The black coldrake hurtled past him, the tip of one wing almost touching the cliff. Amsel knew the coldrake's wings were too big for it to fly close enough to pluck him from the ledge, but the backwash from them could do the job as effectively. Ahead was a narrow chimney, where a splinter of the spire had broken free of the main body. He reached the safety of it just as the coldrake whistled by again. Bracing his back against one side and his feet against the other, he started down it. The basalt was smooth and wet, which gave him little traction, but spared his clothes and skin further damage. Then suddenly he felt rock beneath him. He had reached the top of a rockfall that had choked the chimney. From there it was a relatively easy descent down the jumbled rocky slope. Amsel ran, hopping, stumbling, tearing his hands on the rocks. The mist hid him from the black coldrake, and from the others; he could hear their shrieks of rage faintly above him, and he knew that it would not be long before they found him again.

He studied the rocks ahead. Below the warrens there was a series of thin gorges running along the foot of the cliffs, big enough for a man but too slender for the smallest coldrake. He ran toward them, but as he did, he heard the beating of heavy wings. The coldrake was coming!

Amsel leaped for the cracks that split the barren floor, and tumbled into a wet crevice. He hid within it and glanced out. There was a storm above him, born of angry wings. If the enraged creature could find him, it would seize him—*if* it could find him. Talons swept across the top of the opening, and Amsel ducked. The path ahead was too narrow for running, but if he stood sideways, he could slip through it. Amsel continued. The strip widened slightly, and soon he was able to run. "Only a little more"—he panted—"just a little bit more, and I'll be inside the gorge!" He watched the sky and saw the coldrakes circling above him. He hurried ahead, covered by the edge of the rock. Minutes later, he darted, panting, into the cliffs where a crack widened into a gorge.

"They can't find me here!" he shouted in relief. "They can't find me here!" He looked out through the slender opening in the cliff. "I'm safe!" He thought for a moment of his escape, of how a simple seed pod from Fandora had affected a creature of legend. "I'm safe!" he cried happily again, and he sat down for a moment to rest.

Then he remembered the freezing winds that would come with the cover of darkness.

Night fell a few hours later. Despite his theory that the coldrakes could see clearly in the darkness, Amsel was sure that most, if not all, of the creatures had given up their search for him. The clear palette of the night sky reassured him that he was no longer being chased. He was cold, but he had kept as warm as possible by moving quickly through the gorge. He was quite hungry now, but his pouch was empty. He had discovered all the seed pods were gone when he had looked for some remaining pieces of bread.

"If I can get far enough away to make a trip out to the riverbank," he murmured, "I may be able to find a little vegetation."

A short time later, the gorge opened into a wider valley. To the west he could see the bank of the river. Growing around it were a few rushes and reeds, even a sapling or two, all covered by a thin layer of frost. He peered up at the sky again and sighed. I must have something to eat, he told himself, even if it is no more than a plant. Slowly he moved away from the edge of the gorge, down the valley, toward the riverbank. Fifty feet ahead, he suddenly saw what appeared to be a hairy beast, waiting for him in the darkness. Amsel froze in his tracks, but as he did, he realized that it was not a beast at all, but a sleeping fur that had evidently fallen from the windship when it crashed. "This is most fortunate!" Amsel sighed, quickly wrapping the fur around him. Then, as he reached the riverbank, he noticed something floating slowly along the shoreline. It was a piece of wood covered by a blue cloth. No, thought Amsel, not a cloth, a section of the balloon sails. He retrieved it from the freezing river. It had obviously been carried south, away from the other wreckage of the windship. The piece of wood was a foot wide and a little taller than he was. The cloth from the balloon sail was shredded, and Amsel was at first disappointed that he would be unable to use it except as further insulation from the cold. Then it occurred to him that the wood could be used as the basis for a raft. He now realized how he could use the sail. After gathering several tall reeds and saplings, he would have something with which to tie them together.

"I shall have to risk it," he murmured. "It is far too cold for me to travel much farther by foot."

In the next three hours Amsel busied himself gathering wood and building the raft. The full moon was quite high when he finished. At last he pushed the tiny craft into the river and began his journey southward.

He observed the high cliffs on both sides of the riverbank. "I will watch for the Glowing Caverns," he said. "It may not be long before the coldrakes take flight again. If their attack on Johan was any example of what is to come, then I must, I must, find out the truth behind the legends of the dragons!" Although he was convinced that the coldrakes were responsible, he still had no idea why the children of Fandora and Simbala had been killed. Amsel thought of the horrors he had faced in the north and the war for which he felt responsible.

A quiet weeping filled the canyon, a sound as lonely as the howling winds. Farther north, clouds hid the moon, and though Amsel did not know it, silent wings still searched for him.

•

At midnight, word was sent quickly to the Kameran Valley.

The meeting of the Royal Family had been brief. Monarch Ephrion's objection to the inconclusive and surreptitious nature of Evirae's charges had been considered insufficient. He was unable to divulge what had happened between him and the Fandoran, for it would throw suspicion on his defense of Hawkwind. Similarly, Ceria's mission could not be revealed. He still hoped that she would return to the forest with evidence to explain the mystery of the coldrake's attack.

The Princess herself spoke with compassion and restraint, giving a memorable performance that Mesor would have loved had he been permitted to attend. She received the unexpected support of her husband, and of other Ministers who had been willing to give the miner a chance in calmer times, but who were now deeply concerned and angered by the losses suffered under his direction in the war.

Baroness Alora was also swayed by the news of the losses—Thalen's murder could not be tolerated, no matter how much she admired Hawkwind's effort to seek reforms. He had brought the hot-tempered Northwealdsfolk into the army. She called for Hawkwind's suspension for the duration of the conflict with the Fandorans, but she wished to defer the question of his complete removal.

Tolchin supported the proposal out of respect for Alora's wishes, but it was soundly rejected.

Jibron and Eselle were the last to speak, and it was they who moved for the removal of Hawkwind from the palace on the grounds of treason and inadequacy in military matters.

The vote was unanimous.

Despite Ephrion's protest, Evirae would have the title of Queen.

•

The road that Hawkwind had taken to the Southland had received the heaviest part of the Spring rains, and parts of it had been flooded. Hawkwind now came to one of these parts—a low gully where the road had been completely washed out. He reined up before it and looked about the woods. The sun was just above the horizon. His hawk had flown ahead to search the road for danger. It would have returned to him had there been dangerous animals lying in wait, but he could not expect it to understand that a stretch of water was impassable to him. Hawkwind whistled and the piercing sound cut through the stillness. There was no response. The bird had evidently flown far ahead. Hawkwind turned his horse to the left and plunged into the woods, riding up the slope. His horse picked its way easily through the woods. It had been trained for battle and for the hunt; many times had Hawkwind gone into these woods to hunt for stag and wild boar. It was a dangerous sport, but the courageous animal had never failed or faltered during it. Hawkwind smiled at the memories. Relaxing in the saddle, he let lapse momentarily his habitual awareness of the woods. His first realization that danger was near came when the horse suddenly neighed a warning cry upon entering a small meadow. Then the dark curtain of the forest nearby was pushed aside, and, with a shattering roar, a gigantic bear shambled into view. Hawkwind, in that moment of clarity that comes with a sudden shock, saw just within the trees the dead body of a cub, felled by a hunter's arrow. The bear was obviously full of grief and rage. She roared again, and then charged toward them.

The horse leaped forward, needing space in which to maneuver. Hawkwind's legs tensed, keeping him in the saddle, as the horse gave a mighty leap that carried it over the bear, which rose too late to her hind legs in an attempt to claw it. She whirled quickly and rushed forward again.

Hawkwind barely had time to draw his sword. "Clear!" He shouted, and the horse leaped to one side. Hawkwind leaned low as the bear passed and attempted to hamstring her, but the blow did not cut deeply enough to reach the tendons. Furious at the pain, the bear turned quickly and rose upon her hind legs, leaning on a small tree that uprooted beneath her weight. Hawkwind's horse reared and struck at the bear with its front hooves. The bear struck back; the horse retreated, but not quickly enough to escape four shallow gouges on its flank.

Hawkwind struck again with his sword, wishing he had the long spear he normally used in hunting. His blow did no good; the bear lashed out at the sword and struck it from his hand, numbing his arm in the process. Now there was nothing with which to keep her at a distance. The distraction that other hunters would normally have provided was also missing. There was only one thing to do. Hawkwind leaped from the saddle, whirling his cape from his shoulders as he did so. He ran to one side, shouting and waving the heavy cape with his good arm.

Now there were two targets. The bear hesitated, then snarled and hurled herself at the small, dancing human, ripping furiously at the flapping thing that cracked at her eyes. Behind her, the horse screamed and struck again with its hooves. The bear turned and raised a paw to strike; she was within easy range, and could disembowel the noble beast with one blow. Hawkwind gasped, but before the bear could strike, an explosion of feathered fury about the bear's head distracted her. The hawk had come! Shrieking, all

talons and beak, it wheeled about the bear, then pulled up steeply, wings laboring, out of reach.

The bear turned about in a circle, completely bewildered by this third and, to her, almost invisible assailant. The hawk dipped down again, needle claws stinging the bear's muzzle, while Hawkwind moved quickly to the edge of the forest, picking up his sword. "To me!" he cried, and the horse responded, slowing to let his master mount. Hawkwind swung into the saddle and the horse galloped swiftly back toward the woods. The hawk screamed a final challenge and followed, leaving the bear bellowing furiously in the empty clearing. They heard the thunder of its pursuit, but it could not move as swiftly as they between the trees, and they soon outdistanced it.

Soon they came out onto the road again, beyond the flooded area. Hawkwind slowed his horse to a canter and drank from his canteen. His arm ached, but it was not broken. He had been very lucky, he knew. He gathered herbs for soothing juice to treat the shallow wounds of the horse. As he did so, his hawk perched on the saddlehorn with a triumphant cry. Hawkwind grinned. These two animals had risked their lives to protect him. He knew that he could do no less for Simbala.

The journey ahead was long, but there would be nothing else to stop him. He knew of the Rayan camps; he had heard Ceria speak about Shar Wagon many times. He would find it, he would find Ceria, before the sun set again in the sky. Whatever evidence Monarch Ephrion had directed her to recover would be taken back to the forest by them.

Hawkwind knew that Simbala would support him, if only he could determine the truth behind the war and the dragon.

He stared at the road that threaded toward the Valian Plains. The troops from the Southland would be returning through the Eastern Pass. If he could reach Ceria first, then rendezvous with the caravan, he could be back in Overwood in a day's time.

The bear had not stopped him. The Princess had not stopped him. Come what may, he would return with the means to win the war. He took to the saddle again and, hawk on his shoulder, rode down the darkening road.

Tweel sat sadly on a rock at the edge of the clearing occupied by the Northweald volunteers. He was gazing silently at the moon when Willen approached.

"Vora still refuses to allow us to infiltrate the hills," he said. "You'd think the Simbalese army was cracking their lines, the way he talked."

Tweel ignored him.

"They're not doing a single thing. Not a single thing! Frightened of the dragon, they are—Vora, too. With Hawkwind off on some secret mission, no one wants to make a move. You'd think there'd be a charge! The farmers are just hiding in the hills. We could push them back to the boats in an hour!"

Again Tweel was silent.

Willen frowned. "Vora won't trust us at all!"

"Can't blame them." Tweel grunted. "It wasn't a Fandoran that killed Thalen."

"That wasn't your fault," Willen said. "It was an accident."

Tweel shook his head. "That doesn't change what happened. I'm worse than a fool."

"Now you're going to sit there and brood over it?" Willen scratched his cheek, covered with a light beard. "You're a Wealdsman, Tweel! You can't just sit there!"

"What am I supposed to do?" Tweel yelled.

Willen pushed him off the rock. "Do not forget the reason we came here!" he shouted. "A child of the Northweald was murdered by the Fandorans."

"There is nothing we can do if General Vora stays here."

Willen glanced in the direction of the General and the cavalry, positioned on the other side of the clearing.

"Vora keeps saying we're not a part of his army. Why should we obey his orders? I say we take our contingent, slip into those hills and flush those child-killers out!"

"What about the dragon?"

"Who cares about the dragon. Every one of us is a hunter! We'll see how it flies with a hundred arrows in it! Come, Tweel! Here's your chance to show Vora you can hit the right target!"

Tweel rose quickly and stared at Willen in anger.

Willen's face reddened. "I am sorry, friend. Sometimes my words are said too fast. I'm not the enemy, Tweel." He pointed at the hills. "They are."

Tweel exhaled sharply, and nodded.

•

The two Wealdsmen quickly mobilized the rest of the Northweald troops. Quietly they slipped into the darkness. They moved slowly around the perimeters of the hills, up the large gulleys and ravines that opened into the Kameran Valley. They took advantage of the trees, rocks, and bushes to conceal themselves. Willen knew that Fandoran sentries watched from the hills. He had told the others with him to take their time. On occasion, they took an entire hour to cross ten feet of open space. In the ravines, where darkness pooled thickly, they made their way through unseen dry leaves with no more sound than a breeze. They moved slowly and surely, toward positions in a rough ring around the center of the hills. They would have one chance at surprising the Fandorans, Willen knew. He intended to see that they drove them back to shore.

XXIX

Amsel continued his voyage down the river all night. The journey was ofttimes perilous—his makeshift raft tumbled down shallow rapids and through narrow passes at tremendous speeds. During these times Amsel would cling to the bonds that held the tiny raft and hope that it would not shatter against the rocks. Even with his fur wrapped around him, he was shivering, but in his heart one tiny flame burned, and it was the hope that the dragons did exist. For if the coldrakes planned to descend on Fandora and Simbala, only a creature as large as a dragon could stop them.

His concern was heightened by the approach of a storm. Chill winds began to whip around him, and flurries of sleet occasionally fell. By the full moon's light he could see clouds massing against the sky.

Fortunately, the storm took its time about developing. By the time dawn arrived, the sky was an angry gray, but rain had not yet fallen. Amsel could see lightning among the distant peaks. Although there had been moments of astonishing beauty in the past few hours, Amsel found it hard to imagine a land more desolate than this chilling canyon. The only colors were the white of snow, the pale, pale greens of the infrequent flora that bordered the river, and the browns and reds of the rocks and the cliffs. Despite the danger, Amsel dozed intermittently, for he was bruised and weary. In his dreams, the coldrakes returned, and he awoke frequently to the sound of a whistling wind.

•

The Darkling led his legions through an icy pass in the cliffs to the east. They would hunt for whatever still roamed in these parts of the canyons; they would prepare for the coming battle. The humans were clever, they knew, and their size betrayed little of their murderous ways. The specter of the dragons haunted him. His edict now violated their own, and never, never had he taken a step that far. Yet the dragons were gone, he told himself again, and his brethren would perish without protection from the cold.

A lone emissary had been sent south. It would watch for any more of the humans' cloud ships, and should it find the tiny creature that escaped, ensure that it would not return to the south.

The Darkling moaned as the cold winds chilled his wings. The coldrakes would endure this land, this cold, no longer. The humans had dared to violate what was sacred to them, and in doing so, had invited their attack.

•

Amsel wondered what time it was in Simbala. He knew nothing, of course, of what had happened, but if the sophistication of the palace was an example of Simbalese technology, then the possibility of Fandora's victory was slim indeed. He told himself that if Jondalrun had surrendered, then at least Monarch Ephrion would see to it that Fandora would not be dealt with badly.

He looked up behind the base of the cliffs to the sheer white walls that faced the canyon. Large stalagmites of ice were melting on the higher levels, and they crashed loudly on the rocks below. The ice and the snow extended for miles beyond the top of the cliffs. It was strange how dim light made murky shadows on the snowy walls. At times it almost appeared as if clouds were moving within them. There was a large icy mass ahead, and within it a dark and irregular shape seemed to lie waiting. Fascinated by it, Amsel reached for his spectacles and remembered that they were gone.

He lifted the long pole from its berth between the slats of his raft and pushed it in the water. The river ran slower here, and it would not be difficult to bring the craft closer to shore. He wished to have a better look at the cliffs as he passed by. Glancing up again in his vigil for coldrakes, he saw the skies were empty and pushed ahead.

"I think," murmured Amsel, "that this might be a good time to do a bit of foraging on shore." He was torn between hunger and sleep, and as he pushed the raft toward the river's edge, he decided he would go several hundred feet along the shore before turning back. He hoped to be able to find some small edible plants and at the same time get a better glimpse of the mysterious cliffside ahead.

He docked the raft securely, and climbed up the icy bank. Then he hurried east, keeping his eyes on the wall of ice above him. Several minutes later he saw a sight worthy of the most fantastic legends.

Encased within the ice of the frozen cliffside was a huge winged creature. It looked as if it had been frozen in flight. Although he could not make out its features clearly, Amsel knew that if this was a coldrake, it was the largest coldrake he had ever seen.

He approached it, forgetting to stay close to his raft, and as he saw the creature more clearly, he realized that this could not be a coldrake at all. "Four legs, two giant wings," he whispered. "It is a dragon!"

He jumped. "A dragon! It *is* a dragon!" The legends were true! Dragons did exist! Or at least, had existed, for this creature had obviously been frozen for ages. Still, it made him hope. He wanted to share that feeling, but the canyon was silent save for the sound of the river behind him and the storm above. He once again felt a desperate longing for another human voice.

Then suddenly, the sound of flapping wings assured Amsel that he would not continue his observation alone. He had forgotten his vigil, and, as was so often the irony of life, he had forgotten at the very moment he should have remembered.

A coldrake was diving directly toward him. Amsel started running, his fur blanket dropping on a shattered block of snow. He was about three hundred feet from the edge of the cliffs now, on a sloping floor of rock. The slope was icy and his progress was maddeningly slow. Twice he slipped and fell, rolling down several feet. A flurry of snow pelted him, and thunder rumbled again—evidently the storm was about to start. Amsel dug his boot into the melting ice and started to climb toward the top of the rocky slope. A shriek cut through the thunder. He turned and saw the coldrake hurtling toward him.

What followed was a ballet of terror. Amsel remembered the rocks slipping beneath his hands, scratching and tearing at his clothes as he scrambled up the slope. He had not turned to see how close the coldrake was; his attention was focused on the climb. He barely made it through a crest at the bottom of the cliff, as the coldrake swooped angrily upward to avoid hitting the rock itself. Then, with a wail, it attacked again, and Amsel heard a shriek of disappointed rage as the creature realized it could not pass through the crevice.

Panting, he stared out and saw the coldrake's claws scrabbling for purchase on the loose rock outside the cliff. The leathery booming of its wings echoed through the cavern behind him.

The creature peered through the crack in the cliffs. Its odor filled the passage and Amsel fought a sudden surge of nausea. He dashed deeper into the luminous tunnel.

Minutes later, there was the echo of sliding rock, and the flapping faded. Amsel turned around and glimpsed the coldrake flying away from the cliff. It frightened him to think that one of the creatures had been dispatched for the purpose of following him, but he knew now that he was safe. At least, he was safe from the coldrake.

He looked around the cavern. It was the first time he was able to notice where he was. The passageway was high and quite wide, growing wider as it went farther into the cliff. Evidently this had once been a much larger opening, but had been blocked long ago by a landslide. Regaining his balance and breath, Amsel saw that the walls and floor of the passage glowed. They felt somewhat warm to him, and soothing to the touch. He had no idea what accounted for the phenomenon at first, but closer investigation indicated that the rocks were uniformly coated with some sort of lichenlike growth. Amsel scraped a few flakes from the wall with his finger. They glowed for a moment in his palm and then faded to ash. Amsel instinctively deposited them in his pouch, but as he did, scientific curiosity gave way to childlike excitement. He suddenly realized what he had found!

"The walls are glowing," he said breathlessly, "and this is indeed a cavern!" He touched the lichen gently. "The Glowing Caverns! These are the Glowing Caverns!" According to legends, it was here that the dragons had lived. He had seen a dragon frozen in the ice outside the cliffs. Perhaps others yet lived within them!

Amsel started to run deeper into the cavern, but as he did another thought pushed its way into his mind. If the dragon in the ice had been so close to the Glowing Caverns, why did it meet such a horrible fate?

Amsel had no answer. He descended farther into the cavern, anxious but wary.

The glowing lichen covered everything, and its varying thicknesses produced different intensities of light, from beige to sunny yellow to orange. Amsel wandered beneath natural archways, past huge stalagmites and stalactites. Although winds swept occasionally through the tunnels, the temperature was quite comfortable. "All in all, quite a nice place to make home," he told himself, "but I think it would be quite lonely here." That statement made him blink in surprise. Solitude had always been one of his prerequisites in choosing a home. Yet here he was uncomfortable with the thought of isolation.

Mindful of what had happened to him the last time he was underground, he kept a careful mental map of his route. The large passageway he followed soon joined another, even larger tunnel, and down the middle of this flowed a stream—no doubt a branch of the river he had rafted. The general slope of the passageway was always downward. Amsel walked for some time before the passageway forked. The route he was following sloped down to the left, and he continued ahead into a larger area. As he descended, the stream disappeared into a small tunnel on his right. "I'm getting close to something," murmured Amsel, and as he passed the opening where the stream vanished, he realized that the passageway ended at the edge of a cliff. The noise of the stream faded, and he became aware of another sound replacing it—a vast, slow regular passage of air, like the intake and release of breath. *That could not be,* he thought.

What could take one breath that was equal to ten of his? Then he realized what it was, what it had to be.

The long search had come to an end. Amsel walked toward the edge of the cliff. Looking out slowly, he saw an enormous subterranean chamber illuminated by the glowing lichen. Within it, a pair of fabled wings beckoned silently.

A dragon was sleeping on the gray stone floor.

•

Vora watched Kiorte's windship descend in the predawn light. The Prince rode with a palace guard. Vora knew this soldier bore ill news for Hawkwind. Kiorte and the guard approached, and without a word the guard handed him a rolled proclamation.

The General glanced at the wax seal and frowned—it was the signet of all the royal crests, indicating a fiat by the Royal Family. He opened it, read, and looked up in shock. Evirae was to be made Queen tomorrow! Kiorte had been sent to assume control of the troops.

"I am sorry," Kiorte said. "But it is for the good of Simbala."

"It is for the good of Evirae!" Vora shouted. "She has wrapped all of you in her web! I refuse to have anything to do with this," he continued in a softer voice. "Hawkwind governs Simbala, not your wife."

Kiorte showed no emotion. "Where is Hawkwind?" he asked. "I have papers ordering his arrest."

Vora sneered. "Papers! More papers! She will not have him, Kiorte. Hawkwind has gone to the south to bring back the missing troops."

Kiorte looked appalled. "He has left the army with you?"

"Yes! What else could he do, with your wife accusing him at every turn?" He turned away in disgust.

Kiorte looked at Vora disdainfully. "A true Monarch would never desert his army," he said.

"A true Windrider would not use his wife's ambition to gain control of it!" Vora glared at Kiorte, as if ready to flight.

"That is enough," Kiorte whispered. "There shall be no arguments in front of the men. I suggest we work together in the best interests of Simbala."

"Never!"

"I am in charge of the army now, Vora. It would be foolish for you to turn your back on its affairs."

"The situation is under control!"

"Control? Vora, my brother was murdered!"

These words stung the General, for he felt some responsibility for what had happened. He turned away. "It was the fault of a Wealdsman," he said in a lowered voice. "Not a soldier."

"The Wealdsfolk were recruited by Hawkwind in another attempt to change our ways!"

Vora did not look at Kiorte. "The Wealdsfolk are worthless to us, I agree."

"Where are they?" asked Kiorte. "I wish to see the man responsible."

Vora glanced up. "They are stationed in a clearing behind those trees, awaiting new orders."

Kiorte shook his head. "That clearing is empty. I saw it as I landed."

"You are in error, Kiorte. I assigned them there myself."

Vora sent a messenger to bring back Tweel, but minutes later the woman returned alone. "The Northweald soldiers have decamped," she said. "Nobody seems to know where they have gone!"

•

Baron Tolchin hummed a favorite tune as he strolled down the walk to Evirae's mansion. He observed the sentries outside with amusement, and looked up to the bedroom window. He spied the red-cheeked face of General Jibron inside and overheard the words he was saying to Eselle.

"It is over at last," puffed Jibron. "Tomorrow Evirae will be formally installed as Queen. Kiorte has already left to take over the troops. The Fandorans will soon be driven back to shore!"

The Baron nodded. Although he still felt uneasy about defying Ephrion, he did not regret it for the lives of too many men and women were at stake. He felt the diadem in a hidden pocket of his coat. The whole affair had been an ordeal. He did not wish to see the miner imprisoned, but he knew Evirae would offer no pardon.

He passed the guards and entered the mansion. Above it were the friendly sails of two windships Kiorte had ordered into duty as a defensive measure against the dragons.

•

Although he had not played a direct role in the meeting itself, Mesor viewed the outcome as the culmination of his work for Evirae. All of her petty intrigue he had turned into politic action; his ambition had resulted in her success. With Evirae in the palace, his position and safety would be assured.

He had Couriers spread word, in subtle language, to merchants and officials that there would soon be a change, and that the Princess would remember old friends—and old enemies. Many ignored this veiled threat, but from a few it brought quick response—assurances that those who once sneered at him now were capable of seeing the sterling qualities they had previously overlooked.

Mesor knew that if he moved quickly, he could make himself a fortune in tookas. On the unfortunate possibility that Evirae did not rule more than a short time—the Royal Family would be watching her closely—he would still have those tookas.

It was not long before his new status was confirmed. At just past midnight, the news of Evirae's impending coronation was announced by criers throughout Overwood. Hawkwind was Monarch no more!

•

Dawn had come and gone. The rising sun turned the dew to wisps of fog, giving an ethereal quality to the plains. Ceria sat by the cold ashes of the fire, staring intently into the shining globe before her. She had sat thus for hours focusing her mind on the Dragonpearl, but what she had learned had already been discovered by the Rayan in the past. The people of the wagons who had at first gathered about her in interest had now drifted away to their morning chores. Only Zurka and Balia still waited, the old woman appearing tense as she watched her foster daughter. Even Balia, though pleased by Ceria's apparent failure, was anxious to see if anything more could be learned from the stone.

Ceria was beyond fatigue. Her body seemed distant to her, and she scarcely felt the aching in her muscles brought on by the long journey and the stillness with which she sat staring at the stone.

She had unlocked the same information as the other

Rayan easily enough, and the gently rolling clouds had seemed to part almost eagerly as she watched. She and those around her had viewed within the jewel a green and lovely land. Slowly, as though borne by giant wings, they traveled through the blue of a cloudless sky, over rivers and rugged mountains whose caps were laden with snow and whose sides were thick with forest. Although the scene was blurred and indistinct, it was clearly a land abundant with life. Ceria had felt herself growing closer to it, seeing vast hazy shapes at rest in the valleys beside gently flowing streams. They appeared to be sometimes with four legs, sometimes two. Despite their varying sizes, all had wings. Accompanying this scene, Ceria had sensed a deep peace and contentment. The creatures basked in the sun, bathed in hot springs, and found food among the trees. It was an age-old paradise; the sense of centuries passing was strong as one scene melted slowly into another. The dragons seemed to prosper; the two-legged ones became more numerous, but the larger creatures continued to dominate the land. After a time, however, like a single disharmonious note in a beautiful symphony, Ceria sensed a feeling of dread. There appeared clouds above the dragons' land and she struggled to see beyond them with her mind. Then the rainbow mist closed over the scene and the Dragonpearl returned to a pearly silence. She could not probe further. The tale within the sphere remained a mystery, a story without end, as it had to the other Rayans who had attempted to fathom it.

Now Ceria felt her exhaustion. Her weariness was weakening her concentration. She became aware of the pains in her body and the need for food and sleep. She tried to ignore them, for she knew that if she gave up now she would have to return to the forest without the Dragonpearl. She had to stay awake. She knew the answer to the mystery of the dragon's attack could be found within the jewel. Her fatigue would not disappear, however, and even as she fought to stay conscious, her thoughts became fragmentary and incoherent, and faded into the familiar blackness of sleep.

Zurka held Ceria as she started to slide sideways toward her. Balia continued to stare at the stone. The mist had faded, but the color was not that which it had been when Zurka had removed it from her wagon earlier. Despite Ceria's state, it still seemed to be functioning.

Zurka pressed her fingers against her daughter's neck and listened to Ceria's regular breathing. The color was returning to her cheeks. "She is resting," said Zurka. "There is nothing more she can learn from it now."

"Wait!" gasped Balia. "Look at the stone!" As her stepsister spoke, Ceria's serene expression became troubled, as though she was experiencing a nightmare. Her hand in Zurka's felt suddenly cold, and gooseflesh rose on her arms.

"The stone, Mother! Look at the stone!"

Zurka looked.

At first, she saw only shifting white, as though the clouds inside the stone had been drained of their colors. Then she realized that she was looking at a blizzard inside the sphere. She watched it, and, as others returned to see what had happened, the Dragonpearl seemed to expand, to fill their visions and their minds.

Then again they saw the valleys and mountains of the land of the dragons, now covered with snow. Snow gathered in drifts and fell in avalanches that buried the dragons. They saw the peaceful streams freeze over with ice. As they watched, the scenes of winter continued, terrifying in intensity and puzzling in their meaning. Freezing wind cut through mountain passes. Glaciers moved slowly but inexorably through valleys, their blue ice shearing trees away and scrubbing the mountains bare.

The dragons appeared again, and now there was a terrible feeling of loneliness and fear. The creatures dwelled now in caverns, their numbers much fewer. As the cold grew worse, some began to leave, in small groups at first, then in larger numbers, flying to the east and the west. There came now a sense of loss and agony. The glow of the Dragonpearl grew dimmer. They looked into the darkness and saw the remains of dragons—bones and the dried flesh of gray wings strewn across the floors of the caverns. These corpses, these ghastly relics of the beautiful creatures, were both large and small. As they watched, the scene drew closer and closer, a sea of ivory, and the sense of sadness was overwhelming. . . .

Ceria moaned and sat up. She saw the mist fill the sphere

again and its radiance diminish. She tried to stand, and Zurka helped her to her feet. "The dragons perished," Ceria said in a shocked tone.

Zurka stroked her daughter's arm gently and whispered, "Ceria, you have delved deeper into the Dragonpearl than any other I have known. It is time that you rested."

Ceria nodded, but said, "I must bring it back to Overwood. There is much that we have seen that we do not fully understand. I must show the Dragonpearl to Ephrion. I must prove my—"

"You shall have it," said another, deeper voice. All eyes turned to Balia, who had also risen. There was no anger in her words, but her feelings were evident to all who knew the story of the two sisters. The spectacle of Ceria's triumph had once again undermined her own importance. Had Ceria remained at Shar Wagon, she would have been chieftess. She was favored by all, even Zurka. "It is rightfully yours to take," said Balia. "It is needed by Simbala. You have proven yourself worthy of it. I do not object any longer." Balia started to walk away from those that had assembled. Ceria pulled away from Zurka and rushed toward her stepsister, barely able to keep her balance. Balia turned and caught her.

"Do not be angry with me," Ceria whispered.

"Angry?" said Balia. "I am not angry with you. You have lost little of your skill during your absence. I am as impressed as the others. There is nothing else for me to say."

"You envy me, Balia. Do not deny it."

There was a look of resentment on Balia's face, but she did not argue with what Ceria said.

"You are beautiful," Ceria continued softly. "Far more beautiful than I. You have remained in Shar Wagon and I have not. You have cared for Mother. I have cared more for myself. There is no reason to envy me, Balia. My talent is a gift. I have not earned it the way you have earned the respect of our people. I have come to find a way to help end the war and to help Hawkwind. In doing so, I may be able to prove my innocence to the people of the forest. I come not to compete with you, Balia. Can we not truly be sisters?"

Balia stared at the young woman. Her face was worn and pale and her hair dangled clumsily down the side of her head. Balia knew there was truth to Ceria's words and knew also that the camp could use a friend of such commitment and intelligence in Overwood.

"We have always been sisters," Balia said gently. Then she waved to Zurka.

"Mother!" she called. "Prepare a bed for Ceria!" Balia felt her sister's weight against her and murmured, "I think she is about to faint!"

•

Ceria dreamed of dragons as the sound of hoofbeats filled the campsite. There was much shouting and confusion for a few moments as the intruder dismounted to ask questions. Then the Rayan watched quietly as he walked toward Zurka's wagon.

The noise outside had awakened Ceria and she caught the light of the moon through a window of the wagon. "Balia?" she whispered. "Is that you?

The door to the wagon opened, and Ceria heard a man's voice as she focused her eyes in the shadowy light.

"My love," said Hawkwind. "We must leave at once."

Ceria noticed his scars and the slashes on his cape, but before she could learn what had occurred, Hawkwind silenced her. "Evirae has won the approval of the Family," he said. "We must return to the forest! Have you succeeded in your quest?"

Holding herself close to Hawkwind, Ceria nodded. "Yes, I have found the Dragonpearl. If what I have learned is true, then the dragons threaten us alone. They are not the allies of the Fandorans. They are few in number and I sense that they are frightened."

Hawkwind listened to Ceria's words intently, running his fingers through the Rayan's dark hair. "We must end the war," he said, "and face the real danger. Ephrion has informed me of the truth behind the Fandorans' attack. If the dragons have murdered the children of both our lands, we must find a way to stop them together!"

Ceria looked at Hawkwind in surprise. "How can we join forces with the Fandorans? We are at war with them now!"

"That is why I have come south, Ceria. I must return with the troops from the Southland to defeat them. Then there will be time to convince them of the truth."

"That will not be easy." said Ceria. "A country defeated in war is never anxious to join forces with its enemies."

"Unless the enemy is a common foe," replied Hawkwind, "such as the dragons. You must help me, Ceria. I must regain my title and control of the troops, before Evirae becomes Queen."

Ceria wrapped herself in Hawkwind's cape. "She will never be Queen," she whispered, "not while Ephrion lives in the palace."

•

As Hawkwind fed his horse in a clearing beyond the camp, Ceria bade good-bye to Zurka and Balia. She was still quite tired, but she knew she had no time to waste. The rest of the wagon folk dispersed, save for Boblan, who watched as Zurka handed Ceria the Dragonpearl. "When I saw you had returned, I knew it was for this," the old woman whispered. "I pray you have discovered what is needed to end the war."

"I pray I have too," Ceria replied, "and I only wish I could be grateful for the circumstances that have brought me back to you both again."

Her mother smiled at those words. At that moment, there was a shrill cry in the air above them. Balia looked up and saw a hawk circling overhead as Hawkwind rode toward them through the clearing.

Ceria gazed around the clearing. How peaceful it seemed here—how much she was giving up, it seemed to her in that instant, to return to a world of war and intrigue. She loved the woods and the plains, but she loved Hawkwind more than either.

"Good-bye," she whispered to her mother and sister, and then Ceria turned her horse to ride with Hawkwind toward the missing troops.

•

Willen peered through a curtain of underbrush at a large clearing, within which was a contingent of perhaps fifty Fandorans. Some slept, but most were awake, crouched over the embers of small fires or restlessly moving about and sharpening the farmers' tools they had for weapons.

Willen stared for a moment, then moved silently back into the darkness of the trees. He traveled a prudent distance,

pursed his lips, and gave an expert imitation of a night bird's call.

After a time, there was another shadow among the many that cloaked the woods. Then another, and another. The stealthy gathering spoke, one after another, in tones no louder than the falling of leaves. They told how many Fandorans each had seen in the hills.

Willen listened, then said softly, "There are more than we thought. We have the element of surprise, but we are not enough to rout them."

"Perhaps, now that we are here, General Vora will be inclined to send Overwood soldiers to reinforce our attack," Tweel suggested.

Willen nodded. "Return to him, Tweel. Say that we will attack at dawn, and for his troops to be at the perimeter of the hills, waiting to join us."

Tweel nodded, rose, and seemed to disappear, so silently did he leave.

•

A slight ground mist had risen in the cold predawn hours, adding an eerie touch to the shadow-shrouded hills. Tamark and Dayon entered a small bower where the Fandoran wounded had been gathered. Both fishermen had some small medical knowledge, but there was little they had been able to do for the injured men. They had splinted broken limbs, poulticed wounds, and given rosewine to the invalids to help them sleep.

"This waiting is even harder on my nerves than the battle," Tamark said softly, putting his hand against a feverish soldier's forehead. "There has been no move from the Simbalese for hours. I wonder what they plan."

"Nothing good, I am sure," Dayon replied. He crouched beside Tenniel. The young Elder looked very pale. As Dayon inspected the dressing on his shoulder, Tenniel's eyes opened and stared into his for a moment. Dayon gasped; he had not thought Tenniel would regain consciousness this quickly.

Then Tenniel's eyes closed again.

Dayon smiled. "He will recover." he said.

"Aye," Tamark said grimly. "Recover to live as a cripple."

Dayon did not reply. They turned away from the wounded. The young navigator felt as though the dark mass of trees was closing in on him. Tamark was right—the constant waiting was hard. The stillness of the predawn hour and the mist combined to produce a most uneasy feeling.

As they were about to leave the bower, Tamark's huge hand suddenly closed like a clamp on Dayon's upper arm. "Look!" he whispered.

Dayon looked ahead, and with a chill saw a dark, shadowy form in the trees. It was moving swiftly in their direction.

●

The moon was down, and the coming dawn had not yet lightened the sky. Tweel did not have to worry about being seen by Fandoran scouts as he ran across the width of the valley to the Simbalese camp. He was challenged by a sentry, who refused to let him pass even after he identified himself as a Northwealdsman. Instead, he was escorted into the camp, protesting angrily. Then Tweel saw Prince Kiorte's windship behind the supply lines. His heart started beating like a bird in flight. He was trapped. The flap of Vora's tent was tossed aside, and Prince Kiorte, followed by Vora, stepped into the torchlight.

Several soldiers awake at this hour gathered about curiously, but at Kiorte's sharp command they left the three alone. Kiorte stood before Tweel, face impassive, hands on hips. Tweel, remembering the feel of those hands about his neck, coughed reflexively. Bravely he explained his mission in words he thought most proper and formal.

"Willen of the Northweald has taken an invasion force to the hills." Vora closed his eyes in weary shock, and Tweel suddenly noticed that the General had aged much in the past few days.

The muscles of Kiorte's jaws tightened—whether in anger or concern, Tweel could not tell.

It took considerable fortitude for Tweel to continue. "He requests that General Vora order Overwood troops to ring the outside of the hills. At dawn, the Wealdsmen will attack. With help from the army, we should be able to drive the Fandorans back to shore."

Kiorte watched Tweel, then in a soft voice said, "No."

"No?" cried Vora. "We cannot leave them there!"

Kiorte averted his eyes and exhaled sharply, as if in regret, but when he spoke his voice was firm. "We cannot afford to waste more soldiers in a hopeless attempt," he said. "If the

Northwealdsfolk foolishly risk their lives to be heroes, it is regrettable, but done. It is not the way of Simbala." Kiorte looked at Vora, then Tweel. "I refuse to send more soldiers to be killed. I intend to implement my own plan."

"You refuse to give us aid?" Tweel burst out, forgetting the Prince's anger in his own indignation. "Our soldiers cannot defeat the entire Fandoran army unassisted! To deny them aid is . . ."

"Is what?" Kiorte asked softly, his eyes burning as he stared at Tweel. "Murder? You are familiar with murder, are you not?"

Tweel tried to suppress his temper. "I tried to save your brother's life, Prince Kiorte."

"I am sorry that you did not succeed." Kiorte turned and summoned two Windriders with a snap of his fingers. The men approached and saluted. "This Northwealdsman is to be taken back to Overwood," Kiorte said. "He is to be held until my return."

The Windriders seized Tweel's arms. He struggled uselessly. "General!" he shouted. "Do not listen to him! You must send troops to support Willen! You must send the troops!"

Minutes later, a small windship rose above the edge of the valley and flew east toward Overwood.

●

Dayon stepped back quickly, one hand going to the sword thrust through the rope belt of his tunic. As the figure before him stepped into the dim light of the clearing, he recognized the man, although he did not feel much relief. The man was dressed mostly in black, with a black eyepatch. He was a Wayman. Dayon had often seen him, apart from the rest of the men. He was taller than most Fandorans, and from a distance on other occasions he seemed to be watching the others with an attitude of superiority.

Now it seemed to Dayon that the Wayman's face had been filled with concern.

"Arouse the men," said the Wayman.

"Why?" asked Tamark.

The Wayman frowned. "Do not question me, Elder. I have had much experience at knowing when danger is about to approach. It is my profession."

Dayon nodded. "I feel it too, Tamark. Something is waiting out there."

The Wayman looked at him grimly. "Summon some men and bring them here! There will be trouble before dawn breaks!"

Dayon hesitated; then, at Tamark's nod, he turned and ran back through the bower, down a slope and into one of the clearings where the camps were. Several of the men sprang nervously to their feet as he entered. He saw a few Elders asleep by a small fire. Jondalrun was among them. Dayon hesitated a moment, noticing how even in repose the old man's features did not relax. Should he wake him? He decided against it. His father needed rest.

He turned to the men. "Come with me," he said. "Alert the other contingents—I want ten men from every town. Move quietly!"

The men seized their weapons and moved quickly into the shadows.

•

Willen kept his eyes on the eastern horizon, where it looked slightly lighter—the merest hint of dawn approaching, the dawn that would be the signal for attack. He had remained in this spot for over an hour, not moving except to occasionally, carefully stretch and flex his muscles. His men and women had spread out in a circle that completely surrounded the Fandorans. With the help of the Overwood troops, the invasion would be crushed. They would drive them back to shore.

Willen held in one hand the rainbow fragments of shells that had been found with the Northweald child. He looked at them, returned them to his pouch, and gripped his knife. He thought of a torn, ragged, and bloody dress. A child that had not been his, but that might have been.

Suddenly the quiet was disturbed by the sound of people moving through the underbrush. It could not be his soldiers—they would not make crashing sounds like a frightened stag! Then he heard shouting, growing steadily louder. What was it?

A moment later, he knew.

•

The eastern sky was growing light by the time the men had gathered. "There are enemy soldiers all about us," the

Wayman told them. "I have been walking in the woods, and I have heard them signaling each other by bird cries. We must attack before they do, to turn the tables on them. There cannot be many."

The men quickly divided into four groups, led by Dayon, Tamark, the Wayman, and another Elder. They moved through the woods by the four compass points. None of them had to go very far. Within moments Dayon spied the silhouette of a man in a tree. Simultaneously something whistled in the air, and a man screamed, an arrow embedded in his chest. Shouts rose all about them as the other groups discovered the hidden Northweald troops. The waiting that Tamark and Dayon had found so nerve-racking was over.

•

Lagow had been absent from the clearing when Dayon had given the order. He was still thinking of home as he stood alone in the woods. Then he heard the attack begin. Shouting and thrashing, faint at first, but growing rapidly louder, came from all about. It has started again, Lagow thought. Full of horror, he dashed back to the clearing. He saw that the Elders were awake. Jondalrun leaped to his feet. "They have infiltrated the hills!" Lagow shouted.

"That is impossible!" Jondalrun cried. "We had sentries everywhere!"

"Dayon suspected!" another shouted. "He took men to investigate!"

Jondalrun turned and picked up his sword in his wounded hand, wincing at the pain. "Follow me!" he shouted, and charged toward the sounds of war, followed by the rest. Lagow followed as well, hardly realizing what he was doing. He prayed that this time there would finally be an end to it.

•

The battle of the hills was short, but nonetheless fierce. The Northweald soldiers, expecting to surprise the Fandorans but being instead surprised by them, had lost their biggest advantage. Another factor in the Fandorans' favor was the dawn, which now came to show them how significantly they outnumbered their foes. The fighting quickly disintegrated into small groups scattered here and there throughout the hills.

The Wayman knew that this battle had to be won quickly, before the main troops might decide to move against them.

Though he fought, he fought with regret. He had hoped that both sides might have learned their lesson after the first battle. Evidently this was not to be so.

Jondalrun and the men hurried through the woods and came upon Dayon and his group, fighting the North-wealdsfolk in a large clearing. "Surround them!" Jondalrun shouted.

Willen saw Jondalrun shouting orders. The North-wealdsman was loath to strike a blow at a man his father's age, but the man was obviously in authority.

Jondalrun barely saw the blow in time to parry it. Willen, off balance, stumbled and fell. He rolled behind a bush, where he lay concealed for a moment. The battle was going badly, he realized. Where were the Overwood troops? They should be into the hills by now, shattering the last of the Fandoran resistance. What had happened to them?

It soon became obvious that no such aid was forthcoming. The Northwealdsfolk, disheartened by the fact that the Simbalese army did not come to their aid, and outnumbered by the Fandorans, started back toward the safety of the forest.

"We have them now!" Jondalrun shouted.

Lagow crouched behind a tree, watching the fighting. He would have nothing to do with it anymore! If he could escape from this hill alive, he would leave this battle, leave this war, and try to somehow return to his wife and children. The war would continue without him until they were taken prisoners or killed. To remain or to leave was no longer a question of patriotism—it was a question of sanity.

He hurried around the edge of the clearing, keeping in the shadows, away from the fighting. Between two boulders ahead was an opening in the rocks and dense undergrowth, away from the battle. He would find his way back to the boats and somehow cross the perilous Strait of Balomar.

Lagow reached the natural archway formed by the boulders. It opened into a narrow passageway through the rocks and trees. He could hear no sounds of fighting through there. He hesitated, then looked back at the battle.

The Fandorans were beginning to push back the Simbalese. Lagow saw Dayon, separated from the rest. The youth had seized a length of branch and was using it as a quarter-staff against the blows of a Northwealdsman's sword. Even as Lagow watched, an overhead slash by the Wealdsman broke the staff. Simultaneously Dayon, stepping backward, hit his heel against a rock and fell, sprawling on the damp ground. The Wealdsman drew back his sword for the fatal thrust . . .

"No!" Lagow shouted. He ran forward, hurling himself at the Wealdsman. Surprised by this unexpected interference, the Wealdsman turned and thrust blindly. Lagow felt the blade enter him, sliding easily between his ribs, a shaft of coldness that seemed to numb his body. He fell forward, tearing the sword from the Wealdsman's grasp. Dayon leaped to his feet, holding the broken staff, and swung it against the Wealdsman's head.

Then he knelt beside Lagow, cradling the old man's head in his arms. Lagow opened his eyes and looked up at Dayon. He had the look of a child who has been hurt without understanding why. He gasped, as though trying to say something. Dayon leaned closer, trying to hear.

There were no whispered last words. Lagow's eyes closed.

Dayon laid him back onto the grass, his own eyes blurred with tears. "I know," he told Lagow. "I know it must be ended."

He looked around him; the battle in the clearing was almost over. Jondalrun sat on a log gasping for breath about forty yards away.

"Father!" cried Dayon, "Elder Lagow has been killed!"

"No!" Jondalrun shouted. "That cannot be! He was not fighting!" He stood up from the log and rushed toward his son.

By the time Jondalrun reached him, he had already seen the wheelwright's body resting in the grass. "No," he repeated in a quiet voice, "it cannot be."

Dayon grasped the Elder's arm. "He saved my life, Father. We have pushed the Simbalese back again. We must retreat now before they return! You must call for retreat!"

Jondalrun glared at him. "Do not order me!" he shouted. "I am your father!" Then suddenly he became silent.

Dayon stepped back and watched as his father stood at Lagow's side.

"He always fought me," Jondalrun whispered, "but I will miss that bitter voice."

He turned back to Dayon, tears filling his eyes. "There is

no feeling of triumph," he said. "We have defended Fandora's pride, but there has been more bloodshed than I ever thought possible. Were it not for Lagow, I could have lost you, too."

This defense of the hills had long taken his mind from the reason for the invasion, but memories of Johan came to him now, like the tears upon his cheeks. He remembered the laughing, life-loving child riding on the ox's back after plowing was done, chopping manfully at wood with the small ax Jondalrun had made for him, playing with his friends in the Toldenar Hills near the farm.

He tried to summon up the same wild rage he had felt when he first found his son's body, and realized that he could not. There was none left in him—only a sadness and weariness. It was time for war to end. He looked up at Dayon and said, "We will retreat."

XXX

It is sleeping," Amsel whispered as he peered over the edge of the cliff. "It does not even know that I am here."

He quietly observed the dragon. It was indeed a creature worthy of legend. It slept with its tremendous head on its paws, and two magnificent gray wings folded and peaked like hills around it. It had four legs, not two, and though its size was twice that of the Darkling, it gave an impression of grace and agility belonging to a creature half its size.

Amsel sensed that the dragon had been respected, not feared, in its day, but he also sensed that its day had passed. The dragon gave an impression of immense age. The skin on its wings was pebbled and cracked, and the tufts of hair about its face were snowy white. As he listened to the creature's breathing, Amsel realized that, despite its tonality, it was labored and weak. He felt a sadness each time the dragon sighed, a sorrow unlike any he had known.

Then he noticed the manacle. It encased the dragon's front paw and was connected to a heavy metal chain. The chain itself was fastened to a stalagmite that had been sculptured into the shape of a terraced building on the cavern floor.

Amsel drew in his breath. By the scale of the edifice, it had to have been built by human hands! He anxiously examined the rest of the cavern, wondering at the same time why the creature would be chained. There were arched passageways

417

running through the side of the cliff, and wide stone steps ran down the cavern wall to his left. Throughout the cavern, the stone had been covered by the glowing lichen. Only in the area around the dragon did the stone seem bare; the lichen had obviously been eaten in the creature's search for food.

"I don't think he'll be of much help," Amsel murmured. "I wonder where the other dragons could be?" He started to walk along the edge of the cliff, looking at the dragon instead of his path. Suddenly he stumbled on a loose stone and it rolled over the side.

Amsel held his breath as it plummeted toward the cavern floor. It hit a lichen-covered boulder with a dull thud, but the sound was magnified a hundred times by the acoustics of the high stone walls. There was a sudden change in the dragon's breathing. Then a deep snort resonated through the cavern. Stepping forward slowly, Amsel peeked over the tip of the cliff.

A dark blue eye looked up at him. The dragon was awake!

Amsel saw the creature lift its head. "I've come within a hairsbreath of being eaten by a coldrake," he whispered, "and now I've awakened a starving dragon!"

The dragon lifted its head higher and roared, a noise which sounded to Amsel as if a door to history itself were being opened. Frightened, Amsel sought refuge behind a rock. The roar was repeated again and again, its echoes filling the cavern. Amsel covered his ears. How, he asked himself, could a creature so old possess the strength to bellow the way it did?

Amsel thought he detected a pattern to its sounds. He listened closely to them again and took a tentative step forward. Peeking out again, he glimpsed the dragon struggling against the heavy manacle. The clanking of its chain was lost in the deep, sonorous sound of the dragon's voice. The creature could not reach him, but it continued to roar slowly and deliberately. The cadence was like that of words.

"I . . . smell . . . manscent!"

Amsel listened in astonishment. They were words!

"I smell manscent!"

Amsel looked at the creature in shock. The slow bellowing voice seemed to be talking in a language like that of the Southland!

"He said something about man," Amsel muttered. "If he repeats it, I think I will be able to understand."

Amsel stepped closer to the edge of the cliff and leaned out bravely. As he did, the dragon thrust its head toward him and bellowed again.

Its warm breath washed over Amsel, and he was surprised to find the odor pleasant, though overwhelming.

"You . . . have . . . returned!" The dragon's words reverberated around the walls.

"Returned?" Amsel muttered. "I have never been here." He peered out at the dragon and cautiously repeated the words aloud. "I have never been here!" he shouted. "I am from Fandora!"

The dragon was silent for a moment; then it lifted its head as high as it could. "Slowly!" it bellowed. "Your words are too shrill! Breathe them slowly."

Amsel shouted the words again. At this rate, he thought, my voice will soon be gone. Then, as his last words faded in the cavern, Amsel added, "I seek your help on behalf of the lands of Fandora and Simbala!"

The dragon watched him and repeated the names in a slow, somber tone.

"Yes!" cried Amsel. "That is correct! Fandora and Simbala!"

The dragon lowered its head slightly. "I have never heard of them," it rumbled.

"They have been attacked by the coldrakes!"

The dragon raised its head again. "The coldrakes?"

"Yes!" Amsel shouted.

"Come down," said the dragon.

Amsel blinked. The dragon wanted him to come closer to the cavern floor!

"Come down!" roared the dragon again. "Men built a way long ago."

Although he had observed the stone staircase earlier, Amsel made no effort to reach it immediately. He glanced at the dragon's long yellow teeth. If he was in range, the creature could eat him in a moment. Should he risk a descent to the floor of the cavern? He was convinced the coldrakes' attack on Fandora and Simbala had just started, and that Johan's murder would be followed by more if they were not stopped soon. If the creatures had plans to attack the humans, then it would take creatures as large as a dragon to prevent the coldrakes from journeying south. Regardless of his own safety, he had to find a way to engage the dragon's help. Threat or no threat, he had to learn the truth and discover a way to end the war.

If I stay far enough away, he thought, the dragon would still be unable to reach me. With that precaution firmly in mind, he approached the stairs.

By the time he reached the bottom, the creature seemed to have returned to sleep. Amsel stepped delicately on the soft, glowing lichen. He felt as if he were standing on the surface of the moon, by the way the floor radiated beneath him. It had a calming effect as he walked forward.

From this new position he could see the dragon more closely. He winced at the sight of the manacle around its paw. The metal was rusty with blood. Amsel was baffled. If the descriptions in the legends were true, and it certainly appeared as though many of them were, why had a creature as noble as a dragon been imprisoned?

He was now determined to find out. As he approached the dragon, he estimated the range of its neck and its claws. He edged as close to the creature as was safe.

"Hello," said Amsel.

The creature's horns seemed to move, but it did not open its eyes.

"Hello!" Amsel repeated.

The dragon raised its head slightly and one eyelid slid open. A mirror of midnight blue appeared, and Amsel saw himself in it.

"Come here," said the dragon in a low, grumbling sound that Amsel both heard and felt. It tapped one claw on the mossy floor.

Amsel waited. Shackled or not, that claw was too reminiscent of the coldrake's.

The dragon sighed. "Come here," it repeated in a less imposing tone. "I will not hurt you. It will be easier to talk if you are near."

Amsel took a deep breath. If he went any closer, he would be in range of the dragon's claws. If he did not, the dragon might get angry. "Remember the legends you heard as a child," Ephrion had told him. He took another deep breath and walked forward. He would trust the creature. The dragons of legend had helped the humans. Perhaps this dragon would, too.

"The coldrakes have attacked my people," he said as he approached, making sure to enunciate every phrase in a deep, slow voice. "We need your help, dragon."

The creature moaned. "Do not call me dragon," it said. "That is a man-word."

"I do not know your name," replied Amsel cautiously.

He was now within range of its claws.

The dragon snorted. "We do not have names. That is a custom of man."

"Rather more than a custom," Amsel answered. "There are so many of us that we must have a way to tell each other apart."

"Then the humans have prospered?"

"Yes. There are thousands in Fandora alone—and it is quite small compared to the Southland."

"The Southland," said the dragon harshly. "That is the home of man."

"It is one place where man lives," said Amsel. "Fandora and Simbala are others."

"You are not from the Southland?"

Amsel shook his head. Evidently the dragon had not heard what he had said earlier. "I am Amsel of Fandora."

"Amsel," sniffed the dragon. "That is an unlikely name for a man. Your name should be cold and painful, like the frost. Must I call you Amsel?"

"It is my name," said the inventor.

The dragon moaned. "I will not call you anything at all."

Amsel saw defiance in the dragon's eyes, but there was also a loneliness deeper than any he had known. Amsel felt a sudden sympathy for the dragon. He was old and in pain. Amsel wished to help him, to relieve his torment, but he knew that the safety of Fandora and Simbala was at stake. He had to find the other dragons! He looked compassionately at the noble creature and said, "My name does not matter, but you must listen to what has happened!"

The dragon lowered its eyelids. "There is little man can say to me now, and there is nothing man can force me to do."

"No!" cried Amsel desperately. "Listen to me! The coldrakes have attacked us! The dragons must stop them before hundreds more are killed!"

The dragon lifted its head slightly and inhaled the sweet air of the cavern. "I have governed my race and those without flame for centuries," it said. "They would never defy my edict."

"They have!" shouted Amsel. Then he realized what the dragon had said. This shackled creature was the ruler of the dragons? He had to convince him to help!

The dragon lifted its head suddenly and roared. "The small creatures are timid and without flame. They would not dare fly to the land inhabited by man!"

Amsel shook his head. "Children have been murdered. The coldrakes have attacked both Simbala and Fandora. They have even attacked me!"

The dragon stared at Amsel. "They would never attack," it said.

Amsel showed the dragon the hole in his vest made by the coldrake's talon. "You see!" he shouted. "They *have* done so! You must help us prevent them from returning again!"

The dragon did not reply. It observed Amsel, tapping its paw continually as it did. At last it sighed and lowered its head to Amsel's height.

"What right does man have to demand anything of me? Man has murdered! Man has betrayed us! Man is a fitting partner to the ice and wind."

Amsel would not be dissuaded. He stepped closer to the dragon's head. He spoke loudly, with a pause between each word. "I have risked my life to come here! If you will not help me, then I wish to ask the other dragons. Tell me where to find them." The dragon was silent. Then softly it moaned, "There are no others. I am the last of my race." A sadness filled the tired rumble of its voice. Amsel gasped. "That cannot be!" he cried. "That cannot possibly be!"

The dragon shut its eyes as if to banish the man and the pain he brought. Seconds later, when they opened again, Amsel was still there.

"Leave," said the dragon. "I wish to be alone."

"You cannot be the last!" said Amsel. "The legends speak of an entire race of dragons—proud creatures living in a beautiful land of glowing caverns and forests. What has happened to them?"

There was a slow, rumbling sound, like an avalanche. The dragon's neck rose above Amsel, and the creature roared. "They are gone! Murdered by the frost! Murdered by man!"

The roar echoed through the cavern and left Amsel in shock. He watched the anguished face of the dragon, and he knew that what he had heard was true. This was the last dragon and mankind, somehow, shared the blame. He shuddered and glanced at the manacle. There was a tale to be told that was not part of the legends, a tale that man had never heard.

The dragon lowered its head once more.

"The frost killed and man betrayed," it moaned. Its eyes were distant and sorrowful. Peering at Amsel, it spoke of the history of the frozen lands beyond the caverns.

"Long ago this was a warm land. My race lived at peace here. As the ages passed, the cold winds came. We moved slowly south, leaving our old land. When the frost followed, we were forced into these glowing caverns. The coldrakes, as you call them, no longer lived among us. They were hardier than we and remained in the cold land to the north.

"Time passed slowly, but the cold winds would not leave. Soon our eggs were unable to hatch even in the land to the south of these caverns."

The dragon pulled its chain unknowingly as it talked. "Those that governed before me sent scouts to the land south of the sea to see if it could become our home. They discovered a warm land there filled with forests and lakes, and only on the highest peaks could be found the frost."

"That could be Simbala," said Amsel. "It is a land directly south of yours."

The hoary old head nodded ponderously. "We stayed there only a short time, for the land soon became too hot for any of us to survive."

"The seasons," said Amsel. "It grew hotter because the seasons changed."

"We knew only that we could remain in that land no longer. An edict was issued to the coldrakes to protect them from journeying south. Many of us returned to these caverns, while our scouts were sent farther south to seek

help from the creature who called himself man. We knew man had survived in many lands, and we hoped that his secret would help us to defeat the frost.

"In the southern lands, man was friendly. Yet he knew of no way to defeat the frost. Our scouts remained, hoping to learn something that would help in our survival."

"There was no secret," said Amsel. "Man is different from dragon, as the north land is different from the south. You can survive where we may not, just as a seaworm is able to live under the sea."

"We did not know these things in that time. We were frightened. Fewer young were being hatched. We brought man to these caverns in the hope that he could help us protect them against the frost."

That might have been possible, thought Amsel. The men could have taught the dragons how to keep the cold from the eggs through a careful use of coverings and heat. He did not know if this had actually been attempted, but obviously the creatures had not survived.

"Our scouts were sent to other lands, to the east and west, to search farther for a home, but few returned. Man remained in our caverns, studying us, learning our secrets. There was still hope that man would discover a way to stop the cold winds, but another age passed and we grew fewer in number. Other men came from the south with plans to help us. None did. The last scouts were sent to the west. I became head of those who still survived, and it was in my age that no young were born at all. Many perished from the cold. It was then that man deceived us."

"Deceived you?"

"Man had learned the secrets of our race. He knew of the jewels that had been passed down from each age to the next. There were eight jewels, each from one of the heads of the eight who had governed us in ages past."

"You are from the ninth age of dragons?" asked Amsel.

"I am the last," the dragon bellowed. "I am the last of my race. I betrayed the others to man."

Amsel looked at the dragon in consternation. "You said that man betrayed you."

The dragon signaled his understanding with a short, deep sigh. "We were frightened, for there was little food to be found, and what man had shared with us was almost gone. They told us once again of their plans to help us survive. If they could see the jewels containing the history and secrets of our past, they said they might learn something that could defeat the wind." The dragon groaned. "This was forbidden, forbidden by an edict as old as the early ages, when we lived in the land to the north. In my desperation I permitted man to study the jewels, revealing to them myself the secrets of our past. I hoped only to help those of us left to survive, but man deceived me. They used the jewels to learn our vulnerabilities and they trapped me in this faceless jaw. I could not escape." The dragon looked back at the manacle around his claw. "They left us then, taking with them the jewels. Our treasure, our heritage, was gone and I had been betrayed. Their contents were not meant for mankind, and if man made use of them, they could cause harm. Yet they ignored my warning."

Amsel looked at the dark, corroded metal of the manacle. "Why did not the other dragons help you escape?"

"They tried," said the dragon, "but the jaw would not open. They struggled to find food, to discover a place where the young could be born. There were very few that remained in the caverns. When they left, I was alone. Almost an age has passed since man left these caverns, and still the others have not returned. I should not have trusted man. He was a creature who cared only for his own survival."

"No!" cried Amsel. "Did not some of the men attempt to help you?"

"Man betrayed us," said the dragon. "Man steals and man lies."

"Man dreams!" shouted Amsel. "Men who dream only of wealth might have stolen the jewels, but all men do not dream thus. I care only to end the war of my land."

"Man murders," said the dragon. "We learned of war in the Southland. It kills like the frost."

Amsel was silent for a moment. He thought of how the Elders had put his tree house in flames. Yet this did nothing to dissuade him from his belief. "Was there not a time when dragons used their flames to survive? To fight for their land?"

"No!" roared the dragon. "The flame was never used to

kill or harm. It has been used only for matters of justice."

"Were there never dragons who deceived or who disobeyed the edicts of your predecessors?"

"There were few," said the dragon, "and those were punished. There were times when some sought to mate with the coldrakes, but they were punished. No young were ever born."

Amsel thought about the black coldrake that had pursued him in the warren. Fran its size and intelligence, it could have been the product of such a union, but he did not know if that could be true. Nonetheless, the dragon had once again confirmed his authority with the coldrakes. He had to use it!

Amsel shouted at the dragon, "Man will be murdered unless the coldrakes are stopped. They have killed; they have violated your edict! Would you see us perish as your race has?"

Lowering its head, the dragon looked at Amsel with eyes of sorrow and said, "It is man's own fault for betraying us."

Amsel shook his head angrily. "It will be your fault if the coldrakes invade our land. They will vanish there from the summer heat. Then you will have betrayed dragons, man, and the coldrakes. Is that to be the legacy of the dragons?"

"Leave me alone," said the dragon. "I have suffered more than any."

"I have suffered as well!" cried Amsel. "I have watched my people go to war for something the coldrakes did, something I still do not understand. If you are responsible for those creatures, you must stop them from going south."

"My race is gone," said the dragon. "I am alone. I am no longer responsible."

"You *are* responsible!" "You still exist in this world, and the coldrakes still respect your words!"

The dragon covered its head with its paw. "Leave me alone," it said again. "I wish only to be left in peace."

"There *is* no peace," Amsel shouted. "You cannot live alone! As long as there are other living creatures you must deal with them." These words were unfamiliar to Amsel, but he had learned their meaning well in the past few weeks. "You must help us," Amsel insisted. "You must help both mankind and coldrake." Amsel looked into the dragon's eye. "If you, the last of the dragons, so noble, so respected, so old, will not help then what hope is there for mankind?"

The dragon raised its head and roared directly at Amsel. "I cannot bear man-scent any longer! Leave me alone! I wish only to be left in peace!"

The force of its breath caused Amsel to stagger backward, but he shouted back at the creature as he regained his footing on the covern floor. "I wished to be left alone, too!" he answered, "but the world found me just the same. We cannot ignore it. It seems to me that there is no hope in this world if we do not live together. I have risked my life to reach you. Please help me . . . help men and women who have done nothing to betray you!"

The dragon sighed. "I can no longer fly, and the flame has gone out within me."

"You have your wings," argued Amsel, "and the heat I feel in this room is not from your blood alone."

"I am imprisoned," it said.

Amsel smiled. "Then I will find a way to unshackle you."

"I have tried to do so for ages. There is no way to remove it." The dragon pulled on the chain to emphasize his words.

"If I can remove it," said Amsel, "will you help me?"

The dragon was silent, but Amsel saw in its face something that had been hidden only moments ago. In its dark blue eyes there was hope, centuries old and waiting.

Amsel walked quickly toward the dragon's leg. If the shackle had been closed by man, then there had to be a way for him to open it again.

The shackle was large, so large that Amsel would be able to stand up inside it if the dragon's leg were removed. As the dragon watched him, the inventor found a large hole within the casing of the lock. It was bigger than his hand, and Amsel assumed it was made for the insertion of a key to open it.

He stepped closer and thrust his hand inside. Probing with his fingers, he discovered a series of tumblers that composed the locking mechanism. He had learned little about locks in his readings and experiments, but there had been a time years ago when a Southland merchant had sold him a box that had a keyhole in it. He had studied the device then, and he knew he would have to apply the information he had learned from it now.

He tugged at the tumbler closest to him and managed to

raise it to what was, as nearly as he could determine, its proper height. He then tugged on the next lever, repeating what he had done to the first.

It took time for him to continue this pattern, as the tumblers farthest from him were more difficult to raise. Straining, he stretched his hand as deeply into the lock as he could and pulled the last lever. He pinched his finger as it gave way. He pulled his hand out of the lock and shook it ruefully.

The dragon watched this with a look that resembled amusement, and Amsel softly said, "Move your paw."

The huge paw flexed; the manacle held for a moment, then broke open with a rusty grating snap. Amsel dusted his hands by slapping them lightly together and smiled proudly at the dragon. "Now," he said, "I think we will visit the coldrakes."

•

"There!" said Evirae gaily. "We will have that rusty old box moved and I will put our dresser there!"

Mesor shook his head in disapproval. "That box is a rare antique from the days before Monarch Ambalon. Your dresser is far too large to fill the same space. It will block the window, Princess."

Evirae glared at the Bursar. "Queen!" she said sharply. "You must call me Queen."

Mesor smiled. "As you wish, my Queen. However, the coronation does not take place until tomorrow."

"It is a mere formality!" Evirae answered.

"Perhaps, but until the coronation occurs, you possess only limited authority of office. The Family must not think you arrogant."

Evirae ignored Mesor's cautionary tone. She cheerfully explored Hawkwind's private chamber, opening closets and doors, murmuring plans of redecorating, and always keeping an eye out for any further evidence of treason.

What a life it would be, she thought. She would take the reins of government firmly in hand. She would send invitations to the Southland and Bundura to increase trade; she would travel with Kiorte in his windship to distant lands. Faded banners in the streets would be replaced with new and colorful fabrics and the streets of the Simbalese would be works of art! The children would love gracious Queen

Evirae, and Kiorte would be their hero. Even Ephrion would respect her, and, she would ask his advice on minor matters of state.

Evirae strolled to the chamber's only window and looked out at the verdant courtyard below it. She would walk these grounds as Queen. Here she would give birth to a child, a daughter to perpetuate her role in Simbala's affairs.

"I wish Kiorte were here," she sighed, facing Mesor, "but he will return for the coronation, will he not?" She tapped her nails on the wall behind her.

Mesor nodded. "If Prince Kiorte's maneuvers against the invaders succeed, you will have every reason to expect him."

Evirae, suddenly anxious, said, "Are you hiding something from me, Mesor? Something that I do not know?"

"Certainly not," replied the Bursar. "Why would I be privy to information that you are not?"

"Do not answer me in questions!" said Evirae. "If you know something, tell me!"

"My Queen, do not be worried!"

Evirae ignored the title and pursued him further. "You expect a high-ranking post within the Circle, don't you? You may rest assured there will be a place for you in the stables if you do not answer me now!"

So upset was Mesor by this threat that he promptly composed a reply. "There is one concern that I have," he said nervously, "and that involves the dragons. If Kiorte uses the windships, the dragons may attack again."

Evirae smiled, relieved. "A single dragon!" she said disdainfully. "The windships are more than a match for a single dragon. If that is what troubles you, then there is no trouble at all. The miner has fled the army to join the Rayan in her escape. Kiorte controls our defense. Dragons or no, the Fandorans will be driven out."

"Yes," replied Mesor. "I am sure you are correct, there is no reason to worry."

Evirae smiled loftily. "I do not mind," she said. "It is my duty to concern myself. I am your Queen now, Mesor. Tomorrow's ceremony of installation is a mere formality, is it not?"

"Of course," the Bursar replied hastily.

"Do not forget it. I must see to the invitations now."

Mesor watched as she walked toward the door. He knew

the Family was watching Evirae closely. Her title was secure, but their support was not. If Kiorte did not return soon, they might change their minds.

He would make sure to have a fast horse available for himself, if that occurred.

●

Hours later, in a dark and private chamber on another level of the palace, Monarch Ephrion rested. He was unaware of the sound of the footsteps in the hallway outside, and it was several minutes before a passing guard entered to inform him of two visitors at his door.

The white-haired statesman sent back word with the guard, bidding the Baroness and Baron to enter. He lit a small lamp near the door, and as Tolchin and Alora stepped into the room and greeted him, Ephrion noticed a nervousness on their part. Although the room was pleasantly cool, Alora was fanning herself repeatedly, and Tolchin viewed the antique furnishings of the room with a pretense of interest. Ephrion knew that their presence had a purpose other than social.

"You seem troubled," said Ephrion. "Is it Evirae?"

The Baron shook his head. "We have come to explain our actions."

"There is no need to defend your vote to me," said Ephrion. "Your reasons were made clear at the meeting."

Alora was obviously disturbed. "I voted not for Evirae, but to end the war. Hawkwind was not fit to run it."

"Nor is Evirae," said Ephrion.

"Of course!" replied Tolchin. "But we all know that Kiorte will be in charge of the army, not Evirae. She had already agreed to that before the meeting had started."

Alora nodded. "Kiorte will drive the farmers out with windships. No more fighting need occur."

Ephrion looked at them both and beckoned them to another room within his quarters. He walked to the rosewood desk, above which one large candle sat glowing. In the dim light it cast, Ephrion unrolled the picture of the coldrake.

"Man and windship have been unable to defeat it," he said. "What makes you think Kiorte will?"

Tolchin examined the picture. "It is terrifying, I agree, but even a dragon is no match for the fleet!"

Alora took the scroll from her husband's hands and held it to the light. "It does not look like a dragon," she said softly, "but I have never seen a real dragon as you have, Ephrion."

"I have never seen a dragon either," Ephrion responded. "The creature that attacked the palace was a coldrake."

"A coldrake?"

"A less intelligent creature than the dragons, but related to them nonetheless."

"I have been reviewing the old legends of the Southland, Tolchin, and I am convinced that it is the coldrakes who are responsible for the war."

"Impossible!" said Tolchin. "The Fandorans invaded Simbala and brought the creatures with them."

Ephrion lifted the picture out of Alora's hands and showed it once again to the Baron. "Tolchin," he said sternly, "does this look like a creature who can be ordered about by farmers and fishermen?"

"No," Tolchin admitted, "but what reason could it have for attacking our forests?"

"I do not know," said Ephrion, "but I have sent Lady Ceria to find out."

"The Rayan?" asked Tolchin. "You sent the traitor on a mission to aid us? Have you sent Hawkwind, too?"

Ephrion walked toward the velvet couch. "Ceria is not a traitor," he said, ignoring the reference to Hawkwind. "I have sent her on a mission, and the time grows near when her mission will be in peril. At noon tomorrow, Evirae will be Queen."

Alora was troubled, for there was much she did not know. "What is it that you have sent Ceria to find?" she asked.

Ephrion sat down on the couch. He knew the time had come to reveal what he had done. Ceria would need the help of the Family if Evirae took office. He had high regard for the Baroness and the Baron, and he would risk the secrets he had learned to engage their help.

He had been unable to do so at the meeting, for Evirae would have sent agents to find Ceria. It was too late for that tactic now. If Ceria had reached the Rayan camp and succeeded in her quest, then she would most likely be returning to the forest now. He had to ensure her safe arrival. For that he would need the help of the Family. Hawkwind had spoken of his respect for Alora, and she had always exercised some measure of control over her husband. There was little time left to ponder his alternatives; he had considered them carefully in the hours since the meeting.

"My concern is not for Evirae, but for Simbala," Ephrion said quietly. "The coldrakes have never before journeyed into our land, but I am concerned that what we have seen may be only the first of many."

"Do you mean an invasion of coldrakes?" asked Tolchin.

"I do not know," Ephrion replied, "but we must protect ourselves."

●

The distant sounds of fighting came across the valley to the Simbalese camp with the first light of dawn. Vora and Kiorte stood staring toward the hills. "Prince Kiorte," Vora said urgently, "we cannot simply leave a band of Wealdsfolk out there!"

"What else am I to do?" Kiorte demanded. "I take no pleasure in the Wealdsmen's peril, but they acted without orders. I will not endanger more men and women to rescue them!"

Vora frowned. "Perhaps we would succeed if we aided the Wealdsfolk now! There is little food in those hills. The Fandorans must be hungry and tired. We have been patient."

"No!" answered Kiorte. "Until the troops return from the Southland, we must not take any chances. The Brothers of the Wind have been ordered to the valley. The entire fleet will drive back the Fandorans."

Before Vora could reply, there was a distant, rumbling sound in the forest behind them. Lookouts rushed from their posts as the cries of other men were heard.

"Lathan!" shouted Vora. "Ride yonder to find out what has happened!"

The aide, standing nearby, ran to his horse and mounted it.

For a moment Kiorte ignored the confusion and glanced west at the foot of the hills. "I can see nothing of the Wealdsmen in that fog," he said. "Perhaps they have found a way to retreat."

Vora looked out into the mists, but did not reply. He had suddenly determined what the sound was behind them. He had hoped, he had dreamed, that this moment would arrive. Now, as Kiorte stood unaware beside him, he knew it had.

Hawkwind was returning!

●

"Hawkwind is coming!" The shout went up from a loyal contingent near Vora's tent, and was instantly overheard by Prince Kiorte. Facing Vora, he said, "You knew of this! You have conspired with Hawkwind against the Family!"

"Don't be a fool!" Vora responded. "I have defended Hawkwind against Evirae."

"To defend a traitor is treason itself! I can have you arrested for—"

Kiorte suddenly looked up. There was a colorful explosion of birds from the canopy of trees. Then a hawk soared into view, circling the Simbalese camp and screeching triumphantly. The cry was echoed by blasts from a dozen horns.

"He has found them!" said Vora. "He has found the missing troops!"

From the forest issued a vast procession. Rank after rank of mounted soldiers rode forth, their surcoats and jambs gleaming. War chargers, caparisoned in brilliant tanselcloth, entered the clearing proudly. Behind the first wave of cavalry came the crossbowmen, some riding two to a horse, for there had been no time for a foot march. Grooms and supply handlers had been ordered to unload packhorses and ride them.

They continued to arrive, bright waves breaking from the wooded depths. The beleaguered soldiers sent up a cheer for the miner and his lady, riding in the vanguard. General Vora broke away from Kiorte and hurried toward Hawkwind and Ceria. He noticed the black pouch at the Rayan's side, with a large bulge in it. He wondered anxiously if they had found the Dragonpearl.

As he neared them, Vora called out, "There is trouble, Hawkwind! Kiorte has taken over the troops!"

To Vora's surprise, Hawkwind responded calmly. "Deal with those behind us," he said. "They have ridden for nearly a day without food or rest. I will see Kiorte."

He passed Vora quickly and proceeded toward the Prince. Ceria rode wearily behind him, acknowledging

Vora as the General continued toward a captain of the troops from the Southland. Hawkwind dismounted, and he approached Kiorte outside Vora's tent. "I have brought the troops," he said, "and Ceria has discovered evidence of the true roles of both the dragon and the Fandoran spy. I must explain it to you."

Kiorte glared at him in controlled anger. "You are under arrest," he answered, "for the betrayal of the Simbalese army and support of a proven traitor." He clasped a gloved hand around Hawkwind's wrist. "If only Thalen were alive to see you charged," he added, his voice heavy with emotion.

Hawkwind twisted his wrist sharply, breaking the Prince's grip. "I have returned with the soldiers we need to drive the Fandorans from our shores!" he said curtly. "You have no right—"

"I have every right to arrest you!" Kiorte shouted in return. "You deserted our army!" He turned to a guard and said, "Take him!"

Hawkwind stepped back. "You will not arrest me!" he warned. "I am still Monarch of Simbala!"

"You are no longer Monarch," Kiorte told him grimly. "Evirae is Queen." The guard waited, not knowing what to do.

"Then the Family has voted," Hawkwind said. "Evirae acts quickly when her own plans are involved. Has the coronation taken place?"

"It will occur this afternoon, but it is a formality only. Evirae is Queen."

"It is unlike you to belittle the traditions of our land, Kiorte. Until Evirae wears the Ruby, I am still Monarch. That is Simbalese law."

"Tell me not about our ways, Hawkwind. You have fought them and the Family ever since you entered the palace! Under mandate from the Royal Family of Simbala, I demand your surrender!"

Hawkwind grasped the hilt of his blade. "Kiorte, we have always respected each other. Do not force me to act."

"Then leave peacefully with the guard, Hawkwind. I vouch for your safety and that of the Rayan traitor."

Hawkwind smiled. "I bring proof of Ceria's innocence! It must be taken quickly to Monarch Ephrion. We have little time, Kiorte. It is foolish to continue this argument. We must use the full strength of our army to end this war now!"

Kiorte shook his head as Ceria approached on foot. "The troops will not be our first line of attack. I have ordered the Brothers of the Wind to come from Overwood at full strength."

"That is madness! You cannot face them with the windships alone. You have seen what has happened!"

"There will be more than three windships this time!" Kiorte shouted. "Using a small number was your foolish plan. An armada will flush the Fandorans out into the open. Attempts have been made and failed at ground level. The windships will not fail!"

"They *will* fail!" Hawkwind replied. "The cover is too thick on those hills, and we no longer have the element of surprise! Your Windriders cannot shoot what they cannot see!"

"The discussion is closed!" Kiorte made a sweeping gesture with his hand that underscored his statement. "The fleet should arrive at any time, and this war will be ended when it does."

"The Fandorans will shoot down the windships! Listen to me, Kiorte. The true danger is the dragons. The Fandorans are merely a problem to be dealt with as quickly as possible. We can drive them back with an overwhelming ground force—which we now have! You must listen to me. There are things you have not been told."

"Silence!" said Kiorte. "You are under arrest!" He drew his sword.

"You fool!" shouted Hawkwind. The rasp of metal sounded loudly in the clearing. There was an instant of shocked disbelief, followed by a worried murmur that spread through the crowd as those who could see communicated what had happened to those who could not.

The sound of swordplay rang out over the camp. Men and women climbed trees to better observe the duel between Monarch and Prince. The two fought cautiously at first, testing each other's strengths and weaknesses. Hawkwind knew that the duel had to be ended quickly, but Kiorte's swordsmanship and drive were almost equal to his own. He knew also that Kiorte did not intend to relinquish command of the army to the man he believed responsible for his brother's death.

The Prince swung his blade in a flat, whistling arc that would have disemboweled Hawkwind had he not parried the blow. Kiorte saw the surprise and anger in Hawkwind's face, and heard the disbelieving murmur around him.

Hawkwind blocked another slash, which nevertheless struck with such force that he was driven back several steps. It had become very clear that this was much more than a matter of honor. The Prince, it seemed, was out for blood; yet Hawkwind could not afford to fight—indeed, he did not want to.

He saw the rage in Kiorte's eyes, and ducked as the Prince's sword passed over him, bringing the flat of his own blade hard against Kiorte's side, momentarily winding the Prince. Pressing his advantage, he drove Kiorte back. He would have to end this soon, he knew. He had ridden all night, and he was near to exhaustion.

The Prince locked blades with him and they closed up, face to face.

"You brought this upon yourself," Kiorte hissed. Hawkwind made no reply. Instead, with an effort, he flung the Prince from him and, at the same time, brought his sword up and knocked the blade from Kiorte's grasp. Kiorte looked at where it fell, as though tempted to grasp it and renew the fight. Hawkwind brought his boot down on it.

"No more," he said quietly. "This is not the battle we must fight."

Breathing heavily, Kiorte said, "You are unfit to wage this war!"

"Whether you like it or not, you are going to hear some things I have learned," Hawkwind said through his teeth. He took a deep breath and continued in a whisper. "There is much that will surprise you." He then told Kiorte what Ceria had told him on the long ride back from the Southland—how the Fandoran Amsel had come to Simbala in an attempt to stop the war, how Evirae had imprisoned him without Hawkwind's knowledge, and more. "You accuse me of bad judgments," Hawkwind said. "I admit to some, but so must you."

Kiorte was silent for several minutes. Then he said in a low, tight voice, "She attempted to show me this prisoner once, to win me to her cause. He had already escaped." He looked at Hawkwind uncertainly.

"I do not ask you to accept me now," said Hawkwind. "Merely work with me to win this war. That is of first importance."

A shadow flowed over the camp suddenly, and Ceria gasped as she looked up. Above the eastern woods, cresting the tops of the trees, came the first line of the windship fleet. Balloon sails taut with gas and billowing with wind, the elegant fleet slowly descended over the camp.

Hawkwind looked at the Prince again. "I can finish this business alone, Kiorte, or together we can end the whole ridiculous conflict."

Kiorte nodded slowly. "You have proven your honor. You will have the chance to prove your courage. Nothing more will be decided now."

Hawkwind smiled. "To a bloodless victory," he said, and extended his hand.

Kiorte took it, his gloved hand stained with sweat. "I will conduct the windships' maneuvers from my own craft," he said. "No doubt you will want to direct the troops to arrive in the hills after us."

"I'll have to summon Vora," said Hawkwind. "We'll coordinate plans together." He looked eastward toward the thickening trees. "Where are the Wealdsmen?" he asked. "We may have use for them in our maneuvers."

Kiorte scowled. "The Wealdsmen are no longer our problem," he said. "They have foolishly attacked the hills by themselves."

XXXI

Two shadows filled the passageway of the glowing caverns, the large swallowing the small. Footsteps echoed from the walls, the sound of scraping claws drowning out the touch of tiny boots on the lichen-covered stone.

The Last Dragon moved slowly, the weight of its body heavy on its legs. Amsel followed the path he had taken earlier, having been shown how to reach it from the cavern floor by the dragon.

The passage, wide as it was, twisted and turned through the subterranean landscape, at times barely high enough to accommodate the creature's body. Every so often stalactites and stalagmites shattered with deafening sounds as its massive wings and shoulders pressed against them, while Amsel scurried under the great body to shelter from the debris.

"We are almost there," said Amsel, sighting a familiar pink-and-yellow bend in the tunnel, "but the opening through which I came in is far too small for your body."

"Yes," grumbled the dragon, "the entrances of many tunnels were covered by ice and rock long ago. It was often difficult for us to leave the caverns."

As he reached the entrance, Amsel saw that falling rocks from the cliffs had closed it completely. The dragon saw this, too, and emitted a short, grumbling sound. "Wait," said Amsel, and he ran forward to probe the freshly fallen rocks with his foot. "It is not packed tightly," he said. "You can force it away."

The dragon looked at Amsel. "I am tired," he said with dignity. "I do not wish to move anything."

"You must!" said Amsel. "It is the only way out I know."

"There are others," the dragon replied. "We shall find another that is open."

"No," cried Amsel. "The coldrakes may be flying toward the south at any time! We must reach them as soon as possible."

The dragon sniffed the dusty air. "You do not understand the meaning of patience!" he said. "Man always wishes to act as quickly as he speaks."

Amsel frowned. "That is very interesting," he shouted, "but you have agreed to help us! You must trust my understanding of the problem. I have seen the coldrakes."

This seemed to anger the dragon, and it bellowed back at Amsel. "I have governed the coldrakes for nearly an age! They will listen to my words."

"They will not listen if we do not reach them in time," Amsel replied, and he looked impatiently at the dragon.

The dragon's blue eyes widened. "Very well. Stand back." he said. "Stand behind me so that you will be shielded!"

The inventor happily consented and hid behind the dragon's tail.

The Last Dragon positioned the front of its horned head against the fallen rock and pushed forward. There was a shifting, a dull echo, and then the scraping sound of rocks moving against each other. Amsel could hear the movements of the dragon's ancient frame beneath the white ribbed skin, and the teeth-grating scratch of the dragon's claws against the rock. Then, abruptly, there was an explosion of stone and dust. Amsel looked out between the dragon's forelegs and saw an avalanche of boulders. Tiny fragments of flying rocks scraped his skin, and a thick gray cloud obscured his view and made him sneeze. "The dragon calls himself old and weak," Amsel whispered. "I wonder what he was like in his prime."

Amsel hurried toward the new opening in the cavern, a hole now wide enough for a being of enormous size. As he reached the edge, his companion spoke. "I hope you are satisfied," he said, "for I am now so tired that I can do nothing but rest," and he lowered his head to the rocky floor. Sighing, the tiny inventor looked out through the burrowed exit and was surprised to find that the sky was dark. He had apparently been inside the cavern for a longer time than he had thought. A good thing, too, he told himself, for it had obviously been raining. Black clouds filled the sky, and freezing rain and sleet fell, obscuring the river. Amsel shivered as the cold air touched him.

"I cannot fly," said the dragon. "I must have food and rest."

Amsel looked at the creature and nodded. "There are reeds and grass frozen beneath the riverbank. I could not get to them with my hands, but with your claws you could easily dig them out of the snow."

The dragon moaned. "I wish never to feel the frost again!"

"That is fine with me," Amsel replied, teeth chattering, "but I do not think we have any choice."

The dragon scrutinized the distant shoreline. Then, with a harsh and sudden bellow, it lifted its neck and said, "I *must* find something to eat."

Amsel stepped aside and the dragon stepped forward. Then, with a moan, it departed from the cavern. Amsel smiled as the dragon moved down the deep slope, wings half-spread to aid its balance. The long neck lifted, defying the weather, and the beast walked toward the river. It was difficult for Amsel to tell what the dragon was thinking, but he hoped that it was happy, happy to be alive and needed again—even by man. He trusted the dragon to keep its word. He was also hungry and tired—and cold! He had not realized how much heat there was within the dragon's body. Left alone now on the cavern's floor, he was freezing!

Amsel hurried down the tunnel to crouch in a cozy niche between two glowing rocks. He leaned his head against moss, but even as he cautioned himself to stay awake in the event a coldrake appeared, he fell asleep.

A tapping on the stone awoke him a short time later. The dragon had returned and was now standing in front of Amsel, watching him with what appeared to be an amused expression.

"Did you find anything?" asked Amsel, and as he did, he saw tufts of pale wet grass caught between the dragon's claws. "You did!" he continued. "Would you mind if I take what is trapped between your paws for myself?"

The dragon gently lifted its paw toward the inventor. Amsel removed the grass and ate it.

"The land is colder. I cannot fly."

Amsel shook his head. "If I can survive a flight to the north, then you can, too."

These words confused the dragon. "Man cannot fly," he said.

Amsel smiled. "Man has ships that sail the air like boats upon the sea. That is how I reached the coldrakes' warren."

"Man does not have wings."

"No," the inventor responded, "but you do." Amsel knew he would have to be very persuasive now. The dragon was in no hurry to leave the cavern. Amsel started to walk toward the opening.

"Where are you going?" asked the dragon.

"To the north," said Amsel. "I am going to the north with you. We must not wait any longer!" He continued ahead and was relieved to hear the dragon's footsteps behind him. As he reached the edge of the tunnel, Amsel looked out and saw that the sky was still dark but that the rains had ended. He turned to the dragon behind him and simply said, "We must leave now."

The dragon looked at Amsel, lifted his head proudly, and roared with anguish. "You puny creature! Do you not understand?" it said. "I have not flown in nearly an age. I am tired and I am old."

"You have your wings," said Amsel. "You can still use them if you want!" He started to walk on the icy slope outside the cavern. It was slippery and wet from the rain. The dragon was watching Amsel with its dark blue eyes as a gust of icy wind blew at them both. Amsel continued down the slope, shivering but undaunted.

He looked back and once again shouted, "You *must* fly!" Then he glanced beyond the dragon at the cliff above the cavern. Within it he saw the familiar form of a dragon frozen in ice.

He knew then how to convince the dragon to fly. "Look behind you!" he shouted. "Look up behind you! There is another dragon!"

He watched carefully as the Last Dragon twisted its neck around to observe the sky above the cliff. As it did, it unthinkingly readied its wings to fly. Then suddenly the dragon turned back toward Amsel. It had not seen the other dragon. "Do not trick me!" it roared. "I will not be betrayed by man again!"

"No," cried Amsel. "Look within the ice of the cliff. There *is* a dragon!"

The Last Dragon turned again, and this time it saw the other embedded in the ice. A long, mournful sound emerged from its throat and echoed in the cavern behind them, surmounting even the wind.

The magnificent wings suddenly spread and flexed and spread again. The Last Dragon's head rose proudly, and the monstrous body launched itself toward the face of the cliffs. Slowly, but without hesitation, the dragon floated into the sky.

Amsel gaped at the beauty of the creature in flight. "He is worthy of the legends," he whispered. He regretted showing the dragon something that would bring it such pain, but he knew there would be more pain if he did not.

Amsel found it hard to accept the thought that the creature was the last of its race, and that the dragon frozen in the ice was as close as it would come to seeing another again. "There have to be others somewhere," he said aloud. "They are too beautiful to vanish completely."

He watched the dragon hover in front of the icy cliff. He knew that the creature had once governed both coldrake and dragon, and he was sure that its orders would be obeyed by the coldrakes once they had learned that it was alive.

Amsel hugged himself tightly in protection from the cold, waiting for the dragon to return.

"Johan," he whispered, "I will keep my word."

XXXII

In the barren mountains, where a few wild animals still survived despite the cold, the coldrakes fed. The Darkling had exhorted them to a frenzy of hunting and gorging, knowing that they would need all of their strength for the long flight and the battle to come. While they fed, he spoke to them in their harsh, sibilant tongue. The dragons were gone, never to return. The coldrakes could not be bound to the dragons' edict when the safety of their race was at stake and the actions of the humans could bring the coldrakes to extinction. The Darkling shrieked and circled the others, its angry sound joined to that of the wind.

The coldrakes howled in confusion and anger while the Darkling watched with approval. They would need all of their strength, all of their savagery, in this battle. Each time contact was made with the humans, he became more convinced of what the Guardian and his emissaries had told him. Man was murderous, man could attack them at any time, and, as if the secrets of light and flame were not enough, the human he had captured had escaped. The tender tissues of his mouth still burned from contact with the pods. The humans were small, but their intelligence rivaled that of the dragons. If one creature could escape their warren, then a thousand could surely invade it. They had to be destroyed before they could attack.

The Darkling reassured himself with this thought, but deep within him, burning stronger than his rage, was the feeling that he should enforce the dragons' edict, not defy it. He did not know why. The dragons had vanished. The old order had ended. The coldrakes needed him—born of dragon and coldrake—in the dragons' stead; there could be no doubt that he was destined to protect them. He possessed the secret of the dragons and the endurance of the coldrakes. He could not deny them his help. He shrieked loudly again, aloof and lonely beneath the stars, and watched the feeding continue below.

Before dawn a storm moved into the area, and the heavy winds and sleet made departure dangerous. The Darkling kept his rage under control, though it was not easy—he was afraid that the frenzy he had instilled in the others would lose its edge. It did not; the others watched the storm and shrieked in frustration and impatience. The storm lasted all that day. At last the clouds began to part, and the setting sun turned the steam and clouds crimson. The Darkling flapped his wings and soared high into the dreary sky. The coldrakes would return to the warrens for the last time. Then they would embark upon the long journey south to the land of the humans, the warm land that would soon be their own.

●

The retreat of the Fandorans was to take place in two stages. The first contingent to leave the hills would be supervised by Elders Tamark and Pennel and would consist mainly of those wounded or rendered helpless by their fears. Soldiers from Cape Bage would accompany them, to act as guards and also to prepare the ships for a speedy departure once they had reached the shore.

"We will hold the line until evening," said Jondalrun. "Then we will join you as fast as we can. The Simbalese have learned of our fortitude. They would not dare attack us in daylight."

Tamark shook his head grimly. "Do not forget their dragon. It may attack at any time!"

Jondalrun shook his wristlet defiantly. "They have been driven off once; if they return, we will do so again!"

Tamark nodded and, with Dayon's assistance, began to round up the familiar faces of the men of Cape Bage.

The men remaining were positioned in three groups within the hills, directed by Dayon, the Wayman, and Jondalrun himself. They would defend their line as best as possible, to give Tamark's men a chance to reach the shore. Hopefully, the Simbalese would again be unable to penetrate the cover of the hills. By nightfall, they would be able to escape.

Jondalrun observed some of the men glancing skyward, as though puzzled. Then he heard what they did—a low rumble, like the thunder of a summer storm. He looked up warily; what could be seen of the sky through the foliage was innocent of clouds. The noise did not come from the windships, yet the sound increased steadily, growing nearer. He could not see the valley from his place of cover, and so he dispatched a young man to investigate, whispering, "Up yonder oak, and tell me what you find."

The fellow so ordered climbed quickly into the branches. Those below could not see him, but they could hear his cry moments later.

"Elder Jondalrun!" he cried. " 'Tis the Simbalese troops—far off, but there's hundreds of them and their windships above them! 'Tis far more than we ever dreamed!"

Jondalrun sprang up from the spot in which he had hidden. "Impossible!" he shouted. "We have driven them back more than once! They cannot possibly have . . ."

Now others broke cover, anxious to see what was approaching.

"Get down!" yelled Jondalrun. "Do not let yourselves be seen!"

Some did not listen; they sprang up from rocks and bushes and glimpsed the Simbalese riding straight for the hills.

"Stay down!" cried Dayon. "Stay down until they see you!"

The Wayman chased two frightened soldiers back to the cover of a stand of butterwoods, but as he did he heard the sound of hoofbeats in the brush at the bottom of the hill. In a few moments the Simbalese would arrive.

The morning wore on as the return to the shore was effected as quickly as possible. Most of the wounded were able to walk, but, like Tenniel, they were quite weak and would not be able to go far without frequent rest. Those unable to walk were accommodated by improvised travois and stretchers.

"It will take Tamark the entire day to reach the boats,"

Dayon said to Jondalrun, who stood on a high hill watching the valley.

Jondalrun stared broodingly out over the valley toward the Simbalese camp. The trees and the rising mist made it difficult to see clearly. The rigid old man leaned on a staff, gazing at the forest, his rage still high. He knew many had perished, and he felt the burden of those lost men upon him. How would Lagow's wife be told? How would any be told? Then he shook his head. It was a heavy price to pay for Fandora's security.

Dayon stood silently by his father's side. Tamark had left close to an hour ago, and he wondered how long it would be before the order would be given for the rest of the troops to retreat. "The Wayman says all are ready, Father. I have spoken to the Borgen Town contingent and they wish to depart now. They are worried that the weather will soon make it difficult to escape."

Jondalrun nodded and looked back over the valley. Suddenly he stiffened, staring intently. Dayon followed his gaze. "What is it, Father?"

Jondalrun pointed. "There! Over the trees!"

"It is a rain cloud."

"A cloud indeed," Jondalrun said tensely. Dayon looked closer and gasped. What had at first seemed to be a large gray cloud billowing over the treetops was now suddenly breaking up, scattering into an incredible armada of windships! As he watched, sunlight streamed through the sails and scintillated off the prows' jeweled designs, and the windships' many masts seemed to form a second forest in the sky.

"Give the order!" shouted Jondalrun. "Alert the men! We will defend the hill!"

Among the Simbalese, preparations were being made for the assault on the hills. The troops formed themselves into serried ranks, pennons on lances held proud and high. Archers and infantry composed the flanks, and the center was row after row of armored knights. The Simbalese army, once more at its full strength, was readying for the final battle.

To the rear of the ranks, near the forest, stood Hawkwind and Ceria. It was to be their last moment alone before the charge, and the sounds of final preparations made them both aware of their danger. Hawkwind could be killed in battle, the victim of a Fandoran's sword. Ceria was considered to be a traitor; her safety depended on her ability to reach Ephrion before the coronation occurred.

"I know you will come back," Ceria said to Hawkwind. "We have shared too much to lose each other now. My heart tells me you must return."

Hawkwind held her close and then took her by the shoulders. "You are dearer to me than life itself, but Ceria, I am worried."

"I know," she replied, "and I understand what must be done. Every moment brings Evirae closer to the Ruby. Whatever risk may be involved, I must hasten back to the palace with the Dragonpearl."

"No!" Hawkwind said. "Such a course is far too dangerous. Evirae's agents are still combing Overwood for you. They would not hesitate to take you prisoner, even with the knowledge of my return to the forest."

Ceria pulled away from him. "I must reach Ephrion!" she cried. "I do not fear Evirae's agents!"

Hawkwind drew her back. "You bring a secret too precious to lose, my love. We must ensure its safety. You must wait for me until I am able to leave the valley. Lathan will accompany you to a safe place in the woods, where you will hide. We will return to Overwood together."

"No!" said Ceria. "There is not time! Evirae's coronation draws nigh."

"It is prudent that we go together, Ceria! If I am not present, even the Dragonpearl will be insufficient to stop Evirae's plans. The jewel will only tell of the dragons—I must be there to clear my name. Evirae will find a way to use it if we do not return together. Wait, my darling, for this war will soon be ended."

"I do not wish to wait," Ceria answered gently.

"I will have you stopped if you leave," Hawkwind replied. "I will not lose you to Evirae!"

Ceria saw the love within his dark eyes, and for a moment, all too brief, the war, the scheming of the Family, and the threat of Evirae did not exist for them. Hawkwind embraced her and they were lost in the touch of hands, and bodies, and the richness of their love for each other. When Hawkwind at last glanced up at the waiting troops near

them, it was as though a sword had been thrust through his heart. He heard the dreadful portents of the coming conflict, the rattle of scabbards, the snorting and stamping of war horses, and the sea sound of chain mail being donned.

He compelled himself to release her and turned away to face the waiting troops. "We shall return," he whispered. "We shall return to Overwood together!"

He hurried back toward his tent and appeared several minutes later in a light mail coat, burgnet, and leather leggings. Ceria watched Hawkwind make his way through the ranks, heard the storm of cheers as he mounted his horse beside Vora. His hawk dropped from the sky to his lifted arm and sidled up to perch on his mailed shoulder. Ceria watched, her vision blurred with tears.

•

Kiorte adjusted the gas flow of his windship and leveled off before the others. He looked at them. They awaited his direction. He was in his element, the rustling of the balloon sails, the caressing currents of the wind, the deck rocking gently, but none of these now brought the usual pleasure to him. Without Thalen to share it, flying would not be the same.

Below, he faintly heard the trumpets sound the battle call. He raised the flags that signaled to others to fill their sails. The armada began to move slowly forward. Kiorte gripped the steering levers and looked toward the hills.

•

Hawkwind rode in front of the rows of troops and raised his arm. He was loath to give the signal, but he knew that he must. He had instructed the soldiers to drive off or capture the Fandorans wherever possible. What Ceria had told him during the ride back from the Valian Plains had convinced him more than ever that this entire war was born of a tragic misunderstanding. He knew that it had to be ended quickly and with as little bloodshed as possible. There was another threat to Simbala, far more dangerous than this. He brought his hand down sharply. "For Simbala!" he cried. The combined troops of the Overwood contingents charged toward the Kameran Hills.

•

The filtered sunlight was blocked as the windships passed overhead. The sight of the overwhelmingly vast armada was too much for the Fandorans. Throwing down their mismatched weapons, they began to run. "Hold the line!" Jondalrun shouted, but to no avail. The men had had enough. They fled from what they felt to be certain annihilation. Many thought that the Simbalese had at last unleashed their dreaded sorcery. Others thought the sky was darkened by dragons. Jondalrun looked about helplessly, his army in total disarray. He caught glimpses of mailed figures on horseback approaching and heard the clash and cries of soldiery all around him in the underbrush. A Simbalese soldier on horseback leaped over some bushes before him. The rider raised his sword, but Jondalrun struck first—the blade rang against the other's armor, knocking him from his horse. Before the man could recover, Jondalrun turned and ran toward higher ground, where he could get a better view of his surroundings.

He saw that his line had broken. There was a solid wave of Simbalese soldiers sweeping through the hills, driving the Fandorans before them. Even as he watched, he saw the second line crumble and break. A hundred yards away, his son, Dayon, was disarmed by two Simbalese and unceremoniously thrown across the back of a horse. "No!" Jondalrun shouted, rage blackening his vision. He ran down the hill, sword upraised. There was another crashing in the bushes nearby, and as he turned with sword ready, a brown horse appeared, ridden by a Simbalese woman in chain-mail armor. Jondalrun stood his ground. If this was the way the Sim fought, using women as soldiers, they had no pride at all! He would not be defeated while Dayon still breathed.

The soldier's horse reared as though to trample him, and Jondalrun leaped back against a large boulder.

"Surrender!" yelled the rider. "The war is ended! You have lost! Surrender while you can!" She drew her sword, and the stallion reared once again.

Jondalrun dodged the horse, but in doing so caught his foot in a small hole and toppled.

"Idiot!" yelled the Simbalese rider, and she rode on to find another challenge.

Jondalrun could not tolerate the defeat. He pulled his leg out of the hole and hurried after her.

"Murderous Sim!" he shouted. "Face me!"

The woman's horse kicked out at the yelling man behind

him and caught the Fandoran a glancing blow in the head, grazing his helmet, knocking him heavily to the ground.

"Idiot!" the woman shouted again, and she charged ahead to search for the generals of the Fandoran army, unaware of the identity of the man who lay unconscious behind her.

•

The Wayman continued to fight alone, defending a small contingent of young men hidden in the brush. When at last he had found a moment to rest, he spied beyond the trees a tall Simbalese rider, dressed strikingly in silver and black, surrounded by others who seemed to be of official importance. They carried tall lances on which banners had been hung. I must reach them, the Wayman concluded, before more are killed. He had seen Dayon taken prisoner from afar, and though he did not know the whereabouts of Jondalrun, he knew that any further resistance would be futile. A surrender had to be arranged, and he, physically larger than most of the Fandorans, would at least have a chance to impress the Simbalese in the Elders' absence. There was no longer any question of retreat—the hill was being overrun by Simbalese troops, and nothing could be gained by waiting.

He cautiously started toward the cluster of trees where the dark rider stood. As he drew closer to the gathering, he could see four or five people clearly. Two were obviously guards, a man and a woman, posted at the most vulnerable spots. The other three were on horseback; the tall dark figure was speaking with a bearded man twice his age and girth.

This would be difficult. The Wayman sighed. If he drew near too quickly, they would kill him; if he proceeded with caution, he could easily be caught.

He kept moving, slipping past a pair of Simbalese soldiers in the cover of a narrow hedge. He heard the sounds of prisoners being taken behind him, and he realized that more were being driven back or held captive than were being killed.

This was to his best advantage. The Simbalese apparently wished to end the war as quickly as possible. He continued forward, anticipating the sound of his footsteps by judging carefully the carpet of underbrush and leaves beneath his boots.

Then, only yards away from the nearest guard, he drew his sword and hid behind the slender trunk of a butterwood tree. "Sim!" he cried in a dialect of the Southland which he hoped would confuse the guard. "Defend yourself!"

The guard rushed forward, but as she did, the Wayman slipped through the stand of trees and reached the clearing. By the time the guard had spotted him, he was running directly toward the tall, dark rider.

Then suddenly the male guard spied him and leaped from his horse as the dark rider drew his sword.

"No!" the Wayman cried, but as he gripped his sword, he heard the returning guard behind him. He would have to face them both.

The dark rider was young, and he wore an expression of such intensity that the Wayman expected words of anger from him at any second. The Wayman lifted his sword slowly, wishing only to speak.

"Surrender!" shouted the dark rider. There was a blur in the sky above him, and the Wayman saw a hawk, talons extended, swoop down toward him.

He whirled to evade it, but the other guard was waiting. The bird slashed his jacket and screeched, then soared skyward.

"Surrender!" came the cry from the dark rider again, and the Wayman felt a sword at his back.

"I come in peace," he said, dropping his weapon. The guard retrieved it.

"Then you shall find it." The dark rider lowered his sword. "I am Hawkwind, Monarch of Simbala."

"Hawkwind," the Wayman replied grimly. "I have heard your name."

The dark rider observed the Wayman silently. He was too tall to be a Fandoran, and he spoke with an accent of the Southland. "You are not from the west," Hawkwind stated.

"I am a Southlander, but I speak for Fandora. We seek justice for the murder of a Fandoran child."

"I know the reasons for your attack," Hawkwind responded, "but Simbala is not responsible. There has also been a child murdered in Simbala. We believe the dragons to be responsible."

The Wayman grimaced. "I care not for dragons or windships. From what I have seen, our Elders have been captured or attacked. The bloodshed must stop. We wish only to return to Fandora."

Hawkwind shook his head. "It was Fandora that invaded Simbala. There is now a danger we must all face together."

"Together?" asked the Wayman skeptically.

Hawkwind turned away from him and waved to a stout man on a stallion not far away. "Vora," he cried. "Over here!"

As the General approached, Hawkwind watched the Wayman. He was a man of reason, Hawkwind thought. Vora will be able to work with him in arranging a swift surrender. He glanced toward the valley. With every moment, Evirae drew closer to becoming Queen, and he was impatient to depart.

He had to leave with Ceria before it grew too late. The ride through Overwood would be swift, but dangerous, for Evirae's agents had probably learned of his return. They would be waiting.

•

The windship armada, led by Prince Kiorte, had approached the hills with the intention of augmenting the ground troops, but the soldiers were having no trouble. From his flagship he saw that a sizable percentage of the Fandorans were leaving the hills on the western side, slowly making their way across the meadowlands that sloped gradually down to the beaches. Quickly he ran up a series of flags, and the armada responded to his orders; ten windships stayed behind to help the taking of the hills, and the rest continued on toward the retreating Fandorans.

As in the hills, there was no question about victory. The size of the armada precluded any dispute. The Fandorans saw the dark masses of the windship hulls blotting out the sky and, silhouetted above them, the Windriders aiming crossbows at them. There was not even a chance of running, as most of those retreating were either wounded or responsible for a wounded comrade. No arrows were fired.

Tamark, at the front, looked longingly at the distant beach on the horizon, where the boats were. He knew there was no chance of reaching them now. The retreat had come too late.

Several of the windships descended, headed by Kiorte's

flagship. The Prince climbed down the rope ladder and approached Tamark, who had identified himself to the other Windriders as the leader of this contingent. Tamark looked at Kiorte, reflecting that despite the difference in their height, he was much the physical superior of the thin, pale man, but was still his prisoner.

"By my authority as commander of the Brothers of the Wind and as Prince of Simbala, I demand your unconditional surrender," Kiorte said stiffly. "You may consider yourself under restraint and arrest, and you will—"

"We do not wish to fight," Tamark interrupted wearily. "We surrender! I ask only attention for our wounded."

"That will be done," Kiorte snapped, slightly annoyed at being interrupted. "Since you are the leader of this contingent, you will return with me to Overwood."

Tamark looked past the Prince at the hovering windship, and tried to give no outward sign of the nervousness that suddenly seized him. It is but a boat, he told himself. Still, he was hard put to act casually as he climbed the ladder after Kiorte and watched the ground drop away from him.

Kiorte's windship moved quickly over the trees, back into the main fleet. He would direct their maneuvers, ensuring the capture of any stray bands of Fandorans planning to reach shore. Hawkwind was probably already on his way to prevent Evirae's coronation. He would have to depart soon if he were to reach the Dais of Beron first. He glanced back at the Fandoran, who stood between two burly Windriders.

"At least this foolish war is over," he murmured. "That much is fact, in a time of uncertainty."

He had spoken to himself, but Tamark overheard him. "Aye," he replied softly. "Would that it had never begun."

Kiorte turned to look at him in surprise. " 'Twas your country which attacked us!"

"Not so!" Tamark replied heatedly. "Your windships attacked our children!"

Kiorte stared at him. The man obviously believed what he had said. Kiorte turned back to the steering levers. He gripped them hard. He was remembering what Hawkwind had told him after he and the Monarch had fought, the discoveries Ceria had made of the reasons behind the Fandoran attack.

They *had* believed Simbala to be the aggressor, then. Hawkwind had been correct.

He stared ahead, watching the trees pass beneath the windship. They were moving quickly, he thought. The journey would be over far too soon.

•

Those few hours that Ceria waited in the depths of the forest were among the longest she had ever known. She had become more and more convinced that Hawkwind had been wounded or slain in the hills. Lathan, watching Ceria pace nervously about the glade, wished he could do or say something to comfort her, but he knew that only the appearance of her beloved would soothe her.

Then Ceria abruptly raised her head. "Listen!" she breathed. "Do you hear it?"

"Hear what, milady?"

Ceria did not reply. She listened intently, and a smile spread over her face like the burst of a sunbeam through the tangled canopy. "It is the cry of a hawk!" she shouted.

Now it came to Lathan's ears too, along with the sound of a horse approaching through the woods. A moment later, Hawkwind, astride his horse, came into view. He had shed his armor, and both Lathan and Ceria shouted happily as the familiar figure swung down from his horse. Ceria ran toward him. A moment only did they embrace. "Quickly!" Hawkwind said. "Do you hold the Dragonpearl?"

"The pouch is within my mount's saddlebag," Ceria replied.

Hawkwind nodded with determination. "Then we ride!" he said. "Vora has told me of eight cavalrymen who wait within the forest. They will accompany us to the dais."

He took to his saddle, and Ceria and Lathan mounted their horses. With a leap, once again Hawkwind's dark stallion was on its way, Lady Tenor's borrowed steed following close behind it. Lathan spurred his horse after them, but to little avail. Within a short time they were far ahead, lost in the afternoon light.

"It is like that night near Dragonhead," he muttered, and he consoled himself with the thought that even with one of the swiftest stallions in Overwood, it would be difficult for him to catch Hawkwind or Ceria.

•

From the edge of the abandoned windship station within the palace, Monarch Ephrion stared out at the forest through an ancient skyglass.

"Nothing," he said. "There is no evidence of Ceria's return at all."

Behind him Baron Tolchin waited. "Then we must go on with it!" he said. "The coronation must take place. It would be unfair to ask for further delay. Even if Ceria returns with proof of her innocence, Monarch Hawkwind will still be missing. We cannot reappoint a Monarch who has abdicated his role and fled the army!"

"I do not believe that for a second!"

"Nor do I believe that the Fandoran spy escaped the palace alone. But we must accept certain things if we are to get on with the affairs of Simbala. I do not think Kiorte would lie about Hawkwind's actions. I am sorry, Monarch Ephrion, but I am convinced that Hawkwind has proven himself either a coward or a traitor."

Ephrion was silent, but it was evident that his confidence in Hawkwind had not been diminished. He did not know what the miner had done, but whatever Hawkwind's plans were, Ephrion knew they were in the best interest of Simbala's safety.

"Kiorte has a plan," said Tolchin, looking down at the empty courtyard. "He has summoned the remaining windships to the valley for an assault on the hills. They will drive the Fandorans back before nightfall."

Ephrion shook his head. "The true danger remains."

Tolchin nodded. "Kiorte will deal with the creatures you call the coldrakes, too. The Windriders will devise a plan to trap them."

"You believe that, in light of what I have told you and Alora?"

Tolchin nodded.

"They are giant creatures, but they cannot be very smart. How many can there be, Ephrion? We have never seen another in all our days in the forest."

Ephrion once again raised the skyglass and stared at the road which wound its way from Overwood. "I do not know how many exist or from whence they came, Tolchin—that was what Ceria had been sent to find out." He did not mention Amsel or the related mission on which the Fandoran had been sent, for that would surely have enraged Tolchin and raised even more doubts in his mind.

The Baron glanced anxiously at the door behind him. "The Rayan has obviously been unable to complete her task. I must go now and join Alora in preparation for the coronation. Do not worry, Monarch Ephrion. We will keep Evirae under control." He patted the elder statesman on his back and then turned from the open arch of the station. Ephrion sighed. The Baron listened too much to his nerves, he thought, but there was truth in something he had said. Even if Ceria were to return to the forest before the coronation took place, there was nothing to stop the naming of Evirae as Queen as long as Hawkwind was missing. It was obvious to the Family that Hawkwind had deserted the army, and they would support Evirae's succession regardless of what Ceria might find. The truth about the coldrakes would help end the war quickly, but Hawkwind himself would have to be present to win the struggle for the palace that had so briefly been his.

Ephrion gripped the skyglass firmly. He did not know where Hawkwind had gone, had no assurance that the young Monarch would return at all, but he had not surrendered his hope.

•

"I'm spending more time in the air than I am on the ground," Amsel told himself nervously, staring down at the bleak landscape below. He was crouched in a small hollow just behind the dragon's head, sheltered from the wind by the huge carapace and from the cold by the dragon's body heat. He held on to the horns that formed the serrated edge. It was not an uncomfortable ride, although Amsel felt at times as if a strong gust would send him flying toward the white blanket far beneath them. The Last Dragon had suggested that the safest place for Amsel to ride would be in his mouth, but Amsel had politely declined. It was not that it would have been more uncomfortable—the dragon's mouth was the size of the windship cabin and his palate soft as a duck-down mattress, although admittedly somewhat more moist. His breath was sweet, because he was a herbivore, but Amsel still vividly remembered dangling in front of the coldrake's hissing maw and had decided against it.

The return to the land of the coldrakes, from which he had fled over the course of the previous day, took much less time. The dragon had flown a different route north, above the snowy peaks, far from the edge of the river and canyon. Amsel saw few signs of life—an occasional reindeer or mountain goat hiding beneath scattered clusters of trees, but little else besides the snow. The vast range of ice was depressing, though it seemed a fitting stage for the last days of a magnificent race. In the dim sunlight, Amsel's own home seemed terribly remote. An intense loneliness swept over him, and he was once again surprised by the longing he felt within his heart. He wished for a friend, a companion with whom he could share his thoughts. He was grateful for the company of the dragon, and his conversation. Amsel had begun to think of his huge ally as "he" rather than "it." Despite the rapidity of their flight, however, Amsel was keenly aware of the time they had lost.

When the dragon told Amsel he was thirsty, the inventor could not help objecting to the additional time the descent would take. "We will be in the land of the coldrakes soon," he shouted. "There is water there. Could you not wait?"

"No," the dragon bellowed, "I cannot wait any longer. My throat is very dry." He dropped several hundred feet very suddenly and Amsel felt as if his stomach had been left in the clouds. "Be careful!" the inventor shouted. "This is new to me."

"You wished me to hurry, did you not?" A rumbling sound followed the dragon's question as he swooped toward a basin far below, and Amsel thought for a moment that the sound might be the creature's laughter. He glanced down at the basin.

"It is a lake!" he said, "and it does not appear to be frozen!" He noticed melting snow and siliceous deposits all around its edge, and concluded that it must be partially fed by a warm spring. The dragon's flapping became less frequent. He circled down and landed by the lake. Amsel felt the huge neck dipping forward, and asked to be let off so that he might also quench his thirst. The dragon complied, then politely waited while Amsel knelt by the water's edge. Amsel found the water to be icy cold and refreshing, though with a strong mineral taste. He splashed some on his face, then watched the placid surface of the lake ripple heavily as the dragon dipped and drank. They would make it to the north, he told himself, no matter what obstacles impeded them. The coldrakes would not reach Simbala and Fandora. Amsel frowned. He had discovered the true cause of Johan's murder, but he still did not know why it had occurred. Children had been killed in both Fandora and Simbala. Only children. There was something still hidden here, something he did not understand.

He was becoming lost in thought about the matter when he saw a bubbling beneath the surface of the water several yards away.

"We'd best hurry," he murmured. "If there are hot springs, there could be geysers, too." But before he could retreat, there was a sudden eruption in the lake near him. Amsel scrambled backward over the snow, and as he did he saw a huge head, crowned with writhing cilia, dart toward him. There was no way he could escape it. A fanged mouth gaped wide over him; then there was a whistling sound, and a giant wing struck the monster's long slender neck from above, deflecting its course. A cilium struck Amsel like a whip as the head plunged past him; he shouted in pain and scrambled between two large deposits of geyserite. The creature darted up from the lake to meet the dragon's attack, propelling itself forward with enormous fins. The wave it caused washed over Amsel and sent him sprawling, his eyes and nose full of water.

Coughing and sputtering, he looked up. He recognized the thing that lived in the lake now; in his studies, he had seen drawings of creatures like it. It was a seaworm, a serpent of the ocean. They were rare these days, but at one time they had been the bane of all seafaring lands. He wondered fleetingly how this one came to be in a landlocked lake; perhaps there was a subterranean channel to the sea. The seaworm was easily fifty feet long; Amsel could see loops of its tail rising out of the water. It had wrapped part of itself around the dragon's neck, seeking to strangle its adversary. It made no sound, save for the snapping of the cilia about its head. The dragon arched his neck, breaking the seaworm's grip momentarily, and fastened his jaws upon the scaled, sinuous neck. The seaworm thrashed its body and tail, pulling backward; its weight overbalanced the dragon, and he toppled over onto his left wing. Amsel hid behind the

mineral formations to avoid being crushed. Peering out, he saw the dragon brace himself and pull backward, slowly dragging the seaworm from the lake. He also saw red lines of blood streaming down the seaworm's neck. The dragon shook the worm, and Amsel heard a sharp crack. Then another curtain of spray drenched him as the seaworm's dying convulsions whipped the water into foam. Amsel watched the dragon rise slowly and step away from the seaworm. He extended his left wing and flapped it experimentally. Amsel could see that the effort caused him pain.

"Are you hurt?" he called.

"I am," the Last Dragon said, "but I can still fly. Come quickly, before my injured wing grows stiff. The night draws nigh."

He lowered his head for Amsel to climb upon it. Amsel approached, rubbing his shoulder where the cilium had slashed his sleeve and raised a red welt. He climbed aboard. When he was secure, the dragon took to the air again. He flew unsteadily, favoring his left wing, and did not reach the speed he had earlier. Nevertheless, his determination was evident.

"He intends to help me now, no matter what," Amsel murmured. "The legends about the dragons' bravery are true."

A question occurred to him. He leaned closer to the dragon's ear and shouted, "According to all the legends, dragons can breathe flame. It is obvious from the warmth within you that the flame still burns. Why did you not use it to repel the seaworm?"

He put his own ear against the leathery skin covering the dragon's head, and over the wind of their flight he could hear, vibrating through the bone, the dragon's deep voice.

"It is true," the dragon bellowed, "the flame still burns faintly within me. Only the dragons are so blessed; the coldrakes do not possess it, and it is one of the reasons why they have obeyed our orders. For the Dragonflame is not a gift to be used lightly, or for selfish ends, and never to take a life. From the beginnings of our race have we held that to be true. Within me the flame will come to an end; I will not violate its purpose."

Amsel did not ask further. There was a very gentle but unmistakable tone of rebuke in the dragon's reply, as if

Amsel had inquired into matters that were none of his business. He respected this, and spoke no more of it. Nevertheless, it worried him. If the Last Dragon refused to use his flame, how did he expect to face all the coldrakes, especially with an injured wing?

The dragon would do it, Amsel told himself. He would because he had to, despite the pain, despite the danger. Why, it's the same as I've done, Amsel realized. At first he had considered himself flung by circumstance into the actions he had taken, but that was not entirely true. He had done what he had because he felt that he must. His conscience would have permitted nothing less. Bravery had always seemed to him something found only in tales and songs, and Amsel did not think of himself as possessing it. But now he realized with surprise that perhaps he did.

Though he was terrified at the thought of facing the coldrakes again, he wanted to ensure the safety of Fandora and Simbala, no matter how dangerous it would be to do so. None would perish if he could prevent it. Despite all he had been through, he would see this through to the end, even if it meant his own death. He could do no less.

Then, as though his thoughts had been read, Amsel fancied that the Last Dragon's speed increased slightly, that his wingbeat was stronger. They flew north together into the freezing winds of the land of the coldrakes, a tiny human and a huge dragon, equal in courage.

●

At the third hour of the afternoon, the preparations for the coronation were completed. In accordance with Simbalese law, the affair would take place at the Dais of Beron, where not long ago Prince Kiorte himself had been honored. Throughout the morning, banners had been hung along Monarch's March, and oil wicks within hollow jewels now cast faint kaleidoscopic colors in the shade of the large trees. The dais itself had been polished to a warm brown. Already citizens of Overwood were starting to line the March; many looked forward to the coronation as a symbol that the war would be over soon, but there were others who remained loyal to Hawkwind and harbored the hope, however slim it seemed, that he would still return in time to stop Evirae from gaining the palace.

The miners were angry. Their hero had been removed

from the palace without a chance to protest. Lady Graydawn had sent a contingent by windship to attend, but she herself had not come, and by her absence she expressed her disapproval on behalf of the entire Northweald. Only in the heart of Overwood was there obvious support for Evirae's succession. The Royal Family and Circle were happy to once again take control of the government. Many merchants favored this, too, for the meddling ways of Hawkwind would be ended.

The mood was that of quiet expectation; there was hostility from some, uncertainty from others, but all were aware of the fact that the Family had made its decision. Hawkwind would be a monarch no longer. Evirae would be Queen.

To Ephrion's deep disappointment, there had still been no word from Lady Ceria or Monarch Hawkwind. He thought again of the courageous Fandoran he had sent to the north. There had been no indication of his return.

The elder statesman departed his quarters slowly. Although he refused to give up hope, Evirae's triumph had taken its toll. He felt very tired.

In a small silver chest, Ephrion took with him the Ruby, for in accordance with Simbalese convention, he would be responsible for bestowing it upon the new ruler. He was not looking forward to the task.

Evirae, on the other hand, could not wait. She had anxiously made preparations for the procession from her mansion down Monarch's March to the Dais of Beron. Despite the depopulation of Overwood due to the war, she was confident that most of those remaining would attend. The hours had crept by with maddening slowness, but now, at last, it was afternoon and time for the ceremony to start.

Seated in her parlor at the window, facing the palace, Evirae addressed Mesor while a manicurist buffed and lacquered her long nails to a dazzling shine. "Where is Kiorte?" she asked anxiously. "Where is my husband? Why has he not come?"

The Bursar smiled consolingly. "You forget that there is a war in progress. Prince Kiorte cannot leave anytime he wishes to do so!"

Evirae scowled. "This is not just anytime! This is the most important day of my life!"

Mesor nodded. "Yes, but unfortunately it is more important to win a victory over the Fondorans than to see the Ruby bestowed. The Fandorans still remain in the hills, Princess; so we have been told."

"They are fools," said Evirae, admiring her bejeweled coiffure in the mirror. "I have seen a Fandoran. We have no need to worry. They will never reach the forest; they represent no danger."

"You forget Thalen," replied Mesor. "Obviously he did not view them as casually as you do."

These words stung Evirae, and she turned angrily from the mirror. "That was not my fault!" she shouted.

Mesor replied in what he hoped was a calming tone. "Nobody accuses you, Princess, but you must understand why your husband is absent. He is defending Simbala, but he also seeks justice for the murder of his brother." Mesor looked nervously at Evirae.

"I understand it fully," Evirae replied. "Do you think the burden of the loss has escaped me completely?"

"No, Princess, but you—"

"Queen!" Evirae shouted, snatching a hand from the manicurist and pointing a gleaming nail at Mesor. "You must call me Queen!" As she spoke, the door to her chamber opened and a messenger appeared.

"I bring news of Monarch Hawkwind's return," he said. "He has entered the Kameran Valley with the troops of the Southland."

"Returned?" cried Evirae, paling. "Who spreads such a vicious rumor?"

" 'Tis no rumor! I saw him myself! He has gone with the army to stop the invaders!"

"Impossible!" Evirae leaped to her feet, overturning the fingerbowl. She gripped the windowsill for support. "Hawkwind deserted the troops! Kiorte is now in charge!"

"No longer," the messenger said. "I saw it myself."

Evirae took several deep breaths; for a moment it appeared to Mesor that she would faint, but she rallied and, dismissing the manicurist with a gesture, spoke in a low tone to the messenger.

"Does any other member of the Family know of this? Does Monarch Ephrion know?"

"To the best of my knowledge, he does not," the messenger said. "I slipped away as soon as Hawkwind arrived, and rode hard to deliver the tidings to you."

Evirae pressed several tookas into his palm. "Remain hidden until after the coronation," she warned, "and do not speak of what you have seen to anybody." The messenger nodded and left.

Evirae turned slowly and glared as Mesor. "Why did you not anticipate this?" she demanded.

Mesor spread his hands. "How could I have? You heard the messenger—he is the first to bring the news to Overwood."

Evirae paced nervously. "Hawkwind is still Monarch until the Ruby is upon me! Should he return before then, he can challenge the Family's decision! We must hurry, Mesor! We must not wait! The procession is to start at once!"

"Do not panic!" Mesor responded. "Did you not tell me that the coronation is a formality only? There is no need to worry. You are already Queen."

Evirae kicked the fingerbowl across the jeweled floor of the chamber. "Fool!" she shouted. "Do you believe everything you hear?"

Mesor fumbled his words, desperately searching for a way to convince Evirae not to panic. If she rushed now, the Family's suspicions would be aroused. "According to law," he said, "you are to be the last to arrive! You cannot leave now, Princess! How will it look to the Family if you reach the dais before them?"

"Fool! Have you not been listening? *Hawkwind is coming!* What matters protocol now?" She turned and exited the room in a flurry of silk and perfume. Mesor sighed and rose to follow, then paused for a moment and stared through the window at the palace. He could see the carriages of the Family awaiting their riders, and the people that lined the wide avenue. He knew the populace was fickle. The people had shifted allegiance to Evirae, but if Hawkwind defeated the Fandorans, they would easily be swayed to his side again. Perhaps she was correct. If they did not move too quickly, Evirae's anxiety might seem nothing more than her usual demanding behavior.

He joined her in her black coach, which moved at a smart

pace down the road to Monarch's March. "This is Ephrion's doing!" Evirae muttered. "He sought to postpone the coronation long enough for Hawkwind to return." She stared out nervously through the window, waving perfunctorily at the people. Many looked shocked to see the Princess's coach hastening ahead of the less important dignitaries', but the gossip it caused was a welcome change from the grim news of the war.

Evirae gripped the seat of the coach tightly. Although the cheering outside comforted her slightly, she expected at any moment to see a stallion charging down the road, the dark-haired miner astride it.

•

The balance of the procession departed a short time later. In a large white coach rode Tolchin and Alora, who had returned from the merchants' quarter to accompany Monarch Ephrion to the dais. The elder statesman was unusually quiet, and the Baron took this as a possible rebuke to his continued support for Evirae's future as Queen.

"There is no alternative," he said, in an attempt to console himself and Ephrion. "There is no other candidate from the Family with as much support among the people as Evirae. I will be glad when this is done, Ephrion. Then we will act on your suspicions about the dragons."

Ephrion did not reply. He seemed lost in his thoughts. He opened the silver chest on his lap and looked at the Ruby upon the silk cushion within it. The jewel would not be worn on Evirae's forehead as it had been on Hawkwind's. Her hairdress was too tall for Ephrion to slip the diadem over it, and so the artisans of the palace had made a new and longer chain for him to fasten about the Princess's neck.

Ephrion closed the chest and sighed. However she wore it, he thought, she would not wear it well. Of that he was sure.

•

The procession arrived to find Evirae already there, nervously tapping her foot on the gleaming surface of the dais. People who had come early for a good viewing were looking at her in amusement, annoyance, or both, at this contravention of procedure. The chorus that was to provide music for the affair had started uncertainly when Evirae arrived, then tapered off into disorganized silence when it became obvious that she had come early. In her haste Evirae had forgotten that the coronation could not take place without Monarch Ephrion.

At last the large white coach of the Monarch Emeritus arrived before the dais. The chorus once again started a wordless tune, *a cappella*, a lilting combination of tones that was in keeping with the simplicity of the event.

The people crowding into the clearing maintained a respectful silence as Ephrion, followed by the Family and selected members of the Circle, mounted the steps to the dais. Evirae held her breath as she studied Ephrion's face. His expression was set and he did not look at her, but he seemed resigned to his duty as former Monarch.

Lady Tenor, whose duty it was to announce the beginning of the ceremony, took her proper place on the dais. Much fuss was made over the gowns and costumes of the members of the Family. Whispered compliments floated from Eselle to Alora to Jibron, and Evirae thought she would go mad waiting out the social manners of those in attendance. Spurred beyond endurance and good sense, she turned to Lady Tenor and whispered, "Hurry! The ceremony must be started!"

Lady Tenor stared at the Princess. "This cannot be rushed," she replied with disdain. "You would do well to savor this moment, young woman. A Queen must count patience among her virtues. It is a rare event when the Ruby is bestowed upon a Princess."

"It will not happen at all if you wait any longer," Evirae said beneath her breath. General-Emeritus Jibron and Lady Eselle, already startled by their daughter's untoward behavior, looked at her rebukingly. Evirae nodded at them and smiled as if she had suddenly remembered where and to whom she spoke. She glanced up at the sky. Kiorte, she wondered, why are you not here to support me?

At last, all the members of the Family on the dais had taken their proper places. The singing of the chorus swelled to a final burst and stopped. In the silence that followed, Lady Tenor said, "By decision of the Royal Family, meeting in closed session, let it be known to the people of Simbala that Hawkwind, for reasons considered traitorous to Simbala, has been ordered removed from the Monarchy."

Evirae closed her eyes and filled her heart with the welcome words. At last! she thought. Obviously Ephrion did not know Hawkwind had returned. The formal part of the coronation would not take long. Then the Ruby would be hers!

Lady Tenor continued. "In accordance with the laws of Simbala, this removal will be made final by the appointment of a new Monarch." She looked at Ephrion, and he stepped forward, holding the small silver box that contained the Ruby. Evirae glanced at him, but Ephrion's eyes were distant, as if fixed on another time. At that moment, she felt sorry for him. He had fought against her, but he had lost.

Lady Tenor said, "If any person has reason to deny or gainsay Evirae, daughter of Jibron and Eselle, candidate to the monarchy, that person now must be heard."

Evirae held her breath. The silence in the clearing was intense. It was the longest moment Evirae had ever endured. She was sure that Hawkwind had somehow slipped unseen into the crowd and would now speak. But to her delight there were no cries against her. Lady Tenor continued to wait for a reply.

Unable to endure any more delays, Evirae whispered, "Continue!"

Lady Tenor stepped back with annoyance and Evirae turned quickly to face Ephrion. She was trembling with eagerness. In a moment, it would be done!

Ephrion opened the chest and removed the Ruby on its chain. He kept his eyes averted from Evirae's face, not wishing to see the look of triumph there. He tried to speak, to say the words expected of him before he placed the chain about her throat, but the injustice of the whole affair overwhelmed him then, and he could not speak. Two bright tears trickled down his wrinkled cheeks.

A murmur went up from the crowd, as the ceremony halted.

"Ephrion," Evirae said softly and tensely. "You must speak."

Ephrion finally whispered, "By agreement of the Royal Family . . ." but his voice faltered. He could not bear to bring the removal of Hawkwind to pass.

Evirae glared at him now. He was purposefully delaying the coronation!

"Go on," she whispered angrily. "You must finish!"

Their eyes met for a moment, and then suddenly Ephrion looked past her to the clearing behind the crowd.

"Continue!" seethed Evirae, but now the delay had drawn the attention of the Family.

Ephrion lowered his hands, the Ruby within them. There followed a scream, a shriek that at first sounded to some as if Evirae, in her impatience, had made it. Then it was repeated, echoing through the clearing. The crowd looked back in bewilderment, but the elder statesman of Simbala caught the glimmer of recognition in Evirae's eyes.

"Yes," he whispered too softly for any but the Princess to hear, "the hawk."

"No!" Evirae looked up, terror frozen on her face. Above the crowd, soaring swiftly into the clear blue sky, was the hawk. It circled, shrieking, and Ephrion smiled.

"Hawkwind!" he exclaimed proudly. "Hawkwind has returned!"

The Family watched the clearing with suspicion as the crowd turned in unison toward the rustling in the woods behind them.

"*No!*" screamed Evirae. "Heed not this trick! He wishes only to delay my coronation!" Her father bounded quickly to her side to support her. "Get on with the ceremony, Monarch Ephrion," he warned. "You have defied our decision long enough."

Ephrion did not budge. As he watched, from the edge of the clearing eight riders burst forth, the first holding a banner silver and black.

"Look!" Ephrion shouted. "He comes now!"

There were gasps and cries of excitement as a dark stallion broke through the clearing behind the eight riders and headed for the crowd. Astride it, dressed in a silver-and-black robe, rode Hawkwind.

"He has returned!" Ephrion shouted again, and then he smiled broadly as the red-cloaked figure of Lady Ceria, on Lady Tenor's horse, followed the Monarch toward the crowd.

Evirae, with a cry of incoherent anger, reached out and snatched the Ruby from Ephrion's grasp. Yet as she held it, preparatory to fastening it about her neck, the hawk dived straight toward her in a blur of wings. Evirae stumbled backward into her father's arms, screaming in fright and holding the Ruby out instinctively. The chain tore from her grip as the hawk seized it in its talons and soared back into the sky, the dangling jewel sparkling in the rays of the sun. Evirae wailed, watching the Ruby being carried beyond her reach. Then, drawing herself up and stepping away from Jibron, she turned to her personal guards and shouted, "Seize them! Seize the miner and the Rayan! They are traitors to Simbala!"

The riders had broken through the crowd now to make way for Hawkwind and Ceria. The guards started toward them, but Ephrion ordered them to stop. Whether the authority in the former Monarch's voice or Evirae's own histrionics made them hesitate was unclear, but they did not continue.

This cannot be happening, Evirae thought. The strain has been too much. I am dreaming! She closed her eyes, but when she opened them again, Hawkwind and Ceria were still coming toward her. Evirae watched in helpless rage as Hawkwind swung down from his steed and approached the dais.

She would not be defeated! Evirae looked about wildly. There had to be some way to trap Hawkwind, to stop him. She looked up at the sky, hoping to see Kiorte's windship, but the sky was empty, save for the hawk flying overhead. Ahead of her, more and more of the crowd were cheering Hawkwind!

Evirae watched as the miner took a black pouch from the Rayan and stepped closer to the dais. He raised his arm defiantly, and the hawk circled down to land gently, the chain of the Ruby clenched now in its beak.

In desperation she cried, "Hawkwind is a traitor! He abandoned the army in the midst of battle! He seeks now to deceive us again!"

These words rang hollow with the crowd, and Evirae glanced anxiously for support from the Family. Stunned by the turn of events, none would help. Only her parents stood silently at her side. She was baffled. What did Hawkwind possess within the pouch? What had the Rayan found in her escape from Overwood? In her ignorance, the Princess cried out again. "Hawkwind seeks to deceive us with the aid of the Rayan!"

Hawkwind watched her, his expression unwavering, unreadable. He was confident of victory now. He looked up at Ephrion, standing beside General Jibron. There was pride evident upon the old man's face.

Hawkwind faced Evirae. "Your husband and I have brought the war to an end," he said. "The desertion with which you have charged me was a mission to find the troops we had sent to the Southland. By reuniting them with the contingents of Overwood, we launched a single assault on the Fandorans together. With the support of the windships, we have driven the invaders out of the hills!"

A cheer went up from the crowd. Hawkwind had returned in peace!

Evirae could not believe these words. The miner working with the windships? It could not be possible unless Kiorte . . .

"No!" she screamed. "Do not listen to him! It is a trick. He wishes only to retain his title!"

This charge was greeted by several boos from the crowd. Evirae panicked. Her guards defiant, the Family unsupportive, she now feared that Kiorte himself had abandoned her. "I call for justice," she cried pitifully. "Arrest Hawkwind!"

Hawkwind watched her. "There will only be justice when Lady Ceria is no longer viewed as a traitor!" he said. "She did not flee Overwood to betray us—she was sent on a mission by Monarch Ephrion to find this!"

Hawkwind withdrew a gleaming jewel from the pouch and held it high above his head as a gasp went up behind him. "It is a Dragonpearl," he said, "a jewel of legend! With it we may learn the secrets of the dragons—the reason for their attack against Simbala!"

He stared at Evirae. "It is you who are the traitor, Princess! It is you who have betrayed the trust of our people with your petty schemes and lies! It is you who harbored a Fandoran spy in the tunnels beneath Overwood! Do not deny it!"

"These are all lies!" Evirae cried. "A conspiracy concocted by you and the Rayan! You hold nothing but a shiny stone in your hand!"

Even as she spoke, Ceria, standing behind Hawkwind, concentrated her thoughts upon the Dragonpearl. A swirling and clearing of the rainbow clouds within it followed. Then a billowing darkness became a miniature landscape of gray cliffs and a black spire.

"Look!" Lady Tenor cried. "Look at the jewel!"

Again shouts and exclamations filled the clearing, as the scene within the jewel was glimpsed by many near the front of the crowd. Excited rumors drifted back quickly that the sight within the orb was indeed the lost land of the dragons. Ephrion was silent, transfixed by the phenomenon. Ceria had succeeded in her mission!

"The dragons attacked the Fandorans," Hawkwind continued. "Then the Fandorans attacked us, thinking we were responsible! The real threat to us both is the dragons!"

Ceria, too tired to maintain the image any longer, breathed deeply, and the rainbow clouds returned to the Dragonpearl. The picture she had summoned up was different from those she had seen in Shar Wagon. She would have to try to find it again after conferring with Monarch Ephrion.

Hawkwind stepped forward, Ceria at his side, the hawk now resting upon his arm, as the crowd quieted. Then slowly, with the knowledge of the support behind him, he ascended the steps to the platform.

"We may not both govern Simbala," he said, approaching Evirae. "It is obvious whose acts have been traitorous to Simbala. Concede honorably, Evirae, or you will be disgraced."

"Never!" She glared at Hawkwind and Ephrion, who had stepped forward to take both the hawk and the Ruby from the young Monarch.

"Then I must order your arrest!" He turned to the guard behind him. "Take her!" he said.

Ephrion did not protest the order, but before the guard could reach the Princess she spied a small dark cloud moving against the distant sky. "Kiorte!" she shouted. "My husband returns! He will see that justice is done! Do not dare touch me! Prince Kiorte will make clear the menace you pose to Simbala!"

As the ship began to settle over the clearing, those below could see that, in addition to Kiorte and two Windriders, there was also aboard a short, bald, massively built man in ragged garb. He was obviously a Fandoran.

Few noticed a thin man, dressed in Bursar's clothing, slip quietly through the crowd to the clearing.

The rope ladder was thrown down, and the Prince descended quickly, leaving Tamark aboard with the two Windriders. As he touched foot to the dais, Evirae rushed toward him. "Kiorte," she cried, "you must tell the people of what Hawkwind has done, of how he abandoned the army! Tell the Family that he is a traitor!"

Kiorte looked at his wife for a moment in silence. His uniform was torn and soiled, much as another had been when he had first returned from the war. He did not look angry now, but an expression of quiet determination rested upon his face.

Hawkwind and Ceria watched anxiously and waited for him to speak. Kiorte's word would be accepted by the people—his name was synonymous with honor—and the support of those still loyal to Evirae hung in the balance.

Hawkwind knew that his words to Kiorte earlier had had an effect on the Prince, but he knew not how much. Kiorte's commitment to the control of Simbala by the Royal Family had never been challenged. Now he would have to decide between it and the truth.

Evirae crept forward to embrace her husband, and in that moment Hawkwind knew what Kiorte's answer would be.

He rejected her touch, clasping his gloved hand about the delicate fingers of his wife's hand. Her nails cut into his shirt.

"Evirae"—he spoke in a low and even voice—"Hawkwind has told me of your concealment of the Fandoran spy."

"He knows not the truth!" she cried.

He squeezed her frail hand tighter.

"Hawkwind has told me also of your actions toward Lady Ceria, a woman I do not trust, but nevertheless worthy of justice."

Evirae's face turned crimson. "The charges against her were raised clearly and properly, as you yourself saw!"

"Evirae," said Kiorte, and this time the words were loud enough for even the crowd beyond them to hear, "you know my distrust of Hawkwind and all that he has done against the traditions of Overwood!"

Evirae smiled. "Of course, Kiorte. We have always been in complete agreement on this."

"Then you must also realize that my support of his words must mean that the proof of them is far beyond doubt.

Evirae did not reply.

Kiorte continued, and this time, for the first time in memory of those assembled, his emotions could be felt clearly through his words. "Evirae, you have conspired against the Monarch and his Minister. You urged war for nothing more than your personal gain! You have lied and schemed and endangered the lives of others to reach the position you are in today." He stared coldly at his wife and said, "Evirae, surrender your claim to the palace. You have disgraced yourself and Simbala. You are unworthy of the Family."

Evirae moaned as though wounded and started to stagger away from Kiorte. He had not as yet released her hand, however, and as she pulled back, three long and delicate nails broke off with his grasp. Then the tears began. "Kiorte," she sobbed, "my husband, why do you do this to me?"

"You have brought it upon yourself," he replied. "You are a slave to your ambition." He watched her then, as she stood harbored by her parents, sobbing shamelessly in full view of the people of Overwood.

Hawkwind stepped forward and acknowledged Kiorte's support with an expression of gratitude.

The Prince frowned. "You remain Ephrion's successor," he said curtly. "I trust you will show more respect for the laws of Simbala than you have in the past."

Hawkwind nodded to Ephrion, and the elder statesman approached with the Ruby.

"Not yet," said Kiorte. "My wife has been disgraced enough."

Together with Jibron and Eselle, he led the unresisting Princess down the steps of the dais. Hawkwind and Ceria watched as Evirae was taken through the crowd to a large carriage not far from the side of the platform. Suddenly she stopped and turned back toward them. Her face burning with anger and pride, she shouted, "I know of your past, Hawkwind! I know the secrets in it, and the danger it will someday bring to Simbala! A time will come when the people will cry for your removal! A time will come, Hawkwind, when I shall return here in triumph!" Ceria and Ephrion looked at each other in shock as the Princess entered the carriage with her parents. The horses cantered away, bearing the Princess and her broken dreams away from the dais and back to Overwood.

The words were obviously a childish threat, but Hawkwind seemed oddly troubled by them. He looked up at the windship above the crowd as Kiorte returned to the dais and ordered the Fandoran disembarked.

As the rope ladder descended, Hawkwind faced the Family. Tolchin and Alora watched him, as did Lady Tenor and other dignitaries. Hawkwind had refused to be defeated. It was obvious why he remained a hero to the people of Overwood.

"We face a long and perilous road ahead," he said, turning back to the crowd, "but there will be peace in Simbala once again. We shall defend our shores against the possibility of invasion and attack by the dragons!"

As the Fandoran climbed down upon the dais, the voices of the Family were drowned out by the cheering crowd.

Ephrion smiled, and as the hawk circled the windship above them, Ephrion opened the chain holding the Ruby and clasped it about Hawkwind's neck. "There is no escaping this jewel," he said, smiling. Another cheer went up. Hawkwind embraced Ephrion and Ceria. "We must talk with the Fandorans at once," he said softly. "Preparations must begin as soon as possible." Ephrion then conferred with the bewildered Tamark.

Hawkwind turned and approached Kiorte. The Prince stood apart from him, eyes fixed on the avenue where Evirae had been taken away. Hawkwind was sure he had seen a tear fall from those eyes, but Kiorte turned quickly from him and climbed up the rope ladder back to the windship. "The Fandoran will convey the status of their troops," he shouted. A few moments later the craft moved slowly away from the dais, toward Overwood.

"Where is he going?" Ceria asked.

"I suppose to be alone," Hawkwind whispered, "and then perhaps to speak with Evirae in the privacy of their mansion. He has lost more than most."

The windship disappeared from view and Hawkwind turned to address the crowd. "Return to your homes! Men and women will soon be returning from the battle!" As the crowd slowly scattered, he looked at the woman beside him.

"Ceria," he said. "It seems the miner is monarch again."

Ceria smiled. "There was never a time when you were not," she replied.

Then, in front of the crowd, Hawkwind took her in his arms and kissed her.

XXXIII

The palace was a lonely giant, its glowing lights like miniature moons in the darkness. Although it was well past midnight, there was much activity within, for the people of Simbala now faced the real danger.

On the eighth level of the palace, in the chambers of Monarch Ephrion, the elder statesman met with Ceria to determine the true nature of that which she had glimpsed within the Dragonpearl. Below them, in the private chamber of General Vora, Elder Tamark of Fandora met with three navigators of the Simbalese merchant fleet and Baron Tolchin to examine ancient maps of the sea to the north.

Still farther below, deep within the subterranean tunnels of the palace, two figures walked a winding torchlit passage toward an old and dimly lit door. They were Hawkwind and Kiorte.

"I appreciate your understanding," said Hawkwind. "I do not wish to make things more difficult for you."

"You could not," Kiorte replied. He straightened his blue jacket.

Hawkwind sighed. "I too grieve for Thalen. I wish only that it had not happened."

Kiorte stiffened. "Your words cannot bring him back," he said harshly. "It is best that we do not speak of it. The perpetrator of my brother's murder will be dealt with when order returns to the affairs of my fleet."

"Murder?" asked Hawkwind. "You do not still think—"

Kiorte waved his hand flatly in a motion for silence. "My brother was murdered by the Wealdsman Tweel. I viewed the act with my own eyes!"

"As did I!" said Hawkwind. "It was an accident! The Wealdsman was attempting to save Thalen's life!"

"It is easy for you to see things differently from the ground. I was at Thalen's side."

Hawkwind reddened. "Kiorte, haven't the Wealdfolk suffered enough? Many were killed in their assault on the hill. Only an hour ago I dispatched Lathan to help the man who had originally brought the news of the murdered child!"

"A friend of Tweel's, I presume."

"He is Willen, by name. A hunter loyal to Lady Graydawn. He sought food and supplies for the wounded Wealdfolk stranded in the valley."

"They had no business in the war at all!"

Hawkwind stared at Kiorte and saw the face of a man who had retreated, at least in the matter of his brother's demise, to a private reality. There would be no reasoning with Kiorte about it now; he would deal with the matter at hand and confront the issue of the Wealdsman's safety again later.

"We must speak with the Fandorans about the dragons," he said as they reached one end of the tunnel. Hawkwind motioned to a guard in front of the tunnel door. The man smiled in recognition, leaped to his feet and removed a key from his pocket. As Hawkwind and Kiorte watched, he unlocked the door.

The door came open with a loud squeaking sound. Behind it lay a long, low tunnel, a cornucopia tapering into the darkness. It had been bored into a giant root long ago. On either side of the tunnel were lines of small, arched, wooden doors. In the distant past of Simbala, this had been the prison of the palace, a dreary home for spies and enemies of Overwood. More recently it had become a cellar for wines and jams—a sleepy tunnel covered with layers of soil and dust.

Kiorte stepped inside. The floor was covered with fresh footprints, those of Simbalese soldiers and Fandoran men.

"Come," said Hawkwind. "I have had the leaders of the Fandoran troops sequestered here." He started down the tunnel.

"How did you know which men were in charge?" asked Kiorte. "They wear no garments of distinction or uniforms."

"Some identified themselves; others were described to us by Tamark, the man you brought back to Overwood."

"A barbarous name, but I admit some respect for him. He is here, then?"

Hawkwind shook his head. "He confers with Baron Tolchin as we speak."

"Tolchin!" Kiorte snorted. "Have you lost all sense, Hawkwind? What reason would you have for pairing the Fandoran with the Baron?"

"He is a skilled sailor. We have need of his expertise, as you will soon discover."

Kiorte shook his head. "Perhaps I should not have come. There is much we still do not agree upon, Hawkwind. You have a talent for seeking answers to problems in a manner uncommon to Simbalese tradition."

Hawkwind smiled momentarily and signaled to a guard farther down the tunnel. The corridor was dark and musty, and he wished to join Ephrion and Ceria as soon as possible. First, however, it was imperative that he gain the Fandoran's trust. For what he wished to do was more daring, more unorthodox than even Kiorte might suspect.

•

The sound of footsteps in the hallway roused Jondalrun, and he felt the raw pain of the injury to his head. Dizzily he looked up, and the memory of the battle returned. Faint light poured through a crisscross of bars within a wooden door. He had been imprisoned!

Struggling to his feet, he stumbled toward the door and pressed his gnarled hands against it. The murderous Sim had taken Dayon captive! Anger burned within him. He would not lose another son! As long as he lived, he would fight for Dayon's safety.

He peered through the bars and glimpsed three figures across the corridor, illuminated by the light from a small torch. The first was dressed in a blue robe, the second wore a high multicolored hat. The other, holding the torch, was obviously a guard. He opened the door of another cell and vanished inside. The first two waited.

"I demand to be freed!" cried Jondalrun. "I demand to see my son!"

The man in the multicolored hat turned and shouted harshly at him.

"Silence," he said. "We shall be there shortly!"

"I demand to be freed!" Jondalrun cried again. "I will not wait!"

The man in the hat ignored him.

Jondalrun sat down on the floor of the cell. There was little he could do to protest. They had taken his weapon, of course, but they had left his wristlet. It was obviously as worthless as they had thought. He waited and hoped that Dayon was still alive. Sitting on the damp straw, he thought of the others, of Lagow, who had perished; of Tenniel, the injured young Elder; and of Tamark, who had set out to take the wounded back to the boats. Had the Sim captured the last two also?

Suddenly his thoughts were broken by the sound of footsteps. A key turned in the lock of the cell. Jondalrun struggled to his feet. He had come this far; no Sim would keep him from finding his son! Then, as the door swung back, he gave out a gasp of delight. There, in the hall outside, stood Dayon and the Wayman!

"Father!" the young man cried. "You are safe!" In unabashed relief he hugged his father, holding him hard. "I feared you were killed in the battle!"

Jondalrun's eyes grew moist. He saw Hawkwind and the other Simbalese enter the cell, and he turned away from them. "I, too, was worried," he whispered to Dayon. Over his son's shoulder he glared at the captors. "There was no way of knowing what treachery the Sim had used against you!"

"We are not treacherous!" Kiorte answered stiffly. "Nor did *we* invade *your* land."

"No!" Jondalrun cried, thrusting Dayon behind him. "You sought instead to murder my child!"

Hawkwind interceded then, putting his hand upon the tattered shoulder of the Elder's coat. "You are Jondalrun of Fandora. I have heard much about you from the others."

"Aye!" Jondalrun responded, stepping out of the young monarch's grip. "I am an Elder of Tamberly Town and a leader of Fandora's army! You will treat us all with respect!"

The miner smiled at Jondalrun's manner and said, "I am Hawkwind, Monarch of Simbala. I assure you that we do respect you and your men. Your Elder Tamark has told me of the reasons for the invasion. I sympathize with your plight, for it has been our own."

"Tamark? You have talked with Tamark?"

"He works with us now, as I hope you and the others will, too."

"Never!" said Jondalrun. "I will never aid those responsible for the murder of my son. Nor will Tamark."

"Your child was not murdered by us, Jondalrun. If what we have learned is true, he was attacked by a dragon!"

"A dragon? There is no proof that a dragon was involved!"

"There is proof," Hawkwind replied sternly. "I have brought you all to the palace so that we may find a way to face the threat of the dragons together!"

At these words, Prince Kiorte turned away angrily. "I see no need to humor these ruffians!" he whispered. "Whatever threat the dragons pose, we can face on our own!"

Jondalrun overheard him. "Ruffians?" he boomed. "It is not Fandora who murders defenseless children!"

Hawkwind sighed. The bickering could go on for hours if he did not stop it now. "Guard!" he shouted. "Release the others and bring them hither!"

The guard nodded and headed for the next cell.

Hawkwind stared at Jondalrun and Dayon. "Listen to me, men of Fandora! You have seen what the dragons can do to man. We have discovered that they are a vanishing breed. Those that attacked Fandora and Simbala are the last of their race, struggling to survive! I know not how many more exist, but their numbers can only be few." He glanced back at Kiorte, but he could not determine his reaction. "Your men have been encamped near the hills where you were captured. If you are convinced by what you will soon see, implore them to join with our troops in a mission to seek out the dragons!"

Dayon looked immediately at Hawkwind. Do battle with dragons? Had they not seen enough bloodshed? Only a fool would dare challenge creatures of such size and strength. Still, if the Simbalese were correct, and it was indeed a dragon who had murdered Johan, could they do anything less than make sure it did not attack again? Had that not been the reason for the entire war?

Dayon felt very sad then, observing the expression of his

father and Pennel. If the Simbalese had had nothing to do with the murders of the children, if they had had no design on Fandoran land or commerce, then the entire war had been for naught. They had attacked without knowing the truth at all. It was as he had felt from the start. They should never have gone.

Kiorte waited in the silence with growing impatience. At last he turned to Hawkwind and said, "These men are our prisoners! We need not ask for their help! It is our right to demand it!"

Jondalrun looked up at the Windrider and shouted, "You will demand nothing! There is nothing you can do to make us ally ourselves with the murderers of our children!"

"Do not argue!" said Hawkwind. "There will be no coercion here, Prince Kiorte. The mission we are to undertake requires the willing involvement of every man. If the Fandorans do not wish to protect their children from the creatures, then we shall complete the entire mission ourselves."

Jondalrun scowled. "Dare you mean to call us cowards?"

"No," said Hawkwind, "but there is no reason to ignore our pleas unless, of course, Fandorans fear the dragons."

"Any fool knows enough to fear dragons," Jondalrun responded, "and we also do not wish to embark on a long and fruitless mission. My men are tired. Prove to me that there is reason to suspect a dragon of my son's murder, and I tell you, Simbala's purpose will become our own, whether you like it or not!"

Hawkwind held back a smile. "There is a council meeting to be held this morning," he said. "You and the other Elders shall attend." He looked again at Jondalrun. The Fandoran would be a fit companion for Jibron in his most grudging mood.

Then he turned to Kiorte. "Come," he said, "we will discuss this further outside." The guard was given orders to allow the Fandorans free access to each other's cells.

Returning to the outer tunnel, Kiorte resumed his criticism of Hawkwind's plans. "This smacks of your usual unorthodoxy. What need do we have for any Fandoran soldiers?"

"Do not rush to judgment," Hawkwind answered. "Do you not remember what happened during the battle? The dragon swept down to attack the Fandorans, but then it turned away, as though fearing something. We assumed that the dragon was on their side. We now know that is untrue."

"Yes," Kiorte replied with some reluctance. "But why did it retreat? The Fandorans hardly know how to fight—how would they be able to drive back a dragon without lifting a sword?"

Hawkwind smiled tensely. "I do not know, Kiorte. Yet it would be worth their presence to learn, would it not?"

Kiorte nodded thoughtfully. "I still do not like it," he said, "but I think you may be correct."

•

The Last Dragon's injured wing made for an unsteady flight, and the daylight hours had long since passed when he and Amsel finally reached the wide river basin at the edge of the land of the coldrakes. The icy winds cut through the inventor's tattered clothing. He was tired and cold. More than once he had grown worried that the air currents would sweep him from his perch, but he had held on tightly and prayed.

At last he spied the tall spire, silhouetted in the distance against a lonely moon. "We must head there!" he cried. "Below it lies the coldrakes' warren!"

The dragon dropped slowly, his wings proudly raised toward the sky. "I do not see them," he bellowed. "I do not see any of them at all."

"Wait!" Amsel shouted. "You must get closer to the caverns near the spire! That is where they live!"

The dragon continued north above the river, flapping his broad wings through the oncoming mists. "It grows warmer here," he rumbled. "The ice has not yet made its home."

"It is the hot spring," said Amsel. "The boiling waters run below the spire." Amsel stared out anxiously through the mists, his heart pounding. He expected at any moment to see the coldrakes pouring from the caves like bats. Yet, as he watched, he saw nothing but the spiraling mist. He glanced again at the spire, and fear seized him.

What if the coldrakes were gone? What if they had already left for Simbala or Fandora?

It was not possible!

"We must fly down to the caverns!" he screamed against the howling wind.

The dragon flew lower as they approached the gray cliffs. "The sound of my voice will summon them," he said, "if any

remain here at all!" Then the dragon swung its massive head slightly, as if to remind Amsel how easily he could be flung to the ground. "If this is a trick of man . . ." he grumbled.

"It is not a trick!" Amsel cried. "I am deeply worried! The coldrakes seem to have vanished!"

The dragon lowered his neck toward the darkened caves and roared. The titanic sound nearly hurled Amsel from his perch, and as the echo faded in the wind, there came a muffled cry from the darkness below them.

It was the shriek of a coldrake!

The cry was followed by another, and another. At first Amsel thought that these were echoes of the first, but then he saw three coldrakes burst suddenly from a large cavern. The sight of them sent a chill through him, bringing back the terror he had felt so recently.

The Last Dragon watched the coldrakes soar high above the warren, startled and searching. Then, as the mists cleared momentarily, he roared again, a sonorous, sad sound, a cry from another age. The coldrakes saw the dragon then. Shrieking, they retreated in shock as he slowly planed toward them through the mists. They hovered for a moment near the top of the cliffs, and then dropped, screeching and howling in fear, back to the caves.

The dragon's easy planing changed to a controlled dive as he pursued them. Amsel held on for his life. In the excitement of the chase, the old beast seemed to have forgotten that Amsel still rode upon his head!

"Slow down," cried Amsel, "or you will kill me!" The words were lost in the wind. He closed his eyes as the dragon dived to the edge of the caverns, and wrapped both arms tightly around the horn. A moment more and they would be on a ledge outside the warren.

The creature at last landed, and roared loudly at the mouth of the cave into which the coldrakes had fled. An echo of his voice came back in reply.

"They are frightened," said the Last Dragon. "They feel shame for something that they have done."

Amsel peered cautiously over the carapace on the dragon's head, into the darkness. There was very little he could see beyond the shadows.

The dragon stepped forward, scraping the wet rock with his claws. The stench from within made Amsel gag. Then he heard another shriek, deeper within the cavern. Amsel closed his eyes; he could not bear the thought of another attack. His last encounter with the coldrakes had been nightmare enough to last a lifetime. He had no wish for another. Yet the dragon was his only protection now against the creatures and the cold. If he went deeper into the cavern, Amsel knew he would have to go with him.

The Last Dragon continued slowly through the passage. The sound of his breathing returned softly from the darker depths. Amsel listened. He thought he could hear another sound, a panting, like that of a wounded animal. He searched the darkness of the tunnel from his vantage atop the dragon's head, but again, he could see little more than the cavern walls.

Then, as the dragon turned a bend in the tunnel, Amsel thought he could make out a black shape lying on the cavern floor.

It moved.

The dragon drew closer to it. It was a coldrake! It squealed weakly in terror. Amsel squinted and saw its battered wing draped pathetically over a small boulder. The coldrake was seriously wounded; Amsel knew not how, but it was obvious that the creature could do them no harm.

The dragon addressed the coldrake in a low, rumbling voice, calming in tone, but authoritative. The coldrake shrieked its reply, short breathless sounds. Then the dragon roared, causing Amsel to shield his ears in pain from the booming sounds that reverberated in the cavern.

The coldrake hid its head beneath the shattered sheath of its wing. The dragon spoke again, then turned from the wounded creature and spoke to Amsel. "It is as you thought," he said. "They are gone."

"No!" shouted Amsel.

The dragon looked again at the pitiful creature on the cavern floor. "They have been taken by a coldrake larger than the rest to invade the land to the south."

"That is the coldrake that attacked me!"

"He has departed," the dragon grumbled, "the creatures we have seen are the only creatures that still remain here. They are old and frightened. The others have gone."

"Then we must hurry!" said Amsel. "We must stop them before they reach the sea!"

"They seek to escape the cold," the dragon bellowed, "as we once did. They know not the reason for the edict they defy. They know not that the lands to the south will grow too warm for them to endure!"

"We must catch them before it is too late!" cried Amsel.

The Last Dragon turned slowly away from the wounded coldrake and faced the mouth of the cavern. "If we are to stop them, I must rest. I have flown quite far and I am wounded." He considered. "I must sleep." He started back toward the cavern ledge.

"Sleep?" Amsel fairly screamed with impatience. "You cannot sleep! We must go south!"

"Do not presume to order me," said the dragon. "I shall decide when we leave. There will be time to stop them before the land grows too warm."

"You are thinking of the coldrakes! I am thinking of the humans. I brought you here so that we could stop the *killing!* There will not be time for that!"

The dragon considered for a moment, then moved its head irritably, almost dislodging Amsel. "I must rest," he repeated. "I will not be able to help man or coldrake if I do not rest." He proceeded to lower his head to the cavern floor.

To the dragon's surprise, Amsel suddenly stepped forward, pressed his boot into the tuft of hair above the dragon's left brow, and jumped off.

"If you will not stop them, then I will!" he cried.

The dragon watched Amsel drop to the ground. "You cannot leave! It is too cold for you outside!"

Amsel looked up over his shoulder. The giant regarded him with annoyance, he thought, but there was also a tone of concern in his voice.

Amsel hoped that his trust in the creature would be justified; he did not think it possible that the dragon would allow him to perish in the cold. He turned his back to the dragon and marched down the passage toward the mouth of the cave.

"I am going!" he shouted. "If you will not help me, then I will have to find a way to stop the coldrakes myself!"

He waited as the echo of his words returned. There was no sound from the dragon, save for the regular rhythm of his breath. Amsel turned. It could not end now! Not after all of the struggles he had faced.

He turned then and started back toward the dragon. Moments later, they were again face to face.

The giant lifted his head slowly as Amsel approached, then pulled it back with what almost seemed like amusement.

"There are legends," Amsel shouted, "stories told to the children of my land about dragons brave and strong. None have ever seen such a creature, but many think these stories are true. It is sad that they will know only of the coldrakes, and sadder still that those coldrakes will kill them all!"

Amsel looked into the dragon's wide blue eyes. "You feel responsible for the murder of the dragons," he cried. "How can you rest knowing that the people of Fandora and Simbala will be killed because you refused to act in time?"

The dragon watched him, silent and pensive. At last a low, rolling sound issued from his throat. "Man always wishes to act as quickly as he speaks," the dragon grumbled. "You are angry and impatient, but you are also very brave." The dragon suddenly rose, lifting his body to tower above the inventor. "You are different from those men who betrayed us," he continued. "You have proven yourself worthy of my help."

Amsel nodded quietly. "We must go," he said, "we really must leave now!"

"I do not know if I will be strong enough to face them all," bellowed the dragon, "but whatever strength I have, I will use to stop them."

He dipped his head to receive the tiny passenger once again.

We will face a hundred coldrakes, thought Amsel as he gripped the dragon's horn. The odds were unthinkable—an old and injured dragon against a horde of frenzied coldrakes. Yet if the legends were true, then they would respect the dragon and obey his edict.

As the dragon made his way out of the cavern, Amsel thought again of the giant coldrake that had attacked him. He could not imagine it easily obeying the dragon's words. It seemed to him the opposite of the dragon, but at the same time strangely reminiscent of him.

Amsel glanced out through the shadowed mouth of the warren. He and the dragon would stop the coldrakes, or perish in the attempt. It was his duty, his responsibility to those whom he had endangered—two lands which had gone to war and a small child whose smiling, adventurous face he would never see again.

•

There came a tapping on the rear window of Princess Evirae's sitting room the following morning. She sat alone in the small chamber, lost in self-pity. It was a moment before she heard the sound, but when at last she looked up, she saw the familiar face of her former aide peeking through the window.

"Princess!" he whispered. "I bring news of the utmost importance! Hawkwind plans to join our army together with that of the Fandorans in an invasion of the land of the dragons! He meets with your husband and the rest of the Family as we speak!"

She let him finish, although she had already heard the news from others, and replied sweetly, "Mesor, how good of you to look after my interests."

Mesor smiled humbly. "May I come in, my lady? I regret the rather unusual approach, but I am not in favor these days."

"Nor am I," Evirae answered, "as you would have learned had you stayed long enough at the dais to see!"

Mesor reddened. "I . . . I am sorry, Princess. Surely you understand my loyalty to you remains unchanged?"

Evirae rose from her seat and walked over to the window. Her hair dangled loosely over her shoulders. She looked quite young.

"Oh, Mesor," she said, honeyed and gentle, "how could I ever think you disloyal after all you have done for me?"

Relief was visible on the Bursar's face. "Thank you." He sighed. "I had hoped you would be so understanding, Princess, and I am sure you will view whatever else I may have to tell you with equal compassion."

"Whatever else?"

Mesor smiled nervously. "As a Bursar, I have worked hard to ensure the financial community's support of your efforts to unseat Hawkwind, but . . ." He reddened again. "Princess, I had been depending upon your patronage as

Queen in my own dealings with these same merchants and bankers. The unfortunate return of Hawkwind has forced me to leave certain, shall we say, commitments unfulfilled." He sighed. "Princess, there are many in the Merchants' Quarter who wish me harm."

Evirae shook her head. "Mesor, Mesor, I am surprised. After all the advice you have given me, have you counseled yourself so badly that you cannot find an—"

"No," moaned the Bursar. "I am hopelessly in debt."

"What will these merchants do if they catch you?" teased Evirae. "Surely you do not think you will be hurt?"

Mesor shuddered. "You do not know these merchants and bankers! I will be trampled like a tree bear under a carriage! Princess, you must help me to escape! I cannot even go into the Merchants' Quarter to buy a horse!"

Evirae looked at him with what seemed to be compassion. "All right," she said, "I suppose it is the least I can do for a man of your loyalty."

"Oh, thank you, Princess!" He folded his arms over his chest. "I will prove myself worthy of your confidence!"

"Wait here," she replied. "I will summon a coach."

As Mesor watched, Evirae turned away from the window and left the sitting chamber. She hurried to the foyer of her mansion, where Kiorte's driver was seated.

"Coachman," said Evirae softly, "come hither."

The man rose from his seat. "There is a Bursar in the garden," she said. "You will recognize him as a frequent visitor here. You are to take him to the heart of the Merchants' Quarter."

"Yes, my lady."

"He will protest," said Evirae, "but you are not to listen to him. Do you understand?"

The coachman nodded and hurried out. Evirae returned to the sitting-room window where Mesor waited. "You will be met shortly by Kiorte's coachman. He will transport you—"

"Prince Kiorte's coachman?" asked Mesor. "Will the Prince not be angry?"

"Do not worry," said Evirae. "I take full responsibility for this."

Mesor nodded gratefully. "It may be a long time before I repay you, Princess, but repay you I shall."

"Do not concern yourself, Mesor. Knowing what I have done is payment enough." She heard the sound of the coach coming then, and bade the Bursar good-bye. He would soon learn what it meant to betray her. Someday they would all learn—the miner, the Rayan, all who had conspired against her. Someday she and Kiorte would make their home within the palace. Lost within this dream, Evirae made her way to the bedchamber upstairs, a prisoner of her own anger and ambition.

•

The bright afternoon sunlight streamed through the trees that encircled the palace grounds, but within the conference hall of the palace itself, there was a darkness touched only by the light of the six dimly glowing torches. The meeting of the Circle had started.

At the head of the long conference table sat Monarch Hawkwind, flanked by Prince Kiorte, Baron Tolchin, and Baroness Alora. To Alora's left stood the four Fandorans, nervously watching the proceedings. All had been startled by the sights they had glimpsed within the palace. The artistry and elegance of the tree's interior was at once foreign to them and unforgettable. Tamark had not expected a land such as this—there was such casual beauty everywhere! The Wayman felt a longing for his native Southland and the lovely cities to be found within it. Dayon, though wary of the opulence around him, saw nothing to confirm his father's suspicions that the palace had been the work of sorcerers. Nor could he understand how the people of such a beautiful land could ever fight a war.

Jondalrun kept his gaze fixed resolutely on Hawkwind. Despite his exhaustion, his indomitable pride remained unbroken. The Fandoran still viewed Simbala with suspicion and distrust.

"Maintain your guard, my son," he whispered to Dayon. "I do not like the fact that this meeting takes place in darkness."

He listened closely then to Hawkwind's words as the young monarch addressed the thirty representatives of Simbala's people and the Family itself.

"Advisers to Overwood," Hawkwind said, scanning the darkened hall, "we have assembled here to discuss one of the

gravest dangers to ever face our land. I have learned much since the cessation of hostilities. The dragon we faced in Overwood was neither an illusion nor a tool of the Fandorans. It is a creature known in legend as a coldrake—and it is among the last of a vanishing race.

"These creatures are few, but they are a threat to both Fandora and Simbala. Prince Kiorte and I have both agreed that these creatures must be kept from threatening our shores again!" He glanced at the Fandorans. "We will need as many men and women as we can find to embark on a mission to face the few that remain. These noble Elders of Fandora will decide today if their troops are to join us in this perilous mission. They ask, as I am sure many of you wish to ask, for proof of the danger we perceive." He looked toward a door at the side of the hall.

"There is proof!" he said. "I have seen the secrets of these lost creatures within the heart of a fabled jewel, the Dragonpearl brought to us by a Minister once accused of acts traitorous to Simbala."

A faint light drifted into the chamber, and through the small, open passage Ceria and Monarch Ephrion appeared, the former hidden within a gray cloak, the latter dressed in a simple blue robe. All present watched Ephrion and the Rayan approach Hawkwind. The young Monarch stepped back proudly, allowing them free access to the assembly. Monarch Ephrion nodded. As Ceria watched, Ephrion quickly told of his efforts to discover the truth behind the coldrakes, and of Ceria's heroic mission to find the Dragonpearl. Then he added his voice to Hawkwind's own, calling for Fandora and Simbala to unite in an invasion of the land to the north. Ceria stepped forward and removed the Dragonpearl from her cloak.

The Simbalese representatives watched in fascination as the orb seemed to glow in the darkness.

"This is sorcery!" Jondalrun whispered. "I will have no part of it!" He looked angrily toward the chamber door.

The Wayman gripped his arm. "Wait," he whispered. "I have heard of this stone in legends of the Southland. It has nothing to do with sorcery at all."

Jondalrun grumbled, but remained. Ceria grasped the jewel within her hands. "I will attempt to awaken the pictures within it," she said. "The Dragonpearl is beyond my control, but I shall try with my thoughts to influence what you are about to see." She focused on the jewel, and slowly the mist within it started to swirl.

Several gasped as the rainbow clouds within it faded from burning reds and blues into pastel colors. Then these pale shades drained, too, and a gray stone color emerged in the heart of the Dragonpearl. The jewel seemed to grow as the hard angles of cliffs could be glimpsed within it.

Ceria was lost within the dream of the pearl. "This is the land from which the creatures came," Monarch Ephrion explained. Within the Dragonpearl the cliffs drew nearer, as if seen through the eyes of a coldrake itself. Three pairs of wings streaked through the gray sky within the jewel and disappeared into a cavern. Tamark shuddered as he saw a coldrake lying against a black boulder within the orb, its wing seemingly broken. He thought of the skeleton of the seaworm that had been found at Cape Bage. He had wanted to contribute something to Simbala, to be a part of its history, as his grandfather had been. He had not dreamed that this might be his legacy—to help plan an invasion to a distant land of coldrakes.

What would Lagow say if he were alive? He had so fiercely objected to the dangers of the war; the idea of facing dragons would no doubt have seemed like madness. Or would it? Could any now deny the fact that their children had been killed by these creatures? He had seen the coldrake with his own eyes. He watched Jondalrun as the elder saw the picture within the Dragonpearl. Its mists were swirling again and the scene faded. Tamark looked at Ephrion. The white-haired elder had obviously known many dangers in his life, but had any been so far beyond their dreams?

The young woman who held the jewel now opened her eyes, and Tamark turned his head as Hawkwind rushed to her side.

Ephrion faced the four Fandorans. "Our armies shall venture north whether yours do so or not," he said firmly, "but if you care for the safety of your children, then you must join us."

Tamark breathed deeply. These words would not rest with Jondalrun. As expected, the elder of Tamberly Town stepped forward angrily. "Dare not tell us how to protect our children!" he cried. "It is for their good that we fought this war!"

The hall was alive with voices then, accusing Jondalrun of ignorance and disrespect. Ephrion observed the Fandoran elder. He remembered Amsel's tale of how Jondalrun had charged him with being a spy; it would do little good to mention the inventor now; he would have to mollify Jondalrun to win his support.

"You are correct," Ephrion said softly, to the astonishment of the Family and Jondalrun himself. "We have no right to tell you how to protect your own people. You have journeyed far in defense of your land; do what you feel is best." He watched Jondalrun's reaction to these words. The Fandoran had been looking for a fight; now he knew not what to say.

"Father," whispered Dayon, "we must join them! It is obvious that the coldrakes attacked Johan! I do not wish to set forth on another invasion, but if what the jewel shows is correct, then we will be able to defeat them!"

Jondalrun looked at his son. They had come seeking justice for Johan's murder. That had not changed. He did not understand the sorcerous jewel with the pictures of the coldrakes within it, but the challenge it revealed was clear. The coldrakes were desperate creatures, but large as they were, they were few in number and could be defeated by a large army.

Jondalrun glanced at the Simbalese who filled the hall. They had conspired to murder his men, to drive them back with windships to the strait. Yet now they wished to join forces with Fandora. He did not understand these people or their country, with its city of trees and its women as warriors, but he could not return to Fandora while he knew in his heart that it was still in danger.

There was one final battle they would face, one final journey to put his memory of Johan at peace. The children of Fandora would not be threatened.

Jondalrun looked determinedly at Hawkwind and Ephrion. "We shall go north together," he said. Then he looked back at Dayon with fatherly affection.

•

An hour later, when the room had been cleared of all but the most important officials of Simbala and the four Fandoran Elders, preparations were made for the journey north.

Prince Kiorte's anger and resentment toward Hawkwind had not diminished, and though he was a willing partner to the mission, he remained aloof. His assignment needed little explanation. Under Kiorte's supervision, the Brothers of the Wind would transport both the Fandorans and the Simbalese soldiers from the Kameran Hills and Overwood to the shore west of the Northweald, where the Simbalese merchant fleet was harbored. Working with him would be Tamark and the Wayman, who would ensure the cooperation of the Fandoran troops. It would not be an easy task to get the men into windships, Tamark knew, but it would be done. Hopefully other Elders, such as Pennel and young Tenniel of Borgen Town, would be able to help with the task.

Baron Tolchin and Baroness Alora were charged with supervising the requisition of supplies and food from the merchants and traders of Overwood. Provisions for two armies would be needed. Although the war had severely depleted most, Alora was confident that they would be able to get everything that was needed. Support for the defense of the forest against the dragons ran high but many criticized the use of Simbalese troops in tandem with the Fandorans. Nonetheless, it was quite clear to those who had seen the coldrakes that as many men and women as were available would be needed for Hawkwind's plan.

Among the supplies requested by Hawkwind were oil and yithe rope in unusually large quantities. The oil was discovered in drums behind the stables and in the tunnels of the palace, but the search for the rope continued until a tentmaker from the northern woods made known his supply for sale. Two thousand tookahs later, windships took the cargo to the shore.

●

Jondalrun and Dayon would be responsible for the direction of the Fandoran troops once they had arrived in the north. General Vora and Hawkwind would supervise the movement of the Simbalese army, with captains and members of the merchant fleet.

Monarch Ephrion, cheered by the return of Hawkwind and Ceria, but still concerned over Amsel's disappearance, would continue to run the affairs of the forest in Hawkwind's absence.

●

Hours later, Hawkwind, Ceria, Jondalrun, Dayon, and a small crew flew north, high above Overwood, in a windship from the palace. Jondalrun stood defiantly in the bow of the windship, disguising his fear of the flight with an expression of anger.

Hawkwind approached him. "You do not seem to be enjoying the ride," he said softly.

Jondalrun grimaced. "I will not find pleasure in anything until my men have returned safely to Fandora!"

"You seem to fear this windship more than the dragons, Jondalrun!"

The Fandoran folded his arms over his chest. "I am not afraid!" he said. "I worry for my men!" He turned his back to Hawkwind and glanced out at the cloudless blue sky.

To his chagrin, Hawkwind did not leave the helm. Jondalrun looked down at his arm in irritation. He noticed the bracelet of pods that had so long ago been wrapped around his wrist on the advice of the witch woman of Alakan Fen. "I have no need for this," he muttered. "I was a fool to wear it at all."

"What is it?" asked Hawkwind.

Jondalrun looked at him angrily for a moment and then answered, "A wristlet. It was suggested as a way to defeat you." He tore it off and regarded it with disapproval. "It is worthless." He started to throw it over the side of the windship, but Hawkwind stopped him.

"Unhand me!" Jondalrun shouted. The young Monarch pulled the wristlet from the Elder's hand. "A moment," Hawkwind said, and he motioned for Ceria to join them. Her red cape rippled gently in the wind as she approached.

"What does this mean to you?" asked Hawkwind. He handed the wristlet to the young woman.

"It is nothing!" protested Jondalrun.

Ceria took the bracelet in hand nonetheless, setting the

pouch with the Dragonpearl on the seat behind her. Then she rolled the seed pods of the bracelet in her hand.

"A witch woman said they would protect us against the enemy we did not suspect," Jondalrun said. "Obviously, they did not. Your soldiers murdered many who wore them."

Ceria raised the bracelet slowly to her nose and sniffed the seed pods. "It is a bane," she said quickly, and then sneezed. She took a breath of fresh air and continued, "It is an extremely potent bane, such as that used to ward off bats or —"

"A bane?" Hawkwind stared at Jondalrun. "A woman told you the pods would protect you against an *unexpected* enemy? We were not your only adversary, Jondalrun."

Jondalrun squinted in disbelief. "The dragons?"

"The coldrakes!" exclaimed Ceria. "Perhaps the pods affect the coldrakes!"

Hawkwind took the wristlet into his hand again. "Dragonbane," he whispered. "That would explain why suddenly the creature avoided you in battle. Do many of your men wear these wristlets, Jondalrun?"

The Elder nodded.

Hawkwind handed the bracelet back to him. "If my precautions prove insufficient," he cautioned, "we may have use for them."

•

The coldrakes followed the Darkling south, a black wave against the cloudy sky. As they neared the northern sea, the giant creature dropped swiftly toward an icy cliff, the crimson light of the fading sun trapped within it. They would rest here, then start the final journey to the land of the humans.

The Darkling swooped into the mouth of the caves that riddled the cliff, the other coldrakes behind him, shrieking in hunger and desperation.

They flew together through the abandoned tunnels, but as they did, there suddenly came a squeal of terror from those deepest within the cavern. In the darkness they spied a trail of gigantic bones stretching across the cavern floor. They formed the frame of a dragon.

The coldrakes wanted to take to the air again. Frightened by what they had seen, many turned in fear to leave the caves. But the Darkling reassured them. The bones were not to be feared, he told them; indeed, they were proof, like the creature frozen within the cliff, that the dragons had perished, and that the edict keeping the coldrakes from the south need no longer be obeyed. Gradually the coldrakes were pacified. They folded their wings in respose and slept before the flight southward.

The Darkling flew to the mouth of the cavern and perched itself on the icy stone. The land was quiet, save for the dull booming of icebergs dropping from the cliffs to the waters below, and the wind. The Darkling brooded. They would have to strike swiftly; the humans were too danger-ous to be allowed to attack. He and his brood would sweep over the land, destroying the murdering creatures. He lis-tened to the coldrakes, the dissonant sounds of their breath echoing in the cavern, and he knew they would triumph.

Their time had come; there were no dragons to stop them. The Darkling spread his wings and felt the rage he had held back for so long rush within him.

Soon they would be free of the cold at last.

XXXIV

By the morning, the flotilla was ready for departure. Ancient maps and charts were the main reference for the voyage, as shipping craft rarely journeyed into the northernmost reaches of Dragonsea. There were many reasons for this: sea-worms, though rarely seen, were known to inhabit the waters, and the winds themselves were fierce and unyielding.

As a precaution, Hawkwind had ordered only the largest ships of the Simbalese merchant fleet to be used for the journey.

The transfer of troops from the Kameran Hills had not gone smoothly. Many of the Fandorans were frightened by the airborne journey; others were full of braggadocio, over-eager to prove their courage to Vora's men. It took all the resources of Tamark, Pennel, the Wayman, and other Fandorans to control them. The Brothers of the Wind, in return, had little respect for the ill-mannered, ill-spoken farmers and fishermen, whom they tolerated only out of respect for the mission at hand.

Through Kiorte's efforts, the convoys of windships were kept as segregated as possible—the Fandorans in the smaller windships, the Simbalese army in the larger. Additional ships, taking soldiers from Overwood to their contingents on shore, departed from the heart of the forest.

With the high number of men and women transported, it was not difficult for Willen and a handful of other

Wealdsmen to slip undetected into a ship of Fandoran men. If he were to rescue Tweel, and at last discover the reason for Kia's murder, Willen knew he would have to find a way to get aboard the flotilla for the trip north. He was determined to be present when the Simbalese faced the coldrakes.

When the last of the Simbalese and Fandoran contingents had been shuttled north, Prince Kiorte returned to escort Elder Tamark of Fandora to Hawkwind's ship. He admired the fisherman's perseverance and authority. Although weary and advanced in years, Tamark had directed the two large ships of wounded Fandoran soldiers back across the strait.

Upon those ships rode Tenniel and the Wayman, who had been assigned the task of maintaining calm among the frightened and wounded men. Herbs of a Simbalese physician had broken Tenniel's fever, and he was actively engaged in the concerns of the voyage. For a moment the young Elder's patriotism burst forth, and he wondered whether it would be possible to turn the craft north, to join the main flotilla of Simbalese ships. Then, spying the resolute face of the Wayman, he quickly came to his senses again.

The war had not been what he had expected; nor had his own fate. He looked toward Fandora. They had sought to protect it. Now he would return, to bring the tragic news of the casualties to Borgen Town, and to inform the people of Jondalrun's commitment to the mission north.

On the deck of the returning ship stood Steph and Jurgan, both recovered from their wounds.

"It's all confusing to me," said Jurgan. "First we're fighting them then we're helping them!"

"I like it better this way," Steph smiled, "and I'm looking forward to seeing Cape Bage again."

•

With the arrival of Elder Tamark and General Vora aboard Hawkwind's ship, the fleet slowly raised anchor. It had been decided that two ships would be at the head of the armada—the first containing Hawkwind, Vora, Ceria, Jondalrun, Dayon, and Tamark, and the second with experienced members of the merchant fleet. In the event of an attack, they would break the flotilla into two smaller groups for protection.

A loud burst from a cornet signified the formal departure of the fleet from Simbala's shore. Many cheered; Fandorans peered anxiously from smaller ships at the head ship to see Jondalrun and Dayon conferring with the Simbalese. Many were still baffled—only days ago they had been at war.

More than the concern about the Simbalese sorcery was the talk about the coldrakes. Word of the wristlets had spread quickly through Vora's army, and Fandorans found themselves suddenly befriended by soldiers who had fought against them in the hills.

Kiorte watched the armada depart from his windship. He was uneasy at the thought of a confrontation between the coldrakes and the armada, but he knew of no alternative. From what they had seen of the creatures, Simbala had to be protected.

He adjusted the sails on his craft. He would make sure that the Brothers of the Wind were prepared in the event of any sudden return of coldrakes to the forest.

He tacked south, thinking once again of Thalen.

XXXV

It was evening upon Dragonsea. The fleet, over twenty ships of merchant class, sailed in a V-like formation through the cradling waves. Below the mainmast of the flagship, in a small cabin, a meeting of General Vora, Elder Jondalrun, Elder Tamark, Dayon, and two chief navigators from the Simbalese merchant fleet was taking place.

In Vora's hand was a simple map drawn by Monarch Ephrion. It described the unknown terrain to the north, based on what he had learned from the legends, and it confirmed much of what had been written on other, more recent charts and maps. According to legend, a wide river bordered by cliffs and mountains flowed south into Dragonsea. Under orders from Hawkwind, the Simbalese navigators planned to find the river and use it to reach the land of the coldrakes.

"The quicker we find it, the sooner my men can return home," said Jondalrun.

Vora frowned. "You must be patient! We cannot forge ahead blindly! There may be creatures lying in wait."

"Then we will defeat them!" Jondalrun shouted. "Is that not why Hawkwind wished us to join your fleet? We have strength in our numbers! There are only a few creatures left. We are more than able to defend ourselves against them!"

"Yes," replied Vora with exasperation, "but our men and yours are tired and angry. There have even been fights over those damnable wristlets! We must face the creatures on our own terms, Jondalrun. It would be stupid to subject the troops to unnecessary peril."

Dayon listened to this exchange and smiled. His father was now insisting upon a confrontation with the coldrakes in the same manner as he had insisted upon the invasion of Simbala! He had not changed, thought Dayon, but perhaps that was good. There was a need for men with strong wills in the world. It was the responsibility of others to temper that will with their own judgments. That had not happened with the invasion, but Dayon would make sure now that his father listened to what the Simbalese General had to say.

"The woman named Ceria glimpsed the coldrakes within the Dragonpearl," Dayon interjected. "Perhaps she can learn more about where they are hiding."

Jondalrun glared at his son. "There is no time for such foolishness! Fandora must be protected. We must find the creatures now and ensure the safety of our land!" He turned away from them all and pushed out of the cabin.

"Your father is not a man of compromise," said Vora.

"He has lost a son," Dayon replied, "and a war. What do you expect?"

Vora nodded. "I understand, but I will have to ignore him."

"That will not be easy."

Tamark, standing next to Dayon, smiled ruefully. "It would almost be easier to ignore a coldrake itself." He and Vora looked at each other in understanding for a moment and then returned to the navigational work at hand.

•

Hawkwind stood with Lady Ceria on the foredeck of the flagship, wind blowing gently through their clothes. The Rayan clung to the young Monarch's robe and gazed out into the mist. They could see little; the thick clouds above captured the moonlight, and fog swirled about the deck. Above the crow's nest of the mainmast, the hawk circled, but it too was concealed in mist.

Hawkwind and Ceria watched the clouds floating slowly against the sky. It was quiet, as if time were a stranger to the sea. Only the muted flapping of the ship's sails could be heard over the gently lapping waves. Far behind them, in the shadow of the lateen sail on the afterdeck, a small band of Fandorans awaited the return of Jondalrun. In their midst was a young man, dressed mostly in black, playing a sad tune on a small-shawm.

"The Fandorans are scared," Ceria said softly, listening to the music as it drifted to the prow. "They are far from home."

"As are we all," whispered Hawkwind, "but we must continue. We have not stopped Evirae's plan to make way for the coldrakes. Simbala must be protected!"

"Yes, my love, but what can be done to ease the discontent between our troops and those of Fandora? Many feel as if the war had never ended!"

Hawkwind gripped the wooden hull. "For some it has not," he said, "but they will suffer a fate worse than those who suffered in the war if they do not end their foolish ways. The coldrakes are fierce creatures. We must all work together against them."

Ceria glanced suddenly at the open sea. "Hawkwind," she murmured, "look yonder. A wind is breaking up the clouds far ahead."

Hawkwind peered through the mist and saw a massive movement driving east in the distance. Higher up, another mass shifted quickly toward the west.

"I have never seen such a thing in all my travels," Hawkwind declared. "How could those currents force the clouds in two directions at once?"

Ceria nodded and started to look up at Hawkwind. Then suddenly she felt a coldness, an anger, the same feeling she had sensed when the coldrake first appeared at the palace. This time it was stronger, far stronger. She clutched Hawkwind's robe.

"What is it?" Hawkwind said grimly, but as he spoke the words, he already knew the answer. Through the breaking clouds he saw the shimmering circle of moonlight in the sky. Against its silver surface, there was a sudden flickering, a movement of what seemed to be wings. Then quickly, it was joined by another and another. A black wave—frightening, monstrous, and incredible—swept across the moon.

"It cannot be!" Ceria cried. "What we saw within the Dragonpearl—"

"Heed not the jewel!" shouted Hawkwind. "What we see is real!" He turned toward the main deck, and as he did, there came a distant cry, a shriek of bloodthirsty rage from the darkness.

"The coldrakes approach!" Hawkwind shouted. "We must prepare for our defense! All hands to the main deck! All hands to the deck!"

Ceria watched the clouds, and felt the wind grow stronger. How had they misjudged what they had seen within the Dragonpearl?

She shuddered. The winged horde above defied comprehension. They seemed to swallow the very stars in the sky!

She turned to Hawkwind and said softly, "Beloved, I knew not—"

"I know," he replied, "there was no reason for you to have been aware of this danger, but now we must act!"

Hawkwind stepped quickly toward the edge of the foredeck and shouted orders to those Fandorans and Simbalese pouring out of the hatches from the lower deck. The coiled ropes which had been loaded onto the ship for use in mooring or other emergency maneuvers would now be diverted to a more crucial purpose.

"Bring the barrels of oil from the afterdeck!" Hawkwind shouted, and then he directed Ceria to summon Vora and Jondalrun from the cabin beneath the mainmast. He had a plan, but it would take the full support and courage of both armies to effect it.

Ceria hurried off, unaware that the Fandoran Elder had already left the cabin.

Hawkwind spied him a few moments later, approaching the foredeck through the crowd. He started to call out to Jondalrun, but the Elder spoke first.

"The demons!" he raged, drawing closer to Hawkwind. "Those demons murdered my child! What madness is this, Hawkwind? You cannot defeat them using ropes and oil! Summon your archers! The creatures must be brought down from the sky!"

"There are too many!" Hawkwind said curtly, as torchlight flared up behind Jondalrun. "We must protect the ships! Alert your men wearing the wristlets, Jondalrun. They must be mounted upon the masts to keep the coldrakes from attacking the sails. Enlist the aid of your son and as many of my crew as you need."

Jondalrun glared at Hawkwind. "You have no right to order me, Sim! I am an Elder of Fandora!"

Hawkwind seized the stubborn farmer by his collar. "Damn your title! These creatures will kill us if we do not act now! I have my reasons for the use of the ropes and oil! You must get the dragonbane."

Jondalrun broke free of Hawkwind's grip and scowled. "We shall settle this later!" he said. "My men will help me."

Hawkwind called out then, a shrill sound repeated twice.

As Jondalrun left the foredeck, to find Dayon for the task of procuring the dragonbane, the hawk swooped down from the sky.

"Guard!" shouted Hawkwind. "Bring me a quill and parchment! A message must be taken to the other ships!"

•

The Darkling shrieked his rage as he saw the tiny ships far below him. Man had come to murder the coldrakes, had come as he had told the coldrakes they would.

The howling sound of the creatures behind him confirmed to the Darkling what he already knew—the coldrakes had accepted him as their rightful leader. They would obey his orders, they would destroy the ships of these puny humans as they had destroyed the cloud ship of the human who had entered their land.

The Darkling lowered his neck and started the long descent toward the humans' fleet. As he flew, tiny lights came afire suddenly on the ships. The Darkling howled. Man expected to frighten them with fire; man was scared—he had to use precious flame against them.

The Darkling shrieked a warning to his winged brethren behind him. The devious human who had reached their warrens also had the secret of fire, but it was unlike the dragons' flame. It had burned quickly and vanished. These flames were small below them and they too would disappear. The coldrakes would circle the ships, shrieking, raising the waves, terrifying the humans until the flames were gone. Then the true attack would start.

•

The hawk had taken Hawkwind's message to those craft closest to the flagship, ordering their captains to secure the dragonbane of the Fandorans for the protection of the vessels themselves. Many Fandorans protested, fearful that relinquishing the bracelets would ensure their doom, but this sentiment was quickly defeated through the persuasiveness of the crews and the threat of force to those who remained unsympathetic to a common defense.

Upon the flagship, the wristlets were swiftly fastened to the masts and sails by members of the Simbalese crew. These would hopefully prevent the coldrakes from attacking the ship itself. Other Simbalese and Fandoran troops stood ready with long poles, to which the dragonbane had been attached. These would be used to drive back any coldrakes swooping down toward the deck.

Hawkwind shouted his orders amid the chaos. As the shrieking horde drew closer, some ran back in panic to the hold of the ship. Most courageously held their posts, manning the port and starboard sides, armed with the poles, bow and arrows, spears, and even swords. At a section of the hull near the mainmast, six men, including Willen of the Northweald—unrecognized in the confusion—struggled with long shafts to position an enormous oil-soaked rope in the water around the flagship. The rope itself had been bound to long, thin poles in certain sections, affording it a rigidness against the growing turbulence of the sea.

"Faster!" Vora screamed, and the order was repeated by captains watching similar groups of crewmen around the hull. As part of Hawkwind's plan, the rope had been tied into a circle before being thrown into the water. Willen and the others were pushing it a safe distance from the flagship.

The Wealdsman glanced up at the moon as he worked. The coldrakes would be upon them soon. He shuddered. He had been a hunter for almost twenty years, but never had he seen such terror. The sky was filled with the creatures, and their screams echoed in the darkness. He thought of the murdered child and the horror she had faced. He would fight the creatures—fight them to the end.

The leaders of the troops dealt with the panic on deck. Tamark and Dayon reassured the frightened Fandorans who waited with the poles of dragonbane, while Ceria tended the shocked soldiers hiding on lower deck.

Hawkwind and Jondalrun were at the helm. The Fandoran stared at the coldrakes; the winds were strong now,

but he could hear the sound of the gray wings slicing the air above.

"Give the order!" Jondalrun cried. "They are almost here!"

Hawkwind shook his head. "The rope is not far enough away from the ship. Lighting it now could send the hull up in flames!"

Jondalrun glared at Hawkwind. "Your men are as slow as drunkards! We must take action!"

Hawkwind turned away from the Fandoran and shouted to the captains on deck, "Ready the poles of dragonbane! The coldrakes approach!"

Then he heard a scream, as the first creature, larger than those behind it, swept down toward the ship.

•

The Darkling plunged quickly toward the glowing sail. He would rip it with his claws, signaling the attack on the humans. Then the others would follow, seeking vengeance for that which the humans had destroyed. It would not be long before all the craft were shattered, taking the humans with them into the sea. The Darkling watched the desperate creatures scrambling across their craft in panic and extended his talons. He would be upon them within moments.

Then, suddenly, the Darkling cried out in pain. A smell struck him; the odor was the same as that which had enabled the human to escape his warren. The Darkling felt his nostrils burn with the noxious scent, and he howled, soaring up in rage to summon the others. The coldrakes watched him return, shrieking in fear. He circled them once, hissing his order. They would descend together, driving off the poisonous wind with their wings. Then the craft and the treacherous humans would be tumbled into the sea.

•

Hawkwind watched the giant creature soar upward with relief. "The scent of dragonbane has held it off for now," he said to Jondalrun, "but I fear they will attack again at any moment." The Fandoran stared up nervously. The waves were rocking their ship madly now. Combined with the sweep of the coldrakes' wings, the ship could easily be overturned. With sudden horror he saw two creatures, one black, one gray, break from the mass above them, swooping down toward the afterdeck.

Hawkwind saw this and shouted to the General, ordering at last the circle of rope around the ship to be ignited. As he ran from the foredeck, three archers fired upon the descending coldrakes, but their arrows glanced off the creatures' hides without harm. At midship, three others raised their bows and pulled back on arrows whose shafts had been quickly set aflame. Trailing orange light, the arrows arched over the water and hit the circle of rope held in place by the long poles of the crewmen along the hull. A ring of fire shot up and surrounded the ship.

The crew cheered. It was working!

Above the flames, the two coldrakes swerved suddenly in flight, shrieking and flapping in panic. They soared back to the dark mass of wings.

"The coldrakes are frightened," said Hawkwind.

"Yes," Jondalrun replied, "but for how long? When the flame fades, they can attack us again."

As if in answer, a flash of fire burst suddenly in the distance and was followed in succession by many more, as the other ships of the fleet lit the oil-soaked ropes which surrounded them.

Hawkwind watched the flames rise above the sea. The orange light tainted the bellies of the coldrakes as they soared above them. Then he looked back at the deck and saw Ceria rushing in his direction.

●

The Darkling circled in astonishment. The humans had set fire to the sea! They were even more cunning than he had expected. Was this the reason for the dragons' edict? Were these tiny creatures too devious, and too dangerous for them to challenge?

Shrieking, the Darkling eased the panic of the coldrakes even as he concealed his own. There could be no turning back now. If the humans were to use flame in the war against them, then he would use the secret which burned within him. He spread his wings against the moonlight. The others would now discover the secret of his heritage, the secret he had never dared to reveal.

Circling with the coldrakes, the Darkling prepared for his final descent. He watched the fires in the water below, but did not notice the intruder flying slowly toward them from the north.

•

"Look!" cried Amsel. "Above the sea!"

The dragon stared wearily through the clouds. In the darkness he spied the gray storm of wings.

"It is the coldrakes," Amsel cried. "We've found them, we've found them at last!"

There was a grumbling sound from the dragon as it watched the creatures circling high above the distant fog-enshrouded flames.

"I cannot see through the mists," said Amsel. "What are those lights?"

"I see them no better than you," the dragon bellowed.

"Then we must get closer!" said Amsel. "The coldrakes circled my windship when it crashed—what could they be circling now?"

"I do not know," the dragon answered, "but you have succeeded in your quest. We have reached the creatures in time." He slowed the movement of his wings.

"No," shouted Amsel, "I have not succeeded until we are sure they will not go south! You must continue!"

"You lack patience," the dragon grumbled, and as he did, he raised his neck high above his body with pride. "The coldrakes will obey me," he continued. "Though I am wounded, I am still their leader."

Amsel hugged the dragon's horn tightly as the creature roared—a sound loud enough to summon the clouds themselves. Then Amsel looked out anxiously. The dark circle of wings seemed to shatter in the distance at the sound of the dragon's voice. As far off as they were, Amsel heard a piercing cry.

"They have seen you!" Amsel shouted. "They are coming this way!" Amsel and the dragon watched as a dark stream of winged creatures flew in their direction. The first seemed larger than the rest, and Amsel gasped as the moonlight struck the huge body of the creature that had attacked him in its warren. Then, to Amsel's shock, the dragon roared again and dived toward the sea.

"Where are you going?" Amsel screamed, but the dragon ignored him and cut through a cloud with terrifying speed. Amsel held on for his life.

Moments later, as they dropped out of the clouds, Amsel saw where the Last Dragon was headed. Two score ships, encircled by rings of fire, floated on the turbulent water below!

•

To those aboard the flagship, the approaching dragon seemed to be another of the coldrakes. Then, as it grew closer, Ceria gave a cry of recognition.

" 'Tis a dragon!" she shouted, standing on the foredeck with Hawkwind and the Fandoran Elders. " 'Tis a dragon that approaches!"

The others stared out in shock, for as the winged behemoth drew closer, it was obvious that the creature was not the same as those which tried to attack them. It was large, larger even than the coldrake that had first descended on their ship. It had four legs instead of two, and—

Hawkwind stared in disbelief. "Jondalrun," he whispered, "do my eyes deceive me or is that a man riding atop that dragon's head?"

Jondalrun watched as the dragon spread his huge wings to brake himself against the wind high above the circle of flame. The waves below rocked in response, and a section of the burning rope was extinguished.

The dragon glided swiftly down toward the deck of the ship. Far behind it came the shrieks of the coldrakes, but Jondalrun could not tell if they were the sounds of anger or fear.

Then, in one quick move, the dragon tilted his head toward the maindeck, and a tiny figure swung out from one of his horns! As he plummeted down, the dragon turned, raised his head, and soared quickly back up to the clouds.

Amsel cried for help as he hit the soft, billowing pocket of the topsail, slid down it, and then continued his drop toward the deck. Willen and two others caught the tiny Fandoran. Hawkwind and Jondalrun ran toward him, but it was Ceria who called his name. "Amsel!" she cried. "Amsel, you are safe!"

Jondalrun heard these words and felt as if a madness had seized him. "Amsel?" he boomed. "Amsel of Fandora?" Then he saw a white tuft of hair peeking out from between the legs of two Simbalese soldiers. "Out of my way," Jondalrun shouted, and he broke past them in consternation. A few yards above, being helped to his feet by Willen, was the inventor he had accused of murdering his son!

"You!" Jondalrun exclaimed. "You are not alive!"

Amsel saw the Elder, and though he was dazed, he cried, "I have found the cause of Johan's murder!"

"This cannot be!" Jondalrun shouted. "This man was trapped in a burning tree house! He cannot possibly be here!"

Before Amsel could answer, Ceria happily embraced him. "He is here and he is a hero!" she said. "He is a hero for us all. He has brought a dragon to defeat the coldrakes!"

Amsel smiled uneasily. "It appears as if the war has ended," he said.

"Yes," Hawkwind replied, "but another has begun."

He looked up at the sky. Bathed in the moonlight, brushed by the clouds, were the two gigantic creatures. The wave of coldrakes hovered in the sky beyond them. As the Fandorans and Simbalese watched, the Last Dragon approached the Darkling.

In shock the Darkling shrieked his anger. A dragon still lived—a dragon who had faced the humans' fire without fear! He had arrived in darkness, the Darkling knew not how or from whence he had come, but he knew the dragon had to be defeated. Only then would coldrakes complete their journey south. If the dragon prevailed, the coldrakes would respect his edict and perish—as the ancestors of the dragons had done long ago.

The coldrakes hovered behind him, watching in silence as the dragon appeared.

The Darkling hissed; he knew the respect the creatures harbored toward the dragon. He, too, felt those feelings within him, for the dragon's blood was in part his. In another time he would have deferred to the dragon's presence, but now he would not. The age of the dragons had passed!

The Last Dragon flew toward the Darkling. In adherence to an ancient code of battle, he would circle the creature once before attacking. He did not wish to fight, but it was clear from the dark creature's cries that he would attack. The Last Dragon roared as he swooped through the clouds, making clear his challenge to the frightened coldrakes above.

As he did, there was a sudden shriek from the creatures, and the Last Dragon saw the gigantic coldrake hurtle

straight toward him. He had not circled. His talons were extended. He was attacking!

The Last Dragon was old and wounded; he could not turn away quickly enough to avoid the Darkling's claws which raked him along one side. The sight of blood again drew disapproving sounds from the swarm above. From the boats far below, all could see the silhouettes come together against the full moon. The Last Dragon dropped slightly; Amsel caught his breath, but then the dragon rallied, wings beating strongly, and rose again to meet the Darkling. Hawkwind stared at the creatures; the fire around the ship had vanished in the waves; and a few barrels had fallen overboard in the tumult. If the coldrakes attacked again, they would be relatively defenseless.

The Darkling surged forward, knowing he could give his adversary no respite. He swooped, slashing at the dragon's neck with the claws on the ends of his wings, but the dragon arched his neck, and the slashes whistled through the thin, cold air.

The Last Dragon knew that this creature was different from the other coldrakes. Beyond his size and color, there was an intelligence, a determination to succeed for a higher purpose. The human had been correct; the creature was planning to invade the south!

The Darkling twisted about in mid-flight then, hurling himself upward with mighty wingbeats in an attempt to gore the dragon with his horns. The dragon swerved and avoided the attack, roaring as he did. He was enraged by the coldrake's arrogance. He was old and tired, but he was still a dragon, a member of the race that had protected the coldrakes for ages! He was to be treated with respect. He soared up to meet the insolent creature. The edict would not be defied.

The Darkling did not wait to renew his attack. As the dragon ascended, the Darkling swooped down again, slashing the dragon's wounded wing with its teeth.

The dragon screamed as the membrane of his wounded wing was torn apart, but as he did, he swung his tail forward, surprising the savage coldrake. Then, folding his wings, the Last Dragon dropped to a lower altitude, to gain a few precious moments' rest.

The Darkling interpreted the dragon's retreat as fear. With a shriek of triumph that carried to the boats below, he pursued him. To the Darkling's surprise, the dragon rose to meet his attack. They collided in midair with a sound like a sudden storm. For an instant they fell together, wings beating, stirring the waves far below to white foam. The Darkling clung to the dragon, trying to eviscerate him with his slashing talons, but the dragon used his sharp claws and tail to hold him away. As they fell, the Darkling's gaze met the Last Dragon's. In those calm, blue eyes he saw no fear, no panic; he saw instead determination that would not be diminished by a hundred attacks. He also saw sorrow.

In that instant, the Darkling knew that nothing less than the secret deep within him would defeat the dragon. The dragon would not retaliate; he was still bound by the meaningless laws of an age gone past. The dragon would be vanquished, the Darkling knew, for it was he who had the strength to govern the dawning of a new age—the age of the coldrakes in the warm land of the south!

The Darkling broke from the dragon, soaring high above the sea, and he howled in ecstasy as the warmth he had hidden for so long grew within him. This was as it should be; he was certain of it. The fire would light the way to a new life—a life they would never have if the edict were still obeyed.

The Last Dragon looked up and saw the coldrake's arched body against the moonlit sky. He had struggled against him, but surely not hard enough to drive him so quickly away. He saw the creature stiffen and heard him roar, a sound of dragon, not coldrake.

Only then did the Last Dragon suspect the truth behind the creature's rage. It was nearly too late. A white bolt of flame burst from the Darkling's mouth, hurtling with terrifying speed toward the dragon. He swerved away in a steep and sudden glide, flame singeing only the tip of his wing. The Darkling screeched in fear. He had missed!

In the ships below, those watching thought at first that a star had fallen from the sky. All aboard the deck of the flagship shielded their eyes from the brilliant trail of light. It leached color as it fell, illuminating the ship in stark blacks and whites.

Then the ocean exploded! In an instant, the water was blanketed with fire, as the Darkling's burst of flame ignited the oil that had escaped the barrels floating on the sea.

"Man your stations!" Hawkwind shouted to the crew. "We must stay clear of flames!"

Amsel watched as the combined forces of Fandora and Simbala raced across the deck. Fortunately, the currents had separated the oil from the fleet; there was no immediate danger to the flagship.

Amsel quickly looked up again, but the light and the smoke from the fire had obscured the sky.

"Listen!" Ceria whispered.

From far above the billowing clouds, there came a savage chorus of shrieks. Jondalrun scowled as Dayon faced Amsel. "What is it?" he asked.

Amsel frowned. "The coldrakes!" he said. "They are angry or frightened!" Then, a breeze cut through the clouds, and Amsel saw the dragon's dark wings against the moon.

The Darkling circled in confusion. He had used the flame, but he had failed! His secret was lost! The dragon still lived! It could not be! It was his destiny to defeat the dragon, it was he who had seen to the coldrakes' survival. The Darkling knew there was no way now to mitigate what he had done. In a single, fiery instant he had violated one of the most ancient edicts of the dragons and failed. His rage gave way to sudden panic, and in his panic, he saw the dragon flying up toward him.

He did not need to see the anger in the dragon's eyes to know what he could expect from his adversary now. He had used the flame in an attempt to kill. He could do nothing worse. The dragon would risk his life to punish him.

The Darkling banked sharply away from the dragon, thrashing his wings desperately in the thick smoke billowing from below. He was blinded by it. Something struck hard against his tail. He shrieked in pain and floundered for a moment before catching air beneath his wings. The wind tore apart the curtain of smoke then, and suddenly he could see again. Ahead of him, all about him, were the coldrakes! In their eyes, glowing like embers in the smoke, he saw their rage and confusion. He had convinced them that the dragons no longer existed. He had driven them toward the south.

Now a dragon had returned and he had tried to attack it with flame! The coldrakes did not understand, but they knew that as long as the dragon survived, they would be loyal to him, loyal at the expense of any other creature.

The Darkling shrieked a last, anguished cry, a passionate sound that he had never before made. The coldrakes did not understand what he had done for them. A dozen mighty tails swept across the clouds, and the Darkling felt his wings shatter against the blows. To the accompaniment of the coldrakes' cries, he fell. Below, he saw the burning sea awaiting him. His own kind had hurled him to it—but no, they were not his own kind. They had never been. He had flown lonely and apart, always.

At least there would be loneliness no more.

The Darkling took that thought with him to the flames.

•

At Hawkwind's cry, the others looked up to see a huge coldrake fall helplessly from the clouds. The hawk screeched as the giant plummeted toward the sea. For an instant the Darkling was limned before them; then it plunged into the inferno on the waves. The impact hurled sheaths of orange and red flames, which fell short of the ships. Fiery droplets of oil splashed on board, starting several small fires which were quickly doused.

The crews of every ship watched as the Darkling surfaced in the midst of the flames, raising his burning head. From his throat came a last cry which startled them, a remorseful sound that echoed to the creatures above. Then the fire consumed him. The Darkling sank, and the burning sea closed over the battered peaks of his horns.

The Fandorans and Simbalese stood at the railing of the flagship, stunned by what they had seen. They watched as the ship floated further and further away from the flames. They watched, but the Darkling did not surface again.

•

High above the ships, the Last Dragon slowly circled the coldrakes. He roared with pride, for the horde had respected him; they had rallied against the dark creature whose plans would have caused them to perish.

He told the coldrakes of the reasons for the dragons' edict against entering the land to the south. The heat there could destroy them; the humans were able to survive where they could not. The coldrakes shrieked in sorrow as the Last Dragon told them of the fate of the other dragons. They were frightened, he knew. The cold was killing them. Yet it would accomplish nothing to attack the humans.

The Last Dragon roared again. He would search for a safe home for them, a place away from the cold. He would find it, he told them. Anything was possible if they did not lose hope.

He had seen much courage since his return; he would demand no less of himself. The coldrakes hovered in the moonlight as the fires faded below.

The Last Dragon bid them to return to their warrens. He would soon join them. The Guardian flew out then, and told the dragon of her attacks upon the humans.

The Last Dragon listened, broad wings flapping against the breeze. He roared, vowing to learn the reason for what man had done. The Guardian shrieked her assent and returned to the grey mass of wings. Then the coldrakes turned north and began their flight home in peace.

●

"Look!" Amsel exclaimed. "The dragon is returning!"

From out of the smoke and clouds, the Last Dragon appeared. Blood had dried on his skin where the Darkling had gouged it, and the wounds on his wings were evident in the way he flew. Nonetheless, he settled upon the sea so gently that there was scarcely a change in the keeling of the ships nearby.

Amsel watched the dragon's descent from the foredeck of the flagship, surrounded by Hawkwind, Ceria, Tamark, Vora and Jondalrun. Despite his assurances, many in the crew shrank back at the dragon's approach. Under orders from Hawkwind, a few brave Simbalese women had scrambled up the masts to remove the dragonbane put there earlier. The hawk remained perched upon the mizzenmast as they did.

As the dragon arched its neck toward the prow, Ceria thought about the pouch at her side. The Dragonpearl rightfully belonged to the dragons. She would see to its return.

Far behind her, in the shadow of the mainsails, another also stood with pouch in hand. It was Willen of the Northweald. He fingered the rainbow-colored shells within his bag. He knew now that it was the coldrakes who had murdered Kia, but he still did not know why. A child had also been murdered in Fandora. It could not be mere coincidence. He was sure of it. Perhaps the dragon held an answer. He had to find out.

As the dragon's head loomed toward those standing at the helm, his mouth slowly opened. Then, to the vast amazement of all save Amsel, he spoke!

"The coldrakes have gone," he said, "They were frightened and driven to attack. They will not return."

Amsel smiled. He had told Hawkwind and Jondalrun about his meeting with Ephrion and about his mission to the north. Hawkwind had listened carefully as he had explained how the cold had gripped the land of the dragons and of how the giant coldrake had attacked him. Yet this same information had done little to soothe Jondalrun's anger. "Why was Johan murdered?" he had screamed. "Why did the coldrakes murder my son?"

Amsel did not know. His own anguish over Johan's fate had not diminished, despite his role in helping to save Fandora and Simbala from the coldrakes' attack. Amsel knew that this might be the last chance he would ever have to find out. He stepped toward the prow and shouted to the dragon, in the slow, deliberate voice that the creature preferred.

"These people govern man," said Amsel, nodding toward the elders and the Simbalese behind him. "They are grateful for all you have done, but they ask a question for which I do not know the truth."

"Yes," the dragon bellowed, "there is the question of the murder of the coldrakes' unborn young."

"The coldrakes' young?" the inventor said with surprise. "It was the children of Simbala and Fandora who were attacked!"

The dragon grumbled. "According to the Guardian of the coldrakes' young, their nest of eggs was destroyed by man on his land's northern shore."

As the dragon spoke, Willen slipped quietly forward through those who stood between him and the foredeck. At last, he was close enough to see the face of the dragon ahead. "'Twas a child of the Northweald that was murdered!" he shouted. "She had destroyed nothing! She had held in her hand only shells of the sea!"

Willen hurled his pouch over the railing of the foredeck and it landed near Amsel's feet. As the others watched, he picked it up and shook the contents into his hand.

Amsel examined the rainbow-colored fragments quickly. "They are not shells," the inventor said, holding them up so that the dragon could see. As the creature stepped forward, Jondalrun stretched closer, joined by Hawkwind and Ceria. Behind them, Willen pushed his way onto the foredeck in the silvery light.

"These appear to be fragments of an eggshell!" Amsel continued. He asked the dragon if he were correct.

The dragon roared in recognition and explained what he had learned from the coldrakes.

"Then there was a reason for Johan's murder," said Amsel. "The coldrakes attacked him in retaliation for the killing of their own unborn young!"

This knowledge filled him with sadness, for Amsel knew then that the boy would never have been murdered had he not borrowed the wing. Johan had been an easy target for the raging coldrake that day, flying gently through the sky. The raging coldrake had seen the shattered eggs, had learned that the precious young would never be born. She had attacked madly in revenge, killing the children of Fandora and Simbala in retribution for what had happened. "She knew not of either land," ventured Amsel sadly, "nor that the eggs were probably broken by innocent young children at play." The inventor looked at Willen. "Is that not possible?"

The Wealdsman nodded. "Aye, there are some who play on the northern shores. Kia may have found traces of their mischief while walking there alone. She was not the sort of child to do such a thing herself."

Jondalrun started to weep, the mournful tones of a man who has learned the truth of a tragedy too late to prevent it. His cries were joined by those of Dayon, and Amsel, for the inventor was sure that if Johan had not taken the wing that day, he might still be alive.

Their tears were a sight unknown to the dragon, and he looked at his tiny friend with compassion.

"You have saved more than you have harmed," he bellowed. "My loss is far more than yours. We must despair no longer."

Amsel did not reply. He gazed into the night beyond the

dragon, feeling the burden of his quest slipping away. He knew that it would take far longer for the pain to disappear. Then suddenly, the tired inventor felt a hand upon his shoulder. Amsel turned and discovered to his surprise that it belonged to Jondalrun.

"I accused you of murder," he said stiffly, "but I do not blame you any more. You risked your life to learn the truth." Dayon stood behind his father proudly. It was a difficult admission to make, but he had done it. The healing would begin.

Hawkwind walked forward with Ceria to speak to the dragon. "Perhaps not all the eggs were shattered," he said. "Might it not help if our troops searched the shore on the coldrakes' behalf?"

With a grumbling sound, the dragon responded, "The coldrakes laid their eggs on your shore because their land had grown too cold for them to hatch. It is unlikely that any still remain alive."

"Is it not worth looking?" asked Ceria. "Your numbers are so few already—though not as few as we thought!"

The dragon regarded her with an exasperated look. "It is difficult for me to fly now," he said, "but you are correct. I must make sure that the coldrakes were not in error." The Last Dragon spread his wounded wings and slowly lifted his body out of the water. "I shall return," he bellowed. He flew south, heading toward the Simbalese shore. The crew watched as the dragon vanished into the night.

"If only these things had been known long ago," Hawkwind said to Ceria, "there would never have been a war."

"Yes." Ceria nodded. "If we had all known the truth, the Wealdsman's child would be alive today! There is ample room for nesting ground for the coldrakes."

"Aye," said Tamark, behind them. "'Twas no reason for any of these things to happen. We must learn from this; we must talk to each other to make sure that such madness does not happen again."

I hope we will, thought Amsel. I hope we will talk the next time, instead of fight. There was so much to be learned from the world that to ravage it was indeed madness. We must learn the lesson of the war, he thought. In that way the memory of Johan would be respected.

He blinked in surprise as he realized that he was using the word "we" instead of "they." Others had always been "they" before—Amsel had never thought of himself as a part of them. For the first time that he could remember, he was thinking of himself as belonging—as being a part of something. He had considered himself to be a Fandoran, and he cared about its people, but he had felt apart from them. He had felt alone. Now he felt as if he were a member of not only that land, but of Simbala too—and more! He was a part of humanity. It was something that would take time to fully understand. He wanted to understand. Yet for the moment it was enough just to feel—to have a sense of belonging within him. He smiled. He was very tired. He wanted to go back to his treehouse to rest, but he knew that he could not. It had been burned. He would have to find a new place to live, perhaps, he thought, a place not so far from other people.

Amsel looked at the Fandorans and Simbalese talking together around him. He felt hopeful.

The people of both lands joined in a prayer for peace.

•

It was after dawn when the Last Dragon returned. He landed in the water beside the flagship again. In his mouth he gently bore a single rainbow-colored egg, as large as a barrel. He set it down on the foredeck and those present clustered around it.

"There is a crack within it," said the dragon, "but it may still be alive." The people on deck stepped back as the Last Dragon arched his head over the egg. He breathed out a warm yellow flame. It brushed the egg, playing lightly over it, then vanished. They waited in silence.

The egg shuddered. There was a *crack* and the jagged line across its surface grew in size. Then the two halves fell apart, and there sat a small coldrake, no larger than a pony. It blinked in the light, looking about owlishly. Its wings, wet and shiny gray, unfolded, and it flapped them clumsily to dry them. It looked up at the dragon and made a sound that was halfway between a croak and a chirp.

The people watching began to laugh. It was a hesitant laugh at first, almost a guilty laugh, as though those who participated did not feel right in laughing so soon after so much tragedy. Yet, as the hatched coldrake tried to figure out what use its legs were for, the laughter grew. It sounded healthy, Amsel thought. Healthy and healing. He laughed with them.

The coldrake looked up with a surprisingly human expression of reproach. It flapped its wings again, with growing surety and speed, but it was not yet ready to fly.

"It must be taken to its mother," said the dragon. "I must depart."

Ceria glanced down anxiously and removed the Dragonpearl from the pouch at her side. "Wait!" she said, holding out one legend to another. "According to what we have learned, this belongs to the dragons. I wish to return it to you."

The dragon roared at the sight of the long-lost Dragonpearl. As he observed it, the sphere glowed a bright shade of white.

A hush came over the foredeck. Even the baby coldrake lifted its head to see the jewel. The luminescent white faded slowly to a paler color, soft as a cloud. Then a huge, dragonlike creature, appeared within it. It was graceful, and had wide, lovely wings, but it was different, and somehow larger in scale than the dragon who watched it.

"What is it?" asked Amsel.

The dragon watched quietly in fascination.

"I do not know," he bellowed at last, but there was hope in his voice.

Hawkwind smiled. "It appears as though the age of the dragons may not be over at all!"

"The Dragonpearl contains the memories of eight ages of dragons," said Ceria as the dragon intently watched the clouds within the orb. "There is no telling how old this scene may be."

The dragon heard these words, as accustomed to the humans' speech as he had become, and bellowed, "No! I had learned all contained within the stones before they were taken by man. This was not within them!"

Amsel observed the scene within the Dragonpearl. Although he could see very little beyond the clouded sky, the creature within it seemed healthy in flight. "If he lives," Amsel said excitedly, "then perhaps there are more!"

The dragon watched, then looked at Amsel, and it seemed

as if a smile had blossomed across his age-old face. "I must find it," he said, "for the coldrakes can no longer live in the north. I would value your company on my quest, Amsel of Fandora. You have a quick mind and a loyal heart."

Amsel was surprised that the Last Dragon had called him by name, but the words it had spoken surprised him even more.

Join the dragon in a quest for the home of the creature within the jewel? The question did not seem real, but he thought he understood what had prompted the dragon to make the offer. The Last Dragon was lonely and tired, he did not want to go on such a quest alone.

Amsel looked at the others, and saw Ceria was smiling. These were his friends, he thought; the word sounded strange to him. It would be hard to leave, but how could he refuse such a journey? He was being offered a chance to explore a world!

The Last Dragon was also his friend. He knew the dragon's loneliness; he knew of his sorrow and the coldrakes' plight. He would not refuse him.

"I must return to Fandora first," said Amsel. "I must have food and rest."

"As you wish," said the dragon. "My duty shall be to return this child to the coldrakes' warren. They must be told of our plans. You shall keep the stone until I return."

Ceria placed the Dragonpearl back in the pouch as the scene within it faded. She then handed it to Amsel.

"You will always have a place in Simbala," said Hawkwind, "if you ever wish to return."

Amsel smiled. "I should one day like to see your forest as something other than a prisoner!"

There was laughter from the Simbalese on the foredeck and Tamark shouted, "It would be nice to see it in a time of peace!"

Then, as those on the foredeck watched, the dragon retrieved the baby coldrake and embarked on his flight to the north.

Amsel gazed out quietly at the cool, blue water and thought of the adventure to come and the adventure past. He had set out to find the reason behind Johan's murder and to stop a war, never having dreamt that he would meet a dragon, a princess, or a dark winged creature in a distant land. Yet he had met them all and more. He smiled, hoping, wishing, dreaming for bright days to come. For who was to say where dreams end and life begins?

ABOUT THE AUTHORS

BYRON PREISS, author, is considered to be a major figure in the renaissance of illustrated fiction in America. His company, Byron Preiss Visual Publications, Inc., has produced over a dozen innovative books of illustrated fantasy and science fiction, including the acclaimed *Fiction Illustrated* series, *The Illustrated Roger Zelazny,* and *The Illustrated Harlan Ellison.* The company's most recent books include *The Dinosaurs, A Fantastic New View of a Lost Era,* illustrated by William Stout and narrated by William Service; *The Secret, A Treasure Hunt,* illustrated by a team of respected fantasy artists; and *The First Crazy Word Book,* a children's book with illustrations by Ralph Reese. A native of Brooklyn, New York, he has a B.A. from the University of Pennsylvania and an M.A. in Communications from Stanford University.

MICHAEL REAVES, author, has been a free-lance writer for ten years. He has sold six novels, including *Darkworld Detective,* a Bantam book, and has had over sixty teleplays produced. His fiction and nonfiction stories have been published in various magazines and anthologies, and one of his stories was nominated for the 1979 British Fantasy Awards. He lectures on the craft of writing at schools and colleges and currently resides in Los Angeles, California.

ABOUT THE ILLUSTRATOR

JOSEPH ZUCKER is a native of Blauvelt, New York, and a graduate of Parsons School of Design in Manhattan. His award-winning illustrations have graced both hard and softcover book covers, greeting cards, and magazines such as *Science Digest.* Zucker created many of the major characters and set illustrations of the Ralph Bakshi film *Lord of the Rings.* Dragonworld marks his debut in book illustration.